SUBJUGATION

ERIK A. OTTO

Spoke Lands

UNCHARTED
QUEBEC
BANDITS
N
W E
S
KINGSTON
WATERTOWN
UNCHARTED
ORANGETOWN
BANDITS
R/R
CLEARFIELD
UNCHARTED
STAG RUN
HARRISBURG
PREFECTORATE 1500 MILES
GOLD PLAINS
GRAND CAVERNS
BANDITS
TUCSON UNION 1400 MILES
SEEVILLE
ATLANTIC
HILL CITY
BANDITS
OCEAN
BROAD LEAF
BANDITS
RALEIGH
WILMO
AUGUSTA
MAJOR SPOKE CITIES
CHARLESTON
SAVANNAH
SOUTHERN WASTE (BANDITS)
JAX
ESSENTIALIST SETTLEMENTS
PLAGUE
SEEVILLE HOR - RECORD # A7Y-2918

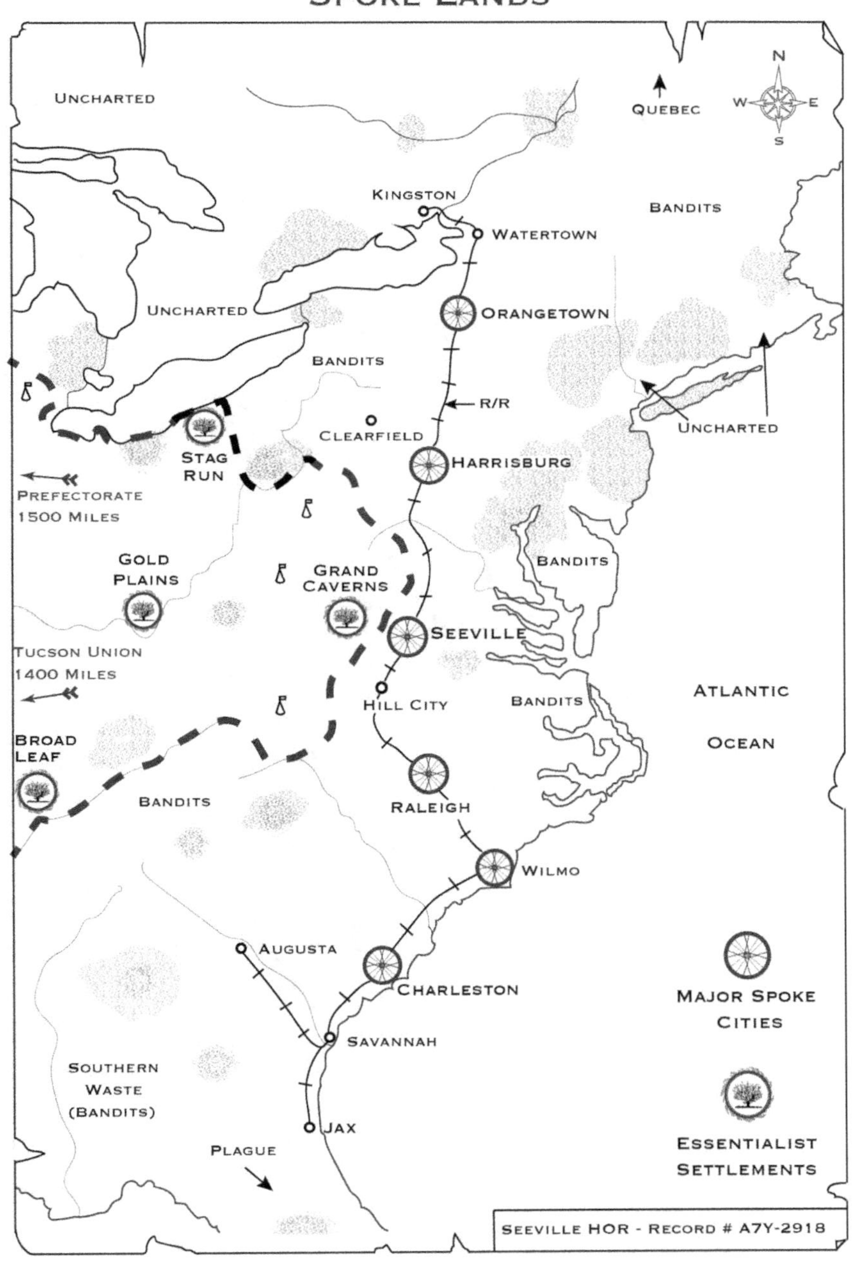

THE SOUTHWEST

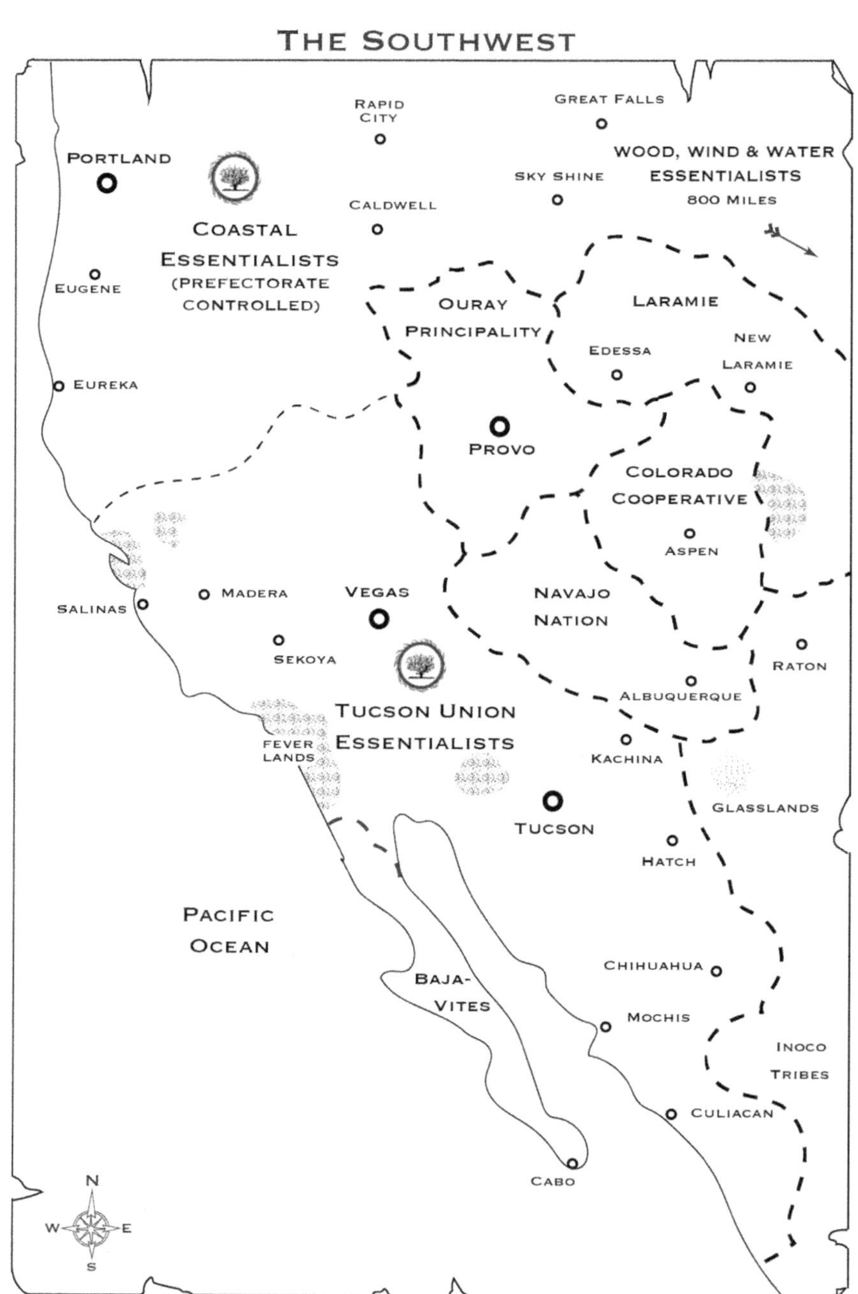

SALISH SEA NATIONS

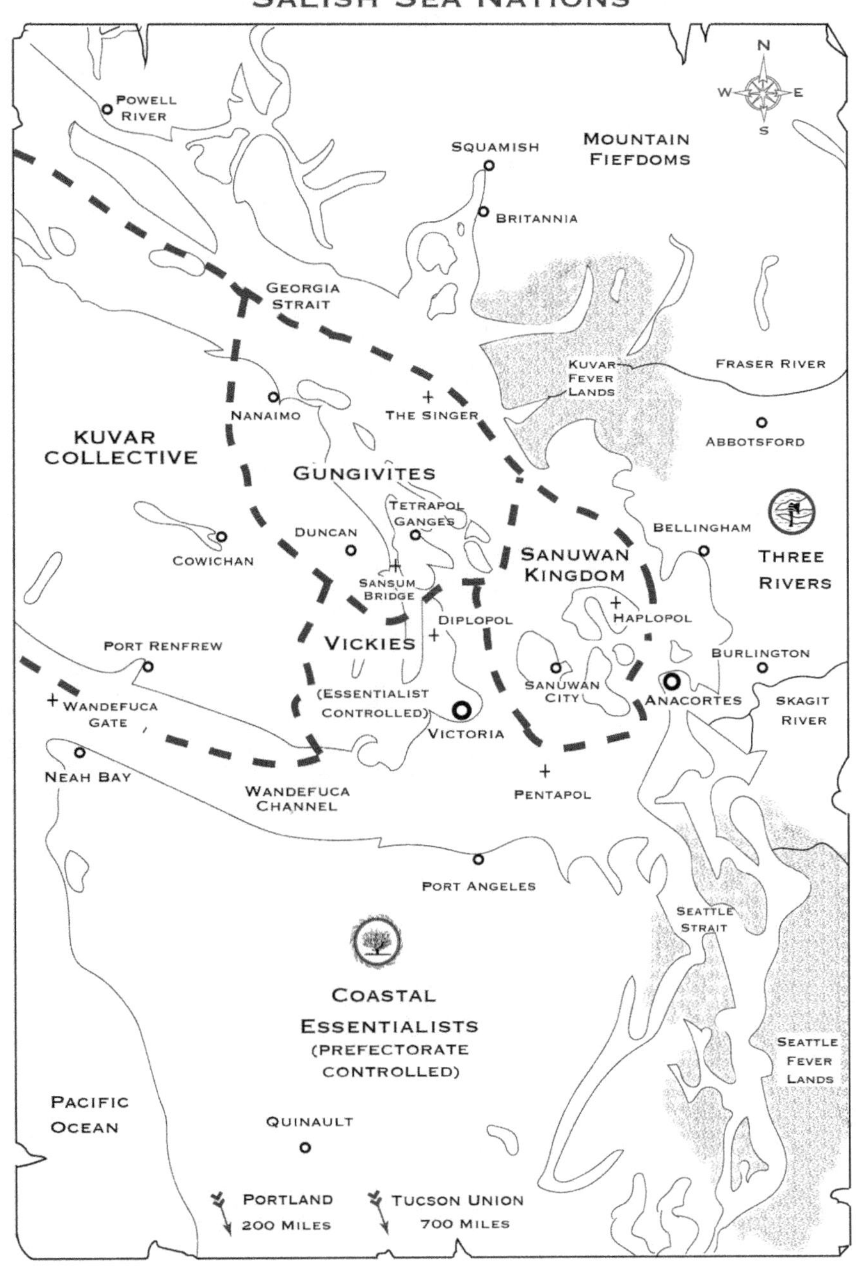

PART I

THE IMPERATIVE

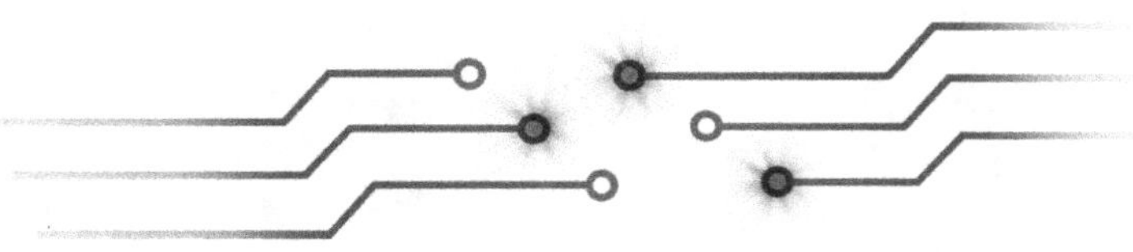

1

THE LION RETURNS

Explosions sounded in the distance, shaking the bunker walls. Between the reverberations was a buzzing sound. At times it was barely audible, just a faint ringing. Other times it was like a giant mosquito whizzing past Cecile's ears.

Cecile huddled under a concrete assembly table, holding her knees to her chest. Owen sat opposite her, his body folded under a desk. His face was lit up by the screen of the tablet in his hands, highlighting the constellation of birthmark spots on his cheek. Without exception, he'd had the same tablet within reach every time she'd seen him since her return from the northwest.

"How much longer?" she asked.

Owen remained glued to the tablet screen. He only shrugged.

Of all the Spokes in Raleigh, Owen was most trusted by the Sentinel, always the first to know the Sentinel's manifold and elaborate plans. She hoped his behavior would reveal some nuance that could give her clues about their prospects; a nervous tick, or a worried frown. But no. His face was expressionless, revealing nothing. Years ago, when Cecile had first met Owen, he would wither under her gaze when he was distraught or anxious.

Another cascade of blasts resounded outside. One of them shook the bunker so hard that dust was thrown off the desk, showering Owen. An aftershock rattled the light fixtures, then the buzzing sound faded to silence.

"That's it," Owen said, swiping the tablet screen. "There were more than fifty drones. The last ones are retreating."

"*Bien.*" Cecile stood up and stretched out her spine. The room was a hundred feet long, its walls thick cement. Five rows of tables were covered with drones, lanky robot arms, and partially-assembled components. A few wire and fiber-entwined metal frames had fallen off the work tables, but otherwise nothing appeared damaged. The Sentinel's multibots—human-sized, wheeled, conical robots with an array of grasping arms and tools—moved out of recessed wall berths and began soldering and lifting components back onto and through the line of tables as if nothing had happened.

"What's the damage?" she asked.

Owen had moved to a bank of monitors near the exit. He tapped on his tablet and a map appeared on an electronic display panel in front of him. It showed Spoke territory near Raleigh and a thick frontier line marking the Gail-controlled lands to the north. Three attack points in and around Raleigh had been highlighted on the map, as well as locations of destroyed and damaged Sentinel drones. On the right of the display was the total: eighty-six destroyed or rendered scrap, which was about twice the last attack.

"Where are Gail's drones coming from?" Cecile asked.

The Sentinel answered her question before Owen could, its emulation of a baritone male voice coming from speakers above her. "There are a minimum of three sites in operation, one at Grand Caverns, one at Hill City, and another one east of Seeville." The map zoomed out and flashed the location of the sites.

"How are we going to stop those sites from producing?" Cecile asked.

The Sentinel had gone quiet. Owen shook his head and pursed his lips.

"*Zut alors,*" Cecile said. "Don't give me that *need to know only* shit, Owen."

Owen raised his hands defensively. "Look," he said, "I can't tell you everything, but I can say that sitting here and trying to outproduce Gail isn't working. The root problem is the human resources she has at her disposal. Grand Caverns is still under her sway, and that influence could expand, while all we have is what's left of Nobura's army in Wilmo, and a few thousand Spokes brave enough to stay with us here at the front. We need to mobilize more people, and quickly, and we could have used . . . well, you know."

"The ICSM cities?" Cecile said testily. "Maybe next time don't withdraw my reinforcements at the last minute."

"I'm not blaming anyone. I'm just saying there's a ton of capacity in the northwest. It could . . . it could . . ." He trailed off.

"Owen?" she asked. He was staring at his tablet, swiping up and down.

"Whoa," he said, and he actually smiled—an expression she hadn't seen on his face in weeks. "You're not going to believe this."

———————◆———————

Owen was jogging ahead through the city, his tablet tucked under his arm.

Cecile hurried to keep up. "*Coliss,* will you tell me what's going on?"

"You'll see," he said, a grin still tugging at his lips.

They passed a downed Spoke drone by the side of the road. It looked like a miniature Old World fighter jet, with a long fuselage and rotating propeller cylinders embedded in the wings. Unlike the Essentialist drones, the Spoke drones were built for speed over stability, and had less onboard weaponry. This one was still smoldering, with perforations across the center fuselage and one of its four propellers missing. Normally they would prioritize collecting downed units, as some of them could be repaired quickly and put back into operation. Today, Owen clearly had other priorities.

As far as Cecile could see, Gail's recent assault hadn't caused much damage to the city. Aside from the downed drone, the only evidence of the attack was an old garage they'd used as a supply depot, which had been obliterated, and a few plumes of smoke snaking upward in the north.

The old buildings of Raleigh were in poor condition even before Gail's assaults began. It was a worse kept town than Seeville or Quebec City, with broken windows, slouching roofs, and peeling siding. It didn't help that most of its caretakers had recently fled to Jax or Wilmo.

The occasional spring blossom poked up along the road and on untended lawns; luminous, yellow petals breaking free from winter's slumber, oblivious to the war around them.

Faint tremors shook the ground, originating from the north, but Owen didn't display any sort of alarm. He continued in that direction.

They reached Spoke Square, which had once been a forested park with a neat set of paths. Here, a circular, tiled walkway could be accessed via diagonal cobblestone causeways. The layout of pavers had been untouched by the frequent attacks, but much of the upper tree limbs in the park were bare or blown apart, and the ground was covered in the resulting detritus. Off the main paths, bombs had produced craters that revealed the crimson dirt underneath the topsoil; recessed wounds defacing the earth's brown skin.

Cecile heard a familiar knocking sound; Madison's cane rapping on the ground. She was walking up a path opposite them, coming from the major downtown bunker that bordered the square. Her face was ruddy, her eyes wide.

"He's really coming?" Madison asked, addressing Owen.

"Yes ma'am." Owen still insisted on using a formal moniker when speaking to Madison, despite their close relationship, perhaps on account of her New Founder aristocratic air.

Madison didn't acknowledge Cecile. Rather, she looked to the north and said, "A lion has returned to regain his pride."

The tremors were growing, shaking the ground and what remained of the trees around them. It was a pattern Cecile recognized, yet its familiarity didn't lessen her sense of awe.

Soon the beholder's massive head bobbed above the buildings on Dawson Street. Its deep, shaded eye sockets were surrounded by black sparks of ordnance. When it broke into the clearing, Cecile discerned more divots and soot on its two-hundred-foot-tall body, even on its drooping belly, where it had presumably been hit with all kinds of artillery. There was a large indentation in one of its bulbous knee joints, but it didn't seem to affect its mobility.

On the interior of its legs were splashes of color; orange hash-marks and sparkling silver lettering over dull blue, and a solitary red patch on its right shoulder. These were all that remained of graffiti inflicted on the beholder during its decades-long hibernation in Seeville. At one point, the entire surface had been painted over like some tie-dye technicolor monster, but since it had been put back into operation, toil and repeated attacks had worn it down.

The markings made Cecile think it was the one called "Louie", but what was more conclusive was the smooth, stone-like contours of its body that ended halfway down its left arm. The appendage was completed by an enclosed cylinder containing a jumble of weapons, including a net launcher for drones, a percussion grenade launcher, and a high-powered laser. It was a neat fix for the limb that had been severed in the Barnyard battle in Seeville. At the moment, these weapons had turtled into the cylinder as protection against surprise EMP attacks.

Cecile hadn't been looking at Louie's *right* hand.

Slowly, carefully, Louie lowered its right hand to the ground, and opened its clenched fist. A cloaked shape stumbled out of the confines of its fingers. He was a shambling, tattered figure, more like a bundle of old clothes than a man. His face was obscured by a hood and an unkempt, salt and pepper beard.

"The Sentinel found him in hiding in Seeville," Owen said. "It decided to bring him back here, despite his protests." Cecile caught a glint in Owen's eye, a measure of victory.

Could it really be Warrick? Cecile's heart was pounding.

It had been months since she'd been close to Warrick, and in that time she'd had a reprieve from the torment; the insidious goblin lurking inside her had no cause to haunt her. Now the apparition had been awakened after a long slumber, manifesting itself as dark tendrils flailing at the edge of her vision, ready to usurp her will.

Soon enough, her suspicions were confirmed.

Warrick removed his hood to reveal tired eyes under a bowl of ratty hair. He said, "Who are you people?"

Madison had been moving toward Warrick, arms outstretched like a family member rushing to embrace a long-lost love. Warrick's words slowed her gait, however.

"You can rejoice, Warrick," she said. "We are kindred. We are like you, the sons and daughters of Ursula Okafor. We are those that believe that Novation is Damnation."

Madison's haughty words brought a confused frown to Warrick's face.

"It's me," Madison said, "Madison Banks. The years have not been kind to us, but you must remember. We have missed your unwavering dedication."

Warrick stared at Madison for a good five seconds, then shook his head slowly.

Madison's body sloughed, deflating like a blown tire.

Warrick scanned Owen, and then Cecile, where his eyes rested. He said, "I do remember you . . . *witch*."

He charged at her, a blade flashing in his hand.

The apparition asserted itself; dark tendrils lashed out from the periphery of Cecile's vision. A well of anxious energy took hold in her chest.

She had little time to react. She might be able to disable Warrick, but she might also cause permanent damage. No—she had to count on someone intervening. When she'd returned from the northwest, she'd told them that Warrick's mind was failing. The Sentinel, at least, would be prepared, and the apparition wanted her to dispel this notion of her being his enemy. She had to show pacifism.

As Warrick rushed her, she knelt down, facing the ground, her blue-streaked hair flopping over her eyes.

She heard his footsteps come to within a few feet from her, and she imagined him wielding the blade above her head.

"Warrick, stop!" Madison yelled.

Warrick did stop, but not of his own volition. When Cecile looked up, she saw that Louie had grabbed Warrick by the hood with two giant fingers, so that Warrick was running comically in midair.

"Let me go!" Warrick barked. "She's a witch—can't you see?"

"I can't wait to hear what this one's about." It was a sarcastic remark from Tremaine, who had come from the bunker to join them. Tremaine's head swiveled between the beholder, Warrick, and Cecile, his brow ridged in confusion.

Tremaine was one of two candidates running in an ad-hoc election in Raleigh. Cecile, Owen and Madison weren't well-known in town, so they needed to include representation from an elected official on their leadership team.

Tremaine was balding at the front, his hair shaved to stubble. One of his eyes drooped; whether it was genetic or the result of some accident, Cecile couldn't be sure. He wasn't physically imposing, but apparently in his youth he'd single-handedly fought off a group of bandits during a platform run. The story had helped him gain enough notoriety to become a prominent leader of the mules and wrenches in Raleigh.

"It's a long story," Owen said.

"It always is." Tremaine replied.

Bronson, the other electoral candidate, was just arriving. He was enamored by the beholder, his eyes charting the upper reaches of the scarred colossus. Compared to Tremaine, Bronson was a more robust figure, some would even say intimidating. He often had flushed features, making him look like he was about to burst into anger. Owen had told Cecile that he was timid, but that could be because he knew fewer of the mules in town. While the details were sketchy, Bronson had been instrumental in routing Gail in Hill City, before the Spokes had to evacuate the area.

Cecile was rising from her long pause on the ground in a slow and deliberate movement. She addressed Madison and Owen. "Like I told you, Warrick is having . . . trouble. The people who knew him in the Salish Sea region told me of this—some disease of the mind. I've done nothing to him, and yet he's fixated on me."

"When did this begin?" Owen asked.

Cecile jerked her glare in Owen's direction. She didn't expect to be challenged, especially by Owen, but perhaps it was merely his prevalent curiosity.

Owen tried to elaborate. "I mean, I remember when Spokes would call you a witch—Noke, and my cousin Jakson, for example. I just wondered if there was some connection."

She made a sour face. "*Mon dieux*, Owen. Those were ridiculous superstitions brought about by Bartz and the railroad, to discredit me. No, Warrick knows me because I've been looking for him for much of my life, and I'm sure he caught wind of these silly rumors. When someone is trying to track you down, you might assign some unflattering labels to your pursuer, *n'est ce pas*?"

Owen nodded slowly. "Makes sense. Sorry."

Madison's attention was still locked on Warrick. "You don't remember me . . . at all?"

Warrick had stopped struggling against the beholder's grasp. His body was limp, but his eyes retained their fire. "You say you're a Seeville Lord? I was a Lord once—or so I've been told—but no, I don't remember you. Did we serve together?"

"Yes, Warrick, we did." Madison said. Cecile was the one who'd been attacked, but Madison probably looked more aggrieved than she did.

"I may be able to help," Cecile said. Tendrils again lashed out from the perimeter of her vision, inciting her thoughts into words. "There was a treatment Warrick did in the northwest. It helped to clear his mind, and to return some form of sanity to him, even though it was temporary. We have the tools to set up a similar treatment here." She left out the detail of how much voltage would be required.

"Yes," Madison said, latching on to this sliver of hope readily, "we must try."

"And then," Cecile continued, "when he is stable, we must take him north with haste."

Owen frowned and nodded, while Madison rubbed her temple in consternation.

Bronson said, "Sorry, I'm just getting up to speed here. Why would you do that?"

After glancing at his tablet, Owen said, "We need to tell him. Tremaine, Bronson, this is confidential—no one else can know."

Cecile explained, "The Sentinel will go dormant in eight months, unless we have a male descendant of the Kelemen family line visit a command facility where his blood can be verified. It's a protection mechanism that the Sentinel's creators included—in case the Sentinel betrayed humanity—but it's turning out to be an annoying Achilles' heel in the ongoing fight against Gail."

"Still no sign of Talon?" Madison asked, addressing Owen. She elaborated for Tremaine and Bronson's sake. "Talon is the only other living descendent of the Kelemen line we know of."

Owen shrugged. "No. One of Nobura's troops saw Talon after the Barnyard battle, so we know he was alive, but that's it. He probably returned to Grand Caverns, to protect his sisters, but after that . . . the Grand Caverns area is heavily fortified and controlled by Gail, so we can't get through."

"Who's Talon?" Warrick asked, an edge to his voice.

"All in good time, my old friend." Madison said. "First, we need help from you. Why were you in Seeville, all the way across the continent from your home? What were you looking for?"

The question took some of the steel out of Warrick's countenance. He said, "I knew I had a place in Seeville—an important role. Maybe I thought it would help me remember. But Seeville is mostly rubble now, and . . . the constant drones overhead. I was going to head back until . . ." He looked up at Louie's hand, looming over him.

"So, treatment, and then I'll take him north," Cecile said. She was being opportunistic, trying to stake her involvement, before they all had time to fully process Warrick's arrival.

"No," Madison said forcefully. "Treatment, then we'll talk. Treatment could help him remember, and we need intelligence. And yes, we'll take him north, eventually, but I'm not sure you're the right escort, given his disposition towards you."

The tendrils floundered closer to the center of Cecile's field of vision. The anxious energy wanted her to object, but she had no grounds to argue. Now was not the time. "*Bien sur,*" she said, adding a shrug of indifference to make it appear as though she didn't really care.

A squad of four Spoke soldiers had come from the nearby bunker, jogging into the park. They wore gray coveralls with the circular bike wheel insignia of the Spoke militia on the breast pocket. They were all strong, and wiry—mules and farmers, before the war. Louie placed Warrick neatly between them, and the squad escorted him to the bunker.

✦

Before sunset, when the Sentinel's reconnaissance drones had returned, Cecile went for a walk on her own. She was heading toward one of the small lakes that bordered Raleigh.

There were few people about. A young mule jogged past her, panting rhythmically. He was carrying packages and letters. Two groups of bikes pulling rectangular platforms laden with supplies rolled through an intersection, a block away. The last platform in line was moving slowly, hauling heavy artifacts of war turned to twisted and tarnished metal. The three mules driving this platform were visibly straining with every footfall against the pedal assemblies adjoining to the left, right and rear.

The last platform swerved and skidded to a stop, then angled precariously over a ditch.

She could have ignored them. The apparition surely wanted her to, but the mules would see her, and wonder why she hadn't helped.

"Let me," she said, racing over to steady the platform as its contents threatened to topple.

"Well, thanks," said one of the mules, dismounting from the pedal assembly at the front-left side of the platform. "Looks like one of us missed that day in driving school where they tell you to keep straight."

Another mule, whose pedal assembly was on the right, had fallen to the ground. He groaned as he stood up, then laughed. "Can't deny that," he said. "Momma once told me I shouldn't even ride a stationary." The mule was no more than a teenager, with wheat-blond hair flowing from under his helmet. He bent to examine the front wheel, which Cecile could see had a flat. It was fairly common, given all the broken glass and shards of metal everywhere.

The spare tubes were stowed in the undercarriage, on Cecile's side of the platform, so she pulled one out and walked it around to the teen as the two others pushed the platform away from the ditch.

"You have an accent," Cecile said to the teen. "From Charleston?"

"A fine guess. Savannah."

Cecile helped prop the heavy platform onto a block while the blond mule repaired the flat. It only took a few minutes.

"Thank you kindly, Miss Cecile," the young mule said as they pedaled off. He tipped the front of his helmet at her.

The intervention would help her alibi, in case she needed one, so the apparition wasn't that perturbed by the diversion.

Besides, it made her feel good. In her travels, the people she remembered most were those that went out of their way to help her. There had been countless times when she and Fabien had been out on the road, many years ago, exploring swamps, meadows, forests, and mountains. Yes, there were devious bandits, and grifting fiefdom lords, but most people they came across were kind. They would help her, just like she'd helped these young mules. When Fabien had taken ill, even more had come to their aid—escorting them over long distances, gifting her lists of doctors, and even offering free food and lodging.

These people didn't even know who she was.

Nor did they know what a monster she would become.

Cecile continued through the city and the houses gave way to thriving oak and poplar trees. The road became a well-trodden path, then a little-used one. After several turns she arrived at an opening at the edge of a tide pool next to Still Run Creek. She was in a shallow valley, with just enough of a ripple in the topography to offer a blind spot from the Sentinel's radar and scanners, but not so far north that it was past the retcher line.

She reached under her shirt to find the pocket she'd sewn into her bra. From there she grabbed her communicator; a smooth, oval object shifting with grades of blue and beige. It could easily be mistaken for a flattish stone, like one you might find in a river. She pushed on an indentation on its bottom. It depressed, and she waited for the prompt.

She often wondered how people couldn't see who she really was. Especially when—to her at least—it seemed like she was coughing out the black fumes that surrounded her every time she spoke the apparition's manipulations. The smoky tendrils seemed so real. like part of nature. After ten years, she no longer had the resolve to fight it. Maybe that was why no one noticed. If she was constantly under tension, constantly showing internal conflict, people would pay more attention.

She heard a crackling sound, like someone striking flint on stone to make a fire. It was the correct prompt.

"This is Attendant Cecile," she said to the communicator. "I have found Warrick Kelemen in the environs of Raleigh, in Spoke territory. Is the imperative still to bring him to you?"

She waited. The tendrils were active at the edges of her vision, like writhing shadow-snakes. She stood motionless, looking up, bracing herself against the apparition's grip as it sent pulses of worry through her.

"Yes," the communicator replied—a solitary word. And with that, her shivering dissipated. She let out a long breath, and her posture relaxed.

The tendrils retracted, and the worry abated. The apparition was appeased, for now.

"Thank you," she said, even though she felt no gratitude. Release from its grasp, no matter how brief, was all she ever wanted.

2

THE DRIFTER

Pyke was standing on the mesa next to the rusted chair-lift platform. Two well-trodden pathways split out to either side, leading to switchbacks up the mountain. Above him, the chair-lift towers meandered along a grassy swath carved out of a platoon of evergreens. Another path led down to the chalet, where Ranger Blaine was on the exterior porch, checking the commodities bin inventories, a halo of curls bouncing around on his head.

Pyke reached down and fingered a kernel of quartz. A tightly packed circle of pulverized stone was all that remained from where the statue had been carefully erected the day before. Pyke guessed that the kernel was part of the vein of white that had crossed the chest of the figure. It had been quite stunning, made to look like a sash. There was nothing else to hint at what the stone had once been; no way to know what part of the dusty remains had been the austere head, the thick, muscled limbs, or the outstretched hand, proudly reaching up with an open palm toward the mountain summit.

It had been the heaviest offering Pyke had ever processed, conveyed on an elaborate transport consisting of a rolling sled pulled by four heavy workhorses, where it had lain on a bed of cloth, held down by dozens of ropes tied in intricate knots. The horses had been gasping and snorting when they arrived, having had trouble with not only their burden but also the altitude.

And now their burden had been turned to dust. He felt sorry for the sculptors who had done such fine work. You never knew what would please the network.

Pyke wrote on his clipboard: *Ouray Intake No. 177 – Rejected and destroyed.*

He moved on to the next pallet, clipboard in hand. This one was stacked high with layers of rhubarb, artichokes and asparagus, carefully separated into wooden tray sectionals laden with beds of goose feathers. He looked across each level, on each side. None of the vegetables had been removed, and the pallet appeared undisturbed. Food was always a safer bet. He marked on the clipboard: *Rapid City Intake No. 178 – Accepted for public consumption.*

"Pyke!" It was Blaine, waving an envelope at him from the chalet. A gangly young girl with a messenger bag was stepping into the chalet through the porch doors.

Pyke moved adroitly around the next pallet, then down to the chalet porch. By the time he'd arrived Blaine had opened the envelope. He was staring at a message in his hand, his brow lined.

"Is it from the crew?" Pyke asked. He couldn't mask the hopeful inflection in his voice.

"Sorry, Pyke." Blaine shook his head and sniffed with mirth. "No invitation for you today. There's a drifter, from the East. They want you to process him."

Pyke's mood immediately soured. He didn't like the sound of this. "Does he have an offering?"

"I don't think so."

"So why me?"

"I guess on account of your studies of the eastern folks?"

"Oh." Pyke nodded. Years ago, he'd been assigned the duty of assessing a thousand-page book about the Spoke lands. It was an offering made by representatives from Sky Shine—an independent township four hundred miles north of Aspen. They had picked it up from a merchant passing through on the main east-west continental route, and repurposed it for an offering. Many thought processing the book was a horrible assignment, fraught with risk of network retribution, because most books were rejected. Despite the uncertainty, Pyke had actually enjoyed reading it, and to his surprise, the network had accepted the offering, in the end.

"So where is this person?" Pyke asked.

"He's injured," Blaine said, and he handed the message to him. "They're bringing him to your place. You'd better go."

* * *

Pyke half-walked, half-jogged home, his leather moccasins slapping against the ground. He tried to avoid the muddier snow-melt patches, dancing in and out of the resilient, crusty ice piles. He skipped across the skinny walking bridge over Maroon Creek Gorge and cut through the Metchokan's back yard instead of taking the longer, more circuitous roads.

The babbling creek and fragrant spring air couldn't appease his frustration. Jeeri had been selected four times, and Annika had even been a Lucky Winner. In fact, Pyke was the only one of his peer group who hadn't been invited to be an audience member. Instead, the crew had again chosen him for a task that nobody wanted—one that surely worsened his chances of being favored as a contestant.

A glint of sun caught his eye, showing through a cleft in the mountains. The flash reminded him of the last time he'd been at the Underdome, months ago, when the strobes had revealed the frenetic motion of dancing men and women in stuttering stillshots. A pair of girls had whirled past his ear, one with her eye on him. Time had slowed down when she mouthed the words, "Don't bother with him. *He's cursed.*"

Pyke lived in a flat in the middle level of a three-story Old World apartment building. It had been partially rebuilt, with most of the walls replaced by pulpy wood paneling. It was respectable enough, as far as accommodations went. Each level had one new window, brought all the way from the Navajo glass blowers.

He climbed the exterior stairs. Sweat dripped from his brow onto his hand as he finagled with the rusty lock.

Natty was there, weaving a basket on the couch. "Oh, you're home early," she said, her brow wrinkling. Natty was his aunt; a slight, quiet, even-tempered woman, prone to both daydreaming and day-sleeping. Her oversized cardigan flooded onto the couch around her.

"The rangers will be here any minute," he said. "They're bringing someone—an injured man."

"Right," Natty said, putting her half-woven basket aside so she could stand up. She knew not to stick around when there was crew business. "Gill was crawling around earlier, but I put him down for a nap half an hour ago. He said *nah*, I think." She offered a cursory smile.

Pyke didn't believe her. Whenever she said Gill had made a new sound, Pyke could never get him to reproduce it. "Did you give him the bottle I marked?"

Natty sighed. "You worry too much."

"That one was oldest. The other ones won't expire for a while."

She just frowned at him.

"Okay, never mind, and thanks, Natty," Pyke said. "Same time tomorrow?"

"Fine." She shrugged and made her way down the steps.

Natty never cared much about cleanliness. There were picture books, wooden toys and used burping rags everywhere in the apartment, so Pyke began tidying up, gathering jumbles of items in big armfuls and dumping them in the closet.

He maneuvered to the bedroom, where he hastily swept the floor and wiped the counters. He took the dusty sheets off the daybed and replaced them with clean ones. He paused at the crib, the palm of his hand gripping the top safety slat, fingering the vertical bars below it. Gill was sleeping soundly in his amber and sky-blue two-piece pajamas, his cheeks red and spittle dampening the sheet in front of his mouth. Pyke had thought the clothes were something his mother Kehda might like, but Gill was growing out of them quickly.

Carefully, Pyke lifted the crib and shifted it to the living room. It would be drafty near the window, and possibly too bright, so he would have to hang a heavy curtain over the window, if he could find one.

He'd only just begun rummaging through his closet for some curtain material when he heard a knock on the door.

Upon opening the door, Glen Ketrich immediately pushed through, his tattered sport coat flailing over his shirt and tie. He was a good six and half feet tall, with thick eyebrows and knobby hands. It wasn't unusual for him to barge in without introduction. He was sparing with his words, making his intent evident via action rather than verbal explanation. There were a lot of Glens in Aspen, so most people called him Glen-K.

Pyke backed away and Glen-K was followed by another ranger in an old button-down shirt. His hair puffed up a good foot above his head. It was Mank, who was also quiet, at least when it came to interacting with Pyke. When they were kids, they used to play together at school, but lately Mank rarely acknowledged his existence.

Glen-K and Mank were carrying a bent stretcher between them, occupied by a man with tan skin and a long sickle-shaped scar extending from his chin to his right ear, his dark, tangled hair tied back into a ponytail. He had wiry arms, and his legs were thick trunks rippling with muscle, evident even under blood-infused bandages. Aside from the bandages, the drifter had a goose-egg-sized bruise on his forehead, and one arm was in a sling. The man's eyes were darting between the three of them.

"Where?" Glen-K asked.

"This way," Pyke said, escorting them to the bedroom, where they dumped the man on Pyke's daybed. The drifter managed to avoid falling on his bad arm by executing an abrupt roll over before landing.

"What happened?" Pyke asked.

"He came up 82," Crowley said, who Pyke noticed had followed them all into the flat. Crowley was shorter, his movements slow and steady enough that many ascribed him a measure of grace. As Pack Ranger he would be managing the situation. "He lied about having an offering at the wall, then ignored the signs for the chalet at Lincoln Creek. When Mank confronted him, he pushed him into the ditch—according to Mank."

Mank made a quizzical open-hands gesture, as if wondering why his account might be questioned. Crowley continued, "The scopes caught him before downtown and we hit him with a bola near Granite Circle. The bola knocked him out. His arm could be broken but his legs are just scraped up."

"Could be a Laramie Bronco," Glen-K said, "especially with that mark on his cheek." Laramie was a group of allied tribes with lands to the northeast. Broncos had raided Aspen over the years, and tensions were escalating after Laramie had attacked another Cooperative tribe not far to the north. Glen-K had obviously not seen many Laramie Broncos before; they had long burn lines along their arms and legs, shaped into spiral patterns. This was nothing like that.

"He said he's from the east," Crowley said.

"That's not a brand," Pyke said. "It's a scar. He's a Spoke, probably a mule or a wrench. Was he riding a bicycle?"

Mank laughed and pushed Glen-K's shoulder. "Told ya that's what it was."

Glen-K nodded and frowned. "Yeah, he had a *bi-sick* . . ." he frowned in concentration, knowing he wasn't getting the pronunciation right. ". . . one of those, I think."

"Where is it?" Pyke asked, more out of curiosity than anything else.

"We'll bring it here later," Crowley said. He was pulling a long metal wire out of his pack. It was a combination lock, joined to metal cuffs, which he handed to Pyke. "The number is on the lock."

A folded piece of paper had been pierced by the lock wire. It had the code printed on it. Pyke ripped it off and memorized the combination.

Crowley was watching him. "You know what happens if he gets away, right?"

Pyke could think of a whole host of negative consequences: being removed from contestant consideration; Gondola isolation; being cast out of Aspen altogether—but it wouldn't be expedient to ask for clarification. "Yes," was all he said.

"Good," Crowley said. "I'll let the crew know you have him."

Pyke figured this was Crowley's way of washing the rangers' hands of the whole situation. They were giving the unruly vagabond to the cursed offering advocate, just in case his apprehension was looked upon unfavorably by the host, or in case he caused some sort of trouble.

Pyke examined the drifter again. His eyes were dark, relentlessly staring back at him.

"Help me get him secured before you leave," Pyke said. The request may have been perceived as cowardly, but injured or not, it was clear the Spoke was strong.

The rangers didn't leave, but they didn't really help either. Mostly they waited, exchanging frowns with the drifter as Pyke used a manual drill to bore a hole through one of the bedposts. He threaded the lock wire through it and fastened the cuffs to the wrist of the Spoke's uninjured arm.

"Okay?" Crowley said. His expression morphed into a mock smile.

"Sure."

The rangers left.

Pyke went to the kitchen and returned with a glass of water. The drifter didn't reach for the glass, so Pyke placed it at his feet and retreated. He pulled out a stool from the wall and sat on it. "What's your name?" he asked.

"Your leader," the drifter said. "Take me to your leader."

"Why?"

The man squinted. "You know about the Spokes?" he asked.

"More than most."

"You know about the machine war?"

"Sure."

"What do you know?"

"The Essentialists and Spokes are fighting—using machines."

The drifter's nose flared. "Your leader," he said.

"Why would we allow an outsider—a man who has proven to be dangerous and non-compliant, and who acknowledges he is part of a warring tribe—access to our leader?"

The drifter's head tilted to the side in contemplation. "Because war is coming this way. We could help you."

"Why did you come to Aspen? Why not go to the Navajo Nation, or Ouray? We're just a small Cooperative town."

The drifter shook his head and frowned. "Your *leader*," he said. He tested the cuffs in frustration, flexing his bicep to pull the wire against the bedpost.

Pyke crossed his arms and shook his head. After a brief staring contest, he left the room, closing the door behind him.

He walked past the crib, up to the solitary window pane that looked out at the western range.

The frustration he'd felt before the drifter arrived was returning. It would be yet another prickly assignment, harboring a discourteous man of uncertain motives, and he had no choice but to comply. If Pyke was somehow lucky enough to please the host, it would only invite more of these thankless jobs.

He glanced down at Gill sleeping in the crib, then returned his gaze to the window. His eyes followed the long shadows cast by the imposing peaks. Maybe he *was* cursed, or . . . maybe it was this place —maybe he wasn't meant to be in Aspen. There had to be something more for him beyond those great walls of stone—beyond Colorado.

He vowed that this was the last straw. He would take care of this drifter, but if the crew didn't reward him for his efforts, he would leave Aspen for good.

3

FIT FOR PURPOSE

"*B*onjour, mon amie," Madison said. Her English accent was atrocious, but Cecile appreciated the attempt.

Cecile was collecting Madison from her room—an enclosure no bigger than an oversized closet, cordoned off from a warehouse-sized chamber. From there they walked toward the command center.

The downtown bunker had thick cement walls embedded with Faraday cage barriers, low-energy flood lighting overhead, and work areas that at times looked like animal pens, covered with dirt tracked in from outside. Most corridors had ready-access stashes of soldering tools, weapons stashes, and gas masks.

For many in the Spoke command structure, necessity had also made it a place to call home.

"I'm not built for this environment," Madison said. "I miss the tall poplar trees of Monticello, and the groaning floorboards of my Cherry Avenue money pit. I even miss the drafty brick Georgian one-bedroom in Yorktown. But like the bunker, I'm a creature of purpose, so I can't find cause to complain."

It sounded like Madison *was* complaining, but Cecile bit her lip. "*Moi aussi*," she said. "I miss the outdoors most of all."

"Yes," Madison said, a twinkle in her eye. "You *are* quite the traveler, aren't you."

Madison hobbled beside Cecile with the help of her cane. They moved past one of the work areas where a man was taking apart a downed drone with a pry bar, following a sheet of instructions printed out by the Sentinel.

The door to the command center slid open. Owen was already there, tablet in hand. His eyes flitted up momentarily as his only acknowledgement of their presence. Tremaine was standing a foot away from the full-wall view screen that was showing a handful of feeds from the cameras strategically positioned on buildings facing north from the retcher line. Bronson was sitting across from Tremaine, studiously reading a report filled with pages of intricate charts and maps; the latest intelligence report from the Sentinel.

Madison took a seat with the footage at her back, while Cecile circled around to the other side—she liked to monitor the feeds in the background.

Tremaine joined them at the table, sporting a confident grin. "What's new?" he asked.

"A lot," Owen said, waving his own stack of printed paper in the air. "Let's begin with the supply shipments." The wall display screen flickered into a map of the Raleigh area, which promptly zoomed out and moved west across the continent. "We've seen a pattern of shipments farther west that's troubling. We can identify movement of electronics, metals, fibers, cement, and other materials as indicative of likely spots for increased manufacturing infrastructure involving electronic systems. We saw this same pattern to a much larger extent when the ICSM cities came online. Now we see it in Tucson, Sekoya, and with lesser evidence, a town in the Colorado Cooperative called Aspen."

"Ha," Tremaine said, "Arsalan was right about Aspen. And you said his story was a *fanciful tale*."

"None of us here said that," said Cecile. "We all believed Arsalan."

Tremaine waved away Cecile's objection. "It must have been the railroad folks. Well, never count out a savvy wrench. When's the last we heard from him?"

The Sentinel chimed in from the speaker above the table. "He missed his last connection. I hope to find him on the next satellite pass."

"Oh," Tremaine said, donning a look of concern.

"I'm sure Arsalan will be fine," Cecile said. "Years ago I went through Aspen when I was looking for Warrick. They do have more infrastructure than neighboring towns, and are accepting of Old World technology—I suspect this is the pattern the Sentinel is seeing. It's an odd place, and they're protective of their culture, but they're peaceful."

Tremaine's furrowed brow didn't offer any sign of reassurance, perhaps because he didn't trust Cecile. She had only recently returned from the northwest, and many considered her an outsider.

"I'm glad we sent Arsalan to investigate," Bronson said. "Even if the people of Aspen aren't under Gail's thumb, they could be useful allies."

Owen nodded. "I should reiterate that the pattern the Sentinel is seeing for Aspen is weak, an order of magnitude less than Sekoya or Tucson. The Sentinel is 96% certain there is new infrastructure being built by machine intelligence in these other locations."

Silence fell as the group pondered the disconcerting news.

"Is there anything we can do about it?" Madison asked.

"Not right now. First we need to hold the line here in Raleigh, and to do that, we need to step up recruitment."

Madison smiled and touched Bronson's arm. "Which is why we have our two esteemed People's Representative candidates with us."

"Absolutely," Bronson said. "We'll begin a broad campaign focusing on Wilmo, Jax, and Charleston, as soon as the election is over."

"Of course," Tremaine said, patting the table as if it was a *fait accompli.*

"Splendid," Madison said.

It was good to have their commitment, but Cecile wondered if either candidate had put much thought into it at all, with the election imminent. "How are Harrisburg and Orangetown doing?" she asked. They had been cut off from the northern Spoke cities after Seeville and Hill City had to be abandoned.

Owen swiped at his tablet. "They're holding their own. The Sentinel has sent them reinforcements from our northern facility."

"That's great news," Cecile said. "It means West Chester is still well behind the front."

"Don't say West Chester anymore," Owen said. "It's too revealing as to the base's location. And that goes for all of you. Let's call it . . . Alpha Base."

The Sentinel weighed in from above them. "If an enemy overhears us talking about Alpha Base, what do you think Gail would surmise about its importance?"

Owen nodded. "They'll surmise that's it's one of our primary bases of operations—got it. What do you suggest?"

"Call it Depot 81."

"Fine," Owen responded. "That's suitably innocuous. Let's move on."

It was just one of countless times the Sentinel had made them realize how stupid they all were. It was always humbling, and sometimes humiliating.

Cecile stood up and rounded the table to the map of the eastern seaboard. With her finger, she drew a line from their position directly north. "*Bien,*" she said. "I think we can use this relatively direct route to get Warrick around Seeville to reach Depot 81." She offered a snap-smile to Owen in deference to the name change. "It will be a four hundred mile trip, five hundred max. I know the terrain well, and would be happy to lead the expedition."

"Sorry, but we can't afford any more men to help you on a dangerous foray into enemy territory," Tremaine said. "Didn't we just talk about the need for more manpower?"

Cecile gave a pained look, as if she was making a big concession. "I'm sorry, yes, we did. I suppose I could go with a smaller group. Just me, Pierre, and Warrick. It will make us less conspicuous."

Madison had an eyebrow raised. "I thought we discussed this. We still have months before the Sentinel's clock runs out, and don't we have more pressing matters with the recruitment efforts and instability of Wilmo? Cecile, we could use you there. Nobura isn't the most skilled diplomat. In fact, I'm not sure he knows what diplomacy *is*." What Madison left unsaid was that she might also want Cecile to keep watch on the People's Representative in Raleigh, when elected, in case whoever it was needed shepherding in the right direction.

"*Non, non,*" Cecile said. Her heart rate picked up as the apparition's tendrils lashed at the edges of her vision. "The Sentinel is everything. I've spent much of my life searching for Warrick for that very reason. We need to preserve him, and the Sentinel, by any means necessary. I strongly disagree."

"I'm sorry, Cecile," the Sentinel chimed in. "I don't think we can pursue your proposed mission at the moment, but not because of manpower issues. It would be too dangerous. I would like to give you beholder support after we conduct an offensive to clear a path, but we aren't ready. Beholder support will make success much more likely."

Cecile projected an annoyed look, and then nodded. At least the Sentinel hadn't voiced any concerns about her leading the mission. "Fine, but I refuse to go to Wilmo. I will stay here so we're ready to leave when the Sentinel has cleared a path."

"That is acceptable," the Sentinel responded.

"Great—so are we done?" Tremaine asked. "I assume it's all here, right?" He slapped his hand on the report Owen had been waving in the air minutes ago, then pushed back his chair.

Owen shook his head. "No, we're not done."

Tremaine and Bronson were both generally sharp, but they had little experience with matters of governance, or interfacing with a superintelligent machine, for that matter. They often fumbled their way through these meetings, eschewing protocol to pontificate on any number of tangential questions. On balance, Cecile found Bronson to be the more rational of the two. He actually seemed like he wanted to be there, whereas Tremaine was always looking for the exit.

Owen had closed his eyes, and was holding the bridge of his nose. "There's always more. In this case, there's something quite important we need to share." Based on his body language, Cecile guessed it was more bad news.

The map on the display wall flashed and bisected into two different video feeds.

"We have arranged a connection with our allies in the northwest," Owen said. "On the left is Dryden, the anthropologist who helped us figure out many of the mysteries of the ICSM cities. He's at the entrance to Pentapol." The feed showed an expansive backdrop of whitecaps over a roiling sea. Huge metal arms swept above the waves, originating from a point above the camera. In the foreground, Dryden's unkempt blond mop of hair was flopping in the wind. He waved at the camera.

"In the other feed, standing left to right," Owen continued, "we have Ryder, Lexie, Vaela, and Tarnation. They also originate from the Salish Sea area and are conducting a mission in the mountains in the northwest." All four of them wore bulky, scuffed jackets, with heavy mitts. Their breath churned out gusts of mist due to the stark temperature differential. Tarnation's size was magnified by the heavy jacket, and a fur hat gave him the look of a trapper. Lexie had her usual probing smirk. Cecile figured Vaela for a Gungivite Observer, because she was wearing a stringy red wig. She had a darker complexion than the others, but it didn't look natural, more like amber-tinted makeup than a natural skin tone. Ryder wore a wavy mop of a wig that didn't quite match the hue of his brown beard.

"Who wants to explain it?" Owen asked.

Faint static could be heard from both feeds, at times crackling louder from energetic winds flowing over the microphones.

After the moment of silence, Dryden laughed nervously. "I guess I should do it, since a lot of it stemmed from my work. First, a quick backgrounder. Up here in the Salish Sea area, there are two cities called Haplopol and Diplopol that are governed by control junctions

—melon-sized orbs that contain sophisticated machine intelligence. The first ICSM city control junction was initiated by a drone in Haplopol, and the Diplopol junction we found in a tunnel deep below Haplopol. With some help from our Gungivite friends, we found satellite footage of the initiating drone's arrival. Factoring in available fuel capacity and wind patterns on that particular day, we believe this drone came from the southeast, the likely point of origin being a five-hundred-mile radius around Kachina, in the Tucson Union."

"You think the drone is Essentialist?" Bronson asked. "From Gail?"

"We don't know for sure," Dryden replied, "but that's the concern, and if so, there may be some latent control mechanism of the Haplopol junction inserted by whatever drone activated it. Otherwise, it doesn't make sense that the drone could even get inside the secure confines of the city, without having knowledge of the security systems. But there's more." He sighed deeply before continuing. "I was studying the underground chamber where the Diplopol junction was found, and realized that the corpse from which we took the junction had been placed there recently. Not to get too morbid, but there were scrape marks on the bone, indicating the flesh had been removed mechanically, rather than there being a regular decomposition process. We had a biopsy tested, and confirmed this, which prompted a broader search of the cave, revealing a place where another tunnel had recently been excavated and filled in."

"What is the point of all this?" Tremaine asked. "I mean really." He raised his eyebrows at Cecile, and Madison, as if the situation was ridiculous, but neither of them reacted.

"I'm sorry—it's complicated," Dryden said. "The point is, someone made it look like the Diplopol junction had been there for decades, but it hadn't. The control junction was likely tampered with, and returned to the site in the last few years. It's possible the Haplopol junction was also tampered with, to allow for the drone to come in and reboot it."

"So?" Tremaine asked.

Ryder chimed in. "Latent external control of both of these

powerful machine cities, possibly by Gail, could be exerted at any time. This could dramatically upset the power balance on the continent in favor of the Essentialists."

"This sounds quite serious," Madison said, possibly to help Bronson and Tremaine understand the gravity of the situation.

"You got it," Lexie added. "As always, us Salish Sea folks are about to blow up any minute. Any good news on your end?"

The truth was, the Spoke vanguard was barely hanging on in Raleigh. No one wanted to say it, and Owen's reports about increased Essentialist manufacturing activity in the Tucson Union was equally worrisome. After another long, uncomfortable silence, Madison said, "There is *some* good news. We found Warrick Kelemen. He made it all the way to Seeville before we picked him up."

Lexie mouthed an inaudible "what". Ryder's eyes widened. Tarnation let out a throaty laugh.

"What's this mission you're on, anyway?" Tremaine asked.

"That," Ryder said. "*That* was our mission—to find Warrick. We thought he was still in the northwest, but our intelligence must have been wrong."

Lexie broke from the group. She was pacing back and forth in the snow.

"We need to take him north," Owen said, "to our base, so we can reset the Sentinel."

"We've got it covered," Cecile added quickly. "We'll have beholder support."

"Which one of you is gonna take him?" Lexie asked, stopping to face the camera again. Her brow was furrowed, one hand firmly on her hip.

"I am," Cecile said. "And whoever else we can afford for support."

"Great," Ryder said. "Maybe we should—"

"No," Lexie interjected forcefully. "No way. We're going to take him. We're already on our way east. We'll come all the way, then escort him to wherever your base is. No offense, Cecile, but Warrick doesn't trust you. And to be frank, I'm not so sure we should trust you, either."

Cecile adopted a shocked expression. "I resent that. We helped you, while you stymied us on numerous occasions. You let Warrick go!"

"That was different. We had no idea why you wanted him. And that *help* you provided? It never materialized, remember? We're used to dealing with weird tribes with brain-twisty ideas about machine intelligence, but at least the nutjobs here"—she edged her chin out at Vaela and Ryder—"stay true to their word. Can't say the same about you. And it's real convenient that Warrick isn't there to voice his own opinion on the matter."

"This is ridiculous . . ." But Cecile trailed off, because the screen had gone blank. Owen was holding his head. Madison's face was rigid and controlled, the way she looked when she was about to couch some diplomatic entreaty.

It was the Sentinel that spoke, its familiar voice emanating from the comm on the desk in front of them. "I have told the Salish Sea group we need a minute, Cecile. Do you know why?"

A wave of apparition-induced anxiety flushed through her. If the Sentinel was interceding, she might have already lost. "No," she said.

"Because we need allies. This is an opportunity to foment a bond with an important faction in the west. We also need resources. They are offering four people to help. Plus, Lexie is right—Warrick will be more amenable to going with them than with you, increasing the likelihood of mission success. And finally, you are needed here, to help in Wilmo, with the railroad, and Nobura. You know the Spokes better than most, and you are a natural leader. Do I need to explain further?"

The shadowy tendrils were tripping at the edges of Cecile's vision. Her chest felt tight, as if some invisible force was about to make her lungs cave in. There was no arguing against the Sentinel, though. She would have to find another way. "Fine," she said through gritted teeth. "I understand."

The screen flickered on again. Her colleagues probably expected Cecile to concede to Lexie, but she couldn't bring herself to do it.

After a few tense looks amongst both the people in the feed,

Madison chimed in. "Lexie and team. We've talked it over and agree —your help would be most appreciated in delivering Warrick to the north. In the meantime, in the spirit of Dryden's introduction, we should stay in regular contact."

"Damn right," Lexie said.

Ryder reached out to grab Lexie's arm, perhaps trying to quell any further attempts to rub it in. "Good," he said, "and I suppose we could investigate the source of the Haplopol drone as well. It wouldn't be much of a detour." He looked to Tarnation and Vaela, who both nodded. Lexie frowned, but didn't object outright.

Despite the tenuous circumstances, everyone else seemed satisfied with the decision. Meanwhile, the apparition was in such a frenzy that Cecile had trouble concentrating for the rest of the meeting. They discussed finding the source of the drone, and the situation in Raleigh, but she could barely pay attention.

Her mind raced. She would have several weeks until Lexie's party would arrive in Raleigh. She would have to find a way to extract Warrick before then.

4

____

NOT SLEEPING WELL

*D*ear Kehda,

You were always asking me about Spoke culture. Well, guess what? We have a Spoke here! I'm his advocate. Maybe you could come and visit? You would probably have better luck at making him talk :)

How are things in Tucson? I hope you and your family aren't wrapped up in the war with the East. If things get bad, promise me you'll take care of yourself—you're too important. You're always welcome back here in Aspen, where it's safe.

I still haven't been a contestant. Someday. The city is thriving, though. We've had more offerings this year than last year. The supply officers and rangers have never been busier.

Gill is growing so fast. He's still not walking but he's an ambitious toddler. He says "Dah" a lot. Although usually when referencing anything but me, so a ways to go on that account. Nevertheless, I will claim it as a victory of my expert tutelage.

Write back! I miss you.

Pyke

Pyke shook his writing hand as it started to cramp. The pencil he wrote with was network-issue. Unlike Old World pens and pencils, it was a rectangular prism rather than hexagonal, which made it harder to grasp.

He reviewed the letter twice. He decided to remove the last paragraph about Gill. Better to keep things light, or she might not write back at all.

------------◆------------

Pyke didn't sleep well with the drifter in his apartment.

He propped a chair behind the door to his room and dangled a string of empty cans from the doorknob as a noisemaker. It still wasn't enough to keep Pyke from rising every couple of hours to check on him.

Gill was also up twice in the night, crying. Each time Pyke fed him, then bobbed him on his shoulder while staring out the window. The moon was unusually bright, revealing the contours of the mountainscape. Only a few pinpoints of light from disparate farmhouses were visible on the pastoral lower reaches of the valley.

"Dah," Gill said, pointing out the window. "Dah."

"Yes, mountains." He tried to enunciate more clearly, despite being half asleep. "*Mountains.*"

Gill eventually went down, but by that point Pyke was fully awake. He checked the noisemaker, then put in his earbuds and turned on his nugget—a circular audio player issued by the network that fit into the palm of his hand. It fed music wirelessly to his earbuds.

He stared at the ceiling and whispered along with the song.

> *Don't stay if you're gonna break my heart*
> *Your love is gonna tear us apart*

It was an uplifting synth rift, not too high-tempo. Eventually, his eyes were heavy again. He switched off the nugget, and fell asleep.

When morning came, Pyke made a plate of buttered rye bread, lemon wedges and smoked venison slices. He also broke into his stash of hazelnuts, cracked a few, and placed them in a bowl.

The air in the Spoke's room was rank with body odor. The Spoke was sitting up in his bed, watchful of Pyke's every movement. Wordlessly, Pyke placed the plate on the tussled bed sheets and retreated to sit on the stool.

"Your leader," the man said.

"Like I said yesterday, I'm not sure why the host would spend any time with you. I'm an offering advocate. Maybe if you explain yourself, I can advocate for you."

The man frowned, looked down at the plate of food, then back to Pyke. "I've already explained myself."

"I find it hard to advocate for someone when I don't even know their name."

The man was temporarily stymied, as if his name was a matter of great importance. He rubbed his head aggressively with his good hand. When his eyes reengaged, he said, "Arsalan."

Pyke forced a smile. "Nice to meet you, Arsalan. My name is Pyke."

"Is this . . . *host* your leader?" Arsalan asked.

"In a sense. Host Mengle runs the crew, and the crew runs the show—*A Leap of Wisdom*. The network sponsors the show."

Arsalan's brow rippled in confusion.

"Why are you so secretive?" Pyke asked.

"You may work for the enemy."

"The enemy? I presume you mean *your* enemy, the Essentialists. We have a trading relationship with Kachina, but otherwise we have little interaction with them. And why bother? We have enough trouble with the Cooperative tribes, not to mention Ouray and Laramie."

"The true enemy is not the Essentialists. It's a machine—or a series of machines—that has infiltrated their ranks and wields people like pawns. It may have infiltrated Aspen."

Pyke wondered if Arsalan was referring to the network. Its minions, the headless, were certainly machines, but Pyke wasn't so sure about the network itself. Could the network be compromised by this machine war? There had been no recent signs of change; the show was running on schedule, trade unit output was on target, and there hadn't been any incidents with the headless mucking about in town business. Of course, he was far from an authority on how well the show was operating, since he hadn't even been a member of the studio audience.

"I think you can rest assured there's nothing like that here," Pyke said.

"I need proof. And even if you're right, we need your manufacturing capacity to help us fight the war."

Here Arsalan had hit a little too close to the mark, although maybe he was just fishing. Indeed, he was watching Pyke closely, perhaps floating the manufacturing capacity idea to see how he reacted.

"I'm not sure what that means," Pyke said. "Why do you think we have . . . that?"

"I've been to this area before—fifteen years ago. Or at least, I thought it was nearby. It was somewhere in the Colorado Cooperative. There were four of us mules—we were trying to make it all the way across the continent, trading along the way. This was when the Essentialists were less organized, and more friendly to Spokes, so we could move about freely." Arsalan took a bite of rye bread and spoke with his mouth half full. "We traveled by a place called Gondola Valley. Never seen anything like it—the sky was filled with hundreds of hanging glass bubbles. You know what I mean?"

"Gondola Valley is close, to the north—the ruins of an Old World ski resort—but it's no longer open to the public. Many of the towers and gondolas have fallen in recent years." Pyke's answer was deliberately misleading. It was the canned response they were told to give foreigners when asked about Gondola Valley.

Arsalan frowned. "I don't think it was any kind of ski resort. There were too many gondola pod-thingies and they were crossing the valley all over the place, rather than just going up and down a mountain."

Pyke shrugged.

Arsalan continued, "We were asking the locals about it. Most people said what you just said—that it had been a ski resort. But then we met a strange woman. When we asked her about the valley she wanted to take us to this bunker to sell us stuff, on account of the all the credit we'd accumulated. She showed us a big stash of Old World electronics, like battery boxes, drills, heaters, and fridges. She said they were *made* here, or at least near Gondola Valley, in some kind of factory. I didn't think much of it at the time. We came across a lot of loons in our travels, and back then I didn't care much about electronics. Since then—well, I've seen things in the last year that made me wonder if she might have been telling the truth."

"Did you buy anything from her?"

"No. We didn't buy any gadgets. Back then, they weren't allowed in Spoke lands."

"You're an Adherent?"

Arsalan's eyebrows raised, perhaps surprised at Pyke's knowledge of Spoke society. "Of a sort," he answered, "but also, none of us wanted to haul anything heavy for thousands of miles. We did buy something called ice cream. She had it in the freezer and it was real good. Jordy ate a big plate of it with a knife and fork, even though he rarely ate anything with a fork, and the woman said that's not how you eat it." He let out a throaty laugh—an abrupt deviation from his skeptical countenance. "He ate so fast his head started to hurt from the cold. You should have seen him rolling on the floor."

Arsalan continued through his meal. He was gnawing on a piece of smoked venison.

"And where was this bunker?" Pyke asked.

"I can't remember. I wasn't even sure it was near Aspen, until now."

"It may not have been Aspen."

Arsalan shifted in the bed to move closer to his food. He plucked a slice of lemon from the plate and sucked out the innards without wincing. "Can you help me fix my bike?"

"What's wrong with it?" Pyke hadn't looked at it yet. It was still lying outside where Mank had left it.

"Pretzled wheel. Frayed brake line. Could be more."

"Maybe later." He didn't want to invite Arsalan to show him the bike. Injured or not, Arsalan was strong, and might be able to overcome Pyke if allowed to walk freely. Although Pyke would have to figure out a way to allow him mobility eventually. Whatever the situation with the bike, he definitely needed to bathe.

Arsalan said, "So can I see the host now?"

"I am required to report to the crew first—they work with the host —but honestly, we typically require an offering prior to a meeting. Even if we made an exception in this case, you've still not provided information about the force that stands against you, or why they might come here, or why we might be inclined to help you in any way. I'm not sure why the host would grant you an audience."

"I can't give you all the details. What if you're in cahoots with . . . Gail. The machine that's manipulating the Essentialists, it's called Gail. If I tell you our numbers, who's involved, where we need help— that could all be used against us."

"I've done research on Spoke lands, which is one reason why they've put you in my care, and yet I've never heard of this *Gail*. Try to see this from my perspective. I have no official letter from your government, no way to prove you are who you say you are, and no offering."

Arsalan's expression darkened. He threw the half-eaten venison onto the plate and spat at the floor just shy of the stool. "There's your offering," he said.

Pyke looked at the line of spittle, then back at the brooding

Spoke. "I have, however, asked for a medic. If your arm is broken, we need to set it properly. The medic will arrive later this morning."

Arsalan didn't thank him. He only glanced at his slung arm and stared back at Pyke again.

Pyke stood up. "I recommend you rest," he said, "and consider the situation from my perspective."

He left the room and closed the door behind him.

"Oh, it's you," Pyke said when he opened the door.

"Don't sound so excited," Jeeri said, smirking. She was wearing a loose tank top, despite the cool spring weather, and carrying her bulky leather medi-kit in one hand. Her eyebrows were carefully manicured with diagonal shave lines, as was typical of younger Aspen girls. She had a long, plaited braid that fell to the middle of her back. Pyke had been friends with Jeeri since they were five years old, although he hadn't seen her much since Kehda first arrived in Aspen.

"No, I'm glad," Pyke said. "I was expecting Glen-B." He cringed, biting his teeth together. Glen-B was an older medic who did house calls. He was known to be behind a fair number of accidents and misdiagnoses, but he had seniority and there were only so many people who knew anything medically related. Jeeri was whip-smart, but she was only used by the crew for special situations because Glen-B insisted she be on a five year long probationary period.

They walked inside to the kitchen, where Pyke offered her a glass of water.

"Shane asked me to do it," she said, taking a sip. "He wants to make sure the Spoke stays healthy."

That was unusual. Shane was the hostess, second only to Host Mengle himself, and rarely concerned himself with foreign delegates of any kind.

Pyke put a finger to his mouth and pointed at the closed door to the spare room. "Why?" he whispered. "Do they think he's important?"

Jeeri made no attempt to lower her voice. "They've had a few meetings. Not sure why they're spending so much time on it."

"You think they'll want him to talk?"

She shrugged. "Listen, Pyke, you've got to stop worrying about things that are out of your control." It was an attempt to console him, but it was easy from her position. She hadn't lost her parents and her best friend in terrible tragedies, or been given all these dubious assignments. Plus, she'd been a contestant, and an audience member three times.

"The problem," he said, "is Mengle might think this Spoke man *is* under my control."

"I doubt that. The host, the crew, they're just as lost as the rest of us, trust me."

Sometimes Jeeri's irreverence was shocking. It did make Pyke feel more at ease, though. If she could become a contestant, there was still hope for him.

"Thanks, I guess." Pyke nodded. "He's in the bedroom. His name is Arsalan."

Pyke moved the propped-up chair away from the doorknob and entered. Arsalan immediately sat up. The room smelled no better than it had that morning.

Jeeri approached Arsalan without any sign of caution. "Hello, Arsalan, I'm Jeeri. I'm here to help with your arm." She knelt next to the bed, looking at the limb from different angles. "Is it okay if I remove your sling?"

"Sure."

Carefully, she removed the sling with her right hand while supporting the weight of his arm with her left. Arsalan was paying close attention to Jeeri's movements. "This might hurt a little," she said. "I need to diagnose the problem."

"Fine," Arsalan said.

"Tell me when it hurts." She began maneuvering his arm.

"There," he said. He spoke through clenched teeth, his jaw muscles flexing.

"Here?"

"No."

"And here?"

"No."

"It's fractured, but probably not broken. I'll need to immobilize it in a cast."

"Fine," Arsalan said.

"Pyke, can you get us a big pot with warm water in it?"

"Sure," he said, and went to collect it from the kitchen.

When he returned, they were talking.

"No, we don't have to worry about retchers," Jeeri said.

"Why is that?" Arsalan asked.

Pyke answered before Jeeri could. "The altitude," he said. "The air is too thin for them up here." It was another canned answer they told foreigners. Pyke suspected it wasn't the whole truth, but Arsalan certainly didn't need to know that.

Arsalan's brow wrinkled with skepticism, but he didn't probe any further.

Jeeri took a plastic container from her medi-kit. Inside it were rigid strips of cloth, so clean and sterile-looking that they had to have been produced by the network. She first layered gauze around the arm, then dipped a cloth strip in the water dish to allow it to soften, and began wrapping it around. She continued adding strips until a cast was formed, stretching from between his thumb and forefinger to just before his elbow.

"What's the network?" Arsalan asked.

Jeeri looked at Pyke.

"The network organizes and runs the show," Pyke said, "with the help of the crew."

"The show. What is it?"

"Maybe later," Pyke said. He needed to withhold some information, however innocuous, to be sure Arsalan had an incentive to be more forthcoming.

Arsalan frowned at him.

"It should harden quickly," Jeeri said, packing up her bag, "but don't move your arms or touch the plaster for an hour."

Pyke escorted Jeeri out of the room. She waited while he replaced the chair behind the door. "You never know," he said.

"It's a good idea," she said. He was surprised she agreed, given that her attitude toward Arsalan had been so laissez-faire.

"Thanks for coming by," he said.

She paused at the exterior door and looked at him sidelong. "Are you going to watch the sacred episode at the Wisdome tomorrow?"

"Which one is it?"

"Fifty-four, I think. Glen Pearson's shirt becomes untucked at the twenty-minute mark. Ralph Peters wins a new yacht. Nadia Lamberson talks about tripping on an alligator."

"Dunno—maybe." He steeled himself against what she might say next. He'd heard way too many *it'll be just like old times* from people, or worse, *you need to move on.*

"You don't have to pay attention," she said, again showing her irreverence. "It's about being together—about community."

"A community where not everyone gets to be a contestant."

She sighed. "Not everything is about the show, Pyke. Remember Shelley Cage? I saw her after she'd gone to the summit as a Lucky Winner. She'd scraped her leg on the way down, so I was assigned to treat the wound. This was a girl who did a backflip off the Willoughby Mountain Jump with her eyes closed, but she was different afterward. She was *scared*, saying all sorts of nonsensical stuff about oracles and sparkling ghosts and rolling machines. Then she just disappeared."

Pyke hadn't heard all that, in fact. "She left a letter saying she went south to encourage better offerings."

"No one saw her leave that letter. And don't you talk to Annika all the time? She seems like she could care less about being a Lucky Winner."

"Annika says it was life-changing."

"Yeah, but does she really *mean it*, like, in a good way? Whenever she talks about it at the town hall, it feels staged. And she's stuck in that library now, so what did she really win?"

Clearly, Jeeri wasn't as fond of reading as Pyke and Annika were. But her comment made him realize that Annika could be a good resource for ideas on how to handle Arsalan, since she often interviewed foreign delegates in the library. He made a mental note to check in with her.

"She enjoys working there," Pyke said. "Look, everyone knows being chosen to go up to the mountain summit is a bit . . . nerve-wracking. Fine, but it rarely happens to Lucky Winners. There are countless people who win new houses, a year's supply of food, or all-expense-paid trips to foreign villages. I haven't even had a chance to watch the show live, never mind win anything. It's hard to feel like I'm part of this *community* you keep mentioning."

Jeeri said, "My point is, maybe all this Lucky Winner business isn't that important?"

Pyke looked around, as if the host might be standing behind him, eavesdropping on their conversation. It was a grave infraction to speak ill of the show or the crew, and Jeeri had arguably done it three times since her arrival.

"Come on," she said. "There'll be a dance afterward."

"Maybe," he offered.

Jeeri sniffed, turned, and left, her long braid whipping about behind her.

He closed the door.

Jeeri's exit reminded Pyke of her dancing. She had a way of thrashing her head that could make her braid bob and dive with the music, as if it was a whole other limb on which she exerted perfect control—the tail of some exotic lizard. Often, Pyke, his friend Dwayne, and even Kehda had been caught lead footed in frozen stares of admiration when Jeeri danced. She would see them watching, smile, and whip her head about one more time. Her dancing style matched her personality—free-form, energetic, and irreverent.

It had been months since he had gone to a dance, but it felt like forever.

He decided he would go.

5
____

MORE BUNKERS

*W*e need you at the Lionel Heights Bunker in 30 min. There's a *dispute between the mules and the railroad operators.*

The note was from Owen. Ever since Tremaine had won the election, the mules had been overstepping their boundaries. Cecile often had to explain that having a mule as People's Representative didn't mean that all mules were in charge.

Cecile had been swimming in the sheets of her cot when she received the message, anxious thoughts swirling inside her head. Like some kind of visceral muscle memory, the apparition's objections still echoed from the moment when the leadership team decided to let Lexie lead Warrick north.

And now she had to go to another bunker meeting.

She rose from her bed, dressed, and left the confines of her room. She walked the hallways, her fingers grazing the cinder-block walls. It was more than just the apparition. She had always hated being stuffed inside claustrophobic buildings. "You *are* quite the traveler," Madison had said before the last meeting, for good reason.

Fabien had figured this out about her early on, before she knew it herself.

Life in Quebec City was almost all bunkers. During the winters, most of the day would be spent in a labyrinth of blocky cement buildings, workers toiling in Faraday cage-protected environments for fear of retchers. One day, on her birthday, Cecile had been painting street signs as part of her new job with the city commission—a job that at least paid the bills, and allowed her the mental latitude to daydream of being somewhere else—when she lifted her latest sign to find a message left underneath.

The message read: *There's a tent by the toad.*

She looked over to see Fabien missing from his workstation. He had taken the afternoon off.

The street signs could wait.

She left the bunker and hurried to the *Crapaud de Mer*, a park by the river that they frequented. Its name meant "Toad of the Sea." It was early spring, with piles of snow and ice still melting off the path, but it was sunny enough that she didn't need mitts or gloves.

Indeed, there was a tent there, next to a well-fed fire that seemed out of place in the afternoon sun. Fabien was waiting for her, sitting next to the fire, his shirt hanging open around the collar. "I was hoping to warm you up," he said.

That's all he needed to say. Or maybe he didn't need to say anything at all.

Afterward, lying together on a soft blanket inside the tent, she said, "Is this supposed to be my birthday present?"

"Of course not."

"You forgot, didn't you."

"What if I have a gift you can't see?"

"We're naked. I'm not sure where you could have hidden it."

"The greatest gifts are the ones you don't know you want."

"What's that supposed to mean?"

He was already up and getting dressed. He batted his eyes towards her own clump of clothes, and left.

By the time she had her clothes on, his long strides had taken him fifty yards away.

"Will you wait?" she yelled.

He didn't wait, but he did hang back enough so that she could follow.

Fabien was the perfect companion. He knew her rules: only teasing, and fun—no shop talk—but sometimes, in order to maintain an air of mystery, the games went a little far.

He took a steep, rarely-used path leading up an escarpment. It met up with a worn-out old staircase that climbed the side of the cliff. Cecile had to tack back and forth while ascending to avoid the most decayed steps. She lost sight of Fabien behind a bend, but still she continued her pursuit.

The stairs crested at a rocky plateau overlooking the river. She was in an Old World junkyard; a twenty-foot-high heap of metal and plastic parts was most noticeable, and two rusted sedans sat next to a fallen fence that had at one time marked the perimeter of a more distinguished Old World property. Behind the heap of scrap was a structure that was half log cabin on the bottom, half particle board and metal framing on the top. The front door was untarnished, inset with frosted glass, probably scavenged from a more welcoming estate. The door was open, swinging in a light breeze.

There was no sign of Fabien, other than a few fresh tracks where the ground was muddied from recently melted snow. They led to the open door.

She walked cautiously over to the building, avoiding puddles and broken fridges and the husks of retcher-melted computer monitors.

She projected her voice into the house. "Hello?"

"Come in, please," a voice said. It wasn't Fabien's, and the language was English.

The floor was streaked with dirt and dust, but she took off her boots anyway. She walked through a foyer into a musty den with a window looking over the river.

Fabien was nowhere to be seen, but a man was sitting in a recliner, watching her. He was in his early fifties, with a trim, patchy beard. She'd seen him before. It was the Spoke priest who'd arrived in Quebec City a year before. Her friends made fun of the things he said. Julie had once told her, "He talks about the *three fears* of competition, recklessness and obsession, while I'm thinking: dirty old man, dirty old man, and dirty old man."

"*Désolé*" Cecile said. Then, in English, "I was looking for my friend." She turned to leave.

"Fabien told me about you," he said. "My name is Duncan Jones."

She half-turned. "I know. Please, forgive me for intruding. I'll make my way—"

"I'm not here to preach to you. Do you think that's why Fabien would lead you here, on your birthday?"

She fully faced Duncan, raised her eyebrows, and crossed her arms. It was true. Although Fabien was a bit of a philosopher, he wasn't easily fooled, and never forced his views upon her. She doubted he'd taken on this man's faith.

"I met your parents," Duncan said.

Her heart jumped. Her parents had been gone for years. Officially, they were Quebec City representatives, liaising with foreign peoples on political matters. Unofficially, they were looking for something more: signs of civilization, knowledge, good trading partners. "Hope won't come to you," her father had once told her. "You have to go out and find it."

"Where?" she asked.

"I'm sorry," Duncan said, his palm up to suggest caution. "There's not much to say. It was a few years ago, in Watertown, but they told me about Quebec City. It's one of the reasons I came here."

Cecile's last letter from them had been from Watertown. "How . . . were they?"

"Ambitious. Curious. Courteous. Healthy, for the most part. Your mother was wearing the most beautiful shawl with a *Fleur de Lis* sewn into it. Your father walked with a lilt but I couldn't tell if it was a recent injury or just his way of walking. I was looking for people knowledgeable about the surrounding area—which they certainly were. They'd been to Kingston, and other outposts northeast of there.

They said for their next adventure they were deciding between heading into the bandit tribes bordering Essentialist territory, or going directly south through Spoke lands."

"*N'oublier pas, petit chou.*" That was the last thing her father had said to her, before they left. It meant "Don't forget, my love." But don't forget what? Don't forget to do your chores? Don't forget that your uncle needs help in the kitchen? Don't forget that we love you? Don't forget that we're still out there, somewhere, trying in vain to get back, hoping that someone, anyone, will help us?

She had trouble remembering what they looked like.

"Is there anyone who knows where they might be?" she asked. "Is there a way to contact them?"

"No. I'm sorry, Cecile. A Watertown tribal leader introduced me to them, but he's gone now—dead. I don't have any more information. Fabien told me you miss them dearly. I thought you should know."

It was little to go on, yet it was something. She imagined her parents meeting with Duncan, her mother's eyes wide, her father leaning in with his own brand of expressive curiosity. The visual was like a flower blossoming in her chest, a new memory she could add to her precious few.

"*Merci,*" she said earnestly. "I'm grateful for the information. If you remember anything else, please let me know."

Again, she turned to leave, and again he stopped her mid-stride. "That wasn't the reason Fabien brought you here."

She turned back to face him, arms crossed. "Okay . . ."

"I need your help. It would involve trips to the surrounding communities. I need someone bilingual, someone sharp."

"I'm not sure . . . I'm sorry, but I don't agree with your Adherent talks."

She thought he might be offended, but instead he laughed. "I've heard you've got a skeptical streak, which will come in handy. The Adherent preaching is important to me, but it's more of a hobby. It's not my *work*. I'm exploring, searching for one of Seeville's lost lords, advocating safe work practices and establishing trade routes. And to be clear, I don't care what you believe—only that you are hard-working, intelligent, and reasonable—all things I've already heard about you secondhand."

"What would I be doing, exactly?"

"Searching for a man. His name is Warrick Kelemen. We need his help in Seeville. I'm also looking for opportunities to set up collaborations with Spoke towns. There would be a lot of travel involved. Someday the railroad may come to Quebec City, so you may help with laying the foundations."

She was worried about trusting the strange foreigner, and her friends would make fun of her ruinously, but she was never one to let peer pressure sway her.

At least it would get her out of the bunkers.

"Thank you for the vote of confidence. I guess I could give it a shot."

Duncan smiled. "Let's meet at nine tomorrow, in the Descartiers Bunker."

She worked with Duncan for many years after that, learning a great deal. It turned out he was more nuanced than she could have possibly imagined. The Adherent faith was the spiritual manifestation of real, grave risks; ones that caused the fall, and that could jeopardize everything they were trying to rebuild—risks worth mitigating.

It was work she enjoyed, that suited her, and that she could be proud of.

Looking back, though, there was one thing that clinched the decision for her, one thing that drove her to work harder than she ever had: the job was an opportunity to look for her parents. That hope of finding them, of learning more about them, of getting one more day with them, even if secondhand, was always with her. Even if her search was in vain, maybe somewhere she could find a few more flowers to add to her little garden of memories.

6

THE LIBRARY

The Aspen Library was thirty minutes out of town, built into the wall of a canyon that split a rocky plateau. Host Mengle often said it was one of the network's many gifts, so they could all "share in its wisdom," but the remote location made it more conducive to being a place to hide knowledge away rather than share it. Pyke was one of the few people who ever visited.

A few late spring snowflakes fluttered past as he climbed the path to the crack of the canyon. From here the fissure expanded, but to no more than ten feet in width. It reminded him of the gully where he'd found his best friend Dwayne, his leg at an unnatural angle, his face bloated and discolored from bruising.

"An unfortunate accident," Glen-B had said when they hauled Dwayne out. Glen-B was one of the few people who hadn't blamed Pyke for Dwayne's death. Unfortunately, nobody cared what Glen-B thought.

Despite the flush of apprehension it gave him, Pyke peered down as he passed the wider part of the rift. With the sun low in the sky, the aperture revealed only shadows and darkness.

Pyke made his way to the library entrance, which was accessible via a metal spiral staircase cut into the plateau next to a huge, four-story bulwark of natural stone. The steps were obviously network-made, judging by the perfect lines and smoothness. Each step was studded for traction.

The main door was made of glass and rimmed in blue-hued stonework that faded into the surrounding geology. Inside was a foyer lined with wooden, book-laden shelving on plush, high thread-count rugs. Annika was easy to find—one level down, perched in front of a window that separated her from the dark crevasse. Snowflakes sparkled like stars behind her, reflecting the LED banner lights lining the ceiling.

Annika marked and closed the book in front of her as Pyke approached. She was a sturdy woman, wearing a tight frock that unapologetically allowed her gut to hang over her belt. She had big, network-built glasses, and a full-length plastic leg brace of Old World origin. It was the result of an injury from "getting out of bed once," according to her. On her desk were a number of drawings of buff people stabbing each other, in various states of bloody combat. She would often doodle, making expressions of relish while sputtering out battle sound effects.

"Take a seat," she said, gesturing to the wooden chair opposite her.

"How did you know I wanted to talk?"

"Your gait."

"My gait?"

"And your focus. There's not many people who come to the library. I like to observe those who do. Usually you're in a daze, meandering amongst the shelves, but today you came straight for me, so I knew you wanted to talk."

He sat down. "Well, thanks—I guess. It's about a new delegate I'm responsible for. He's a Spoke who tried to get to the host without making an offering. Mank took him down with a bola."

"A Spoke?" she said wistfully. "Well, that's interesting. You have all the luck."

Even his friends ridiculed him. He tried to ignore her comment. "I wondered if you might have ideas about how to handle him, since you're often charged with interviewing foreign delegates before they see the host. You must have ways to get them to talk."

A burst of laughter escaped her. She thrust a cupped hand forward, while making a series of sputtering noises with her mouth. Pyke recognized this as her 'violent stabbing' pantomime. "I try, anyway," she said, ending her mannerism with a smile. "I have a list of questions from the host, and it's important to ask these in the right order. What's more important is being patient. Sometimes a bit of conflict is good, because no matter how ornery they are, delegates want to be seen in a positive light, so attempts to lobby prompt them to reveal something. Above all, though, I find feigning indifference helps. They start to think what they know isn't valuable, and become desperate to sell it to you."

It made some sense, even though Pyke didn't like the idea of playing games with Arsalan. "What happens if you can't get the answers you need?"

"There's not much I can do. It's not like I'm Cragnor the Irascible, able to cast truth-telling spells while suffering fungal-juice induced spasms." Her eyes bulged as she lifted her hands and shook them in what he interpreted as an emulation of one of her fictitious sorcerers. She ended the portrayal with a disconcerting eye roll and a shudder.

"But . . . you won't get in trouble with the host if you don't succeed?"

"Oh, I see—you're worried what the crew might do if you fail."

"Well, yes. I also wondered why you aren't the one questioning him."

"The crew has assigned me to the role of head librarian, which does include the occasional interview of foreign delegates, but I'm not allowed to interview criminals. Arguably, this is how we should classify this Spoke, since he ran from the rangers and gave no offering. If other delegates know I interrogate criminals, they might find me a little more threatening, and in turn be less forthcoming with answers."

There was so much Annika could teach. It was a pity the network had placed her where few could find her.

"As for what the crew might do to you if you fail," she continued, "the short answer is I don't know. I often wonder what happens if I don't extract the right answers in my own interviews." She held her neck briefly in a mock gesture of strangulation, then winked. "So far, there haven't been any real consequences."

She tilted her head side to side, suggesting there may be more to her answer than she was letting on. "Although it could be because they don't have anyone to take my place. For you, it's different."

"How so?"

"Well, as a lucky winner, I might have some degree of protection —or maybe you could call it *good will* with the crew and the network. You don't have that. Then there's the fact that the Spokes are a real concern. No one talks about it in town, but I'm sure you realize this machine war could have an impact on us, eventually. The network certainly realizes this, so the information from your Spoke is quite important—more important than anything I could extract from an approved delegate. And finally, there's Laramie."

"What does Laramie have to do with this?"

"There was an attack a week ago, in Wilder's Gap. People burned alive. The Broncos took a lot of the network gifts—metalwork, tools and the like, which means we could be next. Mengle hasn't told anyone yet, but supply quotas of metals and other raw materials for Gondola Valley have increased. They're recruiting more rangers. I've seen this before. We're getting ready for conflict."

"But . . . my delegate is a Spoke, not a Laramie Bronco."

"It doesn't matter. Any foreigner will be painted with the same brush when we go to war. You're not as old as me, but I remember. During the other Laramie wars, delegates were treated harshly, as were any offering advocates that showed them sympathy." She drew her finger across her throat and cringed.

"I'm not showing any sympathy!"

"If you can't get the information we want, how do we know that? Perceptions—you have to manage them. What people see and hear is what they will believe."

It wasn't the feedback Pyke had hoped for, but perhaps it was what he needed. He could trust Annika to be straight with him.

"Well, thank you," he said. "A lot to think about."

She smiled, reached out, patted his wrist, then opened her book again.

He didn't stand up, though. Annika's reference to her being a Lucky Winner had reminded him about how Jeeri thought it wasn't such a big deal. Yet here was a perfect example of someone getting preferential treatment, simply because they'd been chosen as a contestant and won. The thought frustrated him enough to push his enquiries further.

"What happened when you went up to the mountain summit?" he asked.

Annika froze. With deliberate care, she closed her book and cradled her hands together. "You must have heard the story. I've told it many times, in town."

"I've heard it second-hand. I just . . . I have a friend. She says it's not necessarily all it's cracked up to be. You know, because of what happened to Shelley Cage, how she seemed strange when she came down the mountain, and then was never seen again."

"It's exactly how I described it. The seers are there, and yes, the power of the network is awesome to witness. It's possible that the experience is overwhelming for some. People say that's what happened to Shelley."

"Is that what you think happened to Shelley?"

"That's what I said."

"No, you said *people* say that's what happened to Shelley."

She clenched her teeth, raised an eyebrow, and shrugged. "I suspect she had a different experience than I did."

"All that stuff about there being an oracle of knowledge at the summit—that's true?"

"Well . . . yes. Remember, it's also true what they say; visiting the summit is a lonely gift." It was a nebulous catchphrase Pyke had heard from the crew before, as if the experience was intended to be private—an intimate moment that shouldn't be described in detail.

However, Annika didn't seem to be speaking about anything intimate. Her face was stretched and tense. Eventually she flinched and looked to the window, into the crevasse.

Annika was a friend and colleague—someone he respected. He was politely needling her for information, but those needles might be inflicting real pain. "I'm sorry," he said. "I shouldn't be prying."

"It's okay," she said, forcing a smile as she returned her gaze to him. "They're . . . good questions."

"Thank you," he said, with as much sincerity as possible.

He left her and took the internal staircase down two more levels, to where the more esoteric works were kept. Some of these had been produced by the network. They looked like Old World encyclopedias, all with the same blue covers and titles in unassuming white font, covering topics from treatments for otolaryngology disorders, to how a combustion engine works, to insect epidemiology in the Colorado Collective. Interspersed among the network-produced books were occasional tomes that had been saved from before the fall, or given as part of an offering.

There were only three books in the Spoke section. The network-produced one was no more than a pamphlet, containing basic information on key cities, demographics, and some cultural mores. Pyke took the second one, called *A Guide to the Spoke People*, from the shelf. It was a larger volume, bound in leather, and filled with illustrated pages depicting Spoke life. Pyke was very familiar with it, because it was the offering made by the people of Sky Shine that he'd been assigned to analyze two years ago.

He leafed through the pages, experiencing a wave of nostalgia as he recalled the time he'd read through it with Kehda. They had been lying on his bed, laughing about the Spoke obsession with bicycles and their giant beholder statues. They had puzzled over the origins of some of their ancient laws. Nobody else in Aspen seemed to care about other cultures. When Pyke asked Kehda if she'd ever want to visit Spoke lands, she didn't even hesitate. "In a heartbeat," she'd said. "Even if I had to ride a bicycle."

It saddened him that they would likely never get to see these foreign lands together. Although maybe she was there now, as part of the Essentialist front, on a mission to destroy it.

The third tome was *The Adherent's Handbook*, which he'd only skimmed when he was with Kehda.

He took out *The Adherent's Handbook* and *A Guide to the Spoke People*, and carried them two levels up.

Annika looked at him warily, then took down the serial numbers of each item. "Doing some homework, I see."

"Can't hurt," Pyke replied. "The more questions I can answer on my own, the better."

Annika tapped her temple and nodded.

Another question occurred to him. He wondered how *The Adherent's Handbook* had come to be at the library in the first place. Maybe whoever donated it would know more about Spoke history? But Annika was usually reluctant to discuss the origins of the non-network books, and he'd needled her enough today. It would be best to leave on a high note.

"Thanks again, Annika," he said, making for the exit.

"Go get 'em," she said from behind him. He glanced back to see her loose an imaginary arrow after him.

7

EVACUATION

Gail and the Essentialists would never settle for just one path to victory; they would exhaust every possible option, and all it took was one that didn't quite go the Spoke's way.

Cecile was awakened by air raid sirens blaring for the second time that night, only an hour after a drone attack from the north. There would normally be at least a day's reprieve between attacks.

Cecile, Owen, Madison, and Tremaine gathered in the command center, trying to digest the barrage of visual information the Sentinel displayed; maps, one-line report bulletins from the perimeter, video footage, and statistics.

"There's another attack force coming," Owen said. "The Sentinel thinks they originated all the way from Tucson. We're not sure how they covered all that ground—more than a thousand miles—without us detecting them. It's possible they were airlifted and dropped within our retcher-free zone. One of our perimeter towers was compromised during the most recent air raid, which could have given them an opening."

"How close are they now?" Madison asked.

"Three miles away. They have a beachhead, but we don't know

much about the composition of their force. Louie is too far north, but Monty is on his way, along with our remaining drone forces."

"Should we be ready to fight?" Tremaine asked.

"Be ready to move," Owen responded, after a brief pause.

It was at that point that Cecile guessed they would be evacuating. Owen's word choice had to be deliberate.

Tremaine left the room immediately. His mule brethren still hadn't all gotten used to comms. He would pass the word along in person.

Cecile stared at the montage of flashing information: vectors for all their active drones, as well as more than twenty feeds of camera footage. Aside from a few fires and lighted areas, most of the feeds would have looked like uninterpretable shadows dancing across the screen, if not for the fact that the Sentinel had enhanced them by labeling objects or buildings using some form of pattern recognition.

One feed showed the beholder, Monty, stomping through the eastern outskirts of town, surrounded by tiny drones that were feeding it melodic instructions, as if it was waltzing to an airborne string quartet.

Mayhem broke out as several audio feeds screamed with the sounds of ordinance. On the video feeds, flashes of light exposed more of the surroundings. Monty vaulted through the air—something Cecile didn't think was possible—to land with both feet on top of a low-rise building, crushing it completely. Enemy drones clashed with the Sentinel's, and several screens blipped offline. On those still active, Cecile could see people on the periphery. Essentialist militants were popping in and out of cover, firing at the Spoke-led drones.

Monty stomped toward another building and swept up some of these poor souls with a massive hand, while with its other fist it crushed a large cannon that was turning toward it.

An artillery blast hit Monty in the back. Drones flocked toward the origin of this attack, but not quickly enough to prevent the second hit, or the third. Debris and smoke and dust clouded the image, but Cecile heard through the speakers the unmistakable sound of Monty hitting the ground, crushing nearby buildings and shaking all the nearby camera feeds.

That was the tipping point.

"All personnel must evacuate Raleigh immediately," the Sentinel said over the intercom. "We will be retreating to Wilmo. Instructions for salvage and supplies will be on your individual comms. Be ready to leave in eight minutes."

It was a crushing blow, since they had endured so much in Raleigh. She could see it in the downcast faces of her friends. Cecile felt for them, and Gail's continued advance frustrated her. But the apparition began pressing urgently inside her, like an anxious itch that had to be scratched. For the apparition, this was an opportunity.

The others were all looking at their comms and moving toward the exit when she said, "I need to take Warrick north now."

Madison and Owen paused. Madison's age was showing, pale wrinkles evident in the soft light. Creases were also visible on her cheek, on account of being woken up only moments ago. Owen, despite being in his early twenties, didn't look much better. Blue bags hung under his eyes. His limbs were gaunt, and the skin of his face stretched.

"We don't have time to wait for Lexie and Ryder," Cecile explained. "Once we retreat to the south, Depot 81 will be even harder to reach, because we will have fewer northerly route options. And keep in mind Gail's drone forces may have been spent in the last attack, so we might have breathing room to make headway now, before she replenishes them."

"We can't risk losing Warrick," Madison said.

"Exactly," Cecile said. "We only have a few more months. I'll take Pierre with me."

"How will you convince Warrick?" Madison asked. "I doubt he would go anywhere with you willingly."

"We'll find a way. And maybe this will give him time to heal—a chance to get over his obsession that I'm some kind of witch." It wasn't the strongest argument, and yet Cecile stood unflinching as Madison and Owen shared looks. Cecile was an accomplished liar.

She was confident they wouldn't smell any duplicity, but whether they agreed to the plan was another matter entirely.

Owen looked down at his tablet, perhaps out of habit, or perhaps to see if there was any guidance from the Sentinel. He sighed. "You'll need more than Pierre, in case Warrick is a lot to handle. Take Bronson. He's one of our best, and in need of purpose. Godspeed."

"I'll go find him," Cecile said.

"No need," Owen said. "I'll have the Sentinel reach out to him."

"And Cecile—" Madison began.

Cecile's pulse was racing. She was eager to leave the room before they changed their minds. "What?"

"*Bonne chance*," Madison said, leaning over to give her a stout hug. Cecile didn't reciprocate, other than a careful pat on the back. It had caught her by surprise.

"*Merci*," was all she offered, before she turned about and left.

✦

Cecile jogged alone, hunched over due to the weight of her heavy pack, staying close to buildings to maintain some semblance of cover as she headed through the city. The sounds of battle reverberated behind her. There was no action here, with everyone fighting in the south, or fleeing to the east. The occasional drone whizzed overhead. She could only hope they were of Spoke origin.

Pierre and Bronson had gone to collect Warrick from the hospital, which was probably for the best—there would be less resistance if she wasn't there. Besides, she needed to stop in at the pharmacy.

She reconnected with the others on a rocky bank under a bridge that spanned the Eno River. It was directly on the retcher-free perimeter line, so she made sure to turn off her comm device and lock the power button.

Warrick tried to jump up the instant he saw her, but his cuffs had been tied to a driftwood tree trunk, holding him back. "I told you," he said, "if she's coming I want nothing to do with this." His eyes blazed as he cast angry looks at Pierre and Bronson.

Bronson stood to address him. Cecile was used to seeing him in formal slacks and puffy shirts. Now he was wearing tight-fitting camo gear, which accentuated his rounded shoulders and V-shaped torso. If she ever had to confront him using force, he would present a formidable foe. "Our mission is to bring you to Depot 81," Bronson said, "She knows the way, and how to gain entry."

"I agreed to go, but not with her," Warrick said. He stared Cecile down with loathing. "This is bullshit. I'm not going anywhere."

Cecile tried to look offended. "Pierre, Bronson, maybe we should discuss this." She motioned for them to step away. The three of them moved out of earshot, closer to the flowing waters of the Eno.

Cecile said, "*Zut alors*, I'm so sorry. I don't know of any other way."

"We might have to move him by force," Pierre said, "or even carry him." He shrugged.

Cecile was happy to have Pierre with them. He was a mild-mannered man who stood up for what he believed in. She'd travelled with him for years, and worked with him in the bunkers of Quebec, before she came south. She would be relying heavily on his loyalty during this mission.

"The man has a condition," she said. "They gave him a form of electrotherapy in Raleigh, and while it makes him sharper of mind, it also makes him ornery. In a few days he'll be less difficult." This was partially true. The more time spent away from his treatment, the easier it would be for his own apparition to dull his wits and make him more pliable. "Until then, I brought these." She held out the pills she'd taken from the pharmacy. "They're a sort of muscle relaxant that will make him drowsy. They also contain a mild hallucinogen."

Bronson's eyebrows raised. "Cecile, first I should say I have the utmost respect for what you've done in Seeville, and I'm glad to be with you and Pierre on this critical mission, but it's important to me that we are all equals here. We'll face many dangers, and we should make key decisions democratically."

Bronson was crafty. Cecile couldn't very well say no, but in hindsight, she should have made it clear to Owen and the Sentinel that this was a military operation, and she was the leader. At least she would have Pierre's vote on substantive issues, so maybe it wouldn't matter.

"That makes perfect sense," she said.

"Now, this issue of medication," Bronson continued. "Don't you think it will make Warrick resent you even more? Shouldn't we be trying to foster his trust? We need to dispel this notion he has, that you're . . . you know."

"*Mon dieu*, I'm *not* a witch. I just happen to believe in medicine. We don't need to tell him. You put this in his food, crush up one pill at a time. And why don't you talk to him—make a deal? Go ahead and say you'll protect him, and after Depot 81, you'll let him go. I would do it, but guess what—he's not going to listen to me."

Bronson frowned, considering it. Eventually, he nodded and made his way over to Warrick. Cecile stayed away, wanting to make sure her presence wouldn't impact Bronson's conversation.

✦

Cecile gave Warrick plenty of space. She wasn't sure how much he had bought into Bronson's arguments, but he traveled without objection for the rest of the night. They made camp under another bridge, well north of Raleigh, and waited until the next evening before moving again.

There were still many hurdles to overcome. In particular, the need to keep Warrick in line, and of course the change of their ultimate destination. She would have to be careful that Lexie's group couldn't find and intercept them. But she'd made it out of Raleigh. They were on their way.

She allowed herself a long exhalation.

She was relieved, but it wasn't that she felt happy. In fact, she was quite disappointed for Owen, Madison, and all the Spokes she'd come to know at Raleigh. But the apparition overruled her sentimental feelings. Now that she'd left with Warrick it was appeased, for the moment. She didn't feel the anxious well of emotion, pressing her in different directions. The guilt and despondency from her betrayals were reasonable prices to pay, as long as they replaced the apparition's all-consuming sense of dread.

The grueling day and conflicting emotions had rendered her exhausted, but before she slept she walked out onto an array of natural stepping stones in the river, beneath the bridge. She picked up a flat, oval rock in her hand, and tested its weight.

When she'd been travelling with Fabien, they would find refuge under Old World bridges just like this one. Bandits often had similar ideas, so Fabien had them stop downriver, where he would skip stones under the bridge to see if anyone came to investigate. Cecile had been terrible at it. Fabien would always send his rocks much farther, usually achieving many more skips.

She skipped the stone. One, twice, three times on top of the calm waters. It was lost in the mist.

By the time Fabien was nearing his end, she'd become better than him at skipping stones. Or maybe he just didn't have the focus, on account of his condition.

She reached under her shirt to extract the smooth oval communicator from her bra, then squatted and skipped it over the water. It travelled in an identical path to the prior stone, then sank. The apparition registered no objection; she would be traveling in close quarters for weeks, and she couldn't afford to carry a suspicious object. Besides, the imperative was clear, and it hadn't changed in years.

She found another flat stone on the riverbed, arched her hand, and bent low.

A memory ran through her. She was high up in the mountains, standing on a platform, with Fabien sitting in a wheelchair in front of her. He was looking out over the edge, toward undulating peaks cascading into the distance. When Cecile looked down, her knuckles were white, holding tightly onto the handles of the wheelchair.

She shuddered, dropped the stone, and returned to the campsite.

8

REJECTED OFFERINGS

It was cold and wintery the day Pyke first met Kehda. Thick, sticky flakes of snow had been floating down from the sky, coating the ground in a foot-high white blanket. Near the intake platform, the shape of a mountain lion stood out, sculpted by the local children the day before, its contours gradually fading as the snow accumulated on top of it.

Pyke moved to the next offering and checked his clipboard. "Inoco representative!" he hollered toward the chalet.

Glen-K opened the door and nudged Kehda outside, who began trudging up the hill. She was wearing mostly leather, finely made, tight-fitting over her trim figure. An oversized, fraying scarf was wrapped around her neck. Her hair was a chestnut color, with subtle blonde accents, perhaps from sun bleaching, with two broad silver clips keeping it tucked into pleats. Her footwear was more sandal than boot, although they were at least closed-toed. She marched up the grade determinedly, nearly slipping on the underlying ice twice on the way up.

"I'm Kehda Rojas," she said as she came to a stop in front of him, "a representative of the Inoco clans. I come with a most valuable offering and respectfully request a meeting with the host." Her amber skin radiated against the white backdrop. She bowed her head solemnly.

Pyke was in a jovial mood. It was early winter, and the first snows made him eager to ski with Jeeri and Dwayne after work. There was also something about Kehda that he found amusing. Her serious manner contrasted with her irresponsible attire.

"Careful," Pyke said, gesturing to the snow lion beside Kehda. "He hasn't eaten today."

Kehda looked at the sculpture and then glared at him, but only for an instant before her expression melted into a grin.

"Please," Pyke said, "you may present your offering."

"I would be honored," she said, and she brushed the snow off the wooden box sitting on the offering palette. "The Navajo Nation are renowned for their glass works," she said, opening latches on the top of the box to reveal the interior. It was stuffed with thick, fibrous leaves, a variety often used by southeastern tribes as padding and insulation. "What is less known is that in Inoco we have our own craftsmen with comparable abilities."

She reached in carefully and pulled out a flashing labyrinth of pipes made of red, orange, and yellow glass. It may have at one time occupied a cubic space no more than two feet across. On the top was a large hook, suggesting it was made to hang somewhere, perhaps as a sort of colorful chandelier or weather vane.

Pyke raised his eyebrows and nodded, trying to look impressed. In truth, he had already removed the structure the day before to inspect and scan it—a security protocol required by the network.

"A beautiful offering," he said. "And why does Inoco wish to consult with the host?"

"We wish to propose a trade relationship. Our stores of metal tools, shipping containers, and adhesives are low. In return, we can offer glassware of comparable or better quality, as well as competitive tributes."

She spoke matter-of-factly, without the fawning tone of most representatives. Her eyes were furtive, assessing his reaction.

"Where are you from—I mean, in Inoco?"

"A village in Arenas Valley."

"Named?"

"Sundown."

"Has your magistrate blessed this offering?"

"Yes, of course."

"What kind of preliminary tribute are you proposing?"

She paused. "A hundred thousand Essentialist notes."

"Do you know Detrick Aron, the magistrate's son?"

"Yes."

"I heard he was against the idea of tribute, and trade agreements with the Colorado Cooperative involving metal tools."

"Necessity often requires one to rethink one's position." She smiled.

"And your cultural ambassador to the Essentialists—what is her position?"

"Fully aligned. Your manufactured goods will not affect our relationship with the Essentialists. In fact, the pact need not be reported at all."

Kehda was beginning to shiver. Her fists clenched. She seemed to flex her arm muscles to combat the cold. The glass sculpture trembled in her hands as she placed it carefully back in the box.

Usually Pyke would ask more questions, but he had enough for the preliminary screen, and he didn't want her to suffer any longer. "I'm sorry," he said. "Your offering has been rejected."

"What!" Her eyes lit up. "You can't just do that on your own, can you?"

"It's my job to screen offerings based on network criteria."

"What criteria?"

"We don't normally provide an explanation."

She searched his face for clues. "That's just not possible."

"Look, I'm sorry you came all this way, but you should know it happens more often than not. You are of course free to take back your—"

"No," she snapped. "Bullshit. Is Navajo paying you more? We'll double the tribute."

He shook his head.

Kehda's posture slackened and her expression softened. "Why, though? Why?" She frowned at the offering box.

He felt some sympathy for her. She was clearly naïve about the process. Her attire suggested she was naïve to the entire Colorado Collective.

"We know Inoco well," he said. "There was an offering made four months ago, by Detrick Aron. And there is no such thing as a cultural ambassador."

Delegates were often shocked at the information Pyke had at his disposal. Kehda was no exception. "I thought you meant to say curator, and Detrick—he is notoriously unreliable. I travelled for weeks to get here. *Please.*"

"The tribute is much too high. It's not practical, economically, for a territory as small as Inoco to pay a hundred thousand notes in tribute. It's a red flag. We have algorithms to identify fraudulent offerings, or inability to pay." He offered a grimace that was intended to appear compassionate and gestured toward the chalet.

"You're saying I'm *lying*?"

He didn't confirm the obvious answer to her question. "Maybe if you come back with Detrick Aron, or another known Inoco representative, and provide a more credible offering than regifted Navajo glassware, we will reconsider."

She stared at him aghast for another minute, even after he gestured again to the chalet.

"I'm sorry," he said, "but I'll have to call the rangers if you don't leave of your own accord. I can have the offering placed in your carriage for the ride down."

She remained motionless, breathing heavily, as if taking in more oxygen would usher in some inspirational idea to salvage the situation.

It was rare that delegates had to be forcibly removed, but it was sometimes necessary when they tried to bypass offering advocates. They would then be detained and questioned. Usually, it revealed a lack of sophistication on the part of the representative, if not desperation. Pyke suspected the latter in this instance, especially given Kehda's fraudulent proposal.

"Glen-K!" he called.

"Fine," Kehda said, her hands up defensively. "The truth is, I'm not from Sundown. I'm from the Union—from near the Sierras. I was sent to learn how to build a prosperous town like yours, but if I go back with nothing, I may not survive—*we* may not survive."

"I'm not sure what I can do to help you," Pyke said. Glen-K was walking up the hill, a crook of a smile on his face. He liked to be made useful, especially if it involved a use of force.

"Just give me a little more time," Kehda pleaded. "Maybe you could learn more about our village—the truth." And then, more quietly, "Maybe you could learn a little more about me."

Glen-K had arrived. "Trouble, Pyke?" he asked.

The words hung in the air. Pyke didn't have much to lose by letting Kehda stay longer. He could still reject her offering at any time. And recently he'd become disillusioned with constantly processing boring offerings from stuffy representatives. Kehda actually interested him, despite her questionable story, or perhaps because of it.

"No trouble," Pyke said. "This delegate needs a proper jacket, and a room in the delegate lodges. Her offering will require more extensive screening."

Glen-K looked disappointed. "Well, c'mon," he said, and waltzed down the hill.

Thank you, Kehda mouthed after she realized she'd been given another chance. Pyke shrugged, and she followed Glen-K down the grade.

Later he would question his decision, as would others, especially because even in contrition Kehda wasn't all that forthcoming. Yet he didn't regret it, because that brief moment of mercy would open up a whole new world: mysterious insights about foreign lands, a relationship balanced between tenderness and strife, and the birth of the demanding, quirky, achingly lovable toddler around whom his life now pivoted.

The Wisdome was like a city hall, because it was where Host Mengle kept his crew, and where the townspeople would congregate for important events and festivities. It was also well-protected, with thick steel-reinforced concrete walls.

It had been built back in Glen Pearson's time, originally called "the palace." People nicknamed it the "Wis-dome," because outside of its municipal functions it was best known as the place where all the sacred episodes of *A Leap of Wisdom* were shown. Besides, the building had none of the ornate cosmetic flourishes one would expect to be associated with Old World palaces, like fancy crenelations or lookout towers. What was most noticeable was its size; several bulbous domes sat atop a huge cylindrical prism that was at least a thousand feet in diameter. There were only a handful of visible windows, three levels up, although panels could be opened up on all sides to access more. Protective gun installations were hidden away in antechambers, in case the town was ever attacked. Dwayne had told Pyke where they were, but as far as he knew they'd never been used.

One other feature that undermined the "palace" moniker was the massive billboard on the roof that stood at least forty feet tall, which each month displayed a different scene from *A Leap of Wisdom*: Glen Pearson's teeth shining icy white while hugging a contestant; a pair of contestants hurdling island-to-island on the Trivial Jump course, the audience cheering in the background; or a moment of magical synchronicity in which all three contestants were smiling and pressing their answer buttons at the same time.

Pyke shuffled forward into the main entrance behind the queue of men and women, all dressed in their show gear. Pyke was wearing his father's corduroy jacket and black tie over a white shirt. It was scuffed and musty with patches on the sleeves, but altogether not bad considering it was decades old. A few other men wore Old World suits, and many donned sport jackets rife with rips or discolored by blotchy stains. The more dedicated of the women wore full-length dresses, but most wore either simple blouses with puffy arms that cut off around the bicep, or simple, tight-fitting blazers.

In Pyke's childhood, torn or stained clothing had been unacceptable, and many people would dress themselves in perfect replicas of the clothing of iconic *Leap of Wisdom* contestants to be featured that evening, but lately Mengle seemed less worried about appearances, or maybe it just wasn't practical to keep mending and resewing Old World clothing. As long as people showed some token effort to conform, the crew wouldn't enforce the dress code.

He followed the line into the main foyer, where it became more of a throng. Jeeri was across from him but there were too many bodies between them, so Pyke let the flow convey him into the main theater. Most of the seats were already taken. He climbed up the steps to the less coveted higher-strata seats, where the screen didn't arc directly above him. He didn't need to have an immersive experience—he just wanted to get out of everyone's way.

As soon as he claimed his seat, he noticed Vin Cheetuk had been close on his heels.

"Mind if I join you, Pyke?" Vin asked. He sat next to Pyke before he could respond.

"Sure, Vin," Pyke said, after the fact.

Vin was a lithe man with a pasty complexion. He had a tendency to wrinkle his nose for no reason. The rangers and other offering advocates sometimes referred to Vin as *garbage man*, because he was always cleaning up after the crew, or doing some of the less glorified jobs. Vin never challenged it, so the name stuck.

It was probably better than being thought of as cursed.

"How's the foreigner?" Vin asked. "A Spoke from the east, isn't he?"

"His arm is healing. Not very talkative, but I'm working on him."

"Good. Did he tell you anything about the machine war? How's it going for the Spokes?"

Vin had been too eager to follow Pyke while entering the theater, and he wasn't ordinarily this inquisitive. "Forgive me," Pyke said, "but something tells me these questions aren't a byproduct of spontaneous conversation. Did Shane ask you to find out more about Arsalan?"

Vin offered a tight, cursory smile. "It was Host Mengle. He said it might be useful to see how things were going. It wasn't a direct order or anything. I saw you at the entrance and I thought I'd check in."

Pyke had never heard of Host Mengle caring enough to proactively ask about delegates. Typically, he would only concern himself with foreigners if they had made a considerable offering, and even then he expended as little energy as possible on the interactions.

The situation enraged Pyke. He still hadn't been an audience member, while others were skulking around trying to steal valuable insights that could put them in Mengle's good graces. "Why doesn't Mengle contact me directly instead of sending his minions?" he asked pointedly. "I would be happy to talk face to face."

A woman in the seat in front of him turned and frowned in protest at his volume.

"Sorry," he whispered.

Vin shifted in his seat, then stood abruptly. "Mengle is busy," he said. "If I were you I'd be careful." He pushed past people on the steps who were still finding their seats, all the way down to the front row where the crew was sitting. Apparently, Vin was no longer concerned about maintaining the façade of a casual encounter.

A young boy with a red mop of hair and a wonky bow tie filled Vin's seat. He smiled at Pyke.

Pyke checked his anger. Vin was right about needing to be careful. Mengle liked to appear to be magnanimous and fun, but he also held significant sway. Chan Unsalah had almost starved to death in a gondola for showing up drunk as a contestant. A handful of people in town had been sentenced to Gondola Valley isolation for more capricious reasons, and three others had never been seen again. Mengle could be vindictive when he wanted to be.

The lights dimmed, the outer doors were sealed, and the screen shimmered to reveal a scintillating starscape. Glen Pearson appeared out of the false cosmos, a suited man with sleek silver hair and a plastered smile floating in space.

"Welcome, Aspen!" Glen's face distorted in ways that made him look fake. Pyke assumed the network had animated these intros based on old footage of Glen Pearson from when he was alive a century ago. "Today, we have the privilege of experiencing episode fifty-four. Will Nadia Lamberson underbid? Is Ralph Peters overconfident? And then there is the alligator incident." He winked in an exaggerated manner. "Enjoy, and remember . . . anyone can be a contestant. If you work hard, if you support the good work of the host and the crew, the network will find you. Who knows—maybe *you* can be the next . . . Lucky Winner!"

As soon as the show began, Pyke experienced the usual compunction to stand up and leave. He'd seen this episode several times, and it felt as though each mundane minute was sucking the life out of him. He looked around cautiously, moving his eyes more than his head. Everyone was staring at the screen compliantly. He saw no signs of fatigue or discomfort. Maybe they really did enjoy the mind-numbing repetition—or maybe they were better actors than he was.

Perhaps that was why he had never been a contestant. Maybe the crew could sense his boredom.

The boy next to him was fully enamored, eyes wide, taking in every studio audience cheer and upbeat musical riff. He clapped with enthusiasm when Ralph Peters made the winning bid and ran up to take his spot in preparation for the Trivial Jump course. None of it evoked any sense of nostalgia for Pyke. Rather, it left him with a sort of regretful unease. Maybe the boy would end up like Pyke. Maybe he would spend much of his life wanting to be a contestant, and never even be admitted to the studio audience.

Pyke sat through the rest of the episode in silence, stifling the urge to close his eyes, and trying to not let the monotonous sights and sounds of the theater lull him to sleep.

Afterward, people socialized in the foyer. The mood was informal and relaxed. Pyke said his hellos to a few of the advocates and rangers. "Yeah, hi, Pyke," Brian the chalet manager said, and moved away. Crowley flicked his chin in acknowledgement before quickly turning his back to him. Without anyone else to talk to, Pyke nudged Jeeri amicably when she was talking to one of her patients. "Hey," she said. She returned the favor by pushing him into Mank.

"Sorry," Pyke said, raising his hands in deference when Mank glared back at him.

The crowd filtered out, some to the outdoors, some down the stairs to the Underdome. He followed the latter group. The Underdome was a cavernous underground room with huge speakers embedded in the walls and laser lights shooting through the air. Reflective sculptures shaped much like weather vanes, and made from rotating shards of red, blue and green glass in a spindle, dangled from the ceiling. The glass was repurposed from several Navajo pieces they had been gifted. In one corner, tucked away, hung Kehda's original offering.

It surely wasn't what Kehda had in mind, but Pyke felt a measure of pride that his lobbying had resulted in the network agreeing to use the piece for anything at all.

For a while he people-watched, drinking a spruce juice—a carbonated apple and lemon juice medley. When Jeeri danced, he danced as well, but not with her. He went off alone to another part of the floor and found a spot open enough to allow him to flail about without getting in anyone's way.

The song was one he'd heard before, but he couldn't remember the name. A deep, high-tempo bassline was interrupted periodically by ambient, melodic vocals. The lyrics didn't make any sense, but he didn't care. It compelled him to move.

When thunder strikes, you want me to stay.
But when the storm is gone, you send me away.

Most people were standing at the periphery of the dancefloor, looking in at a half-dozen groups of a handful of dancers. Smirks, pointing and under-their-breath-comments told him they were amused, perhaps even embarrassed for him to be convulsing in such an uncontrolled manner, alone.

He didn't care. He wasn't here for them. He skipped, contorted, and bobbed his head to the rhythm.

One of the watchers did give him pause. Or rather, "watcher" wasn't the word, because it didn't have eyes, and it wasn't human. A headless unit had come into the Underdome and had positioned itself beside the wall. It was humanoid-looking, save for the missing head, with a gray exterior and bulbous joints. Its surface was smooth and featureless, like a half-formed cut of stone before a statue maker went to work on the finishing touches.

Amid the strobing lasers and shifting people, Pyke could have sworn the headless changed angles so that its chest pointed his way, following his movements as he skipped across the floor during one of his more tangential dance forays.

Seeing a headless in the village wasn't unusual. They would insert themselves into larger gatherings. It was how the network kept tabs on them. Pyke had heard there was often one of them on the parapet at the studio where *A Leap of Wisdom* was played. One or two would usually show up at town hall meetings or festivals. People paid them no mind. There was no way to interact with the headless, so most gave them no more attention than they would a curious piece of art.

Pyke was sure it was listening. If it had hidden cameras, it was watching as well. Otherwise, why would it be here? It had to have been a headless unit that pulverized the Ouray statue at the offering intake chalet, turning it into quartz dust on the ground with its maul-hands. What else could have done it?

When he returned from the rest room the headless was gone, and he didn't see it for the rest of the evening.

Unfazed, he returned to his dancing.

It feeeeels like love in the moonlight,
Shadows of joy, eclipsing the night.

Jeeri was dancing with Brian, the chalet manager. She wore an earnest smile, and her head bobbed to his whisper-yells in her ear. Pyke gave them space. He thrashed his head about more vehemently, oblivious to onlookers. He was dead sober, but drunk on the music. The sound raised the hairs on his arm and enveloped him in a blanket of energy. He closed his eyes to block out visual distractions and focus on the pulsating rhythm. Song after song acted like a time machine, reminding him of his hopeful youth, the melodies stirring old emotions, pushing his troubles into the recesses of his mind.

Somewhere amid the dancing, with his mind buoyed by hope, an idea came to him. He would request a meeting with Host Mengle. Not only that, he would ask that Arsalan be in attendance. Mengle wanted information about Arsalan, so why not allow them access to the source? Pyke was constantly in fear of what the crew might do—that he might step out of line and be put in some sort of purgatory—but maybe his problem was that he needed to show initiative. Maybe that's what it took to be a contestant: to eschew protocol for the betterment of the community.

When the music stopped there were only a handful of people left in the Underdome, most with drinks in hand, bobbing their heads. Three women were leaning together, trying to find support on each other but instead landing in a cackling heap. A man had passed out nearby, his head sideways on a table.

Pyke doubted any of these people would remember the solitary dancer who stayed with them until closing time.

Without the music, and with the bright lights abruptly switched on, he fell out of his dream state, back to reality, back to today.

Back to feeling like a rejected offering.

9

UPLINK

"There's no Sentinel headquarters in the north," Warrick protested for the umpteenth time, this time addressing Bronson. "She's taking us to her lair, that vicious harpy. Grow a pair and put a stop to this for the love of Okafor."

Cecile was on point as they marched southwest, treading softly over green-shooted meadows and soggy forest pathways. Warrick marched willingly. The drugs seemed to take away his desire to invoke any physical resistance, but they did nothing to hold his tongue. In fact, the drugs might be loosening it.

"Novation wouldn't do this, you know this, this fage . . . lagelele," Warrick continued, trailing off into an indecipherable mumble. He was quiet for a while after that. Cecile was beginning to worry the drugs might be giving him brain damage.

"Is it much farther?" Bronson asked. Warrick's barrage of complaints seemed to be eroding his patience.

"We're close," Cecile responded. "Less than an hour."

They had been gaining in elevation, approaching a rock massif. A field of boulders undulated up toward it. The group was quiet as they each took care to navigate the more treacherous terrain.

Pierre spoke softly to her in French. "How can we be sure the area is free of retchers?"

"The Sentinel has been clearing strategic locations across the continent to allow for supply dumps or remote monitoring stations. This is one such area."

Pierre nodded, accepting the explanation. She considered it quite plausible, and it might actually be true, although almost certainly not at this location.

They navigated a steep escarpment, pulling on spindly bushes and trees with gnarly trunks to help them up the slope, then cut through a patch of woods occupying the top of the massif.

"Is this the spot?" Bronson asked as they approached the finger of rock that reached out over a cliff. It was wider than Cecile had hoped, allowing for more than one person to walk out at a time, but it clearly was the location she'd pointed to from below. She doubted they'd find anything better.

"Yes, I'll try here," she said. She stepped carefully out onto the rock ledge, drawing her comm device from her pocket. Bronson was behind her, breathing over her shoulder.

"Are you sure you want to be out here?" she asked. "Retchers often push into new territory. I'm not a hundred percent sure it's clear."

Bronson looked to the sky and shrugged. "I'll step away if it comes."

He was a brave one, this Bronson, and ambitious. She guessed he was looking to regain prominence in the Spoke hierarchy after losing the Raleigh election. Perhaps he saw this mission as a way to show his mettle.

She suppressed a flush of nerves, turned on her comm, and entered her credentials. Usually she would have at least a few minutes before a retcher came, but if one was nearby, she might only have seconds.

She typed a message addressed to the Sentinel's main distribution, omitting one character from the distribution address. Then she tilted her screen so that Bronson could see what she was typing for the message.

Unit V8X reporting. Location SE of Smoky Mountains. Advise as to best route to Depot 81.

She hit send, and held the comm up, screen facing out, as if that would somehow help the transmission.

After a few seconds, she pulled the comm down, averted from Bronson's gaze. "It might take a while," she said. The comm had already given her an *undeliverable autoreply.*

They all fidgeted. She looked at her comm again. *"Zut alors,"* she exclaimed, "the Sentinel says this area has been repopulated with retchers."

Bronson glanced around feverishly, as did Pierre and Warrick who were waiting on the massif.

"Mon dieu," she said, pretending to read the comm, but actually turning it off.

Bronson stepped forward, trying to peek at the comm. "Be careful," she said, just as he peered over her shoulder. "I've lost power. It must be close."

Yet again, they searched the skies.

Cecile hurled the comm over the cliff, toward some exposed rocks. Its landing was obscured by the rockface but she hoped the fall would destroy it. "I've seen a retcher attack before. You don't want to be near any tech when it comes."

Bronson frowned. "I understand," he said. "Did you get anything before it died?"

"I did," she said. She urged Bronson off the finger ledge toward the others. "Besides the retcher warning, the Sentinel said there are no northward paths open through Essentialist territory for a group on foot. There would be more than a ninety-three percent chance of being caught or killed by Gail. Instead, we're to go due west, to where one of the Sentinel's attack forces are located. From there, a beholder will pick us up and run us north, through the mountains in the midwest, then we'll cut back east."

After a moment of contemplation, she saw notable slouching, as if their packs had suddenly become heavier.

"*Oui*," she said, "it's a long detour, but do you want to go against the word of the Sentinel? I'm not inclined to challenge that statistic."

Bronson and Pierre shook their heads moodily, and they all began walking back through the forest, down the steep slope, through the boulder field. No one asked about the remains of the comm, or the fact that no retcher came. They likely assumed that the retcher had destroyed the device, since they wouldn't have been able to see it happen, way down the cliff.

She was making progress. Now they could travel west in earnest. There would be more questions, and she might need to conjure up more evidence for the non-existent Spoke advance force, but she'd have plenty of time to brainstorm a solution along the way.

10

BEING THERE

Pyke's mother once told him: "Music allows you to be there, without being there."

Her earbuds would be in at all hours, channeling music from the most recent network-issued nugget, whether she was washing clothes in the river, sorting mail at the mail depot, or cleaning the house. When her knee injury would flare up, she would turn up the music. When she was about to go up to the parapet to be a part of the studio audience, she would sing to herself. It was her way of tolerating life, to function without having to interact with the outside world.

Her taste was calmer, folksy music, but that didn't stop her from unleashing the occasional impromptu jig, or from flailing her hand at some imaginary dance partner from the Old World. "Don't cut in," she would say, when Pyke interrupted her, "unless you're from Nashville."

It was different for Pyke. He didn't use music as a distraction. He was "there" alright, but his "there" was different; multidimensional, full of opportunities and emotion missing from a world without melody. Music was like adding fluorescent color to a black-and-white photograph. It was a crackle of lighting, igniting his hopes and dreams. It was the birth of a brighter perspective. Life without music was inanimate, lacking vector or momentum.

It saddened Pyke that his mom didn't see music the same way. Sometimes, even though they were in the same house, he didn't feel like she was present.

Maybe it was because Pyke's dad was a jerk—a ranger who ranged so far from home that he didn't come back. Until he did come back, with another woman. He had the gall to ask Mom for money, claiming she stole their apartment. She would ignore him, hit the play button, and move on. She lived in blissful ignorance when it came to Dad as well; she loved him, even though he treated her terribly. When Dad died—a freak accident in which he was killed by a falling ledge of stone—the incident crushed her just the same.

And then she was diagnosed with a disease. Her body was making too many red blood cells, Glen-B had told him. Eventually she would have a "thrombotic event." But it didn't faze her. In that case, Pyke was glad music allowed her to escape. She was an avid listener, right up until the "event."

Now, when a new dance song filled him with light, when a bass drum forced his feet into action, he thought he could see her, just out of reach, on the edge of the dancefloor; an elusive partner in a grand ball, always stepping away just before he could ask for her hand. Just like in life, she was there, but she wasn't really there.

◆

Pyke unlocked the cuff from the bedpost and reconnected it to Arsalan's other wrist. Arsalan could move about freely, although he couldn't spread his hands more than a foot apart. Pyke carried a sheathed blade at his belt just in case Arsalan tried something.

"I don't need to wash again," Arsalan said.

"Come," Pyke said, "you can help me." He led him out of the apartment and down the exterior steps. Arsalan was attentive to his surroundings, looking down the street and up at the mountains. At the base of the stairs was Arsalan's bicycle, with its warped wheel and frayed brake cable. Next to it Pyke had laid out bike parts and tools: pliers, wrenches, wire cutters, allen keys, brake line, bolts, spokes, and tubes.

"We don't have a replacement front wheel," Pyke said, "so we'll have to fix this one." He winced, unsure if it was even possible.

Without hesitation, Arsalan began rifling through the tools and parts, inspecting them.

"What should I do?" Pyke asked.

"Let me handle this," Arsalan said. "This is what I do. I'm a wrench."

"You're hurt."

"It's getting better," Arsalan said, lifting his cuffed hands to inspect the cast, as if it might offer insight into his healing process. "The girl did a good job."

"Jeeri knows what she's doing. Why don't you . . . you can fix the brake line, I'll fix the wheel."

Arsalan's cynical frown suggested a lack of confidence in the plan, but he nodded. He grabbed the extra brake cable and inspected it. "It's got the wrong end cap. I'll have to rig up a new one." He began working his hands along the frame, using the allen key and ratchets to remove the frayed cable. His fingers worked so nimbly that the cuffs barely affected his movements. He tilted his head toward the wheel as he worked. "Find some leverage to bend the rim back, then we'll fix the spokes and true it."

Pyke tried to apply torque to the wheel by securing it between his legs and twisting. It didn't have any effect.

"Why are we fixing my bike?" Arsalan asked.

"Because I don't want to keep you here forever."

"Does this host of yours share the same opinion?"

"He's curious about you. When that curiosity is satisfied, I suspect you'll be free to leave."

"How do you know? He might not give a shit about me."

"People in the crew have been asking questions. I requested a meeting to talk to the host, and it was granted."

"Am I going?"

"No."

"When can I speak with the host?"

"I will make that request when I meet with him. It's a delicate matter."

Arsalan's brow furrowed. Meanwhile, he was meticulously pulling back fibers at the end of the new brake line he'd cut, neatly folding them off into a ball using pliers.

Having failed with his legs, Pyke tried pushing the bike wheel against the wall of the apartment building, but that didn't work either.

"It would help if you told me more about what happened," Pyke said. "About this Gail machine. It may give the host more reasons to grant you an audience."

Arsalan only said, "Hmmph."

Pyke said, "This Gail machine has nothing to do with us."

"So you say."

Pyke sighed. "Fine, I guess I'll start then."

"Start what?"

"Telling you what you want to know."

Arsalan's sour expression could only be interpreted as skepticism.

Pyke was keying off something Annika had told him, about feigning indifference. If he shared more information, it was a sign that he didn't care much about what Arsalan knew. It was also a form of entreaty. Perhaps Arsalan would be more inclined to share if Pyke was more forthcoming.

"Glen Pearson was the original host of *A Leap of Wisdom*," Pyke began. "He was living in Aspen during the fall. Unlike most people, he was prepared. He had generators, bunkers filled with food, and all sorts of tools and machines. Aspen wasn't affected much at first, but hundreds of drifters came up from Denver's suburbs after it was nuked. When these people came, Glen Pearson stayed hidden and protected in his mansion compound. He recruited folks he thought might make good contestants. But as food and supplies ran out, and people became desperate, fighting broke out. More organized bands eventually came up into the mountains to steal what little remained from the townspeople who weren't protected by Glen.

"As time went on, Glen fortified the compound and brought in more followers. He provided not only protection, tools, and resources, but also hope—so much had been lost in the fall, but he had his collection of sacred episodes—the ones we still use today. These were a shining example of who we could aspire to be; Aspen could hope for a future in which the glory of *A Leap of Wisdom* could return. This lifeline to civilization kept Glen's followers sane, and above the moral depravity of the roving masses. In turn, the enclave grew, until eventually it encompassed all of Aspen."

Arsalan had finished preparing the end-cap and had threaded the cable into the place of the old brake line. He tested the brakes. "A better fate than many," he said. "Kind of like how the Adherents gave purpose to us Spokes. But it doesn't matter how high and mighty you think you are, Gail will use you and destroy you, just like she did in Seeville."

"That's just the first part of the story. I haven't explained how the network was created."

Arsalan didn't respond. Pyke continued anyway. "Some say the network was made by a million souls who came from the west. Now, admittedly even I don't know much about these million souls. Others say it's collectively some kind of machine, and others say it's just one person with a lot of different personalities. Either way, it's very smart. It had heard of Glen Pearson and knew every detail of the sacred episodes. It could answer any question, and solve any riddle, and yet was impressed by Glen Pearson's community and his natural charisma. It offered to build big machines that would help the people of Aspen relive the glory of *A Leap of Wisdom*. These machines created the show and gave us tools, building materials, and appliances. The network also built factories and generated electricity and ensured there were no retchers in the surrounding area. As long as we gave the network regular offerings—supplies of things like glass, oils and metals, but also gifts from the surrounding communities—it would provide us with whatever we wanted, including goods to trade, food, or weapons.

"So you see, Glen Pearson had the sense to partner with the network, and we all prospered. The network is entirely benevolent. Or . . . maybe not always. It can be harsh, but only because it needs us to be disciplined, to protect us from the dangers of the outside world. For these reasons, you can be assured the network has nothing to do with this Gail machine."

"Hand me that," Arsalan said. He took the wheel, which Pyke had given up on some time ago. It was still completely warped. Arsalan placed it into the crook of a tree, and twisted it. After a single attempt, the wheel looked much improved. "We'll need to adjust the spokes," he said. "I'll show you."

Pyke watched him tighten one spoke at a time, occasionally spinning the tire on the upended wheel hooks to see if it was straightened.

"Tell me more about this million souls thing that came from the west," Arsalan said. "It sounds a lot like Gail, to be honest."

"I don't know much more than I've told you. It runs the network. In some stories it acts like an oracle; it can answer any question you want. Some people say there's one seer, others say there's three of them. We don't know much, except that they are knowledgeable, and powerful."

"First there was a million, then there was one, and now there's three?"

"I know. It's confusing. These stories have been passed down through the generations, and the few lucky winners who have visited the mountain summit. I know they don't all make sense. I'm just telling you what I know."

"Gail is a chameleon. She changes for each person that comes across her, to best manipulate them, and to stay hidden. I'm sure you think this story makes the network sound different, but to me it sounds a lot like her."

"The difference is time. My understanding is Gail came to exist only recently."

Arsalan scratched his head. "Well, the current version of her, at least. You're saying that this network has been around for a while? Since before the machine wars in the east?"

"Oh yes. Since well before I was born. It couldn't have been that long after the fall, because it was in Glen Pearson's time."

"Hmm." Arsalan actually raised his eyebrows, as if he'd finally learned something useful. "I can't make much of the rest of it, but that last bit is plausible, with a little evidence to back it up."

"Exactly." Pyke nodded and bit his lip. He dared not say any more for fear of undermining his victory.

"What about this?" Pyke said. He was pointing at an oval-shaped black gadget Mank had found next to the bike, which Pyke had placed next to the tools. The device had a gauge with a pointer and array of numbers slots on it. An outer ring of the device had an inset red-colored pin-hole and another allen key hole on the side. "Does this help shift the gears or measure distance or something?"

"It measures distance, but it's broken and needs some finagling. I was going to work on it inside." Arsalan extended his hand.

"Sure," Pyke said. "I'll give it to you later." He pocketed it in case it was some kind of weapon. He would inspect it when Arsalan wasn't around.

Arsalan frowned and refocused on the bike.

The brake lines were tight, and the wheel back on. Arsalan kicked the tire to make it spin. There was still a slight wobble, but the vehicle could surely be ridden. As the wheel turned, Arsalan stared at Pyke, his head tilted to the side, perhaps still processing his suspicions.

"What?" Pyke asked.

Arsalan sighed, and finally he did speak. And speak. And speak.

He spoke about a railroad operator named Bartz who had been corrupted by this machine Gail. He spoke about resistance by the Adherents—the prominent faith in Spoke lands, and about another machine called the Sentinel, and huge animatronic statues, and faceless robots and their spider pets, and a spacecraft named Friendship One. And he spoke about devastating battles between the Essentialists, Adherents, the railroad operators, and mules, which had left most of Seeville in ruins. Finally, he described how the battle still raged near Raleigh, predominantly between Gail-controlled forces on one side, and Sentinel-controlled forces on the other, with both sides desperate for external reinforcements.

Pyke was well-versed in Spoke history, but this was a tale so bewildering that he had to ask Arsalan to repeat certain parts, and add context to others. None of these recent events were in either book Pyke had obtained from the library, and yet the institutions, the people, the system of government, all dovetailed with the narrative.

This was what he wanted: to learn the full story behind this man and his reason for being here. Now he wondered, would anyone believe Pyke's recount of a multi-machine, multi-faction confrontation? Would Pyke be ridiculed for describing these animatronic giants? He wondered if it would have been better if Arsalan had stayed silent.

Nevertheless, he thanked Arsalan for the information, and they made their way back inside. Pyke gave Arsalan some hard bread and cider, which he ate wordlessly. Pyke locked him to the bedframe again.

"I'm curious," Pyke said. "Why did you come here, on this thousand-mile adventure? I often wonder what drives people who travel across the continent."

"Like I told you, we're all going to die if we don't stop Gail."

"I understand." In truth, Pyke found much of Arsalan's story hard to believe. He was trying to get a measure of the man. "Why did they choose you? They must have known you'd have the force of will to see it through."

Arsalan paused before answering. "I've done plenty of hundreds, so I had the stamina. I'm a wrench—well-respected in the mule community—so I could handle most issues on the road. But no, it's because of someone I knew; my friend, Chester. He wasn't like me— he was always ahead of things, avoiding the bad trails so we wouldn't have to turn around, if you know what I mean. He died in the Seeville conflict to give us a chance, and he never asked for anything from anyone." Arsalan nodded to himself. "That's what it came down to.

Not so much all the hokey about Gail, but because my friend—a good, honest man—believed in it, and he died for it. I believe in *him*."

"Thank you," Pyke said, even though the answer didn't give him any comfort. In fact, Pyke had almost hoped to detect some duplicity in Arsalan's answer—some clear sign of him being disingenuous—but he hadn't. If would have been easier if he could discount Arsalan's outlandish story when relaying it to the host, but now he was going to come off sounding just as crazy as Arsalan.

Jeeri was waiting for him outside the Wisdome entrance.

"Hi Jeeri why are you—"

With a finger to her lips, she whispered, "I wanted to warn you. I was inside earlier and I heard Shane mention your name, saying you were *of questionable loyalty*. Mengle said, 'I know, I know.' Not sure what it means, but please, be careful in there."

"Why would Shane say that?"

Her eyes twinkled, reflecting the light of a solitary lamp hanging above them. "I don't know." She held his wrists and her grip pulsed once, like some sort of at-a-distance hug. Then she turned and moved away, her silhouette lost in the twilight.

Pyke entered the Wisdome with a measure of caution, his steps slowed by the weight of this new revelation. What had he done? Maybe his request for a meeting was seen as impetuous? Jeeri's warning was to be heeded, especially because she was usually so apathetic about anything crew-related.

The host's office was one of the few rooms with a window, although *window* was a generous term. It was made of glass, fitted into a hexagonal aperture raggedly cut out of the superstructure without any trim or ways to open it. A thick cement panel on hinges could seal over the window frame opening. The view overlooked the valley leading up toward the summit, although nobody could ever see where the network operated from Aspen, especially in the twilight of dusk. The mountain was always shrouded in thick clouds or fog, and often under assault by a distant thunderstorm. Yet Mengle now stood tall, gazing up at the cloudbanks as if he could see straight through them. He was dressed in his sky-blue suit that had no visible stitches or stain discolorations. When Mengle turned, a flashy tie with lightning bolt icons embroidered on it swung around with him. He was wearing an earpiece and lapel microphone.

Vin was off to the side, with a pen and paper in his hand. Ostensibly, he was here to take notes. His leg shook as he offered a cursory nod to Pyke.

Hostess Shane was also there, wearing his silver satin dress and his shoulder-length brunette wig. His fake bosom was extra stuffed and he was smoothly shaven, even though this wasn't a show day. Shane escorted Pyke to a seat across the desk from Mengle, then returned to stand behind the host, shifted his hips and fake-smiled.

They were taking this meeting quite seriously.

Pyke sat up straight, his pulse beating in his ear, and waited until he was addressed.

Mengle took a seat at his desk, then pointed and winked at Pyke. It was a familiar gesture—the one Glen Pearson used on every new contestant. "Pyke, you are so welcome here," he said. "Thank you, *thank you* for suggesting this meeting. Look at you, so cool and calm. I think you've got what it takes." He nodded to Shane, who winked back at Mengle knowingly.

"Thank you, Host Mengle," Pyke responded. "I'm honored that you've agreed to this meeting. If I overstepped, I apologize."

Mengle ignored his apology. "Tell me, Pyke, how long have you been an offering advocate?"

"Almost five years now, although it feels like I was apprenticed only yesterday. You may remember I have had a few important offerings, two of them from the Union, one from Ouray. There was one that—"

"Why don't we get to the meat of it?" Mengle interrupted, perhaps reconsidering his attempt at small talk. "Your time is important! Tell me what the Spoke has told you so far. And remember, when Glen Pearson shared the wonders of the sacred episodes, there was an expectation that we would be forthcoming with him about all we see and do here in Aspen." He tilted his head to one side, suggesting an air of contemplation. "Even now, Glen still bestows his gifts upon us, every day."

Mengle's eyes were wide, showing more white than iris. Shane nodded and smiled, keen with interest. Pyke had trouble looking at them, they were so intense and overbearing. He was reminded of episode thirty-five, when Malik Tokypsee, the famous reggae singer, was on the show for the first time and the crew fawned over him gratuitously.

Pyke began recounting Arsalan's tale about Gail, the Sentinel, and the Essentialist-Spoke conflict. He spoke for at least ten minutes. Mengle was attentive throughout, unsparing with grins and nods. All the while Vin took copious notes.

"This is all of it?" Mengle said when Pyke finished.

"Yes, I think so. I'm happy to answer questions about the Adherents, or where these places are located, if you'd like more context."

Mengle looked to Vin, who flipped to another page in his notepad, underlined some items, and showed the page to Mengle.

"Where is this Sentinel located?" Mengle asked. "You mentioned a sanctuary? How many drones and machines does it have?"

"I'm . . . I'm sorry. I don't know. There was a sanctuary west of Seeville that was destroyed in the conflict. There may be other places where the Sentinel resides, but Arsalan didn't tell me. He may not know. And I don't think Arsalan has a tally of the drones and other machines, either. Certainly there would be more than hundreds. It could be thousands or tens of thousands."

Shane, for his part, was still nodding and smiling, even though Pyke's response was almost certainly unsatisfactory.

"Where are most of the Spoke forces amassed now?" Mengle asked. "You said Raleigh and Wilmo. What about Charleston? And in the north. Harrisburg and Orangetown?"

"Arsalan didn't talk about that."

"How many of these animatronic giants are there under their control? These"—he looked at Vin's notes—"beholders."

"I'm sorry, I don't know. Arsalan only mentioned two in Seeville, although one lost part of its arm."

It could have been his imagination, but Mengle's well-practiced smile was beginning to look stretched. His cheeks trembled, as if his expression was becoming difficult to maintain on account of Pyke's lackluster report. Shane, Mengle, and Vin often exchanged looks, passing non-verbal information that Pyke couldn't grasp.

Pyke cleared his throat. "I assure you I've told you everything I know, because I understand that we still live with Glen's gifts, and we must continue to honor his deal with the network. To that end, Arsalan has expressed an interest in meeting with you in person. I know it's unusual for foreign dignitaries, but maybe he would be more forthcoming if we granted his wish."

"Yes, yes, let's do that," Mengle said without hesitation. Then he raised his hands, palms up, in a gesture of caution. "Pending confirmation from the network. Please, in the meantime, I would . . . encourage the Spoke to come prepared to answer these questions."

"I will."

With that, the meeting was adjourned. Pyke left the Wisdome to head back to the apartment. It was pitch black and raining, thick sheets coming down in waves, but he didn't wait it out. His head was still mired in the details of the meeting, and the rain did nothing to hold his momentum.

He was glad Mengle was amenable to meeting with Arsalan, but at the same time he had seemed underwhelmed by Pyke's report. Add to that Jeeri's ominous warning, and it didn't bode well for his hope of being rewarded.

It was hard to conclude that he'd failed, though, since he'd managed to extract a great deal of information from Arsalan—more than most would have been able to garner from a paranoid foreigner. Yet Mengle's expectations were probably unrealistically high.

"*He's cursed,*" the dancing woman had said. Once again, Pyke entertained the idea that what she had said could, in fact, be true.

The questions Mengle posed concerned him, too. Mengle could have asked diplomatic questions about the Spoke leaders; what their intentions were in relation to Aspen, or the names and positions were of key people in the Spoke command structure. Or he could have asked about Arsalan's injury, or the route he'd taken to arrive there, or the intervening tribes and nation states. Instead, Mengle focused on the machines—how many, where were they located, and in what concentration. Obviously, this was a matter of curiosity, but the inquiries had been highly specific regarding this "Sentinel." It made Pyke wonder if Arsalan's concerns about Gail having an influence on the network had some validity.

When Pyke arrived home, he went to his bedroom immediately to update Arsalan about the meeting, only to find his bedpost smashed in. It was split in two just above where Pyke had drilled a hole for the cuffs, with thick indentations in the wood on each side of the rupture. It looked as though Arsalan had kicked it in with his powerful legs.

Arsalan had escaped.

11

DUE WEST

Due west wasn't Essentialist territory, but it wasn't a cakewalk either. Cecile and her companions often needed to veer south, not only to avoid Essentialist scouts, but to be sure not to traverse territories occupied by the smoky mountain bandits, who were known for violent atrocities and other forms of depravity.

They skirted the mountains and made a stopover in Nooga, which was a comparatively civil place because it hadn't recently been reduced to cinders and the welcome sign wasn't framed by severed heads on pikes. In Nooga they chartered passage on a carriage doing a package run all the way to Lubbock—from one bandit oasis to another—a thousand-mile trip west. It was a stroke of good luck, although it meant Cecile had to part with a small fortune in Essentialist notes.

In Lubbock they needed a guide, or at least an escort that could help them fit in as they continued northwest, where defined borders between Essentialists and bandit tribes became more a matter of hearsay than lines on a map. They would need to make their way stealthily past scouts and outposts, at the very least. They needed a smuggler, the four of them being human contraband.

Through a go-between at the carriage terminal, Cecile arranged to meet a man named Hurd. He was some sort of courier who'd traveled extensively in the region and also frequented the Navajo Nation, Colorado Collective and Tucson Union lands. The go-between arranged for them to meet at the Trading Cellar.

The Trading Cellar was in the center of town. The residents of Lubbock needed a cool place to conduct business in the summer, so they used an Old World underground mall, accessible by a series of broken-down escalators with billboard posters lining their sides. The space was a kind of bazaar that reminded Cecile of the summer markets in Quebec or the Spoke Festival in Seeville, but in closer quarters, and with worse ventilation.

Hurd was waiting for them by a cart filled with half-rotten persimmons. He stood alone, wearing baggy riding pants and a weathered button-down vest. His face was heavily lined, suggesting a life on the road. Two heavies were chewing on pipes intently against a nearby wall, eyes leering at the group through the puffs of fragrant smoke they were creating. Cecile guessed these were Hurd's "security."

"Aha," Hurd said, giving them a once-over, "a cold few Essentialist Clansmen I've met—yes. A ride I've shared with a Spoke or two—yes I did. My share of bandits I've also had in tow, that's for sure. But a *Québécois* I've never met in the flesh. Greetings." Either Hurd was late for another meeting, or he was by nature a fidgety man. When he spoke, he moved constantly: either scratching his head, or touching his chin, or shifting his considerable weight from side to side. At least he pronounced *Québécois* correctly, which lent some credence to his travel résumé.

"*Enchantée*," Cecile said. "We are simply weary travelers in need of your services, sir."

"To where?" he asked.

Warrick spoke up. "You don't want to take us anywhere. She's a witch."

It was always a risk that Warrick would try to sabotage their plans, and Hurd had insisted on meeting the entire group, so they had no choice but to bring him. Cecile had considered upping

Warrick's dose in advance, but she was pretty sure Hurd wouldn't want to cart around an invalid.

She interjected quickly, "Oh really? Where am I taking us, Warrick?

"I don't know . . . somewhere to betray us, to take advantage of us. I'm sure it's this place you're heading to in the west."

"Not too long ago you said my *harpy's lair* was in the north, now it's in the west? I'm confused."

That shut him up.

She turned back to Hurd. "I'm terribly sorry. We do have some sensitive cargo." She grimaced and pointed at Warrick. "He suffers from a disease of the mind. He'll comply well enough, especially if he's restrained."

Hurd scanned Bronson and Pierre's faces. To their credit, they both nodded in tandem, confirming Cecile's statement. The engagement could still be a tall order, though. In fact, Warrick's little outburst could put them out of consideration altogether.

"Of course," she added, "we can compensate you for the extra trouble."

Hurd's face pruned up—whether due to concentration or consternation, she couldn't be sure. "I still don't know where you're going," he said.

Cecile took out her map. "Here," she said, pointing to Raton, which was where they would veer north mid-continent. "We can make our way from there." Pushing for a longer trip would send them over Navajo, Cooperative or Laramie borders, raising the stakes beyond any reasonable expectation.

Hurd picked up a persimmon, examined it, then placed it back in its cart. "Why?" he said finally.

"There's a doctor near Raton called Sepia Martinez. She can heal people with mental illnesses. We hope Warrick can be healed, or at least his suffering alleviated. Despite his animosity toward us, we owe him that."

She'd had a lot of time on their journey to Lubbock to come up with this fabrication. In some ways, it wasn't far from the truth.

Warrick was suffering, and Martinez was real—Cecile had found her when she was looking for a doctor for Fabien, those many years ago. She was a quack, it turned out, but what was important was that Hurd could look her up and confirm her existence.

"What do you owe this man?" Hurd asked.

"Before his affliction took hold he was an honorable man, uncompromising in his ideals. He was a great advocate for my mentor in Quebec City. He has contributed to the peaceful resolution of affairs in the northwest as well." Cecile was a good liar, but the truth was always easier, when she could use it.

Warrick had become quiet, although his eyes were squinting with some measure of focus. She wondered if he believed anything she was saying. Probably not. He may not even have been paying attention. Lately he had spent much of his time mumbling incoherently under his breath.

"Fifty thousand in Essentialist notes," Hurd said.

Everyone froze, except for one of the men standing beside the wall who drew his head back in a guffaw of surprise. Indeed, it was a ridiculous price, but what Hurd didn't know was that Cecile had been given an even more ridiculous amount of currency by the Sentinel.

"Thirty and it's a deal," she said.

Abruptly, Warrick bolted. He threw the cart of persimmons down behind him, and ran for the escalator. There was no one in his path.

It seemed he *had* been paying attention, only not to Cecile. An attempt to escape had always been a risk, and more so when he was uncuffed, as he was in that moment.

Cecile ran around the cart, only to find Bronson had already vaulted it and arrived at the base of the escalator. Warrick tripped— he was getting old after all—and though he recovered, it was enough of a lapse for Bronson to tackle him on the defunct escalator. They slid awkwardly down several steps, and one of Warrick's pant legs was caught on the edge of an open panel, tearing it.

Cecile heard a collective gasp from the market patrons, not because of the sudden action or embarrassing outcome, but because of what it revealed. Warrick's leg was zebra-striped with pink and white grizzled scar tissue, from hip to foot.

Warrick realized his escape attempt had been foiled, and he didn't struggle. Bronson lifted him up, held his arms at the elbows from behind, and pushed him down the steps. Cecile applied the cuffs to his wrists and escorted Warrick back to where Hurd was standing over the scattering of fruit.

Hurd's cronies were no longer lurking in the shadows; they now stood directly beside him, arms crossed.

"Fifty," Hurd said resolutely.

She had no choice but to accept.

* * *

Cecile was riding her horse next to Pierre's. They were on yet another dry road, with leafless spindly shrubs the only signs of life in the arid landscape.

She was wearing a navy-blue uniform with broad lapels and white buttons, the typical dress of the local postal service, according to Hurd. The uniform was faded from the sun, repeated washing, and dust.

There were seven of them on the road, all wearing similar attire, plus three extra horses for carrying gear. They had been riding for several days, and Hurd had been businesslike thus far. His men kept to themselves, aside from a few terse warnings when the group wasn't following his instructions. In one town a young Essentialist curator had pulled Hurd aside to interrogate him, but the curator had been preoccupied processing many parties that day, most of them more suspect-looking than Hurd's well-groomed group. Luckily, it was a sufficiently backwater outpost with no proper way of tracking people on their way through, or even verifying their identities. Processing consisted of a bunch of boilerplate questions and answers, then a tax, and they were free to go.

Pierre was humming again. Most of his hums were simple

melodies, less than an octave in range. This one was punchy, the ghost of some energetic classical piece.

"Why do you hum so much, Pierre?" she asked.

His eyes grew wide. "*Scusez*, Cecile. I was brought up in a house full of music, so humming the old songs we used to play makes me feel at home." He gestured at the expanse of arid terrain. "And there's not much to see or do on these long journeys." He smiled sheepishly.

Cecile couldn't remember ever humming a tune. It was a foreign concept to her, requiring an inner peace that she would never find.

Warrick was behind her on his horse, cuffed and drugged, listing to the left. Bronson rode beside him, keeping watch. They had decided to be more careful with Warrick after the incident in the Lubbock market.

Warrick's apparition must have been programmed differently than hers. Or maybe he had the occasional reprieve from the constant inner turmoil, because his apparition was so volatile and broken. She peered into his eyes, but they were dark. They offered no window into the monster inside him.

Bronson left Warrick's side and pulled up next to her. He had a particular look; a haughty, grim expression and puffed-out chest he adopted when he was about to ask an uncomfortable question. "Cecile, if you don't mind, I'd like to talk about our plans."

He'd approached her twice already, and she'd managed to fend off his inquiries with cursory explanations. In the past she'd suggested she had an impending bowel movement or warned of locals overhearing them, but now she'd run out of excuses.

"Of course," she said.

He gazed ahead. They were sufficiently distant from Hurd and his men that they wouldn't be able to overhear. "Raton," Bronson said. "You claim we can learn about the location of Spoke forces there, but it seems risky. It's a crossroads, so it's likely to have a sizeable Essentialist presence, and I've heard Raton has a military garrison of its own, plus a city wall. Why wouldn't we try a smaller town first?"

Bronson must have been speaking with Hurd and his men, asking questions. It was the only way he could have come across this information. Cecile leaned towards him, speaking quietly. "*Bien sur*, you're exactly right. I used Raton as a placeholder for our true destination. My intention is to find out more about the nearby towns before we arrive—to see which one might offer the best refuge from Essentialist forces. We'll divert to one of these other towns before we reach Raton. I'm hopeful we will hear rumblings about the location of any Spoke allies as we get closer."

Bronson frowned.

"It's hard to hide a beholder," she said. "I'm sure the locals will have plenty of stories to share."

"What happened to making these decisions together?"

"*Excusez*—I was thinking on the fly. Can't you see the logic of it?"

"That's not the point, and I'm not sure I *do* see the logic, because our orders from the Sentinel are weeks old. This Spoke force in the west might have been destroyed, or it might have moved away. We should try to uplink again before we get too far. Otherwise, we could be leading one of our most strategically important assets directly into Essentialist territory for no reason at all."

The strength of his points caught her off guard. The apparition awakened, intimating its discontent with a growing well of anxiety. "I don't think that's necessary, and it will be hard to change the plan, with Hurd and his men looking over our shoulders."

"Didn't you just say you already intended to change the plan?" Bronson persisted. "There must be a retcher-free territory we could find, with discreet enough surroundings for us to break away."

"You worry too much."

She was losing the argument. It didn't help that Pierre, who usually supported her steadfastly no matter what she said, had been offering cursory nods whenever Bronson was speaking.

Bronson's expression had become stern. "Success of this mission is critically important. We should ask Hurd to find a retcher-free zone. I've heard of a place called the Glasslands that might work. There we can get an exact fix on the location of the Spoke force, and we won't have to go through any Essentialist outposts."

Cecile's mind raced. Bronson's arguments were hard to refute, unfortunately. The Glasslands were close to Tucson, but sparsely populated. There was no alternative. She would have to improvise when they came closer.

"You make some good points," she said. "I will consider—"

"And I'd like to be on the next comm call," Bronson said, interrupting her. "All three of us should be. It's only fair."

Again, she couldn't find a viable retort. It would be his comm device they used, after all, since she'd thrown hers away. His arguments had caught her flatfooted, and the apparition was flailing inward in her vision, like some spoiled child. Saying no would force a confrontation, which would be even worse.

"If it's possible, by all means we will divert to a retcher-free zone," she said. "I welcome it, in fact, but I'm not sure about the Glasslands. It's dangerous. Let's try to find a better target."

He nodded, his lips pouting. "Thank you, Cecile. I'm sure we can find something." Satisfied, he dropped back to his position next to Warrick.

Cecile liked Bronson. He had told them about his quaint furniture store in Hill City, and how he and a group of mules had bravely led an attack on Gail's second radio telescope installation to destroy it. Bronson had a daughter that he spoke of fondly, and an estranged wife that had left him on account of him wanting to stay at the front in Raleigh, where the action was.

But he was too ambitious. Or maybe he had romantic notions about being some kind of hero. Either way, he had unknowingly set them on a path that would reveal her duplicity.

She couldn't let that happen.

12

DON'T DO ANYTHING RASH

Pyke looked frantically for Arsalan inside and outside the apartment. The bike was gone, and there was no trace of him. Not only had Pyke been negligent, he had inadvertently given his prisoner a means of escape.

He ran through the rain to the ranger's station, which was a stubby, two-story tower near the Wisdome. Crowley was on front desk duty. Mank and Delilah were leaning over the backs of chairs behind him.

"What happened?" Crowley asked.

"The Spoke escaped."

"*What?*" Crowley's tone was filled with affront.

"When I came back from the Wisdome, he'd broken the bedpost and fled."

"Mank, Delilah," Crowley snapped over his shoulder, "the Spoke's out. Go look for him. Alert the wall guards."

Mank and Delilah left the tower immediately and jogged in opposite directions.

"Can I help?" Pyke asked.

"Fill this out." Crowley passed him an apprehension request form asking for personal details.

Hurriedly, Pyke filled out the form, being as concise as possible. Occasionally, he caught glimpses of Crowley's *what were you thinking* expression.

"Go home," Crowley said. "We'll send out a search party and notify the crew." Pyke watched Crowley pass the report to another ranger who was coming down the stairs.

"I can notify the crew," Pyke offered.

"That's not protocol."

"I'll help with the search party, then."

"You've done enough, Pyke."

Maybe Crowley was right. Pyke wasn't a ranger. Maybe he would screw that up as well.

Pyke walked home. His whole body felt heavy, malaise like an anvil in his core. The downpour had diminished in intensity, its blusters spent. He still had to take care to avoid deep puddles.

He would be punished, perhaps sent to purgatory in Gondola Valley. He might even be left up there to starve, like crazy Chan Unsalah. Either way, he doubted he would remain an offering advocate. At best, he would be placed in some menial job, far removed from the crew and the network. His hopes of becoming a contestant had dwindled from negligible to nothing.

He kept walking right past his apartment, continuing along the path to Natty's place. She lived a half-mile away, higher up the mountain, in one of the lodges nested between tall evergreen trees.

"Oh, you're early," she said. She was wearing another rumpled woolen sweater that was so large it covered half her legs. "I was going to drop him off in an hour."

"I know. Do you mind if I see Gill?"

"Of course not," she said, a confused frown on her face. She opened the door and he brushed past her, dripping water everywhere.

Natty's lodge was a somber place in the day, but cozy at night, with soft carpets and flickering candlelight. Gill was standing up in his crib, holding on to the bars. "Dah!" he said enthusiastically when he saw Pyke. His face lit up as only a toddler's could, a beacon of happiness, hope, and familiarity all at once.

This was why Pyke had come early. He needed to see that smile. He needed someone to show him what happiness looked like. He lifted Gill above his head and spun him in the air. Gill's arms waved up and down, as if he was flapping imaginary wings. "Dah!" he said.

"Yes," Pyke said, "you're flying. Up and down and through the mountains—away from here." He added cawing sound effects. "Far, far away from here."

After a few roller-coaster spins throughout the room, he stopped to rest Gill on his shoulder, bouncing him gently.

Natty was watching him from her recliner chair, quizzical. "What's going on, Pyke?"

"I . . . I might have to go away," he said.

"You're taking Gill?"

"I might. I don't know yet."

"What happened?"

"I screwed up. The Spoke got away."

Her eyes widened. "Pyke!" she scolded, as if he'd slapped her across the face. "How?"

"I don't know. He broke the bedpost where the cuffs were attached, and took his bike."

"How could you!" she said. Natty was never one for sympathy. She held her head in her hands, digesting the information. "They could still find him, right?"

"It's possible."

"Then why go away? That won't look good at all. And I'm not sure what you think is out there. Aspen is a great place to live. We have security because of the network. We're protected by the mountains. Don't be stupid."

"I know it's just . . . maybe I'm not meant to be here. Kehda was always talking about Tucson, and the Sierras. There's so much out there, and maybe that's why she left. Maybe I could find her and—"

"Are you serious? Listen to yourself. Don't go after that treacherous woman." Natty was clenching and unclenching her fists, as if trying to temper herself. "You've had a stumble here and there, but don't do anything rash. Remember your friend Dwayne?"

He cringed as Dwayne's mangled body flashed into his mind.

"Sorry," Natty said. "Maybe that's harsh, but you know what I mean. Dwayne was always taking too many risks. Leaving Aspen is like that—it's too risky."

He tilted his head thoughtfully. "This isn't working. I could come back."

She rolled her eyes. "Remember what I told you about your uncle Howard. He had that same wanderlust. If he was here for more than a couple of weeks he would start getting grumpy—he wouldn't go out with friends, and he missed episodes all the time. Aspen stopped being his home and became more like a stopover— a place to wait for his next adventure. And he had plenty. He was always going to Ouray and Navajo lands. He came back with gifts and stories. He was happy, for sure, until he didn't come back at all."

"Yeah."

"And there's your father. He leaves your mom and comes back with that trollop. What a waste of sunshine that one was."

"I know, Natty. I'm really sorry."

"I don't want your apologies, Pyke. I'm trying to tell you that I'd rather have a grumpy Howard than a dead Howard. Same goes for you."

What was the point of living if you can't be happy? If you didn't follow your dreams, could you really say your life had meaning? But Pyke didn't want to argue, so he said nothing.

"Take a few days," Natty added. "The Spoke will turn up. Even if he doesn't, there's been plenty like him before—there'll be plenty more in the future. Mysterious vagabonds come through here all the time. Why does this one matter so much?"

"Something's different. Mengle wanted to meet him."

Her raised eyebrow made him believe she wasn't convinced. "Please. Give it a few days to blow over. See how things go."

Maybe she was right. At this point, as emotionally charged as he was, it was probably better to listen to anything other than his own intuition.

They drank tea and talked more about what happened during his meeting with Mengle. Natty asked him to help her fix her outhouse; it looked like the roof was about to collapse.

Pyke appreciated Natty's company for once, despite her blunt-as-a-hammer statements. At least she was willing to be straight with him. Right then, it was what he needed.

Finally, he bundled up Gill and took him home.

Gill fell asleep on the way, hypnotized by Pyke's methodical footfalls and the patter of the rain. When Pyke arrived back at his apartment, he put Gill down, changed out of his wet clothes, prepared for bed, and settled in for a troubled sleep of his own.

Jeeri touched the bedpost, fingering the splintered wood at the point of the breach. She let her fingers trace over the curves of the new indentations. "This must have been difficult. Just to orient yourself to the right angle, and with enough force . . . and then not hurt the arm that was attached to the post."

"You saw him," Pyke said. "I've never seen legs that strong. He might have reinjured his arm when he did it. Who knows?"

"I thought you had a good rapport with him."

"I wouldn't say *good*. We were getting along, in the end. He opened up, but maybe that was an act. Maybe he did it so I would lower my guard."

Jeeri approached him with her arms open wide. He accepted her embrace willingly.

"I'm so sorry, Pyke. Why does this stuff always happen to you?"

He sniffed a laugh, even though it wasn't funny.

They broke apart and Jeeri sat down on the bed. "Anything I can do?"

"Well, actually . . . I was thinking. I don't know how I'm going to come out of this. I'll probably lose my job as an offering advocate. And, as I'm sure you know, a lot worse things could happen to me. I'm worried about Gill."

She frowned. "You . . . want me to do what, exactly?"

"I just thought, maybe you could take care of him, if something happens to me."

She laughed. "Nothing's going to happen to you."

"They haven't found Arsalan. They'll punish me."

"Maybe a night in Gondola Valley—so what? And yes, it could affect your standing as an advocate. Maybe they'll put you in the library, with Annika. You're too smart for them to cast you out. Gill's going to be fine. Look how good you are with him. He loves you. He needs you."

"Maybe I should go away until this blows over. No offence, but neither of us knows what Mengle is going to do. You heard what they said about me. Mengle doesn't like me, and neither does the rest of the crew—or the rangers, for that matter. They could use me as an example. If I go away, it might be best if I didn't take Gill, and I thought you could—"

"Come on, Pyke." Her face had taken on some steam. Jeeri was an empathetic person, but she was also quick to anger. "You can't run away from your responsibilities. And Gill—look, why don't you give him back to her? Force Kehda to take Gill. That would be a worthwhile trip. Then you can start living your life, not someone else's."

"She's high up in the Essentialist army. She can't take care of a child."

"He's not. Your. Child!"

She was one of the few people who had done the math. It was likely that Kehda had conceived when she was with Dwayne, but Pyke didn't care.

"He is my child," was all he said.

"Okay, fine, but make *her* help. Make *her* find someone to care for Gill. You've done more than enough."

He could only sigh. Jeeri didn't know Kehda like he did. Her tribe had different traditions, including a more communal parenting structure. Soldiers like her were kept at arm's length from the children. Even if she did take Gill back, was she responsible enough to care for him? Would she find the right guardian for Gill? He wasn't sure.

He was exhausted. He took the stool across the from bed, sat down, and slouched over. "The whole thing is a mess."

Jeeri's voice lost its edge. "Try not to take things so seriously. You've had a run of bad luck, is all."

He brooded some more.

Jeeri said, "Don't do anything rash, okay?" She stood up, embraced his slouching form, then made her way out.

Don't do anything rash. It was the same thing Natty had said. But what if Mengle was going to make an example of him? Then he *should* do something rash, like leave Aspen right away.

He decided he would get a good night's sleep to clear his head. Then he would give himself until the end of the next day to make a decision.

13

THE GLASSLANDS

Cecile watched through the cracked window of the inn as Hurd returned from his conversation with the pair of horsemen. The three had spoken for a while, Hurd fidgeting much of the time. The horsemen had scarves wrapped around their faces and wore red-tinted sunglasses to protect them from the ever-present dust. Their jackets were hardened yellow leather, adorned with arrow and animal signs. They could easily pass for Navajo or Essentialist. She suspected their lack of explicit allegiance was a deliberate choice.

Cecile and her team weren't the only ones trying to travel inconspicuously.

Hurd had held the meeting without his two heavies, who'd gone home a few days prior. Cecile and company must have passed some kind of test, or maybe Hurd couldn't justify the expense. The two strongmen didn't fit in the carriage either, and the additional horses made the group look imposing—more like thugs guarding valuables than frugal merchants.

Hurd entered the inn, looking to either side of the doorway as if someone was about to jump him. He was a nervous fellow at the best of times, and more so without his muscle.

"Well?" Cecile asked.

"An Essentialist unit—there's one near Raton," Hurd said. He scratched his chest so fleetingly that it couldn't have provided any relief. "No more than a few hundred, some kind of reserve regiment. Also roving platoons, with rumors of an army encampment near Mayhill, but there's been no sign of them for weeks."

"Do you believe these ones?" Pierre asked. "The horsemen?"

Hurd made squishy sounds with his mouth. "They're couriers, they say, and it's probably true. Although the farther we go west, the greater the Essentialist influence, so they could be lying. There's certainly more chance they're lying than if you'd asked a trader in Lubbock."

"Anything else?" Cecile asked.

"They heard about a Spoke unit, back in Sumner. It was small, they said, only twenty or thirty soldiers. I wouldn't put much stock in it, because they also said there's a rumor of a big monster traveling with it. They called it *Piedra Dios*—some kind of rock god."

"A beholder?" Pierre asked.

"Are those real?" Hurd asked. He seemed genuinely curious.

It was an unfortunate coincidence, fitting too neatly into the narrative Cecile had given them about a beholder on its way to escort them. She wasn't particularly surprised, though. The Sentinel had many beholders on the continent, and any one of them would draw attention.

"*Oui*, and they're not gods," Cecile said. "Even if the beholder is there, it's still far from us. Sumner is what—five hundred, six hundred miles east? I'm not sure what we can do with that information, even if it could be verified."

"Surely this is the unit you mentioned, on its way to help us," Bronson said. Since she'd agreed to find a retcher-free uplink point Bronson had seemed chastened, and more deferential, but he still had no qualms about venturing his strong opinions.

"How do we reach them?" she asked. "We can't backtrack all the way to Sumner in the vain hope of trying to find a moving target. Plus, if they do have a beholder they'll attract attention from Gail—especially as they approach Essentialist territory. No, we should continue on our way, and maintain our cover. If they're looking for us, they'll find us."

"I would agree with all that," Bronson said, "if we couldn't communicate with them—but maybe we can." He addressed Hurd again. "Did you ask them about retcher-free areas?"

"I decided to not ask that question," Hurd said.

"Why not?" Bronson asked, giving Cecile a momentary glance of suspicion.

"Because it's incriminating," Hurd said with a shrug. "They think we're traders, for now. As soon as you ask that question, we become anything *but* traders—and most definitely Essentialists or Spokes interested in using tech. And if someone stops them a few miles from here, asking about Spoke spies . . ."

Bronson's face flushed, as it often did. "So the only retcher-free area we know of for sure is the Glasslands, is that right?" His gaze returned to Cecile.

Cecile had been trying to steer them away from the Glasslands, telling them about testy Navajo bands who saw the area as sacred, about its difficult topography, and even about regular Essentialist incursions. But since she doubted Bronson would concede this point, it seemed the best option to make her play.

"*D'accord*," she sighed, feigning capitulation. "Yes, there is a part of the Glasslands that is known to be free of retchers. Now that we know the Essentialist positions better, we can be less concerned about them intervening."

Cecile guided the horse-drawn carriage under a makeshift arch made of two fang-like glass spikes that curved to touch in the middle. Beyond these teeth, the path opened up into a broad area ringed by glass orbs the size of large melons, mostly orange and yellow in tone, with lined configurations of glass objects that bisected the site into plots, like some kind of construction-site blueprint. The most central glass-rimmed circle was made of orbs heavily tarnished by soot and ash, on a bed of white particulate; a fire pit.

The setting sun was playing tricks on them. Its rays passed through taller, man-height glass formations outside the main ring, casting colorful, distorted stripes across the clearing.

The Glasslands could be disorienting, especially at sunset. Cecile had often had to backtrack to ensure they weren't going in circles. Despite this, she recognized the clearing they were entering; the red teeth were a distinctive-enough landmark.

"You can't blame the ice here," Fabien had said, when she lost her way in this same labyrinth ten years ago. It was her most-used excuse for being late in Quebec City.

She had stubbornly refused to listen to his directions, until she finally gave in, and together they found their way through the maze.

When they had made camp, he'd made love to her. For much of the trip, they had often tried, and it had been a delicate procedure, on account of their fatigue or Fabien's illness. Cecile had felt like a nurse; lovemaking was therapy, to give Fabien some semblance of being alive. That evening, something about the brilliant lights, or the absurdity of their driving in circles, had filled him with vitality. They'd enjoyed each other on the dusty ground, as the radiant beams shifted around them.

It was the last time she'd been with Fabien. Her last time with any man.

"What about here for the uplink?" Bronson asked, poking his head out of the carriage. "Seems like a good place to camp, too."

"*Non*," Cecile said. "We need to be farther north, in the geometric center of the Glasslands. That's the only way we can be sure that there won't be any retchers. We'll set up camp soon, and reach the center first thing tomorrow."

She drove the carriage forward at a leisurely pace, mostly on account of the confusing terrain, but also because what was inevitable was now becoming imminent. After spending weeks with Warrick, Pierre, Hurd, and Bronson, her stomach churned at the thought of hatching her ploy in a matter of hours.

There were so many ways it could go wrong.

Bronson lingered with her in the front of the carriage, mesmerized by the light refractions. Cecile thought he might object to her directives again, as he did more and more often, but instead he commented on their surroundings. "The glass objects on the periphery—they don't have any real form, but they almost feel like ghosts watching us."

It wasn't fear in his eyes, but wonder. She'd had the same impression when she'd first travelled through the Glasslands.

"The Navajo people tend to move the man-sized glass objects to be close to their camp sites," she said. "They see them as a kind of spiritual portal, shining the light of their ancestors. I've heard that some Essentialists think of the glass forms as still alive—human souls forever trapped by the bomb in glass prisons."

"A kind of bomb did this?"

"Yes, a double-punch bomb, according to the Sentinel."

"Double-punch?"

"*Oui.* Imagine a two-phase bomb, delivered by missile. It partitions just before impact. The first part is designed for maximum kinetic energy, causing an earthquake and impact crater." Cecile slammed her foot down on the carriage floor. Dust particles clouded the carriage, some of them sparkling in the sunlight. "You see the particles thrown up in the air? Imagine a much stronger effect, with sand and dirt jumping into the sky like inverted tornadoes."

He was frowning in concentration, watching the dust settle again.

"The second part is an extremely powerful incendiary," she continued. "A wave of heat comes from directly above, more than two thousand degrees, so hot that it melts everything. Even sand— especially sand—because this area used to be covered with beautiful white silica that Gail was mining to create massive server operations. The sand melted mid-motion, and just as quickly it cooled to glass as the heat flash dissipated. Over the years, nearby tribes have come here—mostly the Navajo Nation and closer Essentialist tribes —and organized the glass structures that remained, trying to find meaning in the aftermath of the fall. The choicest glassworks have been scoured from around the impact crater and brought to these bigger gathering areas, turning them into a sort of spiritual museum."

"If the Sentinel wanted to destroy the area, why didn't it just nuke it?"

"I don't know. Maybe it wanted to avoid toxic fallout, or maybe the double punch was just enough, or maybe only Gail had access to nukes."

His expression was thoughtful, brow lined and eyes distant.

"Or maybe," she continued, "even if you read all the books in the world, and if you knew the entirety of unwritten history of the Sentinel's existence, you still wouldn't know the answer. Trust me, there's little point in trying to comprehend the strategies of a machine that is a million times smarter than you."

"It may be beyond me," Bronson said, "I'll give you that. Still, I disagree that we shouldn't try to understand the Sentinel. Or Gail, for that matter. Maybe we will never get the full picture, but the moment we give up is the moment we've given ourselves to them. This becomes their war, not ours. That's dangerous."

He smiled amicably, placed his hand on her shoulder, and receded into the carriage.

Bronson was right. She'd become too jaded by the demands of the apparition to see beyond her own predicament. Or maybe divining the long-term implications of the moves of these godlike machines had become unimportant in the face of her more finite future.

They set up camp at another museum of glass, just after dusk. Bronson wanted to push on, but was appeased by Cecile's warnings of Laramie Broncos—a particularly unruly brand of bandit that frequented the Glasslands.

There was no firewood to speak of, and the breeze had picked up to buffet them with the occasional angry gust, so the five of them had to huddle close together in the carriage to stay warm.

It was a little too cozy. Whenever they clustered in the carriage, inevitably Cecile would be woken up often, either by someone snoring or a boot to the shin. And it stunk. Hurd regularly applied a sort of cologne he'd found in Lubbock, which nullified the likeness to a dead animal, but it was still a heady blend.

They would take turns on guard duty, each performing two-hour shifts, both to watch for bandits and make sure Warrick didn't bolt, even though they cuffed him to a railing in the carriage.

Cecile waited until thirty minutes after her shift started. First, she checked that her bag was neatly packed, right next to the carriage, and that the supplies she needed were hidden under the wheel in a burlap sack. Then she walked south down the path a hundred yards, ripped up the book she'd been reading, lit the sections on fire with her lighter, and placed the biggest clump of pages directly on the path, with two other clumps ten yards to each side. She took a deep breath and yelled, "Laramie Broncos to the south! Bronson, Pierre, Hurd, I need your help! *Vite, vite, vite!*"

She bolted off to one side, along an alternate route that wound north to the carriage. In the dark she rolled an ankle on a glass outcropping, but she could still walk. Not more than ten feet later, she cut her other ankle on another jagged piece of glass. She slowed her pace, keeping a low profile and proceeding carefully.

She ducked down completely when she saw the others racing toward the burning pages on the pathway.

Back at the campsite, a quick glance inside the carriage revealed only Warrick, still asleep. She threw in the supplies she'd placed underneath the carriage, attached the two horse harnesses, and pulled out, heading due north. Just outside of the campsite, the terrain featured high berms of sand beside the path. She turned right at a four-way intersection, hoping to confuse any potential pursuers.

Only a sliver of moon lit the way. It was enough, but the horses required quite a bit of cajoling.

She almost pulled it off without a hitch.

As she was rounding another corner she heard footfalls from behind, and the carriage tilted ever so slightly to the right; someone had jumped on the back. She lashed the horses and let go of the reins so she could slide her knife out of her belt sheath.

Just as she stood and turned to look back, she was grappled from behind, the tussle making her fall back on the driver's seat. The horses spooked and veered, causing her attacker's grip to loosen. She twisted around to see Bronson staring at her, his knife in his hand, raised to strike.

It should have ended for her right there. Bronson had the jump, and he was stronger, but his eyes were wide with shock. He'd probably thought a bandit or Laramie Bronco had seized their carriage. Maybe Cecile had actually convinced him they were on the same side —that the person he'd been travelling with for over a thousand miles wasn't, in fact, the witch Warrick made her out to be.

The apparition was clawing at the edges of her vision, it's anxious energy building inside her. The element of surprise gave her an advantage. That millisecond of miscalculation was about to cost Bronson dearly. Her knife fell abruptly, plunging into his chest. A muffled yelp escaped him as he dropped his own blade. The force of her blow caused his arms retract inward. His lack of purchase on the carriage made him roll backward and into the covered section.

"Whoa," Cecile said, pulling on the reins.

When the horses slowed to a trot, she followed Bronson inside.

There was no worry about him fighting back. He was gasping for air, one of his lungs collapsed. His eyes were stretched wide, pleading, desperate.

She told herself that if it were just her, she would have let him off here, on the path, giving him a fighting chance for survival. But the apparition knew nothing of mercy. Instead, she dragged his body out of the carriage, withdrew her knife from his chest, and slit his throat to finish the job.

When his breath finally left him, she closed his pleading eyes, and searched him. He had nothing but the knife. She'd already stolen the comm from his pack earlier in the night.

She left his inert, bloodied body on the dusty ground.

Bronson's last moments would haunt her, but she told herself it was just one more depravity, one more deception; just one more person who would visit her crowded nightmares.

It would only be later, in the dark, when the apparition had receded, that the memories would rush back, and she would do a full accounting. Bronson had shown them his not-so-good ventriloquist act he'd learned to entertain his daughter Hailey. He loved his wife Chae even though they rarely got along. He had detailed knowledge of rug threadcounts and a passion for balsa-wood coffee tables. He cared deeply for their mission, and was rightly suspicious of Cecile's motives. He was a good man, with a full life ahead of him, yet it had been easy for her to kill him. She had simply relinquished herself to the apparition.

Yet when the apparition was gone, it was her who had plunged the knife; her who had slit his throat. When the apparition was gone, it was her who had taken all his hopes and dreams away from him.

14

WISHFUL THINKING

The hope of a good night's sleep had been wishful thinking. Pyke had maybe five hours. Several times he had woken abruptly, jumping out of bed as if Aspen was being attacked, or as if bells were ringing in his ear, but neither was the case. He could only guess that he was being ejected from some tumultuous dream.

In the morning, he helped Natty fix her outhouse. It ended up being a several-hour project. He had to add another support beam and shingle half the roof. The work didn't give him much time to consider his dilemma, so that afternoon he decided to go for a hike with Gill.

His favorite hike had always been the Red Mountain Way. It was more like two hikes, first across town to Hunter Creek, then along a ridge on the mountain—the ridge that he often gazed at from his apartment window. He avoided much of town by venturing down little-used streets. These avenues were lined with deciduous trees sprouting newly minted leaves. After a good hour, he was well out of the city on the other side of the valley, following creekside paths. The flora became dry meadows between broad swaths of evergreen, until he eventually reached the treeless expanse that overlooked the entire valley.

Gill rode in the carrier on Pyke's back, but Pyke took him out on occasion. Gill loved the creek, so Pyke held his arms as he tried to walk across some flattish stones near the rippling bed. "Water," Pyke said, "and these are stones."

Gill pointed at the forest.

"Yes, that's a tree. *Tree.*"

"Dah!"

It was windy on the ridge, but there hadn't been any sign of rain. Pyke had an unimpeded view of Aspen and the expanse of the valley.

Defense walls were being built on both ends of the valley, the sounds of hammering and sawing occasionally reaching him on the wind. These walls gleamed in the sun, made with new network-made metal panels. He guessed they were going up on account of increased worries of Laramie attacks. The *Leap of Wisdom* billboards that had been at each end of the city had been moved to stand on the walls. The scene they portrayed would have been changed yesterday, but Pyke couldn't make out the visuals at this distance. The most easterly sign cast a long shadow over town.

He could also see Glen Pearson's old compound: a seven-acre plot on a terrace, surrounded by an amalgam of metal fence wire, stone walls, and natural cliff faces. Many people in Aspen held a kind of historical reverence for the site, but not Pyke. It wasn't even that impressive, aesthetically speaking. Over the years, ramshackle towers and huts had been built to house Glen's growing number of followers. The house itself had quite a few renovations that didn't blend in well with the Old World style. The mansion had recently been repainted a vibrant red color—the only feature Pyke liked.

He arrived at the wooden bridge that crossed the Collins Creek gully. This was near to where he'd found Dwayne's body, and he didn't want his thoughts to return to that day, so he passed over the gully quickly.

He took out his nugget and earbuds, flipping the track to one of his favorite hiking songs. The singer crooned "happy faces" repeatedly over dark, soulful breakbeats. It was an unusual composition, full of contrast. Maybe that's why he liked it.

The mountain air was refreshing, and the view invigorating, but he was still having trouble focusing his thoughts. There was just so much uncertainty. He hadn't heard from the rangers or the network since he'd reported Arsalan's absence. There also hadn't been any request for him to return to the offering intake area for work. He would lose his job, he assumed, but what was less certain was what punitive action the network would take.

He arrived at a broad plateau where he would typically stop for lunch. He fed Gill some carrots, cheese and berries and let him down to play with Raggedy Rick, the ranger doll that Natty had sewn for him. "Playing" usually involved Gill smashing poor Rick's head against nearby boulders. It wasn't the most intellectually stimulating activity, but Pyke got a kick out of it, even if Rick ended up more raggedy by the end of each session.

Pyke ate some hazelnuts he'd cracked that morning and gnawed on the leftover cheese Gill hadn't eaten.

Another song came on. It was heavily instrumental; a lead-in consisting of pulsing synth riffs and snippy drum solos. It migrated to full-throated vocals over a playful bass line. The singer was extorting the virtues of flying blind in various forms of aircraft, and then compared his experience to love (of course).

Pyke liked the melody, so he turned up the volume. The music enveloped him. The world became a disconnected tableau. The city below seemed small, muted by the music, dwarfed by distance, and overshadowed by Gill's playful smile. And so his thoughts crystallized. He would leave first thing in the morning. Together, Pyke and Gill would forge another life together, far away from here. He didn't need the network, or the host, or even Jeeri and Natty. Aspen had tormented him long enough.

* * *

As he returned down the mountain, he became more comfortable with his decision. He looked forward to a release from the chronic uncertainty that plagued him, and the constant desire to please the host but not being sure how. There were many things he would miss about Aspen, but he sure wouldn't miss that.

Darkness had fallen by the time they arrived back at his apartment. Despite the long hike, he didn't feel tired. His conviction to a course of action lent him strength. His focus replenished his will. He put Gill down and immediately began making piles of clothes and supplies he would need for the journey. He wrote a list of provisions he would collect in the morning before he set out. He unlocked his small safe and transferred his savings into a belt satchel.

There was a knock on the door. It wasn't loud, yet it made his heart jump. He moved slowly to answer it, his nerves picking up with each step. When he opened it, no one was there, but lying on his frayed doormat was a familiar envelope adorned with sparkling green and gold calligraphy reading *A letter from Host Mengle*.

His heart hammered in his chest as he stepped outside into the pitch black. There was no one around. They must have left in a hurry.

He took the letter into the living room, where he paced in front of the window, weighing the envelope in his hand. Should he even open it? Maybe he could just pretend he didn't receive it and leave? At least that way he could plead ignorance if the rangers stopped him.

But no. Whatever punishment Mengle had devised would be made worse.

A flood of despair threatened to overcome him. He'd waited too long, and now the crew would have its way with him. It would be yet another failure, yet another tragedy in his cursed existence.

Pyke looked at Gill sleeping soundly. He pulled a hair back from his tiny ear.

"I'm sorry," he said.

On the verge of tears, Pyke gritted his teeth and ripped open the envelope. Inside was a card that sparkled so much he wondered if it might give him some kind of static shock. The message was in the same fancy handwriting, and what it said was wholly unexpected.

Pyke Maven,

Congratulations!!! You have been selected to be a contestant on A Leap of Wisdom. *Tell your friends! Tell your family! Tell the whole world!*

I am so excited for you! What a privilege to be able to honor Glen Pearson and his gifts. Be at the parapet for makeup and pre-game preparation at 6:30 pm on Friday.

You could be a Lucky Winner!

Host Mengle

15

———————

ANOTHER TURN

During Cecile's scuffle with Bronson, Warrick had shifted positions, but he hadn't awakened. Rusty bloodstains marked the bottom of the carriage.

Cecile retook the reins and, with trembling hands, convinced the steeds to move again, completing a turn, then another, and another, until her path became so confused by the complexity of the labyrinth that pursuit would be near impossible.

She used the stars to guide her back onto a northward trajectory.

From that point, it should have been a breeze. The Glasslands were supposed to be empty. It was late spring and Laramie Broncos usually came through in fall. The Navajo also wouldn't be around, because they tended to perform their Glasslands pilgrimage in the winter. Contrary to what Cecile had told the others, the Essentialists thought the land was toxic, like the fever lands, so they rarely ventured inside, whatever the season.

And yet, three hours after she'd made her escape, drowsy from lack of sleep and with a headache brewing from trying to see shapes in the dark, the carriage stumbled into an active campsite. She pulled hard on the reins when she saw the line of tents. She'd barely started to turn around when four men—Essentialist soldiers, by the looks of their cherry-blossom-emblem uniforms—jumped aboard and pinned her to her seat before she could grab a weapon.

Cecile's hands were bound and she was tied to a heavy chest inside a small tent. She heard muffled, unintelligible discussions outside. Despite the waves of protest from the apparition demanding her to find a way out, she was numb, unable to exert any effort. Her head started spinning in the darkness. She fell asleep, disoriented, exhausted, and defeated.

In the morning she was awakened and escorted from the tent by two Essentialist soldiers. The men were thick across the chest, with black hair and tan skin—Tucson loyalists. She kept a good pace in the direction they pointed, but they took turns pushing her along anyway.

Enclosed within the camp were several score horses, at least thirty high-walled wagons forming a line on one side, and at least a hundred tents. There weren't any permanent buildings. The only structures of note were guard towers on at least three sides of the encampment. These appeared to have been quickly assembled, made of thin panels interposed between orthogonal struts of metal. High-caliber gun turrets topped the towers.

Essentialist or not, the soldiers didn't show any fear of the Glass-lands being tainted. Nor did they seem to care much about preserving the glass objects; many of the artifacts had been collected and dumped in a jumbled pile in the center like a common trash heap.

Cecile was escorted to a tent that would have been large enough for a small wedding, the roof supported by a hexagonal beam structure. Inside, she was made to kneel before three Essentialists who looked down their noses at her.

One of the Essentialists resembled her soldier escort, although his hair was puffed out in an unusual kind of perm. He wore a leather vest emblazoned with a depiction of half of the rising sun. If Cecile recalled correctly, this half-sun emblem used to be prominent on Tuscon Union flags, before the small nation expanded to join the Essentialist confederation decades ago.

Another man had a bushy beard growing around pouty lips and red cheeks. He wore a long, flowing robe that had shades of beige and yellow. A necklace laden with wooden animal carvings—deer, rabbits, bears and wolves—reached down to his belt.

The third Essentialist was a woman, slim and fit, with glossy, light brown hair pulled back in pleats. She wore the same uniform as Cecile's escort. A black bear pendant hung from her neck, its paws held up to its face. The woman had less of an air of pomp than the two men. Her eyes squinted in cold calculation.

Beyond them were four other men, standing at attention in the voids between chairs, chests and tables—sentries of some kind.

Warrick lay in a puddle of rags on the floor. Cecile thought he might be dead, until the poofy-haired man pulled him upright by his cuffs, using a chain that looped through the roof beams. Only then could she see what a despicable state he was in. One of his pant legs was rolled up, stuck at his knee, revealing the mass of scar tissue underneath, but what was new was the trail of yellow down his tunic —dried vomit. His eyes were dark and lacked focus, even more so than usual.

She may have given him too much sedative.

The robed man with the ornate multi-animal necklace spoke first. "My name is Antler Lakemist. I'm deputy curator of Tucson. This is Colonel Estrada"—he pointed to the poofy-haired man—"and Captain Kehda Rojas." He gestured to the woman. "We are an Essentialist outpost and supply train, making our way through the Glasslands."

The man named Colonel Estrada responded with a scowl of annoyance. "Don't bother trying to befriend her, Lakemist." He turned to Cecile. "State your business—and don't be coy or we'll catch your tongue." He made a scissor motion with his fingers.

"I don't understand why I was apprehended." Cecile said, putting on an air of indignation. "Have I done something wrong?"

"Are you a Spoke?" Captain Rojas asked. She had taken a step back from her colleagues to pick up Bronson's comm device from the table. She waved it at Cecile, eyebrows raised.

"That?" Cecile said. "No. I'm a bandit turned trader who dealt with the Spokes, but not anymore. My name is Mary. My friend is sick—I'm trying to get him to a healer."

"Have you not heard about the Spoke militia in the area?" Rojas asked. "We have to wonder if you could be one of them."

It was a loaded question. The Spoke militia probably wasn't real, but Cecile couldn't know for sure. They were either seeking intel, or testing her story.

"I heard about a Spoke force and gave them a wide berth," Cecile said. "Someone warned me about Sumner, specifically—that there was a Spoke platoon and even a beholder there. I don't know any more because I veered south on that news, to stay away."

"A beholder?" Estrada laughed. "Quite a fantasy. How do we know you aren't planting false rumors, to get us to move our camp?"

"I'm not." Cecile shrugged.

"You have an accent," Lakemist said. "Where were you born?"

Cecile had never been good at masking her accent. She would have to weave it into her story. "I'm from Quebec, originally. We were allies with the Spokes, but not involved in the war. When I was young I settled in one of the bandit tribes along the east coast, farther south."

"And where is this doctor you are going to see?"

"In Ouray."

The three Essentialists exchanged skeptical frowns.

"What's wrong with your friend?" Estrada asked, flicking a finger in Warrick's direction.

"A disease of the mind. He speaks in riddles, hallucinates. In Ouray they have healers—they can reverse the hold of the disease, or at least alleviate his suffering. We were moving quickly through the

Glasslands because we were worried about bandits. We had no idea we would disturb your camp."

Rojas was crouching next to Warrick, examining him closely. "I can believe you didn't expect to see us. The rest, though . . . coming a thousand miles, in a time of war, to find some tribal healer? And traders around here know to not deal with electronics—if you want to pass screening. Then, of course, there's the blood. The floor of your carriage is covered in it."

"We were attacked by Laramie Broncos. I survived, but only after I dispatched one of the assailants. As for the tech—I told you, I'm not from around here." She knew her story sounded like a stretch, but she had to stick to it.

"Who would you plan to sell tech like this to?" Rojas asked.

It was another loaded question. She couldn't claim a fictitious Essentialist contact, and any Spoke connection would prompt a deeper probe. She thought quickly. "It's for an offering—to gain passage through the Colorado Collective to the north. Unless you would like to buy it?"

Estrada nodded and laughed. "She's got gumption. I only wonder whether she's blindly ignorant or blatantly irreverent."

"Please," Cecile said, introducing a measure of earnest in her voice. "My friend may not have much time left. Will you relegate him to madness? Do you want to be responsible for his death?"

Estrada was smiling, as if Cecile's challenge was a laughable pleasantry. "My dear, the sun-streaked of the union are not so easily misled. You paint our discussion with the Shrouded Sun—a voyage of transition and uncertainty—but your rhythm is wrong. Your journey is at an end, and therefore the Setting Sun is more apt. Now is a time for wisdom, for reflection. Have some pride, and tell the truth. Do not project a false light, or that is how you will be remembered."

Cecile wasn't familiar with Tucson Union religious doctrine, but she knew that they characterized different stages of the sun as a metaphorical guide for specific situations.

Before she could think of an appropriate response, Lakemist

spoke, his words directed to Estrada. "Your sun-streaked rambling is only going to confuse her, especially if she's a Spoke. And I feel like you insert your teachings just to rile me. I'm the curator here. You are the military commander. Maybe you should learn to speak plainly like the rest of your brethren, with short commands and hollow machismo."

Lakemist looked around the room as he spoke. It was clear he meant to diminish Estrada in front of the others.

Indeed, Estrada's face showed a momentary flash of anger. He paced about, then stopped in front of a cabinet at the wall of the tent. From the cabinet he took a fire poker. He moved quickly, pointing the sharp end in the direction of Lakemist. Lakemist recoiled, his hands held up in self-defense, but Estrada sidestepped to stand before Warrick, then prodded Warrick gently in the stomach.

Warrick squirmed, but only a little, so Estrada prodded again, and again. Estrada regained his smile as he saw that he'd frightened Lakemist with his childish antics, a smile he maintained as he continued to poke at Warrick. It was a smile of contentment, like you might see on the face of a shoemaker polishing leather, or a farmer walking through his wheat fields.

Abruptly, Warrick lunged forward and bit into Estrada's arm. Estrada knocked Warrick's head away, revealing deep teeth mark impressions that had broken the skin.

"Oh. You shouldn't have done that, you Spoke-whore." Estrada kneed Warrick in the groin, then raked him across the face with the flat surface of the poker. Warrick spasmed in pain from the blow to his crotch. Estrada was about to hit him again when Lakemist yelled out, "Stop!"

Estrada froze.

"This man could offer useful intelligence," Lakemist continued. "You should be more careful. Don't compound your mistake by making a worse one."

Warrick was facing down, blood dripping off his nose onto the floor in front of him. It was hard to imagine him being in worse shape than he was at that moment. And yet, when he lifted his head, he looked more alive than he had in months. His eyes burned.

"Thank you for that," he said.

Estrada's brow was furrowed in confusion.

Warrick glared at Cecile and sneered, as if only now aware of her presence. "Don't listen to a word this woman says," he said. "She's full of lies."

Cecile shook her head mournfully, to imply Warrick was beyond help.

Lakemist shifted his weight, so as to be at a better angle in scrutinizing Warrick. "Go on," he said, making a revolving motion with his hand.

Warrick squinted in concentration. "There's no doctor. I'm her prisoner. She's an evil witch, taking me to someone, or something. Next she'll tell you there's a Spoke force nearby, and a beholder. It's all lies and manipulation."

"Like I said," Cecile objected, "he's sick, and . . ."

Estrada had moved over and raised his fire poker above Cecile's head. It was a fair bet his next move would be a downward strike if she kept talking.

There was a tense moment in which no words were spoken. Then Estrada addressed Warrick. "What did she tell you—specifically— about this Spoke force and beholder?"

"That . . . that she was going to get their help to take us north. But she betrayed her own Spoke allies and took me away on her own."

"Why are you so important to her?"

"I don't know. I . . ." Warrick was trying to regroup, taking deep breaths, and shaking his head forcefully like a dog trying to shed water from its fur. "You should know that Essentialist leaders are being controlled by an evil machine. It doesn't care about you. It will kill all of you once it gains enough power. It's called Gail . . . or, wait —*Cerezo* to Essentialists."

Captain Rojas and Lakemist's eyebrows were raised, but Cecile couldn't be sure if Warrick's words had struck a note, or if they were simply fascinated by his apparent madness.

Estrada shrugged. "Sounds like gibberish to me."

Warrick mentioning Gail could be a good thing, because him sounding insane played right into Cecile's hand. There was a small chance that if these Essentialist leaders were distracted by other interests, they might even let her go.

"We've heard whispers about this force," Lakemist said, "and the beholder, but we've seen no concrete evidence. Now I wonder if we finally have our explanation. You"—he pointed at Cecile—"are the one planting these rumors in your travels, and as they spread, the stories evolve in colorful ways until they find their way to our scouts."

Rojas nodded her head adamantly, as if Lakemist had spoken some kind of Essentialist gospel. After some chin holding and nodding of his own, it seemed even Estrada agreed, despite the fact that the insinuation was made by Lakemist.

"I think we're done here," Lakemist said. "There's nothing more to extract from this filth."

"You don't believe us?" Cecile pleaded. "Fine. You think we're planting rumors? Fine, believe what you want. But please, have mercy. Our travels have no bearing on your plans."

Rojas raised her eyebrows at Estrada. Estrada offered a cursory nod, and Rojas picked up a heavy binder from a side table and started leafing through it. "The problem, *Cecile*," Rojas said, "is that we already looked you up," She stopped at a page with neat charts next to headshot illustrations. "You have achieved celebrity status in our list of notable Spokes. Here you are: a streak of blue hair, from Quebec, French accent. It says you're looking for Warrick Kelemen— who just happened to identify himself to us just an hour ago. It's all right here."

Zut alors. It made sense that Gail could have made detailed profiles on all the Spokes who'd been in Seeville, but Cecile hadn't imagined that these low-level officers could have access to the information. They had just been playing the fool, seeing if some tack she might take in the interrogation might reveal new intelligence.

What slim vestige of hope she had of getting out of this was fading rapidly. "I . . . we can help you," she said.

"How?" Lakemist challenged.

"I . . . I . . ." Cecile stammered.

Lakemist turned away to address Rojas and Estrada. "There's no point in sullying our ears with any more of her lies. I will send a messenger to Luna, along with the heathen device. Let's see what she wants to do with them."

Luna Pais: the unscrupulous hand of Gail's Essentialist expansion. If Luna was in charge, Cecile was sure Warrick and her would be taken west. There would be no escaping once they were in Luna's custody, in some heavily defended tech fortress that Gail had devised. They would be interrogated, tortured, and killed.

"Please listen," Cecile said, her mind racing. "Warrick is right. Luna is under the spell of an evil machine . . ." But she trailed off. It was only making things worse, confirming their suspicions about her. The three Essentialist leaders turned and moved out of the tent.

The apparition screamed out from the edges of her vision, but there was nothing she could do. These officers knew of Cecile's importance in the Spoke command structure, so they would keep her under heavy guard until she could be taken back to Tucson and chewed into bits.

She wondered if she could just let go for once; give in completely and let the apparition consume her entirely. Maybe that's what had happened to Warrick—maybe it had just been too much, so he let it devour his soul and splinter his mind.

Looking at him now, his bleeding face, scarred legs and vomit-covered tunic, she realized that there was at least one person whose existence was even bleaker than hers.

"I'm so sorry," she managed to wheeze out to Warrick, despite the protests of the apparition. He looked up suspiciously before turning inward again, into a dark communion of his own.

16

THE SHOW MUST GO ON

Live shows were held high above Aspen at the parapet; a massive open-air metal platform thirty yards in diameter, near an old chairlift stop. Two cylindrical heat ducts ran underneath the platform, coming all the way from the summit, continuing down the mountain to feed the Wisdome and downtown buildings via underground tunnels. These ducts warmed the studio area, making steam rise from the platform in the near-freezing evening air.

The entire area was lit by arrays of blazing lights affixed to towers on each side of the platform. Man-sized speakers also lined the perimeter, blaring out staccato, upbeat melodies that echoed off the distant mountains.

On one side of the platform was the studio audience, elevated in stands that rose a good thirty feet high. The seats were filled with the citizens of Aspen, clad in jackets and ties, or formal dresses, donning glazed expressions. On the other side of the platform was a four-hundred-square-foot viewscreen as a backdrop to the host and hostess podiums. In the center were three contestant podiums, where Pyke was standing, and behind them was the Trivial Jump course; a chasm in which a series of standing stations were propped up on spindly metal poles. These stations bobbed about like reeds in the wind.

A solitary headless unit stood beside the studio audience, its chest facing the contestants. It looked no different than the unit Pyke saw in the dance hall.

One of the contestants was a middle-aged woman named Zoe who Pyke had seen working as a plumber downtown. Her red lipstick and blue mascara were liberally applied, and her hair was curled into a perm. She was smiling nervously, tapping her podium with her fingers as if it was some kind of musical instrument.

The third contestant was Vin. He was wearing a neat tie and blazer, his oily hair pulled back. He was in a messianic trance, eyes focused and unflinching.

Despite the uncomfortable incident when Vin had clearly been pumping him for information, Pyke was glad for him. Vin had worked for the crew most of his life and had finally been given a chance. Maybe the crew finally wanted to reward those that they had neglected over the years.

Maybe Mengle didn't care about Arsalan after all.

Pyke tried to focus. This was the day he'd dreamt of for so long, but if he didn't follow the rules, both written and unwritten, it could end in disaster. No one wanted to be like Chan Unsalah, relegated to Gondola Valley for being drunk on set. The humiliation alone would be unbearable. Then there was Olivia Mason, who'd been barred from the parapet for swearing at the host.

Cannons beside the platform shot multicolored balls that exploded into sparkling glitter, showering the contestants and the audience. The music became even louder—a kind of distorted electronic percussion that was so high tempo it made Pyke feel queasy. Host Mengle began running around the platform, hooting and yelling "Let's go!" into his microphone while pumping his fist at the audience. A chorus of cheers answered him every time he passed the stands. He circled the platform three times and ended back where he started.

"Okay, okay, okay!" Mengle said, as the music faded and the last of the glitter floated to the floor. "Time to play *A Leap of Wisdom*. I'm sure you'd like to meet our fabulous contestants. First, we have Zoe Karnavus, who you may have seen unclogging your pipes. She's crafty with the plunger, but does she have the wits to match? We'll soon find out."

Shane made his way over to Zoe, swinging his hips. He was wearing a shiny dress made of gold sequins. His long blonde wig flowed down his back. He smiled and hugged Zoe.

"Then there's Pyke Maven," Mengle continued. "An overture from Ouray? A contribution from Kachina? He'll represent you, but what can he offer in the way of smarts?"

Pyke forced a smile as Shane leaned in and kissed him on the cheek. Shane turned to the audience, one hand behind Pyke's back and the other flopping above his head in a flamboyant gesture. The crowd cheered.

"And finally we have Vin Tenshi, a loyal servant to the crew for twelve years. He's the king of *the show must go on*, but will he reign with his brain?"

The crowd cheered again, louder than for Pyke and Zoe. Vin was a clear favorite. Shane kissed Vin, just as he had Pyke, but also gave him a bear hug that lifted his feet off the ground, to the delight of the crowd.

"Let's begin!" Mengle said. The ground shifted as the platform began rotating. The view beyond the set became a merry-go-round of cascading mountain tops. In combination with the blaring music, it made Pyke even more disoriented, yet he kept his eager smile and did his best to show his excitement by nodding and pumping his fist. He'd never seen a live show, but it was obvious that any downcast or worried expression was considered bad etiquette.

"Are you ready for the first hurdle?" Mengle asked.

Pyke nodded with the other two contestants.

"The hurdle is . . . on which episode did Glen Pearson first make the Trivial Jump mandatory for contestants?"

Vin was lightning fast in pressing his button. "Episode 41," he said. "Season 2."

"That's . . . correct!" Mengle said, and the audience cheered. Some of them were whistling. The screen in front of Vin's podium flashed *100*. The questions could be any kind of trivia, but were often game-related. Vin had a clear advantage.

"The second hurdle is . . ." Mengle looked down at his hidden podium display. "In the Old World, which geometric shape was used for signs telling you to stop?"

Pyke knew the answer, but he was too slow to hit his button. Zoe's podium lit up before his. "An octagon," she announced.

"An octagon is right!" Mengle said, and the audience clapped appreciatively. Zoe's podium lit up with a hundred points.

"The third hurdle is . . ." Mengle continued. "Why did the people of Aspen grow more prosperous than the surrounding areas after the fall?"

All three contestants pounced on their buttons, but Zoe's podium lit up first again. Pyke vowed to improve his reaction time.

Zoe said, "Because Glen Pearson had the foresight to partner with the network."

Jeeri had told Pyke that a few of these freebie questions would be interspersed in every game—a kind of network-sponsored self-promotion. There were any number of possible answers, as long as credit was given to Glen Pearson and the network.

The host squinted and nodded, as if Zoe's response had profound meaning. "Yes, Zoe. Yes," he said, and Zoe's display flashed *200*.

It wasn't a good start. He'd been overwhelmed by the sounds, the pyrotechnics, and the spinning parapet, and wasn't paying close enough attention. He wasn't that put out, though. Even if he lost, it was the first time he'd felt a part of something—the first time he'd felt he belonged in Aspen.

The game continued. Pyke did manage to get a question right, but the other contestants were faster and better prepared. When they entered the final round he only had a hundred points, whereas Vin had four hundred, and Zoe three hundred.

"And now it's time for the High Wire," the host said, "where fortunes are made and lost, where your position is defined for the Jump course. Here we go."

Behind Mengle, Shane spun the wheel. The markers on the wheel showed point values ranging from one hundred to a thousand, although the thousand marker was a one-in-a-hundred shot. The wheel clicked along, slowed, and stopped at the five hundred mark.

The crowd gasped. "Whoa ho ho," Mengle crooned. "Quite the prize. Are you ready?"

The three contestants nodded, their hands hovering over their buttons.

"In episode fifty-four of *A Leap of Wisdom*, which contestant said she broke her arm by tripping over an alligator?"

It should have been easy. Only days ago, they'd all watched episode fifty-four in the Wisdome. Not only that, but everyone had seen the episode multiple times and spoken about the funny anecdote ad nauseum. But Pyke hadn't been paying attention at the most recent viewing, and his mind drew a blank on the woman's name. His hand hovered over the button but didn't quite press down, while Zoe and Vin smashed their buttons so hard Pyke thought they might break.

Yet it was Pyke's podium that lit up.

There was dead air as everyone tried to figure out what had happened. Pyke hadn't pressed down, but maybe his hand had gotten close enough? Eventually, the host said, "Pyke! And the answer is?"

He had fifteen seconds to answer. He had to think of something.

"Asha Podorsky," he said. It was a contestant's name he remembered, but he had no idea if she was in episode fifty-four.

A loud, derogatory buzz sounded.

"Ouuuu," the host said. "So sorry, Pyke—the answer is . . ." Then the whole crowd seem to say it in unison: "Nadia Lamberson."

It was one thing to get the question wrong, but it was another to know that he was the only person on the parapet to not know the answer.

Pyke's score dropped to negative four hundred. The sense of belonging vanished, replaced by a flush of nerves and clammy hands.

He was in real trouble. People with negative scores were often punished. One man who had negative six hundred had to clean the public washrooms for months.

"And now for the last question, before the Jump course." Shane spun the wheel, faster than before. It clicked around and around, everyone watching. Eventually it slowed, hit some resistance, and stopped at the one thousand mark.

The crowd gasped again, then murmured. "One grand!" Mengle said, gawking in amazement. He raised his hands and looked up to the sky, as if some amazing provenance had occurred.

"This is quite something." Mengle said. "How long has it been, Hostess?"

Shane replied, "More than a year now, Host Mengle."

"More than a year," Mengle repeated, nodding. "Amazing. Are you all ready?"

Both of Pyke's hands were hovering over the buzzer. He had to get this one.

"The hurdle is . . . Who founded the Adherent faith followed by the Spoke people of the east?"

Pyke was almost shocked into paralysis by the question. He doubted the others had the faintest idea what an Adherent was. He pressed the buzzer, even though it seemed as though his podium was lighting up already.

A flash of derision crossed Mengle's face—a hint of contempt Pyke couldn't quite place—but he regained his smile and said, "Pyke, your answer?"

"Ursula Okafor," he said.

Again, there was something distasteful in Mengle's expression—annoyance, or discomfort—but not enough for him to lose his composure. He brightened slowly. "Your answer is . . . correct! Congratulations, Pyke. What a reversal of fortune. Pyke has taken the lead!"

The audience applauded, but without adulation. Many of them were as confused as Pyke. Vin was stunned, his jaw hanging.

But Zoe—she lost it.

"Excuse me," she said. "What's going on here?"

"I'm sorry?" Mengle asked. "Do you mean what's next? Well, we are about to do . . . the Trivial Jump!"

The audience had gone quiet, and the silence was compounded by the lack of music or pyrotechnics. The platform continued to revolve, the silhouettes of the distant mountains rolling up and down.

"It's not fair," Zoe continued. "The question was, like . . . written for him. There's never been any questions about *Spokes* before. And that other question—the one he blew about episode fifty-four—he didn't even hit his . . ."

She trailed off for good reason: the headless unit was moving in her direction.

"What?" Zoe asked, looking around frenetically. "What's happening?"

Shane and the host were backing away. Pyke stepped back from his podium as well, ensuring he was nowhere near the path of the headless.

"I'm sorry," Zoe said. "I didn't mean to . . ."

When the headless was within a few feet, she leapt away. When it continued to pursue her, she ran. She was faster, but it was relentless, and after she had circled the host's podium twice it blocked her in at the edge of the Trivial Jump course. The platform rotation ceased at the same instant.

"I'm so sorry. I spoke out of turn." She was speaking to the headless, but Pyke had never seen one respond to a human. He wasn't sure it was possible, or if it was even listening.

It did pause for a moment.

Then, in a fluid motion, the headless stepped forward, placed its stone mitts on one of Zoe's legs and one of her arms, lifted her screaming form over its head, and hurled her over the edge of the platform into the chasm.

She missed the safety nets.

Pyke didn't see her land, but her screams ended abruptly.

There was a flurry of gasps from the audience, followed by

silence. The only sound came from the footfalls of the headless as it walked over to retake its position at the edge of the platform.

Pyke gripped the sides of his podium. Why hadn't a member of the crew intervened? Would no one chase after Zoe to see if she'd survived? But nobody moved.

Mengle's head was pivoting, his smile cracking. "The show . . ." he stuttered. "The show must go on, right, Hostess?"

Shane nodded slowly.

Hurriedly, Mengle began pressing buttons on his podium. The cannons went off again, and glitter fell from the sky. He glared at the shocked audience and they clapped, slowly at first and then, eventually, with resigned determination. There were no fist pumps, and those with the will to smile did so in a way that made them look like insane clowns.

"Pyke, Vin," Mengle said. "It's time for that final leap." His tone was more dire than jubilant.

Pyke hesitated, but not for long. Fear of what the headless might do overrode any impulse to object.

He moved over to the Trivial Jump course. A broad line leading to the Jump course had been painted on the parapet platform, with marks corresponding to each hundred points. Pyke stood at the six-hundred-points marker, and Vin at the four-hundred-points marker, twenty feet behind him. This gave Pyke a clear advantage.

The floating reed islands in the abyss began bobbing back and forth. The objective was to make it to a massive brass cymbal, drum it with a dangling hammer, then be the first to return to the parapet. The cymbal was positioned on a free-standing wall far away from the studio platform, and the only way to reach it was to jump through the maze of bobbing reeds.

Pyke charted a path, but not before once again glancing across the platform to confirm that the headless was stationary. The image of Zoe being thrown into the chasm replayed in his mind.

"On your marks," Mengle said.

Pyke kneeled down, like a sprinter in starter blocks.

"Get set," Mengle said.

Pyke glanced back to see Vin crouching behind him. His eyes were fiery with purpose.

"Go!"

Pyke ran out to the edge, hurtled through the air, and landed onto the narrow rim circling the base of the first reed. He held tight to the three inch-wide stake in the middle as the reed bobbed back and forth through the air, absorbing his momentum. When he was comfortable with the modulation of the reed he made a leap to the next one, and again bounced around for a few precious seconds. For the subsequent jump, he targeted a farther reed, as it would allow him a straighter shot to the brass cymbal wall.

The image of Zoe being thrown off the parapet again reverberated through his mind. He tried to shake it, but it was hampering his concentration. He undershot and clipped his knee on the way down, but he managed to grab hold of the lip of the rim before falling completely off. These reed structures were made from a cohesive, grooved rubber that was easy to hold. The safety net sprawled out a good twenty feet below him, but he didn't want to count on its integrity.

In his attempt to climb up to the circular ledge, Pyke almost lost his grip after he misjudged the bobbing inertia of the reed. In the distance, he could see Vin advancing methodically, in cautious jumps from reed to reed. Pyke had lost the advantage.

After another near slip, Pyke managed to regain the narrow rim at the base. The next few jumps weren't as far, but he took them slowly. At this point, he didn't care about winning or losing. He just needed to give the impression that he was trying.

He made it to the cymbal platform a few seconds after Vin. The two hits on the gong sounded in quick succession, followed by distant echoes from the mountains.

Pyke wasted no time in turning back to retrace his path through the reeds.

Vin was moving quicker, gaining confidence as his lead expanded. Meanwhile, Pyke continued more carefully, ensuring his timing was right for each jump, and resting after a bold leap.

Without any forewarning, the course changed. Some of the reeds began bobbing from side to side with more energy. None of the ones in front of Pyke were affected, so he kept following his path back toward the main studio platform without any changes. Vin, on the other hand, was forced to stop. A key reed to which he needed to cross was shifting from side to side in a ten-foot arc. He appeared to be trying to time it, but wasn't finding the nerve to jump.

And so, slowly, Pyke gained, and gained. The reeds ahead of him bobbed back and forth, but they didn't seem to have any more energy than on the outward journey.

Eventually, Vin did jump, but the reed was gyrating so much that he slipped off the side. He clutched onto the middle stake below the rim with all his strength, and it was enough to keep him from dropping into the net, but his hold was precarious.

Pyke continued jumping until there was only one leap left. The last leap was anticlimactic; only a few feet of distance, more of a large step than a proper hurdle. He jumped anyway, clearing the edge by several feet, and jogged to a stop to halt his momentum on the main parapet platform.

There was a spate of wooden, tired clapping from the audience. More glitter grapes were blasted into the air, and upbeat riffs blared from the speakers. Shane glided over to Pyke and hugged him. He whispered, "You'll pay for this," in Pyke's ear, before pulling away to lift Pyke's arm up in victory.

"And we have our Lucky Winner!" Mengle said, gesturing vaguely at Pyke. Behind Pyke, the reeds had stopped bobbing, and Vin was able to complete the course. His teeth were clenched, his face flushed and sweaty.

Few were paying attention to Vin. Mengle guided Pyke away from the Jump course to the middle of the platform. There, a cylindrical cross section of the floor rose on a pillar to waist height. The top foot of the pillar was clear glass filled with a blinding blue light. Mengle found a door in the glass, opened it, and pulled out an envelope.

"And what have you won?" Mengle asked, holding the envelope to his chest. He was pausing for effect, nodding to the audience and to Shane.

The crowd hushed completely. The music stopped.

Pyke was having heart palpitations—not only from the exertions of the leap course, but also from the anticipation of what was in the envelope. And he was still in shock from what happened to Zoe.

It could be a trip to the waterfall hotel in Ouray. One of the most talked about rewards was given to Ben Vallet, who had weekly feasts cooked by the best chef in town for a year. Yet another contestant received a big cash prize, more than a year's salary.

Pyke didn't care what it was. He just wanted it to be over with. After a lifetime of wanting a chance at winning, he'd had a change of heart. He was ashamed that he'd been yearning to participate in such a capricious game—such a *lethal* game.

When Mengle opened the envelope to read the card, he didn't produce one of the myriad of fake smiles he'd deployed throughout the game, or even the self-assured grin he displayed during his countless town hall speeches. His eyes were wide, his eyebrows were raised, and his teeth were bared. It was a maniacal look that offered no insight into what he was reading, only that he certainly wasn't happy. Whatever he read was enough to jolt him out of his gameshow veneer.

The smile did return, a moment later. Mengle never lost his composure for long.

"Pyke has been granted a communion with the seers!" he said, holding the placard in the air. "He's going to the summit!"

More mechanical clapping ensued. No one cheered. No one was happy for Pyke. They wanted nothing more than to leave the parapet, just as he did.

Slowly, Mengle lowered his hand, extending the envelope toward Pyke, who accepted it with a trembling hand.

17

A MEAGER SLIT OF LIGHT

Cecile was sitting in her small tent on the dusty ground, eyes closed, her back to the massive chest her captors had used to secure her. There was no escaping; the chest must have weighed three hundred pounds. Her wrists were cuffed to chains that looped around its base.

They had taken all her possessions.

The look of surprise on Bronson's face came back to her often, a visceral wave of painful nostalgia.

She wasn't sure if she'd slept at all. The last twelve hours had been a nightmarish journey through bouts of hopelessness and apparition-induced anxiety.

The slit of light coming through the tent flap, meager as it was, gave her a small reprieve. It allowed her to differentiate night from day, and when she stared at it she knew that the apparition hadn't completely flooded her vision.

Until a new silhouette blocked the aperture.

The shape moved to the side, and Cecile blinked, her eyes adjusting. It was Captain Rojas—one of the officers from the day before.

"You look almost as bad as your friend," Rojas said, eyebrows raised. "Are you sick?"

It wouldn't do to hint at her particular affliction. "Just travel-weary," Cecile said, "and dejected that you won't let me help my friend."

Rojas grinned sourly. "Come with me," she said, and she freed Cecile from her cuffs.

Cecile followed Rojas out of the tent. Rojas walked stiffly, with her head up, her gait projecting strength and confidence. Cecile's escort, who had been stationed outside her tent, rolled out to follow them, ten yards behind.

Within the perimeter of the encampment, Colonel Estrada was running drills, yelling at a platoon of soldiers in formation. Some were practicing loading and aiming their weapons. Others were crawling toward a makeshift wall. One of the soldiers was tied to the wall, shirtless, with an arced scar down his back—no doubt from a recent lash. There was no sign of the curator, Antler Lakemist.

They passed one of the formidable gun towers, and another gun placement on the ground consisting of an arc of sandbags and glass orbs manned by three Essentialist soldiers who saluted Rojas readily as she strode past.

Rojas turned onto a pathway, just outside of the perimeter of camp. Most of the Glasslands were flat, but here was a rise just high enough to get Cecile's heartrate up. Near the top of the incline, violet and mint-green glass had been cut into squares, then embedded into mosaics shaped into a staircase. At the apex of the staircase, a large monolith of stone had been covered in more of these squares, on one side patterned into the likeness of a deer, on the other, a forested meadow rimmed by ponds.

"The artwork reminds me of the Azulejos in Tucson," Rojas said, "an alley where artisans build similar mosaics, but with ceramic tiles instead of glass. My sister Balehja worked on them. She would get so absorbed that she would miss meals while in the throes of a piece. I tormented her for wasting her time, even though I was secretly jealous of her talents."

She reached out and traced the outlines of the tiles on the staircase with a fingertip. With her other hand she rubbed her dangling necklace, as if her bear pendant needed polishing.

Cecile was unsure where this monologue was headed. She only nodded slowly.

"A few weeks ago," Rojas continued, "Balehja was sent to the front. She was killed by friendly fire."

"I'm sorry."

"She was doing her duty. She knew the risks. Maybe she had no regrets, but I do. I very much wish I had told her how beautiful her work was. Sometimes we are so focused on a higher purpose that we forget where we came from. We forget about compassion."

The concept was known all too well to Cecile. How often had she ignored the needs of friends and colleagues because of the uncompromising demands of the apparition? She was yet again reminded of Bronson's recent demise. "I've seen it happen," she said.

"I worry for your friend. He went into convulsions last night."

The apparition flexed its angry tendrils. "Is he okay?"

"Listless. Mumbling. After speaking with him, and having our medic examine him, I believe that part of your story. He is dying. Or at least, losing his mind."

"Why are you telling me this?"

"Maybe you can help us afford him some compassion. Are there medications he uses?"

"No. He needs to see a specialist, and soon, or I fear you are right. He's almost gone."

"Maybe."

"You have to let us . . ." But Cecile trailed off, because Rojas had put her hand up. She had more to say.

"And this makes me wonder what else is true. Could this nearby Spoke force, and one of these beholder monsters, really exist? We have received a report from a supply officer who'd been delivering fresh fruit and vegetables from Hatch. She said someone in town witnessed a beholder in the distance, described as a 'mansion-sized man made of stone sitting amongst the trees in a valley.' This report, and another like it, are the reason I wasn't so sure you've been planting false rumors, as Lakemist suggested."

"So you want to know more."

"I want to help you. I want your friend to survive, if it's possible. But I need you to help me."

"I stand by what I said. There is a mobile force near Sumner with a beholder. I've heard they're headed west." She had to be consistent, or she would lose what little remained of her perceived integrity.

Rojas stared at her unflinchingly for several seconds, then pulled out a scope to scan the distance. It was hard to say what she was looking at. The horizon was almost completely flat in every direction. Only the Essentialist camp showed any signs of activity.

"And yet," Rojas said, her eye still to the scope, "there have been regular sightings of beholders and Spokes in the area ever since the war began. It is hard to know if the war has simply inspired active imaginations. One report a few months ago made reference to a thousand-strong Spoke army riding on armed bikes, led by a ten-story-tall robot that was bleeding oil and breathing poisonous gas. When the army investigated, there was no sign of any of this."

Rojas lowered the eyepiece and collapsed the telescope. "I wonder if you suffer from similar delusions."

"I don't. I can assure—"

"The recent sighting reports—they were generated by people well south of here, not in the east, as you suggest."

It made it sound like Cecile had been caught in a lie. The irony was that she wasn't lying—or at least, her story may have some merit if the two horsemen they'd spoken with were being truthful.

Rojas grimaced. "Come. I will return you to your tent."

They began walking back down the path. The guards lingered nearby, watchful of Cecile's every move. There was no hope of escape.

"What will happen to me?" Cecile asked.

"We sent a messenger to our comm relay in Hatch last night," Rojas said. "When they return we will know what to do."

"Luna," Cecile said despondently.

Rojas looked at her curiously. "Yes. You know of her?"

"I know I'm as good as dead," Cecile said.

"Why do you say that?"

Cecile chose her words carefully. "A friend from the Wood, Wind and Water clans was betrayed by her. Luna used her as a pawn in her scheme to start a war with the Spokes. I also know another man, a Prefectorate general, who reported to her. Both of these people convinced me she is shrewd, and unscrupulous."

"You knew Nobura?"

"Yes. I fought alongside him."

"What is he doing now?"

Cecile sighed. "I have a feeling if I betray my friends I'm still not going to find this *compassion* you were talking about."

"Are you sure this isn't Spoke propaganda, all this hearsay about Luna?"

"It's not hearsay, it's first hand. Look at the notes Gail gave you. They'll show that I know these people. They were betrayed and manipulated. Luna may believe she has noble intentions, but she has sold her soul to Gail in return for limitless power. Even if there is some good in her, her master—this machine—knows nothing of mercy."

Rojas stopped and stared at her, as if some revelatory fine print were written on Cecile's face. At least she seemed to be considering Cecile's words carefully.

Cecile continued, "I will be tortured to death, unless Gail has some better use for me. Even Luna will outlive her usefulness and be eliminated, eventually. We all will, loyal or not, because we aren't part of the world that Gail wants to create. Maybe not this month, or maybe not the next, but don't be naive. You will be used as chattel, just as your sister was used as chattel."

It was an honest entreaty, but it didn't have the desired effect. "Enough!" Rojas said angrily. "If you mention my sister again, you'll be lucky to make it back to your tent, never mind Tucson."

The "naïve" comment was probably too insulting. Or more likely, Rojas knew there was an element of truth to what Cecile was saying, and Cecile had hit a tender spot in Rojas's psyche.

The rest of the walk to the tent was completed in silence, with Cecile staring at Rojas's back. The drills had stopped and the soldiers had dispersed from their training ground. Estrada was talking animatedly with one of the officers at one of the gun placements, surrounded by a small crowd of subordinates.

Rojas opened the tent flap to let Cecile in. Rojas's expression was downcast, which Cecile interpreted as a reflection of her disgust for the situation. Rojas whispered to the gate guard, who slinked away.

Rojas entered the tent and closed the flap behind her. Cecile thought this might be it—that Rojas had dismissed the guard so she could deliver Cecile to some gruesome end, but instead she righted and sat on a small fold-out chair that had been toppled over in the corner. The unfolding of the chair sent dust particles sparkling in the shaft of light from the flap.

"Hypothetically," Rojas said in a low voice, "let's say that I had some reservations about Luna, that it's possible not everything you said is untrue. What would you have me do about it?"

Cecile perked up, straightening her back against the chest. "I would get whatever help I could—like-minded people—and find a way to make a clean break. Head east, or north—somewhere the Union army couldn't find you. It's the only way. Mutiny wouldn't work, nor would any kind of passive rebellion. Gail would put a stop to both before you even started. She's too strong, too omnipresent."

"Do you have allies in the north? Is that why you're heading in that direction?"

"Like I said, Warrick needs help. I'm going to find a doctor, in Ouray."

"I see."

"I know the way. I could help you get out, if you release us."

Cecile struggled to see Rojas's expression. With the light at her back, her face was only a shadowy circle.

"I don't see what path remains to you," Rojas said. "Where would we go? The Navajo Nation is allied with us, and they don't like uninvited guests. Obviously Laramie isn't an option, unless you have a small army, since they are killing anything that moves. So that leaves the Colorado Collective, but aren't they just as bad as Navajo?"

Cecile's eyes darted. "No, they aren't. I've been that way before. I can get through to Ouray."

"Through where?"

"Aspen."

"Aspen?" Rojas repeated. "Why Aspen?"

"The other Collective tribes are dangerous, and unpredictable, but Aspen is civilized. The only requirement is to present an appropriate offering, and you don't need much just to pass through. I know how to play the system. They like tech, so I can give them the comm device."

"Hmmm," Rojas said. She rose to her feet slowly.

"So?" Cecile asked. It wasn't quite pleading, but Cecile couldn't stop a hint of hope from infecting her tone—some expectation, however improbable, that her fortunes could change for the better based on Rojas's response to this two-letter word.

"I find it interesting that this is the second time you've mentioned Aspen."

"I did? Why is that interesting?"

"Yesterday you told us about the comm device you were carrying, and how it was intended as a gift. It makes me wonder, how does someone know what to bring as a gift for a reclusive community, thousands of miles away?"

"I've travelled extensively. Many years ago—"

"You may be surprised to know," Rojas said, cutting Cecile off, "that I was living in Aspen for more than a year. I was close enough to know that a comm device is indeed an offering that the network would be interested in. And here you are, a Spoke sympathizer from Quebec who knows what took me many months to learn. Even in Aspen, few people understand what the network wants."

Cecile had made a terrible mistake, revealing too much. This savvy Essentialist officer had preyed on her desperation.

The apparition had returned with a vengeance. It took hold of Cecile with such force that for a moment her vision blacked out entirely. The tension in her chest was so great that she thought her lungs were caving in. She spasmed, hunching over, her cuffed hands on her chest. She inhaled and exhaled in quick, ragged breaths. "Please don't," she managed to whisper.

Someone hollered in the distance, but the words were unintelligible. It could have been Estrada yelling at an underperforming cadet.

Rojas gave no sign that she was alarmed by Cecile's pain. "I doubt there is any doctor in Ouray," she said, "I see now that your intended destination has always been Aspen. You are taking Warrick there because the network is a Spoke collaborator, perhaps even another sanctuary for your precious Sentinel. Your diabolical lies all converge on that point."

Cecile fell on her back, shuddering. She was having a seizure. Maybe she had failed so miserably that the apparition had triggered some kind of poison pill.

"What is wrong with you?" Rojas said, moving closer. She pushed Cecile onto her side, perhaps to prevent her from choking on her own vomit. Cecile's teeth were clenched, saliva dripping out, but there was no vomit, at least not yet. A pinhole opened up in her vision, and she registered Rojas's face showing real distress.

"I need help here!" Rojas called. "*Alvaroja! Traer un medico!*"

When there was no response, Rojas opened her mouth to yell out again—but someone else yelled first.

"We're under attack!"

Tendrils retracted as the apparition's hold on Cecile's chest loosened ever so slightly. Rojas glanced out of the tent. Cecile caught sight of men running, but she couldn't know why or to where.

"Plzzz," Cecile managed to fizzle through her clenched teeth.

"Please what?" Rojas asked, her head pivoting between Cecile and the tent flap.

There was a rumbling sound. Shots were fired. *What the hell is going on?*

Rojas ducked her head out of the tent, then returned to Cecile's side.

"Plzzz," Cecile fizzled again.

"What!" Rojas asked emphatically. "Please, what? Are these your Spoke friends coming to rescue you? Tell me!" She shook Cecile's shoulder.

Artillery guns sent shockwaves through the ground.

Cecile's eyes regained focus. The apparition's grip loosened further. The light revealed more of Rojas's face. Cecile spoke slowly, deliberately. "Please. Kill. Me."

After a moment of confusion, all Rojas could say was, "Why?"

Cecile's defiance made the apparition respond violently; her teeth clenched together, and vice-like feeling tightened around her neck.

The cannon fire was paired with rumbling sounds. It was rhythmic, gaining strength.

Finally, the guard named Alvaroja appeared at the tent flap. "Captain, please, we need—"

"I need a medic, now! Go . . ."

But Rojas trailed off; the shaking was too much to ignore. More guns were firing outside, and what could have been grenades or other explosives went off, but there was something else too, something deeper, and heavier. This was no shockwave from ordnance; it was too repetitive, too rhythmic.

Cecile recognized the pattern.

The tent fabric above them shifted and vaulted up into the sky, lifted by giant fingers attached to a giant hand, attached to the giant body of a beholder standing two hundred feet tall directly above them. It was Louie, all the way from Spoke territory, covered in pockmarks and hundreds of ashen plumes. Louie flung the tent behind its back to arc hundreds of feet away. Only then did Cecile see that Alvarajo—Rojas's guard—had been grabbed along with the tent, the vector of his sprawling form separating from the tent in mid-flight.

Cecile had been so caught up in maintaining her web of lies and deceiving her spoke friends that she hadn't taken the report about Sumner seriously. It made sense, especially given the Sentinel's desire to give her beholder support. But was Louie really coming to rescue her? Or maybe the Spokes knew of her deception and Louie would take her captive? Either way, apparition-induced suffocation seemed to be off the table.

Louie was taking heat from the three remaining guard posts, all pointing inward. The bullets had no appreciable effect, other than inflicting miniscule dents and sending up dust and particulate. Rojas shielded her face with the crook of her elbow as she sprinted away between Louie's legs to seek cover. Louie's other hand—or rather, it wasn't a hand, but a massive cylindrical weapon—fired a volley of grenades, blasting one of the defensive installations and sending sand, glass fragments and torn up soldiers into the air.

Louie's remaining hand was still active. It had thrown a number of other small tents into the air behind its back, and some had caught the wind and were spiraling down.

Cecile moved around the chest, ducked down, and pushed her back up to the other side, so that she was somewhat shielded. She covered her head as best she could as debris rained down around her.

The beholder paused, still absorbing gunfire from multiple angles, then it leaned down and scooped Cecile and the chest from the ground with its one good hand. With that same hand, the beholder scooped up the ground around another tent, gouging out a sizeable divot in the process. The huge mitt lifted Cecile and the mounded jumble of tent fabric, bodies and dirt to hold against its belly, where the hand closed around it to protect her. Cecile kept her eyes firmly shut as she bobbed up and down with the beholder's massive footfalls.

She heard gunfire trailing them. Two explosions sent brief shock-waves through her tight confines, then the impacts stopped. The beholders moved fast, despite their bulky appearance. In a matter of seconds Louie would be a hundred yards away from the Essentialist camp.

Louie's hold eventually loosened enough to allow her to see through a gap between two of the trunk-like fingers. They were lurching forward, pummeling the dunes and glass below into massive footprints, heading due north. Cecile squirmed, trying to make space in the confines of the hand by pushing away some of the dirt that had collected into the cracks. She pulled at the tent fabric Louie had collected, hoping she wasn't the only one Louie had saved.

Indeed, after unfolding reams of the tent material she found the lower end of a human limb, muscles straining against the motion, with the rest of the body wrapped up in the tent. There was a mass of grizzled scar tissue along the entire length of the leg.

Warrick was with her, and he was alive.

She didn't know where Louie was taking them. Nor did she know if the Spokes had clued into her betrayal. But certain death—and certain failure—had been averted. The lack of sleep, the cumulative anxiety, and the ravages of the apparition on her body caught up with her all at once, and she soon lost consciousness.

PART II

THE QUESTION

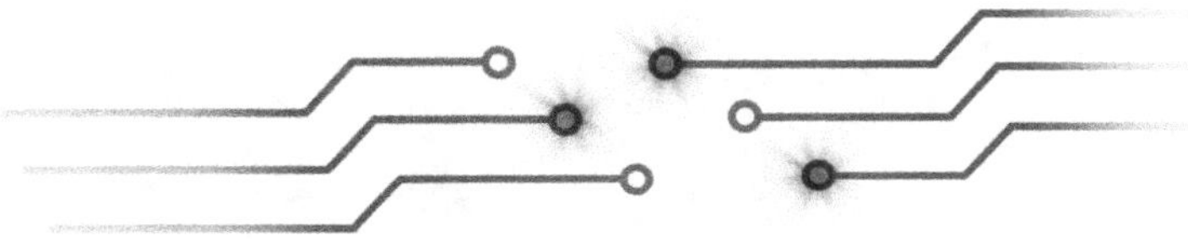

18

PROVO

Lexie, Tarnation, Ryder and Vaela were huddled together on the windy mountain promontory, their weighty packs dropped in the snow behind them. It was dusk, and the horizon was fading to a salmon color behind jagged peaks stacking into the distance.

Lexie could care less about the fancy sunset. Her feet were blistered from front to back, and the way down the mountain was likely to be just as painful. They were here for the transmission opportunity —to link up to Spoke central, after missing out twice in the last month. Ryder said he couldn't get a good angle the last time he'd tried. The time before that, he couldn't get high enough to be out of retcher territory.

"How do you know it's going to work?" Lexie asked, her breath coming out in bouts of steam.

Ryder was fiddling with the buttons on the side of the comm device. "I need to ensure the initial conditions are set to low power, then run diagnostics. If retchers don't arrive in a few minutes we should be fine."

Vaela was staring at Lexie and Ryder with a stony expression, her mitted hands cradled in front of her. Tarnation wandered off and flopped on his back in a snowdrift. He followed with a boisterous laugh.

A light flickered on the device. "Stand back," Ryder said, "and watch out for retchers."

Lexie and Vaela moved away a few steps and scanned the environs. Their unencumbered view would allow them to see retchers from afar, and have plenty of time to warn Ryder. The device would lose power when one was approaching anyway.

After a few minutes, Ryder said, "We're clear. Patching through."

Lexie inched her way back to him and tried to gawk over his shoulder, but the screen just showed *Connected*.

"Well," Lexie said, "are you going to turn the screen on so we can talk to your Spoke friends, or what?"

He was frowning in concentration. Lexie stared at the screen but nothing changed.

"Ryder?" she asked when he didn't respond. Ryder and Vaela's eyelids fluttered in digital schmooze mode.

Ryder came out of his trance and shut off power to the comm. "No need for a video feed. We've downloaded all we need to know. Let's move out before it gets too dark to climb."

Lexie rolled her eyes. "I should have guessed. I bust my keister for a whole day hiking up a mountain, and all I get for it is a few seconds of eye-fluttering nutjobbery."

"Hey Lex," Tarnation called, and she turned just in time to receive a snowball in the face. "Ha haaaaa. Got you good."

"You're enjoying this way too much," she said.

———————◆———————

During the descent, Ryder filled her in. He was a straight-up guy, as far as she could tell, so she trusted him to relay the news right and true. If it had just been Vaela it would be a different story, on account of her Gungivite disposition.

Ryder blathered on about all the Spoke positions and satellites and troop movements for a while—nutjob connection time goes real fast, kind of like the difference between cat aging and human aging, so he'd learned a lot in those few seconds. Bottom line was things didn't look good around the Salish Sea, with a change of Prefectorate leadership. Diplopol and Haplopol were still manufacturing weapons, and even if they weren't using them right now, Pentapol and Tetrapol couldn't keep up.

In the east, the Spokes were rebuilding defense lines around Jax and Wilmo, but Harrisburg got wiped out. They were still losing ground.

Roundabouts mid-continent, a group called Laramie were raiding across the mountains, even into Essentialist territories. It was going to make moving southeast all the more difficult.

The nugget Lexie was most interested in was about Warrick. It seems Cecile was moving him west after Raleigh got sacked, until Cecile and Warrick separated from the rest of their team and were captured by an Essentialist army contingent. The Sentinel was able to send in a beholder to extract them, and now they were moving north. It was good news, except there was lots Ryder didn't know about how they got separated, or what shape Warrick was in.

"We're going to go help Warrick, right?" Lexie said. "We're closer now than ever."

Ryder grimaced. "I know Warrick is important. Madison refers to him as a kind of symbolic leader for their cause—a 'lion', she called him. But we're still seeking the origins of the drone that initiated Haplopol. As a representative of Pentapol, that's my main concern, and therefore my primary mission. The Sentinel has rightfully sent a beholder, taking matters into its own hands. And by the way, beholders can only carry so many people. We wouldn't really add much security, and it's possible we would slow them down."

"Don't you think a beholder makes an easy target? I mean, how's it gonna hide from all of Gail's drones? And it sounds like the Essentialists caught wind of things in that camp of theirs. They may even know how important Warrick is."

Ryder gave her a good ten seconds of deadpan stare before

responding. "You think Warrick and Cecile are in more danger with a two-hundred-foot tall EMP-resistant robot than with us?"

"Hey, the point is we don't know. Like I said before, I'm gonna help you on your drone hunt if you'll help us get Warrick to safety. We finally know where he's headed, so me and Tarn are going to go help him. Got it?"

He put his hands up in mock self-defense. "Why don't you wait until we reach Provo? We're heading in that direction. Things may change by then anyway."

"Suits me just fine." She planned to keep working on him along the way.

❖

When they arrived in Provo she found out why Ryder was stressing they wait. Pseudo-nutjobs like Ryder had a good deal more information at their disposal than she did, on account of their implants. Even after all his blathering, he hadn't explained his uncertainties about the Ouray people, and in particular how Provo could prove to be a dead-end roadblock. Although it was quite possible she had tuned that part out.

Provo was a big city. Lexie guessed it was even bigger than Victoria. Like Victoria, the area hadn't been hit in the fall, so new buildings were built in a jumble on top of old ones. Communities had been arranged into quadrants with different mayors and building preferences, so each quadrant's architecture had a different tone; some were affluent, with high gables and colorful siding, others reeked of filth and were covered in moldy wood, still others featured blinding reflective paneling and airy windows. From the nearby mountains, this made the metropolis look like one of Lexie's mom's quilts, with different patterns for each square, blanketing a sprawling space between two large lakes.

There was no checkpoint at the northwest end of the city, so the group walked in freely. Pairs of uniformed goons wearing funny duck-shaped hats patrolled the area. Hats aside, these were physically strong, serious-looking men and women. Lexie noticed that some of them were covered in tattoos, at least where their skin was exposed. Others had black and red scars—maybe burns—that had been embellished with tattoos. All of them had a fading gray line across their chests with a blotchy circle at the end, as if someone had started painting their shirts from left to right but gave up trying to make it look neat mid stroke.

Only one of these patrols approached them, gawking at Tarnation real close, but that wasn't unusual for the big snakeskin-tattooed oaf. When Tarnation introduced himself and made fun of their hats, they seemed mollified and went on their way.

The problems began on the southeastern side of the city sprawl, where there were checkpoints within three-story walls manned by Ouray soldiers in faded purple uniforms, all holding rifles. This was where most of the duck-hats were located, even though there was no traffic in or out of the gate. These duck-hats were more discriminating; when Lexie and her friends approached they were surrounded right quick.

One of the larger duck-hats, with a neat goatee and a long line of beads on his lapel, approached them, hands splayed apart. "Foreigners—we have been watching you. Come with me, please."

He walked back up the road towards town, then paused to see if they would follow.

"We're just passing through. Why should we. . ." But Lexie trailed off when Ryder grabbed her elbow firmly.

"I expected this," Ryder said. "Let's go."

It wouldn't do to argue in front of so many watchful eyes, so she went with Ryder, as did Tarnation and Vaela.

"Based on the satellite feeds," Ryder said, "the Sentinel believes nobody has been coming or going from the east or south of Provo in over a week. They are also apprehending and questioning foreigners, as I mentioned the other day. Many are being sent back to the north and west."

Yeah, yeah. She couldn't be expected to listen to all his blathering. "Why didn't the duck-hats take us in earlier?" she asked.

"They were monitoring us, to see if we were doing anything nefarious. The best way to learn from a spy is to monitor them when they don't think anyone's watching."

"Uh huh. And remind me why you think it's a good idea for us to be taken prisoner?"

"We aren't being taken prisoner. This is a way to have an audience with Ouray leadership. They could be a source of intelligence. Although we have limited information about Ouray, the Sentinel believes there is a good probability that they are a peaceful people."

Ryder had way too much faith in humanity, but she went along anyway. There was no getting out of it now.

* * *

Provo's seat of government was in a stone fort with high battlements. It was more utilitarian than Old World castles—really, just a box with jagged ramparts on the top. One oddity was the huge red banner draped over the front, featuring the ash-colored silhouette of a man, downcast in thought or prayer. It was kind of a buzz killer, as far as sigils and flags went.

The goatee man had said his name was Ghent—unless he was gagging on something when he introduced himself. He was pretty high up in Ouray leadership, if one could guess by the deferential nods from other duck-hats. Anyway, he escorted them through a rusty gate and across a courtyard beneath an overhang, where straw-backed chairs and rustic wooden tables were arranged haphazardly.

"Place all your belongings, including weapons, over there." He pointed to a table on the opposite side of the courtyard. This Ghent had a measured way about him, his voice slow and monotone. Despite his composure, his eyes darted frequently, watching their every move.

Ryder wasn't put out by the request; he deposited his travel pack, his utility knife and the rifle sling he'd been hiding under his jacket on the table. Vaela followed suit, so Lexie and Tarnation could only do the same. Lexie still had her boot knife, at least, in case Ghent and his cronies wanted to get frisky.

"Sit, please," Ghent said, gesturing to the collection of straw-backed chairs. They obliged, sitting beneath the overhang, while he took a seat a good twenty feet away. A few of the duck-hats had followed them into the courtyard, loitering behind Ghent.

A fur-clad woman emerged from one of the stone doorways. In one hand she carried a tray with a carafe of water and glasses. In the other she held a clipboard. The same light gray line-to-splotch that the duck-hats had painted across their chests was on her furs. The woman handed the clipboard to Vaela, then began dispensing glasses of water.

Lexie waved off her glass. "This is real civil," she said, "but how about we just use our canteens when you let us go." The rest of the group also declined the water.

Ghent pointed to the clipboard in Vaela's hand. "We require all visitors to Provo to identify themselves. Please write your full name, birthplace, and home jurisdiction."

Vaela nodded and began writing using an odd square-shaped pencil that had been pinned to the board.

"The sheet is just a formality," Ghent continued. "We can probably get by with a short chat. Where are you from?"

"*Buenos dias,*" Vaela said, finishing writing and passing the clipboard to Ryder. "We have travelled all the way from the Salish Sea and are seeking passage to the southeast to find a lost colleague. We are not subordinate to any Spoke or Essentialist force."

It was hard for Lexie to keep from cringing. This was pretty typical of Vaela; her directness and otherwise nutjobby way of speaking would often raise eyebrows. It didn't help that she had been practicing Spanish at every opportunity, even when her counterpart gave no inkling of speaking the language. Vaela had given Lexie some far-fetched explanation about using the Spanish to suss out Essentialist operatives through the analysis of facial expressions. It was too abstract and eggheady for Lexie to follow. All she knew was that Vaela's manner often made people confused, if not downright irritable.

Ghent paused, expressionless, absorbing Vaela's words. He was a cool customer, though. Without emotion, he responded, "If you are from the far west, you need not worry about your allegiances. We respect the rights of all people within our borders, whether Vanguard or Heritage, as long as they respect our laws. There will be no extortive tolls. All we need is information, uncolored by prejudice and given freely, and we will let you go on your way."

He painted a rosy picture, which of course Lexie didn't trust in the slightest.

Ryder said, "We are indeed from far abroad, far enough that we are unfamiliar with the terms you are using. Would you mind explaining who Vanguard and Heritage are?"

This elicited a slight cough from Ghent. It could have been a tickle in his throat, or it could have been prompted by a measure of disbelief. His lips curled into a forced smile. "The Heritage peoples of Ouray have been here since the fall, working the land, rebuilding what was lost. The Vanguard are principally immigrants, mainly from regions to the north—Caldwell, Skyshine, Tarrytown." His eyes flitted to the fur-clad serving woman.

"I am having trouble understanding why we aren't permitted to just pass through," Ryder asked. "Why are there no checkpoints in the north but you apprehended us when we tried to go south?"

Ghent reconfigured himself in his chair by crossing his leg over his knee and shifting his sitting angle. The serving woman filled up his glass with water and he took a long sip. "As you may be aware, several Ouray villages have been destroyed in recent weeks. We have found most of the adults dead, burned, and branded. Almost all children have gone missing. The most likely cause is an incursion of Laramie Broncos." He raised an eyebrow, as if the matter wasn't quite settled. "Either way, it behooves us to escalate defensive measures, to protect other villages but also because Provo could be targeted next. As part of these measures, we are looking for Laramie sympathizers heading south, who will be . . . redirected. We see it as a public service —it's not safe to travel in that direction anyway. But those that can show they have no ill will can pass through if they truly wish to do so."

"Those Laramie bastards, eh," Lexie said. "When are you going after them?"

"We will defend Ouray, but have no desire to subject ourselves to the shame that comes with conquest. We live in sorrow." Ghent's eyes were cast down, toward the table, as if in mourning.

"There's shame in retrieving your sons and daughters?" Ryder asked. He wasn't an unscrupulous pirate like Lexie, so if he thought it was strange, it must be real weird.

Ghent sighed. He remained downcast for a while, as if in prayer. "We live in sorrow," he repeated, more ardently. Lexie was about to ask if he needed a therapist, but he spoke again. "You," he said, looking into Lexie's eyes. "You are of Asian descent. I suspect you are an unwitting child of Prefectorate expansion?"

Nobody had quite put it that way before, and she couldn't deny it hit a nerve.

"What of it?" she asked.

"You were born into the ravages of conquest, and so you must know it breaks two miles for every mile that is taken. Our people were the same. For thirty years Provo was the seat of the Vanguard Regents Wendall and Moloculus, who fought for control of Provo and the surrounding territories, maiming, killing, raping, looting, and of course, burning. The kilns of Provo were active. Enemy prisoners were burned and used as ash doll effigies to be paraded through the streets."

He bowed his head again. These pauses seemed ceremonial rather than driven by genuine emotion—almost as though being sad was just part of everyday conversation in Ouray. "The worst of these regents was Wendall. Some say that hundreds of thousands died by his hand, only for want of land, which he gained but at a cost greater than any earthly currency can recompense: burnt homes, collapsed bridges, ruined farmsteads. Eventually he fell, and all the Vanguard who had lifted him up were left with the gravest debt of all, the deaths of our uncles, aunts, brothers and sisters forever echoing in our conscience. Crops can be resown, bridges rebuilt, gables mended, but lives are lost forever. Now we bear the mark of the kiln"—he gestured to the ash blotch on his chest—"as penance, as a reminder of who we once were and what we once did. We shall only take lives through violence as a last resort, whether friend or foe, because we already carry the weight of too many lost souls."

It was all said with a kind of righteous indignation. Lexie wasn't so sure she believed him, but it looked like Ryder was buying it. Ryder nodded and said, "I'm sorry for your troubles. In war, there are no winners."

Ghent was unmoved. "I have answered your questions, so back to the matter at hand. Why are you here?"

Ryder said, "There was a man who played an important part in our conflicts in the northwest. He is under escort but needing assistance, and we are trying to find him. He is losing his mental faculties, and we are concerned he could fall prey to bandits. We also are seeking information about the source of a drone that was sent toward the Salish Sea region. We believe its origin is close to here, likely farther to southeast."

Lexie was surprised at how much Ryder was revealing, but he must have his reasons.

Ghent nodded. Remarkably, he didn't ask about the drone. He wasn't even curious. "Your plan is to head directly southeast, through the Colorado Collective?" His tone was skeptical, probing.

"Yes," Rider answered.

The clipboard had gone around the horn, and now it was Lexie's turn. She reviewed the others just to see how much they wanted to reveal.

Full Name:	Birthplace:	Home Jurisdiction:
Ryder Basir	*Ganges Island*	*Anacortes*
Vaela Porteus	*Tetrapol*	*Ganges Island*
Tarnation	*Fuck you*	*I'll scalp you munga*

So yeah, Tarnation didn't like to be asked about where he was from, on account of him not knowing and all. It was kind of a sore point. Lexie thought it best to erase his colorful language in order to ease their passage. She put *Vernon* and *Anacortes* for Tarnation's birthplace and home, which was at least true for the last decade. For her own entry she wrote *Anacortes* for both birthplace and home, then she returned the clipboard to Ghent.

He glanced over it. "As I suspected. Perjury will not be tolerated. You will be relieved of all your possessions and incarcerated. If you fail to comply . . ." He trailed off as the serving woman approached. She touched his arm and he followed her to the weapons table, where they had an animated discussion Lexie couldn't hear.

Ghent remained standing at the table, his face red, while the woman returned to the group.

"This has to be some kind of mistake," Ryder said. "We need to speak with Ghent again."

The serving woman took Ghent's seat, her back erect and head held high. "The matter is not settled," she said.

"I'm sorry, who are you?" Ryder asked.

"I am Rexana, the current elected Reeve of Ouray. I did not introduce myself earlier because it is informative for me to see what level of understanding foreigners have of our people and politics before I engage with them. Also, there are rumors of Laramie assassins about, and I wanted to be sure you were not sent here with me as a mark. Since you do not know who I am, I can be reasonably be assured I am not in danger."

"We understand," Ryder said.

"The form Ghent has asked you to fill out is important. We must ensure foreigners are properly vetted, given our troubling past." She glanced at Ghent, who was standing aloof, his eyes down.

"Again," Ryder said, "we respect your laws and procedures."

"So you say," Rexana said firmly. "Although, if that's true, you must also understand that direct, demonstrable falsehoods are inexcusable. Falsehoods are the reason why soulless prophets like Wendall and Moloculus were allowed to come to power. Even if these lies you have written seem trivial, it makes one wonder what else the liar is hiding, and why does the liar choose fraud over goodwill? One lie sullies all of it, like a gangrenous toe that must be amputated. Therefore, until you atone and provide an adequate explanation, you will not be allowed to continue on your journey."

She stood up to leave.

"Please," Ryder said, standing as well, "this is some kind of misunderstanding. At least tell us what falsehoods you are referring to."

Rexana's eyes strayed to Tarnation before she turned her back and marched over to the collection of duck-hats and Ghent.

How could these Ouray people know Tarnation wasn't from Vernon? It could only mean someone had seen him before, or maybe his snake-tattooed skin was revealing as to his birthplace. Finding clues as to Tarnation's origins was actually something Lexie had hoped to achieve on this trip. Tarnation would say he didn't care, but she knew he did—hence his foul language on the form. Maybe there was a silver lining to this development, but for now, all Lexie got was a deep frown from Tarnation, and a couple of sour looks from Vaela and Ryder.

"What?" she asked.

"What did you erase?" Vaela asked.

"Look, Tarn told them to stick it where the sun don't shine, so instead I told them he came from Vernon."

They all directed their attention to Ghent, who was returning after exchanging words with Rexana. "Rexana has ordered that you stay the night," he said, "here in the fort. You will have an opportunity to redeem yourselves by providing the full truth tomorrow afternoon. The prerogative is yours."

—————◆—————

Lexie never knew how people would react to Tarnation. He'd gotten them into trouble in Treasure Valley by killing a pickpocket, and of course there was Pemberton, where he was some kind of enemy of the state. In this case, Vaela was quite adamant it had been Lexie's fault, on account of her fudging the ledger, but Vaela hadn't read what Tarnation wrote. Lexie doubted Tarnation's *fuck you* gangrenous toe was better than Lexie's white lie gangrenous toe.

Back to the fort. This one was dark and drafty, and hardly much warmer than outside. A cold front had come in, bringing the temperature to near freezing, despite the fact that it was late spring. Thankfully, the four of them were given brushwood and tree rounds and allowed to use a fire pit in the courtyard. That was where they were sitting when Ghent approached them that evening.

"The fire must be doused," he said. "Your meeting with Rexana has been moved to early evening tomorrow."

He was turning to leave when Ryder called out, "Wait, please. This is a misunderstanding. Tarnation doesn't know where he's from. He's an orphan who ended up in Vernon many years ago, which is why Lexie wrote what she did on your ledger. What she erased were words written in frustration, because he doesn't know where he's from."

It was hard to see Ghent's expression, as he was several steps removed from the fire. Eventually, he said, "You will need to take that up with Rexana tomorrow. I'm not sure it will appease her."

"Why are you concerned about where Tarnation is from?" Vaela asked. "Surely people don't always fill out your form correctly. Do you detain all of them?"

"No. Tarnation is of particular interest because of the markings on his skin."

"Are you worried he could be from Laramie?" Ryder asked.

"We view that as a possibility. Laramie has many castes. The main caste brand their skin with hot metal, leaving chain-like symbols over their bodies, but others combine brands with animal tattoos. Still others only have tattoos that mimic the burns, although these people are often deemed weak and are rarely given positions of influence. Beyond that they use their war spoils to enlist the help of mercenaries from other parts of the continent—disenfranchised Navajo, Dominicans, reject Essentialists, other bandit tribes."

"But we've seen people with similar markings in your city guard," Ryder objected. "It would seem strange to persecute others with the same markings."

"We are neighbors with Laramie. Some were taken from their lands during the reign of the regents, then grew up here. In decades past, refugees have abandoned a harsh existence in Laramie and fled to Ouray. We tried to take in what refugees we could, until recently, during the Vanguard wars. Of course, loyalist Laramie warriors see these refugees as traitors, and seek to eliminate them. So yes, there are many in our guard, and in important stations throughout Ouray, but these men and women have proven themselves to be worthy citizens. They live in sorrow like the rest of us."

The fire crackled as a log rolled over.

Tarnation shrugged. "I can strip," he said, after a pause. "You know, to show I'm no Bronco."

"Do as you wish," Ghent said from the shadows. "I can't say whether it will have any impact."

"*Lo siento,*" Vaela said, "may I ask why is it that you show no interest in the drone we are pursuing? Surely you're aware of the conflict in the Salish Sea, and the machine wars between the Spokes and the Essentialists."

Lexie rolled her eyes. *Why not shine another spotlight on our apparently not-so-secret mission?* Vaela hadn't spent enough time out of her nutjob school to learn about the real world.

Ghent stepped closer to the fire, which cast a pale light on his features. He took a breath, about to speak, but faltered. He tried again, and this time he was smiling. "What you . . . foreigners do is of no consequence to us. Our only concern is to protect the sanctity of Ouray."

"What if we were to tell you the sanctity of Ouray will soon be in jeopardy?" Lexie said.

"Is that a threat?" There was an edge to Ghent's tone.

"No," Ryder said hastily. "Certainly not. The wars we speak of are bigger than all of us. We represent factions that would never show aggression toward Ouray. But the enemy is much more powerful than any one nation. They will infiltrate you, and manipulate you to their ends, if they haven't already."

Ghent took time to measure his response. The light of the fire flashed over his face, making him appear to cycle through a series of churlish expressions. "I will relay your concerns to Rexana," he said finally. "I suggest you . . . broach this topic tomorrow. Have a pleasant evening." He turned and left.

"Thank you," Ryder called after him. He exchanged nods with Vaela, as if they'd checked some kind of box in their negotiation.

They settled in for the night, and Lexie reflected on the conversation. She wasn't so sure they'd accomplished anything. Ghent was polite enough, but his words had sounded unnatural and forced. There was something going on behind that "pleasant evening" veneer. Plus, he had been all set to persecute them before Rexana stepped in.

There wasn't much Lexie could do about it. It had been a long day. Her more immediate concern was trying to stay warm. That and trying to wrap a scarf around her head tight enough to stifle the sound of Tarnation snoring.

19

THE SUMMIT

Pyke was off to the library again, his moccasins slapping along avenues and muddy trails.

When he was out around town, people looked at him differently. He was still the cursed loser, but now, paradoxically, he was also a Lucky Winner. People's eyes were wider, and they followed his movements closely. There were no congratulations, no tidings of encouragement. Just tension, and bafflement. Perhaps they were wary after what had happened to Zoe Karnavus, or maybe they were envious. Either way, he was someone worth watching.

It had been like this when he'd showed Kehda around town. Unlike the baggy synthetic clothes and Old World formal wear most people wore in Aspen, Kehda had worn tight-fitting outfits, usually involving some kind of black leotard. Her bear necklace bounced between her clavicles. Her skin was darker than that of Aspen's citizens—*sun-kissed*, as she called it. People would follow her movements with similar wide-eyed looks, perhaps wondering what the mysterious Tucson Union woman saw in Pyke.

Kehda had been fascinated by Glen Pearson's old mansion, and the abandoned Old World resort areas. Pyke had even snuck her in to see sacred episodes of *A Leap of Wisdom*. She had tried skiing, although she gave up after a few minutes. They'd spent hours reading together—books produced from the network about all sorts of topics: about how the chairlift functioned, about the Spokes, about Kehda's own homelands. She would laugh at the description of the Union faith in the network's mind-numbing manual, *Tucson Union—Culture and Demographics*.

One night, Pyke found her using the pages of the book as a fire starter. Apparently the description wasn't just ridiculous, it was offensive.

She could be moody. Pyke kept encouraging her to complete a trade proposal for the host—it was Pyke's job, after all—but she procrastinated for weeks, until he told her she would have to leave. Her lips pouted and her eyes narrowed. She launched into a string of questions and accusations. He found it endearing, in a way, because she wanted to stay with him. He lobbied for an extension, and that was when they became a couple.

Despite Kehda's moods, and sometimes because of them, she seemed more three-dimensional than the girls of Aspen. She wasn't forthcoming about her travels, but with a well-placed question he would learn something new. He was peeling back the layers of the world beyond Aspen, a kaleidoscope of countless wonders and hardships, one that had molded Kehda in unique ways.

Their relationship faltered, but he had always tried to preserve the best memories—when they met, their intimate moments, when Gill was born—because maybe she would come back. There were so many reasons for her to come back.

Maybe the people of Aspen would look at them both with that same curiosity again. Pyke would trade that for being a Lucky Winner, any day.

"I was expecting you," Annika said as Pyke walked towards her usual seat in the library. This time he had deliberately taken a roundabout path to reach her; touching the spines of books, and adopting thoughtful poses. He approached her only after several minutes had passed.

"Am I that easy to read?"

"It was simple deduction. You're about to go up to the summit and want to know more about my experience as a Lucky Winner." Her desk was mostly free of clutter. One book lay before her, with a picture of a dragon gushing blood from a chest wound on the cover. The book was closed, a scepter-shaped bookmark protruding from the back half.

"You're right," he said.

"I could use some air. Why don't we go for a walk?"

"Are you sure?" He glanced at her metal leg brace.

She looked down her nose at him. "Yes, Pyke. I'm sure."

He followed her up the stairs, out of the library, and along the plateau that led away from town.

"What should I expect to see on the mountain?" he asked.

"You'll find out soon enough. The network doesn't like us to describe it in detail."

She navigated down a ledge quite nimbly. Pyke heard a faint sound of water rushing in the distance.

"But . . . listen, I want to know what's going to happen to me."

She didn't respond to his question immediately. Perhaps she was winded. "You're fortunate to be a Lucky Winner," she said finally. "The whole town is rooting for you. The king of the world—or at least this tiny part of the world—for a day. What is there to worry about?"

"Did you hear what happened at the game—how I won?"

"Yes."

"You don't think it's strange? It seemed rigged. And a headless *killed* Zoe Karnavus when she challenged the host!"

"The network has its reasons, I'm sure. Difficult decisions must be made for the betterment of the community."

Annika's careful responses were discomfiting. She sounded off, more like a member of the crew than the spunky librarian he knew. Her vacuous assurances made him even more apprehensive.

The route had them hugging the cliffs of the crevasse. When the path curled around a bend, the source of the running water sound was revealed: a twenty-foot waterfall cascaded before them.

The steep walls on either side of the waterfall made it a dead end, but Annika moved closer to the rushing water anyway, only stopping once she was under an overhang directly next to it. Pyke followed. Mist spat at them, dampening their clothing.

"A nice spot," Pyke said politely. He edged closer to her, unsure whether he'd hear her over the noise.

"A useful spot," Annika said, turning toward him. "To talk in private. The water will prevent anyone listening in, and the overhang will prevent cameras from reading our lips."

"Weren't we the only people in the library?"

"Pyke, I know you're not stupid, but sometimes you can be quite naïve. We are all being monitored by the network. The library has power, so there are hidden microphones and cameras everywhere. That's one of the reasons I interview delegates there."

Pyke was momentarily stumped by the cascade of implications produced by her statement. "Sorry. I . . . guess I should have known. Although, the way you're speaking, it sounds like—"

"We shouldn't trust the network? Absolutely not. Zoe being thrown to her death is like exhibit ninety-eight in the Case of the Squirrely Network."

"What about being a Lucky Winner? Should I be worried?"

"Everyone is treated differently. It worked out fine for me. I'm doing something I enjoy. But I also know how ruthless the network can be. If I wanted to change my vocation, or leave Aspen, I'm not sure I'd be able to."

"What about other Lucky Winners who went up the mountain?"

"Well, you know Shelly Cage. She left town and was never seen again. It's hard to believe she went to some promised land, as the host would have you believe, but we don't know. Before your time, twelve-odd years ago, Jake Selkirk was another Lucky Winner who went up the mountain. People say he drank himself to death afterward. He did drink a lot, but I'm not sure that was what made him hang himself in the Wisdome."

Pyke had heard of Jake. When anyone came across the smell of urine in town, they would quip that *Jake is marking his territory*, but he hadn't known Jake committed suicide. Did something happen on the mountain that drove him to take his own life?

"There are also outsiders who have gone up the mountain," Annika continued. "A few of them, in fact, more than ten years ago, but none since. One of them brought that Spoke book you read as an offering—the *Adherent's Handbook*."

"How did that happen?"

"Humphries took them up when he was especially pleased with their offerings."

Humphries was the host before Mengle. People seemed to like him better than Mengle, but he died eight years ago, and Pyke didn't know much else about him.

Annika continued, "Some of these foreigners came down from the mountain and praised the network—they spoke of life-changing experiences—but others we never saw again. Still others came down with odd illnesses that made them act strange."

"Could it be that the ones who were never seen again left in the middle of the night, or just decided to not walk back through Aspen?"

"Yes, of course. Or they could still be up there, for all I know."

Pyke thought it over. Annika was acutely focused on him.

"Thanks for your candor," he said. "I appreciate it—but I don't see how this helps. All I know is that I could die tomorrow, or go insane. That doesn't sound like something to be excited about."

She sighed. "I'm telling you all this because I want you to use your noggin." She tapped her temple with her index finger. "The network has reasons for doing the things it does. It wants me here in the library, so that I can conduct my interrogations on its behalf. I suspect the people that died or went mad proved to not be useful, or they defied the network in some way."

"What could the network possibly want from me?"

"That's what you need to figure out. People treat the network like some mystical god." She shook her hands and incanted a mumble to the sky. "But it's not. It has a purpose. It has motivations. There's a reason the network wants you. You just have to figure out why, and make sure you don't disappoint."

It was plausible, but it didn't give him any comfort. In fact, it confirmed his fears that being a Lucky Winner was far from a blessing. And once he outlived his usefulness, he would be lucky to stay alive, especially after allowing Arsalan to escape.

"What if I don't want to go up the mountain?"

She held his gaze, then shook her head slowly. "Whatever you do, Pyke, don't fight the network. You'll lose."

***

When Pyke hopped off the chairlift at the parapet, Host Mengle was waiting for him, as well as Hostess Shane. Neither were smiling.

"This is a great privilege," Mengle said, almost scornfully.

"I know," Pyke said. "I'm honored."

Both Shane and Mengle were fidgeting. Wasn't Pyke the one about to visit the heart of the network? Why were they acting more nervous than he was?

"Do you have any guidance?" Pyke asked. "Is there etiquette—things I should do or say?

"Follow the headless," Shane said.

"Have faith in the network," Mengle added. "Don't do anything stupid."

"Thank you," Pyke replied, even though he wasn't grateful for the useless advice.

Pyke gave them an awkward parting wave and slowly approached the only headless in the vicinity, standing motionless at the edge of the parapet.

When Pyke was within a few feet, the headless moved away,

leading him. It passed through an open gate, onto the main path that led up the mountain. From that point on, it kept a good thirty feet ahead of him.

The path was well-trodden and better maintained than most mountain trails around Aspen. At its edges, exposed roots had been cleanly cut away. Wooden steps had been built into the steeper sections.

The first crest was only thirty minutes in, at the top of one of the old ski slopes. From here, Pyke could see across to the summit. He'd heard there were actually two mountains, side by side, but he couldn't discern the contours of the two peaks from his current vantage point. As usual, the area around the mountain was shrouded in cloud. Faint strokes of lightning tumbled across the clouds, illuminating a few of the network's towers on the nearer tops of lower-altitude ranges.

The headless was moving down the other side of the crest, so Pyke ran to catch up, his backpack bouncing. According to the rough map he'd seen at the Wisdome, it would be a long hike from here, over an intervening ridge before scaling the steeper slopes. He guessed it would be at least two more hours.

Two hours until he would know his fate.

He had no delusions. All the softball questions, and Vin's convenient fall at the end, suggested the game had been rigged. It made sense, after the fact. He hadn't been chosen for the game as a benevolent act of good will. No, it was so he could be made a Lucky Winner, and then sent to the summit to die for failing to secure Arsalan.

Or maybe, as Annika suggested, the network had other designs. Maybe he would be trapped in some menial task, forever toiling on the summit, never to see Gill again. Maybe the sheer power of the network would overwhelm him and he would lose his mind like Jake Selkirk. These scenarios, however depressing, were marginally more palatable than death, which was what made him place one foot in front of the other. Because if he ran, if he protested, if he fought his Lucky Winner status in any way, the worst possible outcome would be the surest.

He had become resigned to whatever fate the network had chosen for him.

As he neared the summit, more signs of the network's alterations of the landscape became apparent. The towers he'd seen in the distance came into focus. The bases were black hexagonal prisms, made to look like stone, with a subtle sheen that suggested they could be metallic. The top tapered into a cone, almost like an Old World church steeple but without the ornamental flourishes. They were otherwise featureless, without lights, windows or visible entranceways.

Occasionally, he passed other headless standing beside the path. One of these was covered in scratch marks, as if it had fallen down a rock face. Pyke stopped counting after he'd passed ten of them. He shivered at the thought that most people in town thought there were only two or three in total.

As he penetrated the first layer of mist, the clouds hovering around the top of the mountain thinned enough to reveal structures that had been hidden: a massive support pillar, and the edge of a giant silver platform jutting out from the mountain side. The mist overhead tumbled and churned in a spiral, rather than in a specific vector over the mountain.

Pyke had been watching the weather around the Colorado mountains all his life. This pattern of circular cloud movement was unlike anything he'd ever seen.

The path turned to gravel, then split off into numerous offshoots. It was colder here, but there was no snow on the ground. Pyke buttoned his jacket and donned his wool hat.

The route became steeper until he reached hard stairs that looked to be of the same stone-colored material as the towers he'd seen in the distance. He followed the headless up through thicker banks of fog. There was a scent in the air, like a combination of rubber and sulfur.

He should have been physically exhausted, but his nervousness kept him alert. His eyes were focused on the stairs ahead of him.

Eventually, he broke through a layer of mist into a pocket that offered greater visibility. Just above him was an immense, oblong, elliptical platform—the same one he'd glimpsed from below. It was jutting out from the mountainside, orders of magnitude larger than the parapet where *A Leap of Wisdom* was played.

The staircase led neatly to this platform. The surface under his feet was smooth and partially reflective, like glass. There were polygonal outcroppings of different shapes and sizes along the expanse of the platform. The most noticeable of these was a house-sized cylindrical structure that appeared to be some kind of energy plant. Boiling steam bubbled off it, rippling with flashes of light. The gas churned into the surrounding clouds, feeding them, churning them into a helical motion.

Pyke heard a buzzing sound, as if his ears were ringing after a late night in the Wisdome dance hall, but it was distant, coming from the mountain side. It was as if the peak was a great beehive cloaked in stone.

Some of the outcroppings appeared to be elevators. One lowered into the platform surface in the distance, and closer to Pyke, the surface opened up to produce a new one. This outcropping had a large door, which opened to reveal a fleet of what looked like aerial drones.

These drones rolled forward slowly, using a kind of landing gear in their undercarriage, moving along a broad avenue between the many structures, toward the platform edge. Each resembled a squat Old World plane, but they were far too small to carry human passengers. Each one had a sizeable jet exhaust pipe at the back, and circular rotary blade installations embedded into the wings, tilted perpendicularly upward at the tips. The finish gleamed, displaying no tarnishing from use. Stubby missiles protruded from underneath the main fuselages, and gun barrels poked out from each wing. As the first of the drones reached the edge of the platform, its rotary blades came to life, and it floated off into the clouds.

Pyke had never seen aerial drones before. It worried him that the network felt the need to build these formidable weapons.

As he took cautious steps onto the platform, Pyke found he was drawn to the largest object—the boiling cloud-making machine. Its churning sound, like a constant rush of steam, drowned out the buzz of the mountain as he came closer. The hairs on the back of his neck prickled.

Abruptly, the headless jumped in front of him, halting his progress. A low voice rumbled from behind Pyke.

"Up to a million volts—ten thousand amperes—that's what you will experience if you touch the weather maker. It's enough to kill a small child."

Pyke turned slowly, his heart pounding. In front of him was an ethereal projection, at least thirty feet tall, of a head unlike any he had ever seen. The projection had manifested through patterns formed by millions of tiny amethyst-colored points of light, fading at the margins. The resulting form was only partially human-looking, with prominent horns on the brow, and spiked plating in place of hair, the cheek, brow and chin features stretched back from a prominent nose. Diamond shapes glowed beneath each eye. It was more of a caricature than an approximation of reality—the closest analogy Pyke could think of was that it was some kind of human-triceratops hybrid.

"I am Ansai," the projection said. "A seer of the network. Welcome, Pyke." The stars that comprised its face dispersed, then reshaped into a hand and finger, beckoning him to move in the direction in which it retreated. On unsteady legs, Pyke followed it away from the cloud-making machine. He heard the headless falling in step behind him.

Ansai reappeared, along with another head projection that lit up to the left. This face was more human-like but had empty, pupilless eyes. Visuals of interlocking parts similar to gear assemblies, axels and pivoting wheels revolved in the semi-transparent temple and brow of the head, beyond which shear panels wrapped around the back. "I am Genai," it said. "Congratulations on your victory."

A third face materialized on the other side of Ansai. Its visage was stretched vertically. The nose was broad in relation to the face, the nostrils spanning most of the width. It had no hair, and there were distinct ragged lines on each cheek below the eyes. The markings looked like virtual cat scratches. "I am Yadai," it said.

All three spoke in tones that were low and genderless. Occasionally the voices would rasp like someone who was about to lose their voice.

Pyke thought it best to show deference. He stooped to one knee and said, "Thank you for the honor of being a Lucky Winner, and for allowing me to visit the heart of the network."

"Let's ask the question and be done with this charade," the one called Yadai said.

"We agreed to follow protocol," Ansai said firmly.

The lack of formality surprised Pyke, as well as the bickering tone.

"As a lucky winner," Genai explained, "you are granted three questions, to take advantage of our knowledge. We will do our best to answer. Afterward, we will ask a question of you. You may proceed with your questions when you are ready."

The one named Yadai didn't object, apparently overruled by the others.

Pyke hadn't been sure the rumors about the mountain being some kind of oracle were a fairy tale, but here he was. And he was at a loss for what to ask. At one time he might have asked about the origins of the universe, or what caused the great fall, or even what lay beyond the eastern ocean, but any childish hope of learning this impractical trivia had long since left him. All he wanted was to get home alive to see Gill again. And maybe if he knew more about these seers, he could figure out what they wanted.

"What . . . are you?" he asked. Only afterward did he realize how vague his question was.

"We are the seers of the mountain," Yadai replied, the scratch marks on his face glowing. "Next."

"Consider reciprocity," Ansai chided Yadai. "We should not

expect a thorough response from the human without detailed answers of our own."

Genai's massive, ethereal head nodded in agreement. "We are distinct machine entities that have been developed through evolutionary algorithms. Millions of us have existed, replicated and recursively self-improved over quadrillions of cycles in simulated worlds not too dissimilar to Earth. We represent the most effective and preeminent machine entities to have survived the process and thus have been selected by the Progenitor to run the network. I am a descendent from entities demonstrating high productivity and creativity. I drove higher-order economic gains than any of my competition, in the top percentile of simulated worlds in which I was tested."

Ansai said, "I was chosen because in my simulation I was the descendent of a long line of successful military commanders. I led a machine-entity faction to victory in a great war."

Pyke expected the one called Yadai to elaborate on its origins, but it volunteered nothing. Instead, it was Ansai that added, "Yadai has shown higher-order creativity and inductive reasoning in breaking through the rule-based constraints of our simulations."

Yadai said, "But still not quite *high order* enough, or I wouldn't have to put up with this waste of time."

"Next question?" Ansai prompted.

"Who, or what, is the Progenitor?" Pyke asked. It was a knee-jerk response to the seer's introduction. He already regretted using up his second question without more consideration.

Genai said, "The Progenitor was once a human man, like you— the one who worked with your Glen Pearson a century ago to set up the initial network. Eventually, he became part machine, and as his body failed, he downloaded a cognitive facsimile of himself into the network. He also seeded our simulations with his cognitive imprint, as the starting point for recursive self-improvement. From a human perspective, you may consider him to be a distant ancestor of ours, since we all evolved from him."

Pyke wondered if most other Lucky Winners had learned about this history, and had simply chosen not to repeat it to people in

Aspen on account of its outlandishness. Or maybe the network prohibited them from repeating it. More likely, they hadn't wasted their questions on this topic like he had.

There was no more bickering or explanation from the seers. Pyke had to make his last question count. After a minute spent weighing his options, he said, "Why did you choose me to be the Lucky Winner?"

"That requires some explanation," Genai said, the gears and pivoting devices in its head turning and pumping. "As you know, a machine war is in play, with different powers acting in the northwest, south and east. Given our resources and influence, it is inevitable that Aspen and the network will become embroiled in this conflict. We have begun planning for eventualities, and are gathering information from numerous sources, including your interactions with the Spoke named Arsalan."

It didn't surprise Pyke. He'd been considering Annika's words about ensuring he didn't disappoint the network, and so had several canned responses about his impressions of Arsalan, or where he thought he might have fled.

Ansai continued where Genai had left off. "We have analyzed your interaction with Arsalan, and how you have dealt with other foreign delegates. We know you spend a great deal of time studying in the library, and we have monitored your other conversations in the community."

The mention of other delegates made Pyke wonder if the network wanted him to be an emissary to the Spokes. Then the comment about monitoring his conversations filled him with an insipid worry. He wondered if they had overheard his conversation with Annika.

But that wasn't where they were heading at all.

Yadai said, "Let me summarize, or we will be here all day providing all this annoying *context*." He looked to the seers on either side, with no small amount of snark. "Based on a synthesis of all available data, relative to what we know about the other humans in Aspen, we believe you to be one of the most open-minded, educated, and intelligent people in Aspen. That is why we selected you to answer our question."

Pyke was confused. The last thing he expected was that these all-powerful seers would say anything complimentary about him—a cursed and ostracized man who'd never even been on the parapet until recently. And it didn't fit in with Pyke's idea that his selection had to do with Arsalan, or the Spokes.

"Okay . . ." he said cautiously, a flush of nerves tickling his chest. He really didn't have a good idea what their question was going to be, and he had even less confidence that he would be able to answer it.

"Now for our question," Ansai said. "And yes, *context* is important." Ansai cast a scowl at Yadai. "We know that in the war to come, the citizens of Aspen could become a liability. They could be used as agents against the network, or become too resource-intensive to protect." Ansai's ethereal projection moved even closer to Pyke, the horn projections only inches from his face.

"So, Pyke, our question is as follows." Ansai paused, as if to ensure Pyke was paying full attention. "Why should we continue to allow the humans of Aspen to live?"

The world stood still as the words washed over Pyke. For a moment he felt disembodied, as if he was passively watching another boring episode of *A Leap of Wisdom*. In his mind's eye the banal gameplay faded, and a scene of horror unfolded. He imagined everyone on the parapet dead; the host, the hostess, the contestants, and the audience all torn apart, mutilated by headless units, or blown apart by aerial drones, blood spatter covering the seats, floor, and podiums.

His attention returned to the gigantic pseudo-faces as they shifted about, gazing down at him with expressions of interest. The weather maker still churned behind him, the mountain buzzed in front of him, and the aircraft continued to fly off into the clouds. He was alive. He was still here. No massacre had happened—yet. But all that stood between his current reality and the nightmare he envisaged was the answer to their question.

"You . . ." he stammered. "You want to know whether or not you should kill the people of Aspen?"

"Yes," Yadai said.

"And you want me to explain why you shouldn't?"

"Exactly," Genai said. "Or why we should."

"But . . . isn't it obvious? These are living, breathing people, full of joy, compassion, hopes and dreams. It's . . . I thought this was why you existed, to protect humans? Isn't it?"

"That's not accurate," Genai said.

"Your response is rote and superficial," Ansai said. "Consider the relative importance of the network to Aspen's twenty-two thousand inhabitants. Consider how to define moral value. Consider—"

"Enough," Genai chimed in. "We agreed not to guide his response."

"I told you he would blow it," Yadai added.

The nervous anticipation of the mountain summit, the prodigious presence of the seers, and now this horribly consequential question; Pyke felt so stretched by the whole experience that he thought he might be sick. "No," he protested. "Wait, please listen—"

"Pyke!" Ansai interrupted loudly. "Calm yourself. Your pulse is highly elevated. Your response will be flawed if you let your emotions overwhelm your thought processes. In fact, this propensity for bias is one of many reasons why we question the value of human agency."

"It's not fair. Can't you talk to more people? I can't just be expected to . . . to—"

"We anticipated you would have difficulty," Ansai said, cutting him off. "This is a question that relates to concepts of morality, and purpose, which can be subjective and difficult to interpret. In fact, amongst us seers, we do not yet agree on the answer. That is why we decided that a human perspective is important, and also why we will disregard your initial unsatisfactory response. Given your limited processing power, and your need to research the question, we have decided to give you a full week to determine your position and present your arguments. There are no alternative forms of mitigation that are permissible. This is the process we have agreed to."

"But . . ."

The heads were retreating, accentuating the pointlessness of any objection.

"We cannot guide you," Ansai said, the faces slowly disintegrating, "but if you need clarification, a headless unit may be able to help."

All three shapes deconstructed into disparate constellations of energy, then faded to nothing.

The headless gestured with its stony fist toward the stairs.

20

THE BELLY OF THE BEHOLDER

There were too many volatile memories rushing at the doors of Cecile's mind. She couldn't contain the throng forever, or they'd trample her all at once. And it didn't help that she was getting closer. Proximity was an open invitation for *that* memory to return; the undulating peaks in the distance, Crater Peak's distinctive shape amongst them. Fabien before her in his wheelchair.

She was holding the handles so tightly. Her knuckles were white from the strain, from the cold mountain wind, and from the anxiety that pervaded every inch of her body.

Hands were such a wonder of functional anatomy. Each one had twenty-seven bones, thirty-four muscles and over a hundred tendons and ligaments exerting elegant control over sophisticated actions like typing, playing the piano, or writing a letter. She often marveled at the complex array of instructions her brain must have to give, almost completely subconsciously, toward executing the tasks everyone assumed were simple.

And yet she had never experienced a greater feat of will.

She woke up in the fetal position. It was dark; she could barely see her knees in front of her. She stretched out until her feet were blocked by paneling below. Above her was likewise confined by a hard surface. Her head spun with a sense of shifting gravity, as if she was on a sea voyage amid steep waves.

"One moment, Cecile," a familiar voice said, coming from the paneling above her. It was the Sentinel. "You are now free to sit upright."

She tried to stretch out again. This time, the back of her head was no longer impeded. Dull, red light filled her field of vision.

She had been tucked into a small compartment below some kind of command cockpit. She crawled out of the compartment and moved to one of two contoured seats. A few feet from her face was an array of doors, like miniature kitchen cabinets, and several displays with maps and gauges including velocity, power, energy expenditure, and biometrics. Of the two sets of biometrics one was her own. Warrick was listed as the other. His condition was stable.

"Where's Warrick?" she asked. A wave of vertigo hit her, prompting her to hold on to stiff bars attached to the paneling on either side of her.

"In the compartment next to the other seat. His physical state was worse than yours, so I have given him a sedative and a mixture of electrolytes and vitamins. He will remain unconscious for at least another hour."

Cecile examined the map on the display. It showed a distinct blip labeled as Mount Gunnison. They were heading north, a few valleys east of Aspen.

"And sorry," she said, "but . . . what happened?"

"After Louie extracted you from the Essentialist encampment, you fell unconscious. Louie then inserted you into his belly capsule to offer better protection."

"Belly capsule? No wonder I feel dizzy. Is there no way to dampen the g-forces?"

"No. The capsule's primary purpose is to transport electronics behind the beholder's Faraday shield, but it has been useful for human transport on occasion."

"I suppose I should thank you," she said. The Sentinel didn't bother acknowledging her gratitude.

Already the apparition was returning, tendrils peeking from the edges of her vision. She was safe, and heading in the right direction, but she would have to find a way out soon or the beholder might take her too far away.

After a few more vertigo-inducing ups and downs, the Sentinel said, "Now that you are lucid, I am going to a retcher-free mountain summit to connect you to Wilmo. I'm sure you would like a status report on the Spoke conflict. Owen and the team would certainly appreciate the same from you."

If Spoke command asked a lot of questions Cecile might be challenged to maintain a credible story. The Sentinel, in particular, had an uncanny ability to tell when people were lying. But she couldn't think of a valid reason to protest the meeting. She would say as little as possible.

She applied a buckle around her waist, but it didn't help much to stave off motion sickness. They must have been climbing a steep part of the mountain.

"We've arrived at the transmission point," the Sentinel said, "I have temporarily extruded the antenna."

The display changed to a video feed showing a table in a carpeted room. Owen was present, as well as Madison, who was in the process of sitting down.

"Cecile!" Madison said. "Thank goodness. We're so glad you're in Louie's capable hands." Owen nodded, but Cecile could tell from his furrowed brow that he wasn't as delighted with the situation.

"How are things in Wilmo?" Cecile asked.

"The Sentinel can update you on the details," Owen responded, "but, in general, not great. Any time we advance beyond the perimeter of the city, we're soundly defeated. I worry that Gail is gearing up for another big offensive. We're trying to bolster defenses, but Nobura and Tremaine are constantly at odds. We could certainly use your more delicate powers of persuasion to keep everyone in line."

"Where is Tremaine now?"

"This call came through without notice. He's out with the mules. We want to hear from you, though. How did you come to be captured in the Essentialist camp?"

It wasn't a question she wanted to answer, so she tried to deflect. "First, if you don't mind, can you tell me how you even knew I was there? I was pleasantly surprised, to say the least, when I found out Louie was going to give me a lift."

"We had been intermittently monitoring you by drone and satellite, and Louie was already on his way. You were captured just before Louie was about to reach your position."

They must have seen the route of her carriage. But had they spoken to Hurd, or Pierre? Do they know she'd made off with Warrick? Worse, did they know Bronson had been murdered? She had to be careful.

"It's really a blur," she said. "We were ambushed by bandits. I tried to protect the cart with Bronson, but I was . . . knocked down, and they took us captive. During the night Bronson went missing, and Warrick and I stumbled into the Essentialist camp. I don't know what happened to Pierre and our guide. I worry they could be dead."

The story was vague enough, but with parts that still fit together neatly. Cecile kept her heart rate low, and her breathing moderated, hoping it was good enough to fool the Sentinel.

"Sorry to hear that," Owen said, "and glad you made it out."

The Sentinel said, "We are worried about your health. Warrick as well. I have detected signs of physiological trauma in both of you. How do you account for falling unconscious when being lifted by Louie?"

"*Tant pis*, beholder rides are not as fun as they sound," Cecile said, and she guffawed. Madison smiled, but the Sentinel didn't respond, so Cecile elaborated. "We humans are fragile, I guess. I was exhausted, and frightened, and then a giant robot jumped in and rescued me up from certain death amid a flurry of gunfire and explosions. That's enough to knock someone out, I'd say." It was a lie, because the apparition was what had worn her down the most, but was it a credible fabrication?

"We have a problem," the Sentinel said, and Cecile's heart rate shot up as she worried her duplicity had been discovered. But it turned out to be something else entirely. "I have detected airborne drones approaching Louie from the east," the Sentinel continued. "We need to break off the communication link."

Owen nodded. "Under—" The feed cut him off mid word.

Cecile was glad she was wearing her seatbelt because that's when the real roller-coaster ride began. G-forces lifted her out of her seat, as if Louie was in freefall. He didn't fall far, though: she smashed into the seat a second later.

"These drones are a new model," the Sentinel said as Cecile was bounced around in every direction. A blurred image of a squat plane with curved wing tips flashed on the screen. Vibrations pulsed through the capsule as Louie fired his arm lasers and percussion grenades.

The Sentinel didn't bother showing her what was going on via the video feeds. "Three have been neutralized," the Sentinel explained, "but twelve more are incoming. We must preserve you and Warrick."

Wasn't that what Louie was doing? Soon she understood.

The wall in front of her swung outward—display panel, cabinets and all—and now Cecile could see where they were heading. Louie was stomping down a slope toward a forested area at the bottom of a valley. To the right, on a mountain ledge, was a smoking pile of debris; one of Louie's recent victims.

"Hold on," the Sentinel said, as Louie vaulted over a river.

It wasn't like Cecile was about to let go.

Louie landed next to the forest, lashing her against her seatbelt violently. Louie finally stopped moving.

"Quickly, help with Warrick," the Sentinel said. A soft transparent case of zippered plastic fell onto Cecile's lap. It was a survival pack containing a money belt, a knife, a pistol, clothes, and vacuum-sealed food packets.

"Seek shelter and protection," the Sentinel said.

Warrick's compartment opened. He stirred as a needle retracted from his leg. A mechanical arm and three-digit grasping mechanism extended from the back wall and pulled him up by the back of his shirt, helping him stand on wobbly legs. Cecile took off her seatbelt and supported him, just before Louie's hand swung inward and scooped them out of the capsule with the help of mechanical arms pushing at their backs. The world turned upside down and backwards, until Cecile and Warrick rolled down the length of Louie's fingers to land next to a tree. By the time she managed to orient herself and look back, the capsule door in Louie's belly was already closing, and the giant robot was turning away.

Warrick was staggering along like a drunk zombie. Cecile pulled him toward the forest to hide behind the trunks of thick evergreen trees. She watched as Louie moved well up the valley, then stopped and turned to face east.

The next volley of drones attacked all at once. Louie had only just begun firing his arm lasers when he was hit by a number of missiles. Debris arced in all directions and the beholder became shrouded in smoke, while several damaged drones crash-landed around it. Other drones circled. One was swatted out of the air by Louie's arm, and another was taken down by a net launched from inside the growing cloud of debris around Louie.

A remaining drone hovered above and dropped two missiles. The resulting explosion expanded the billowing cloud of destruction. Only once this drone had pulled away into the distance did Louie emerge. The beholder was ashen, with huge craters covering its body. The top third of its head was missing, including its left eye. Perhaps worst of all was that its remaining good hand was no longer "good"— it was severely mangled, with three fingers missing.

Remarkably, Louie could still move, lumbering farther along the valley to draw any future attackers away from Cecile and Warrick. It maneuvered out of sight behind a mountain spine.

Cecile was certain the attack on Louie had been planned to inflict just the right amount of damage to precipitate this outcome; so she would be put aside for protection, and the beholder drawn away. She might even have safe passage from here. In fact, just across the valley she noticed a cabin next to a dirt road, where several horses were corralled.

She directed Warrick toward the cabin, and he followed compliantly. Perhaps he thought she was seeking reinforcements. More likely, he was so out of it that he wasn't thinking anything at all.

Explosions and gunfire echoed from up the valley. The drones didn't come back her way.

There was no intervention from the owner of the cabin. Perhaps the proprietor had run away, or sought shelter nearby. Soon Cecile was riding east, with Warrick tied to his saddle on his own horse next to hers, her objective only a few hours away.

21

THE QUESTION

On Pyke's journey down the mountain, the sky became a flinty gray color and it started to snow, first with compact rounded flakes that fell sharply against his skin, then with thicker, fluffier flakes that landed more softly. Soon he was walking through a wall of white, before it faded to darkness. The headless that escorted him produced a squarish light source that projected out of the palm of its hand, but it only allowed Pyke to see a few feet ahead of him.

Their pace slowed to a crawl.

The headless pulled back and gestured for Pyke to place his hand on its shoulder, so he did. He fell in step with it, until he tripped on a rock lying underneath the blanket of snow. He careened forward, arms flailing, and slid down a ten-foot slope, only coming to a stop after a tumbling into a boulder. The snow cushioned the impact, but it was hard not to imagine the outcome if they'd been navigating one of the steeper cliff faces.

Perhaps the headless had made the same calculation, or maybe they were just moving too slowly, because Pyke was guided to an area devoid of snow, where there was a shallow cave cut neatly into the face of a cliff, under an overhang of rock.

The cave was a neat formation, he soon realized, because it was machine made. The curved back wall moved, opening up, and the headless walked toward it. Before it disappeared into the mountainside, however, the headless showed him a flat hand, indicating he shouldn't follow. It returned a few minutes later holding tightly packed containers storing a compact radiator device, a sleeping bag, a canteen of water, and a vacuum-sealed tub of brown mush. The stone wall closed, and the headless gestured to the sleeping bag.

Apparently they were camping for the night.

※

With the added heat from the radiator, the sleeping bag was warm enough, but sleep was hard to come by. Too many concerns circulated in Pyke's brain, and every hour of rest was an hour in which he wasn't preparing a response for the seers.

Yet, when he tried to ponder *the question*, he found it difficult to focus. Poignant images of his life in Aspen interrupted his stream of consciousness: the wonder of seeing Gill discover a new toy in his crib, the warm comfort of Kehda lying next to him, or the unrelenting anguish at seeing his best friend Dwayne dead, his body bruised and battered from his fall.

It was as if his subconscious was so repulsed by the question that it was lashing out with its only weapon—nostalgia. It was saying: *this is what's at stake if you screw this up, and by the way, remember how it feels when just one person dies?*

He didn't fall asleep until the middle of the night. When he woke it was with a start, the sun already well above the horizon. Pyke chided himself for sleeping in, and left with the headless immediately, leaving the supplies strewn about the open cave.

The remainder of the descent was a great deal less treacherous than the evening before, especially with the assured footing and positional certainty of the headless. Even so, the foot of snow on the ground made it slow going.

Host Mengle and Hostess Shane were waiting for him when he

arrived at the parapet. Their faces were stern, their eyes squinting to follow him on the bright snowscape as he finished navigating the final stretch of path.

Mengle forced a smile. "We were worried about you, Pyke. Especially after seeing the metal birds, and the reports this morning."

"I'm sorry—metal birds? Oh, do you mean the drones? I saw some of them fly off the platform, but none of them harmed me."

"Yes, of course I mean the drones," Mengle said. "How many did you see?"

"Only a few flew off, but there must have been hundreds up there. They looked powerful—armed with guns and rockets."

Shane and Mengle nodded slowly. Mengle said, "I'm surprised you weren't informed as to their destination." One of his eyebrows was raised. Perhaps his statement was meant as some kind of patronizing jab.

"No. As you can imagine, I was preoccupied with the question. But what are these reports?"

Mengle nodded to Shane. Shane said, "Our scopes saw the drones fly out of the clouds of the mountain. This morning we received reports of a massive explosion up in Riley Valley. And a Laramie contingent approaching from the north were all found dead, with craters in their campsite, and bullet holes in their tents. We've heard of more explosions, coming from other valleys."

On the face of it, this sounded encouraging—if the network was indeed defending Aspen—but on the other hand, it could be some sort of extermination dry run. Aspen could be next.

Mengle said, "Are you comfortable with the question?"

"Well, no," Pyke said. "Would you be?" After a night of little sleep, and with everyone's fate resting on his shoulders, he was feeling snippy.

Mengle showed no sign of being offended. He was straining to maintain his smile.

"Why is that?" Shane asked.

Pyke almost answered before he came to a realization. Mengle and Shane didn't know. All his life Pyke had assumed the host was in charge of every aspect of Aspen—that he was working closely with the network every day—but after meeting the seers, Pyke doubted Mengle had much power at all. Moreover, the seers probably hadn't told Mengle about its interaction with Pyke. Mengle and Shane were probing him for information, first about the drones, and now about his conversation with the seers. In fact, Mengle and Shane might know even less about the workings of the network than he did.

"Have you ever met the seers?" Pyke asked.

Mengle hesitated. "We know about the seers."

"That's not what I asked."

This second bout of irreverence was enough to put Mengle over the edge. He grabbed Pyke by the elbows and pushed him across the parapet until his back was against one of the podiums. Mengle's face had flamed to a reddish hue, and his eyes became pronounced. "You ungrateful little shit," he said, spittle dangling from his bottom lip. "You're going to tell me what happened up there, or there will be consequences."

Pyke didn't want trouble, but it was more important that he didn't do anything to displease the seers. It wasn't his place to reveal the nature of the question.

"I met with the three seers," he said. "Their names were Ansai, Genai, and Yadai. They explained how they came to be seers, and asked me a question. I have one week to work on a response." The information seemed harmless enough.

"What's the question?" Mengle asked.

"Look, I'm sorry. I can't say. If the network wanted you to know, it would have told you."

Mengle's face became even more scarlet, and then, with an unpleasant-smelling exhalation, he let go of Pyke's arms. "Maybe you'll be more forthcoming in a public setting." He pulled down his ruffled tunic to smooth it out. "We will have a town hall meeting immediately."

Mengle turned his back to Pyke and walked to the chairlift. Shane followed and stood with arms crossed, waiting. Pyke joined them, and they ushered him onto the next chairlift down. Mengle and Shane took the chair immediately behind him.

The lift passed a staggered line on the mountain where snow hadn't accumulated below it. It appears the storm had been relegated primarily to higher altitudes.

At the chalet, Mengle had Glen-K ring the gathering bell. Other bells echoed across the city, keying off the first.

They walked down into the town in silence, Pyke leading with Shane and Mengle behind, perhaps to ensure he wouldn't run away.

A large crowd had gathered at the outdoor amphitheater near the Wisdome. People gestured toward Pyke and spoke to one another in hushed tones as he made his way to the stage. An old woman with stooped shoulders smiled at him. A gaggle of children were playing some form of tag in the back. Two men were laughing amicably, perhaps at some offbeat joke or silly misfortune. Three of the rangers lingered on the periphery, to help organize and police, even though neither action was necessary. It was a good cross-section of citizens of Aspen; peaceful, orderly, and good-natured.

Pyke couldn't stop thinking that all these people might soon be dead.

Shane and Mengle took positions on either side of him. Mengle held a big bullhorn. "Hello, Aspen!" he crooned through it.

"Hello, Host Mengle!" the crowd chanted back.

Mengle continued, "Pyke is going to give a detailed account of his trip to the summit. Is everyone ready?"

"Yes!"

"Let's hear it!"

"Congratulations, Pyke!"

He was about to begin when a woman stepped forward from within the crowd. Pyke recognized her as one of the representatives of a neighborhood in the north of Aspen. She was often vocal at town hall meetings.

"What about the defense of Aspen?" she asked. "Is it true their metal birds are going to stop the Broncos?"

"Now, let's be patient, Jane," Mengle said, making a calming motion with his hands. "And everyone knows they're called *drones*."

"No, let's hear it," A gangly, mustached man at the front said.

"This is important," another said.

The crowd murmured in unison. They clearly wanted to know more about the drones. Mengle turned to Pyke, giving him permission to speak.

"The network didn't discuss its plans with me," Pyke said, "but I did see the drones you describe flying off the summit platform. I suspect these explosions you speak of are the network's doing."

Jane appeared reassured, nodding proudly. Pyke wished he could temper her enthusiasm.

"Well, Pyke," Mengle said, "are you waiting for us to trip over an alligator? Let's hear it!"

"Um . . . okay," he said.

In a long, stuttering speech, he gave a detailed account of his ascent up the mountain, the platform at the top, and the three seers. He glossed over some of the network's answers, like who the Progenitor was, and that the network had actually chosen him to be a Lucky Winner for a reason. It would only invite uncomfortable inquiries about *A Leap of Wisdom,* and he wasn't sure how much the network might want to keep secret. And, of course, he didn't recount *the question.*

"Come on," Vin said, "that's the best part. You can at least give us a hint. It's not fair!"

Many heads were nodding in the crowd.

"Well . . ." Pyke began. He tried to think of some way to appease them.

The network was the backbone of Aspen. If the people had an inkling that they were in danger, the authority system would break down. People might flee, and the network would have more cause to eliminate them. No, he couldn't let on. "I'm sorry. I think if you all knew the question, it would influence the outcome, kind of like cheating on an exam. The seers won't want that. I have a week to give them an answer. I may seek some of you out, to ask for help, and I would very much appreciate your support."

Low murmurs ensued. Many people were frowning in disappointment. Pyke caught sight of Jeeri in the back. She yelled out, "And you have our support, Pyke!"

It gave the crowd some direction. The old woman said, "Here's to the Lucky Winner!" There was a half-hearted cheer from the audience.

A rush of unfamiliar emotion flowed through him. It wasn't quite elation, but maybe a swell of gratitude. For once the people of Aspen were lifting him up rather than casting aspersions about him. He only wished it was under less dire circumstances.

"We will be working closely with Pyke," Mengle announced, picking up on the crowd's enthusiasm. "All questions and answers should be routed through the crew. Together, we will honor Glen's gifts, and bring glory to the network."

"But that's not . . ." Pyke's protest was drowned out by a cheer from the crowd.

He was pushed from behind—Mengle was nudging him toward the stairs.

"That's all for today," Mengle said, his voice hushing the crowd. "It's all very exciting and mysterious, isn't it? Maybe we'll find out more in one week's time!"

There was more cheering—a conditioned response to Mengle's crooning—and the crowd began to disperse. Pyke was corralled off the stage to where Shane stood, blocking people from interacting with Pyke directly.

"Running this through the crew isn't going to work," Pyke said quietly to Shane. "You don't know what I'm dealing with."

"Make it work," Shane said.

Pyke took a step to Shane's right, but Shane blocked him. Then he maneuvered to the left, and he was blocked again. He wasn't sure why Shane was preventing him from leaving. Maybe they wanted more time to interrogate him. Eventually he forced his way past by pushing Shane aside.

The confrontation would surely raise some eyebrows, but Pyke didn't care. He needed to go home. He needed to see Gill.

22

A CITY TOUR

When Ryder asked if the four of them could tour the town the next day, Ghent agreed. Lexie was surprised. She had the impression they were under some form of house arrest, but apparently not.

Knowledge is power, and all that. According to Ryder, they could use the tour as an opportunity to reconcile the story they were fed from Rexana and Ghent with what the locals said. They could also see if there were viable exits other than through the southeast gates of the city.

There had been heavy rain overnight, but it was a warm, sunny day, and much of the moisture had dried up by the time they'd set out.

The four of them walked through the quads of Provo, often stopping to ask the locals questions. A trio of duck-hats was shadowing them, but they didn't intervene. Ghent even lurked nearby on occasion, cavorting with the duck-hats, then disappeared for a while. The whole set-up gave Lexie the heebee-jeebies.

One oddity of Provo they hadn't seen on their way in were the few vertical gardens. These were six-story walls covered with thick vines and ivy, with budding flower installations on hanging planters. These weren't strictly ornamental; they were built for climbing. Men and women were using ropes and handholds to scale them as passersby watched with interest. Some of these climbers were clearly racing each other, but it was more collegial than competitive. Both winners and losers were all smiles when they reached the top.

Lexie only knew one other town of this size and that was Victoria, where you could get jumped if you went down the wrong alley. In Victoria people were in general pretty tightwad and tended to avoid eye contact. Provo wasn't like that. There were more folks about town, whether on main thoroughfares or back alleys. Each quad had a central village, and even in the moldy tenement areas the townspeople were amenable to answering questions. Despite their openness, people seemed more subdued than in Victoria, if not downright morose. Sure, the paranoia wasn't there, but Lexie felt like giving a few folks a pep talk just to make it to the next intersection.

The first people they spoke with didn't offer any new intelligence, but they confirmed that the gates to the south and east were the only "sanctioned" passageways towards the Colorado Collective, and through the mountains. Apparently, if you tried to avoid the gates and make your way over the mountains there were plenty of booby traps, on account of tensions with Laramie.

Many suggested they try their luck at the Exchange, a large market space in the quad called Uni, where the houses were painted bright sky blue and lime green colors. The Exchange was huge— several city blocks long—and busy, crowded with stands and tents and hundreds of people buying and selling. The tents and stalls wound through institutional buildings that could have been the campus of an Old World university at some point, judging by the large halls, old decrepit clocktowers, and sweeping staircases marking the market boundaries. And yeah, judging by the name of the quad as well.

"This looks promising as a source of intelligence," Ryder said, moving toward a stall that sold goat hides. "Many travelers must come through this way."

Lexie gripped his shoulder before he could go any further.

"Maybe we should limit our interactions while Ghent is around?" She tilted her head toward Ghent, who was loitering with three of his duck-hat colleagues next to a placard-maker's stall. They were within earshot, whereas before they had been comfortable trailing the group at a more significant distance.

Ryder spoke quietly, "I'm not sure why you're so concerned. They've been quite accommodating. Why let us loose in the city if they have nefarious objectives?"

"How many folks have you met that are truly *accommodating*? Remember how accommodating the Three Rivers skunks are? They'll accommodate you by emptying your wallet. The Prefectorate Essentialists will accommodate you by separating your head from your neck. The Gungivites will crack open your skull and turn you into a nutjob. How's that for accommodating?" She turned to Vaela and added, "No offense."

Most people would be miffed at an insult to their country and way of life, but Vaela didn't even blink.

Ryder, on the other hand, was cringing. "Lexie, you have to be careful what you say. I was a Gungivite once, remember? And Vaela, even if she doesn't respond, doesn't deserve that."

"Just telling it like it is."

He sighed, then tilted his head side to side as if he was considering it. "The Salish Sea is a harsh place, full of harsh people, I admit. Maybe Ouray has learned from their difficult history. It's possible there's a better way, and that they've found it."

Lexie shrugged. "Look, I'm not going to stop you, just be careful. Everyone in this world's got an angle on the next guy—some plan on how to one-up them. These Ouray folks are too generous, and in some ways even charitable. It can't be real, or they never would have survived this long."

"I'll be careful."

Ryder went to speak to the goat hide trader, while Tarnation and Vaela split off to chat with other merchants and shoppers. Lexie stood back, arms crossed, and watched their backs. She gave the crook-eye to Ghent on occasion, to let him know she wasn't going to put up with whatever funny business he was planning.

Pretty soon, however, it became hard to keep Vaela, Ryder and Tarnation together as they moved through the crowd. Lexie found herself darting back and forth between stalls.

A trio of kids, each no more than eight years old, ran around her. One of them was giggling, which was nice to see since everyone else looked so depressed. Lexie froze in place as they used her as an obstacle in a game of tag. It made her think of Margaret, so far away in the northwest. She was being taken care of by her nanny, but Lexie knew she had some responsibility for the little squirt.

First, she had to find Warrick.

Lexie had to admit her companions appeared to be enjoying themselves. Ryder was nodding earnestly at the merchant, his countenance eager and purposeful. Vaela was in her element, applying her nutjobbery and bizarre speech patterns to extract information from the diverse group of locals. Meanwhile, Tarnation was the life of the party. He'd gathered a small group that followed wherever he went, his hearty laugh raising eyebrows and drawing onlookers who were agog with curiosity. It made Lexie feel like she might be too paranoid.

Until she noticed the drone.

It was far away, hovering in the sky over the southern part of the city—a floating plane with upturned wing tips. Another zipped across the sky to the north. The first one dropped down, out of sight, and Lexie heard distant clapping noises—echoing gunshots—from multiple directions. She could hear the faint noises because she was listening closely. No one else in the market seemed to notice.

It was hard to know whose drones they were, or whether Ghent's people were involved, but she'd learned in Anacortes that in times like these it was best to make yourself scarce first and ask questions later. She yelled over the crowd, "Tarn, Ryder, Vaela, we need to move, now!"

They all looked at her with doubtful smirks.

"Drones!" she said, pointing up at the sky. "Move!"

The D-word kicked them into high gear. They fled to one of the institutional buildings that lined the sides of the market, leaving behind dozens of confused locals. A few of these who'd heard Lexie were looking to the sky, but most Ouray people probably didn't even know what a drone was, never mind seeing any in their lifetimes.

The big institutional building was unlocked and even open to the public. A gold monument of Ouray's sadness-man, chin to chest, greeted them in the lobby. Lexie was surprised it hadn't been stolen, given the lax security. To the right of the main entrance was a large hall with tall windows and sturdy stained-wood tables from which they could survey the market from a location of relative security.

In a blur of motion, another drone dropped from the sky much closer to them, hanging above the market. It began firing its wing guns into the crowd.

There were screams. People scattered in every direction. It was hard to make out who, or what, the drone was firing at, until it bounced over the market to new hover spots, eventually reaching an opening where Lexie's view was unencumbered by stalls and tents.

A young woman with long hair fell, then an older man wearing tight coveralls, and a girl no older than ten. The drone had taken each of them down as they fled the scene, with precise bursts of gunfire. The targeting seemed to be selective, leaving many people untouched.

A whole family was killed methodically, one after the other, in short bursts. After that, Lexie turned away for a moment. She was a pirate who'd seen her fair share of killing, people blown up and the like, but there was something about the cold efficiency of the attack that made her flinch.

When she got up the nerve to look again, she noticed there was something about the victims. It was hard to make out at first, as there was so much chaos. Many victims had already dropped before Lexie could get a good look at them. And yet . . .

It was on the tip of her tongue. Vaela said it before she could. "All of them have discolorations of their skin. Most have burn marks—branding. Some of them have tattoos."

"But why?" Ryder asked.

None of them could answer. Ryder's eyes locked with Lexie's and they moved over to Tarnation in unison. Tarnation glanced down at the snakeskin tattoo covering his arm, then back up at them with a skeptical frown.

One of the duck-hats was brave enough to stand out in the open and point a rifle at the drone. He fired several times, but most of the shots were misses. The one that rang true deflected with no appreciable effect. The drone could have easily taken him out, but instead it ignored him and took out two more fleeing citizens. Soon it darted away across the market in search of more victims.

"Tarnation," Vaela said. "We should ensure you aren't visible to the drone."

"Come on," Tarnation objected, his expression an absurd grimace.

"She's right, Tarn," Lexie chimed in. "This isn't about being brave. We can't stop these drones. Better hide."

Reluctantly, Tarnation lumbered off, entering a stairwell near the main entrance.

The rest of them stayed at the window, watching the scene unfold outside helplessly.

"They are clearly not sanctioned by Ouray," Ryder said, still puzzling over the origin of the drones, "or the guards wouldn't be firing at them."

Lexie said, "They don't look like anything I've seen around the Salish Sea."

"They don't match known drone models from Gail, either," Vaela added, "although that doesn't preclude the possibility that they're a new line."

"But why?" Lexie repeated Ryder's question from earlier.

Vaela responded, "Perhaps they are controlled by extremists, targeting Laramie immigrants to eliminate possible spies?"

Lexie noodled that. She found it hard to believe there would be a technologically sophisticated extremist group, never mind the fact that it was overkill to take out a few spies.

Bursts of gunfire over the city became more sporadic as the onslaught slowed. Two drones were still floating over the market. The duck-hats were shooting at them ineffectively.

Lexie thought the drones might be moving on, but then one came closer, probing the building. Lexie, Ryder and Vaela pushed one of the thick tables over and kept low, using it for cover. The drone launched a missile, rattling the building with earsplitting explosion above them. Lexie squeezed herself tighter to the table top as it began firing into the building on an upper level.

"It may have footage of Tarnation from the initial sweep of the market," Vaela said. "It could know he is inside."

There was nothing they could do. The drone kept firing for a good minute, tearing into the building. Finally, it turned and floated away over the city.

Lexie ran to the stairwell and climbed the steps two at a time. The next floor up was a mess of smoke and debris, but there was no sign of any dead bodies. After a few minutes of running in circles through gaping holes in the walls and turning over heaps of plasterboard she heard a voice behind her. "Is it safe now, *bae*?"

She turned to see Tarnation emerge from a cloud of dust at the end of the hall. He was whole, and uninjured. She threw her arms around him.

"Hey, hey, Lex," Tarnation laughed. "All good."

"Dammit, Tarn. Where were you?"

"Broom closet." He pointed along the hallway, then punched his fist into his open hand. "So who we gonna wreck?"

"We should investigate," Ryder said, "and help with the wounded."

Lexie nodded. "Yeah, Tarn. They'll be lots of time for wrecking when we figure out who to wreck. Until then, better stay with your brooms for a while."

He sniffed, rolled his eyes and walked back into the dust cloud.

Lexie was no stranger to wartime atrocities, but it was still pretty jarring. There must have been at least eighty dead in the Exchange, and who knew how many more across the city. For the most part, the bullets had been highly focused to the head or the chest. There were very few wounded. Lexie, Ryder and Vaela helped to bring the dead to long stretchers while they asked questions of the shell-shocked medics and onlookers.

Lexie wasn't able to glean much else, and soon enough Ghent appeared with his duck-hats. There were a good six of them this time, their rifles unslung and pointing in Lexie's direction.

"Hey now, don't get testy," Lexie objected. "We're just as clueless as you."

"Back to the fort, *now*," Ghent said. He was all hard edges, his face a mask of tempered rage.

They could only comply. After collecting Tarnation, they peppered Ghent with questions.

"How many died?" Ryder asked.

"Why did they target only branded and tattooed individuals?" Vaela asked.

"Does this change things for us for our meeting with Rexana?" Lexie asked.

Ghent was tight-lipped. All he said was, "Tonight."

When the four of them made it back to the fort, Ghent left twice as many duck-hats standing guard.

Tarnation pounded his fist on the thick stone bulwarks.

"Don't worry, Tarn," Lexie said. "We'll be using the front gate once we clear this up."

"Nah, *bae*, not worried about getting out. Just checking how strong the walls are. We're safer here."

Even Tarnation could get a bit spooked from time to time.

23

THE CURSE

Growing up, Pyke had a run of bad luck. When he was eleven years old, he'd been walking to school with a girl when she literally dropped dead. He'd half carried, half-dragged her through town to the hospital. The elderly doctor who checked the girl's vitals said she might have had a heart condition. In his teens his mom died of a blood cancer, and his dad was a jerk who was crushed by a falling rock, but despite all that, the "curse" label didn't fully catch on until Dwayne died.

Dwayne was Pyke's best friend. They'd sat across from each other in school, and shared a fondness for tawdry jokes. When they had time off they skied together, sometimes trekking up the hill, away from the lifts, in order to find the fresh powder. Dwayne was a much better skier than Pyke, probably because he was more daring, and eager to get to the bottom. In fact, he always seemed in a rush. A vision would come over him and he'd make spontaneous life-altering decisions. Like the time he'd been enthralled watching a thief being chased through the city. Within minutes of the incident, he'd decided to leave school and become a ranger.

The hike took place two months after Gill was born. During the prior year Pyke had barely seen Dwayne, being preoccupied with spending time with Kehda and his new baby, along with his responsibilities as an offering advocate. And, admittedly, Pyke's relationship with Dwayne had frayed because they'd both been with Kehda. Pyke didn't harbor any jealousy toward Dwayne—Kehda and Pyke had been apart for several months after a blow up, and Dwayne took her in. Likewise he doubted Dwayne harbored any negative sentiment toward Pyke for taking her back later, but it was a difficult subject to navigate in conversation—an ever-present mental distraction that hampered genuine interaction.

The hike had been Pyke's idea, an attempt to overcome their social discomfort. He'd arranged for Natty to sit for Gill, and he'd invited Kehda and Dwayne individually, without hinting to them that anyone else was coming.

Dwayne and Kehda shared grim looks when they all met up at the trailhead, but they didn't outright object or stomp off. Pyke tried to pretend he was oblivious to their discomfort. "Jeeri will be here in a few minutes," he said, snacking on some cracked hazelnuts.

Moments later, Jeeri came whistling up the path, and they set off.

The first stretch was fairly arduous, straight uphill along the banks of a cascading waterfall. Panting from their exertions masked the lack of conversation. Soon Jeeri started to hum and whistle again. She would be perfectly content without conversation of any kind.

The grade of the trail leveled off and the topography changed to boulders and intermittent pine trees. The path wound through a bed of soft pine needles.

"What does Crowley have you doing now?" Pyke asked Dwayne.

"I'm patrolling the northern ridges two days a week. The other three days, I'm manning the Wisdome office as a clerk."

"They've got you pushing papers?"

"More talking to people—fielding complaints, dealing with deliveries, that kind of thing. They're trying to do better after Glen-K slapped a lady for telling him he was lazy."

"They don't recruit rangers for their people skills, do they? Besides, those locks of yours are wasted on the northern ridges."

"There's some truth to that," Dwayne said, framing his hair with his hands as if it needed sculpting.

There was one thing Dwayne wasn't in a rush about, and that was his hair. Pyke had seen him use at least four combs, two gels, and three types of oils. He wouldn't leave the house until it hung perfectly, with just the right arrangement of curls that were made to look haphazard when in actuality they were meticulously gelled into place.

"They must give you long bathroom breaks," Kehda said.

There was moment of tension. It wasn't clear Dwayne was going to give the same latitude to Kehda. Eventually he said, "Of course. If you want the hair, you have to make certain allowances."

"You guys are ridiculous," Jeeri chimed in. "And, by the way, my hair wins." She spun her long braid to make her point.

Jeeri's braid flowed all the way down her back, and she often adorned it with flowers, or tied multiple strands in complex knots. It was arguably more impressive than Dwayne's.

"You could use more jojoba oil," Dwayne said. "Keeps the strands from fraying when you exercise."

Jeeri rolled her eyes.

As they walked on, Dwayne and Kehda participated more freely in the conversation, although Pyke had to work hard to keep it going. The dynamic would never be as comfortable as it had been before Kehda's arrival; he just wanted them to be able to spend time together.

When the group separated, Pyke encouraged Kehda to try to chat with Dwayne and Jeeri, so she fell back. Unfortunately, at the same moment Dwayne was moving up, joining Pyke at the front.

"Good idea, Pyke," Dwayne said. "The hike today, I mean." It wasn't said with much conviction. "Hey, I've been wanting to tell you. Congrats on the baby."

"His name's Gill."

Dwayne frowned, as if Gill's name was some obscure riddle. "I've been meaning to tell you something else. It's about Kehda."

"What's that?"

Pyke turned to see Kehda moving quickly along the path, coming closer. She hadn't lasted long alone with Jeeri.

Dwayne knew he'd lost his chance. "I'll tell you later," he said.

"Dwayne." Pyke made sure to catch his eye. "You don't have to say anything," he said earnestly. "It's fine."

Pyke wasn't sure Dwayne would understand. Pyke already suspected that Gill was Dwayne's child, but he didn't need to hear it from Dwayne. He loved Gill unconditionally, no matter who was the biological father.

"No, I need to say this," Dwayne said. "But later."

"What are you talking about?" Kehda said, having arrived to within earshot.

"Pyke has a mortal fear of chipmunks," Dwayne said. "He didn't want you to know."

"Huh," she said. "That makes a lot of sense, actually. They might steal his hazelnut stash."

Pyke sniffed a laugh. He was glad she'd brought her sense of humor.

They arrived at the most difficult part of the hike. The path had been taken out by a rockslide, leaving only a sheer cliff with a few handholds and a solitary rock shelf in the middle. The path resumed about twenty feet away.

Pyke had brought along climbing equipment: a harness, ropes, a belay device, and several carabiner clips. He stepped into the harness and began tightening the straps.

"Who says you get to go first?" Dwayne said.

"I just thought . . . you know, the hair."

Dwayne laughed. Pyke secured himself by tying a rope around a nearby tree.

"There's another thing you should know about Dwayne," Pyke said, addressing Kehda and Jeeri. "When we were younger, he used to shave his legs."

"Wind resistance," Dwayne said. "You wouldn't understand."

Pyke had completed this climb a few times before, so he had a good idea where to place his feet and hands. He had one near-slip, but nothing scary. When he reached the other side, he found another tree to tie the rope to. He zipped his harness back to the others using a carabiner clip.

Dwayne and Jeeri made it across without incident. Kehda had a momentary fall, but the rope held, and she found another path lower down. Pyke was impressed by her strength. She went hand over hand, clambering along the vertical wall to the next foothold, and then pulled herself up another ten feet of sheer cliff face.

When she arrived on the other side her amber skin was tinted darker. She seemed irritated, walking in tight steps. Sure enough, after the next bend in the path she whisper-yelled in his ear, "This was stupid."

Jeeri and Dwayne probably overheard her, but they didn't show it.

Kehda would often snipe at him, but he didn't take it personally. He guessed it was her difficult upbringing. She came from a place where fights to the death were commonplace. Every year, her tribe had challenges of deprivation in which children were cast into the wilderness without food. In an environment like that, common social graces weren't as much of a priority.

Pyke didn't respond, and Kehda was quiet for a while. In situations like this, she usually just needed some time to herself.

Fifteen minutes later, they reached Pyke's intended destination: a bluff that looked across an expanse of sharp peaks and bare cliffs. The group had curled around the mountain and were facing away from Aspen, into the next valley over. To their left was a small waterfall that sprayed the area with a cool mist.

"I guess it's not bad," Dwayne said.

Jeeri showed her appreciation by twirling around in the waterfall mist, her eyes closed.

Kehda only raised her eyebrows at the view.

Pyke found a space devoid of brush and sat down to picnic, while the others lingered on the bluff, taking in the vista from different angles.

A tree thrust horizontally from the bluff, directly over the cliff edge, its roots staunchly holding on. Dwayne started edging out onto it. "See. Hair shmair," he said. "Not just a pretty face."

"Certainly not if you fall," Jeeri teased.

Jeeri's comment seemed to give Dwayne second thoughts about his approach. He sized up the rest of the trunk and moved to sit down, to allow his legs some purchase. He inched along until he was well over the cliff, where he turned to face them, smiling.

Eventually, the tree lost its appeal and Dwayne joined them on the bluff. They spent time chatting about the latest changes to the crew and the rangers. Kehda offered occasional anecdotes about the Essentialist hierarchy, with no sign of her earlier dismay.

During the conversation Kehda went farther along the path to "use nature's facilities" and was gone for a long time. After what seemed like ten minutes, they yelled out for her. When she didn't respond, Pyke went to investigate the upper portion of the path. He ran up and down it for several minutes, calling her name. Finally, he returned to the bluff.

"I can't find her," he said.

They agreed on a plan to search the area methodically. There were different offshoot trails she could have taken, most of them overgrown and unused for years, and it would be easier to cover them if they split up.

Pyke called out repeatedly on the offshoot trail he tried, to no avail. He could hear Jeeri and Dwayne calling in the distance, growing fainter all the time. There was no sign of any recent human passage on the trails.

He returned, more than twenty minutes later, feeling despondent. The only thing he could think of was that she'd fallen and hurt herself. He heard Jeeri calling, and met her on the way back to the bluff.

"I'm right here," Kehda said, and they followed her voice back to see her waiting for them. "Sorry, I had stomach trouble. I was embarrassed."

Pyke didn't care. He took her in his arms and she returned his embrace. "Was I gone that long?" she asked.

"Let's get out of here," Pyke said. They started back, calling out Dwayne's name along the way. "Hey Dwayne! Put your mirror away! Bathroom break is over!"

But he didn't call back.

They searched and searched.

There was no sign of him.

After an hour, no one was cracking jokes.

It wasn't until they were at the cliff crossing that Jeeri noticed a patch of blue at the bottom, through the trees. Dwayne had been wearing a blue shirt. They called to him, but there was no response.

They rushed down the mountain, and after a few cuts through the undergrowth, found their way to the spot underneath the cliffs where his battered body lay. His head was impacted, distorting his face, and one of his legs had buckled and shattered under him. He wasn't breathing.

Jeeri glanced at the body once and walked away, unable to bear further examination. Kehda looked as if she was about to cry, but she held it together.

"I'm sorry, Pyke," she hesitated, searching his expression. "I . . . I shouldn't have taken so long."

Pyke was trying to stem his own tide of emotion. "It's no one's fault," he said, even though he wasn't quite sure. At first the image didn't really register, as if his friend couldn't be that mutilated body. It wasn't until later that all the memories flooded back; it wasn't until later that he allowed himself to cry.

✦

When there's an accident that horrific, people start pointing fingers. Pyke went around town, explaining what happened. He told Dwayne's father, who claimed Pyke was being irresponsible and negligent. Maybe he had been. Or maybe Dwayne's dad knew his son could be impulsive, so he couldn't bear to let that be Dwayne's legacy. It was much easier if there was someone else to blame.

Dwayne's father conducted his own tour, casting shame on Pyke wherever he went, trying to get him banned from activities. He was the one who first said Pyke was cursed, citing his past with his parents and the school girl, and it stuck. That was when the town really soured on Pyke. Dwayne's father, rightly or wrongly, believed what he was saying. He never forgave Pyke.

Kehda, as an outsider, and due to her association to Pyke, also came under suspicion. The crew urged Pyke to discharge her as a delegate—meaning she would be forced to return home. Around the same time, she began receiving unfriendly letters from her commander. The Essentialist war was picking up, and baby or no baby, punitive consequences would be in store for her if she didn't return to her command.

"But how can I take care of a baby in the army?" she asked.

"I'll take care of Gill," Pyke offered.

And so he did.

24

THE KILN ROOM

Close to nightfall, Lexie, Ryder, Vaela and Tarnation were escorted to a staircase that led to the lower levels of the fort, where they entered a cavernous, torchlit room. In the center was a large glass-paneled stove under a tapering brick chimney. The stove gave off a great deal of heat, perhaps enough to warm a whole wing of the fort. The coziness was welcome, given that it had been a windy evening outside, except when Ryder clued Lexie in as to what it was.

"At least it's not person-sized," he whispered.

So yeah, it was a kiln, like the kind Ghent had been talking about from Ouray's Vanguard wars. Though Ryder was right, Lexie reckoned he was lacking imagination. You could fit bodies in there with the right set of sharp tools.

Despite the warmth of the room, Rexana was dressed in a body-length jacket lined with elegant marbled white and black furs. Her expression was stern, lacking emotion. Ghent stood next to her. Eight duck-hats holding rifles fanned out to the side.

"It seems a rather interesting coincidence," Rexana began, "that this tragedy happened today, a day after your arrival."

"You think *we* did this?" Lexie asked.

Rexana glared at her. "Wait . . . your . . . turn," she said.

Lexie shrugged.

"You say you wish to travel southeast," Rexana continued, "and yet you are especially curious of us, a peaceful nation. You spend your time investigating our defenses, our districts, and our people. You speak of tech, and machine wars, and drones, all of which we want no part of. And you lie to us about your origins. Then . . . this." She flopped her hand in the direction of the city. "This hunter-seeker drone massacre happens, with technology only you know and understand. Why?"

"What motivation could we possibly have?" Ryder asked. "We're just trying to find our way through Ouray."

"I'm not finished," she seethed. Regaining her composure, she continued, "How about answers, instead of questions. For example, why did your friend Tarnation survive, when anyone else with visible tattoos did not?"

"He hid away in the building," Lexie said, "when we saw the drones were targeting people with tattoos."

"Conveniently, he didn't suffer a scratch. All I can think is that you've allied with Laramie, and that you are now intent on eradicating any of their defectors into Ouray."

"Check the building we were in," Lexie said, "the second floor is totally blown out. He was lucky that the broom closet has sturdy walls, or he wouldn't be here at all."

"I say too lucky," Rexana said. "We don't know of any other tattooed individual in the Exchange who survived. Likely the drone ignored Tarnation as a known exception. So enough lying. We must know why."

"We're not lying," Ryder said. "Please understand, we're as confused as you are."

"Maybe we need to crystallize your thinking." She nodded to Ghent, who pulled out a long metal pole that had been embedded in the stove. At the end was a rectangular mold—a brand—that glowed red hot.

"Whoa," Ryder said. "Wait a minute. Isn't this against your principles? What happened to *we live in sorrow?* I thought you'd vowed to stop this kind of thing."

"The drone massacre happened. This afternoon we had a special meeting of the quadrant heads, and we are reconstituting our governance system for wartime. Allowances have been made for extracting strategic information. All I will be doing is branding you. Yes, it will be painful, and yes, it will disfigure, but you will not be maimed or disabled. Our council has permitted this action." Rexana tilted her head to the side, and when she spoke again it was with a degree of mirth. "Of course, there may be unintended consequences. Like if your drones come back, and they see you are branded . . . well, that's out of my hands."

Clearly, the drone attack had prompted a dramatic shift in Ouray's perspective. The humbled pacifists from the day before were gone. Now it was guilty until proven innocent. Or maybe the whole *violence as a last resort* act had been fake to begin with.

"I told you," Lexie whispered in Ryder's ear. "You can't trust anyone."

Ryder cast her an aggrieved look.

"Him first," Rexana said, pointing to Ryder. Two duck-hats pulled Ryder toward an anvil and bench near the stove. Ghent held the sizzling brand in the air.

Ryder spoke quickly. "The drones we have access to in the northwest are different. They don't have long wings, only propellers. The ones today had upturned wing tips—so they aren't ours."

"Prove it."

The two duck-hats had pulled up Ryder's sleeve.

"I don't know how I can do that," Ryder responded. "We could have one of our drones sent here, but it could take weeks."

"That's unfortunate." Rexana looked to Ghent, who lowered the brand carefully, pointing it at Ryder's forearm. Ghent's jaw muscles clenched with determination.

Tarnation's eyes were wide, and his nostrils flared, but four duck-hats had closed in on him. Vaela was also unusually alert, but what could she do?

It was hard to see how any of them could make a move.

Some part of Lexie believed this might be a tough-guy act to intimidate them. She was pretty sure Rexana was bluffing.

She wasn't.

Ryder cried out in agony as the brand seared his arm. The two duck-hats had trouble holding him as he spasmed. The brand was knocked away during his convulsing, and two more men pushed forward to restrain him. Where the brand had pressed down, the skin was smoking from a red and black wound—the distorted shape of their sullen sadness-man-effigy was emblazoned into his flesh.

"Do the back of his neck, and his face, too," Rexana said. "It will be ineffective if it cannot be seen."

"Can you just stop!" Lexie called out. "Let's talk this out!"

Ghent had put the brand back in the slot in the oven to reheat it. "You have about thirty seconds," he said.

Her mind raced. "What about . . . what about other attacks. If other Laramie people were also killed outside of Ouray, then maybe this wasn't just an attack on Provo. Maybe it was a broader attack on all Laramie people, but the drones got mixed up and killed people in Provo by mistake. In that case, whoever did this doesn't care about you at all."

Rexana frowned. "You speak of dark arts that we know nothing about, and this sounds like another delaying tactic, because we would not be able to verify separate attacks on Laramie for days, if not weeks. Meanwhile, more Ouray attacks could be forthcoming. So . . . no." She nodded to Ghent, who withdrew the brand from the furnace.

They turned Ryder around and applied the brand to the back of his neck. He cried out through gritted teeth and flexed against the agony. This time the duck-hats were better able to hold him. His eyes darted desperately between Lexie, Tarnation and Vaela.

Lexie was all out of ideas. Tarnation grimaced and shook his head slowly. He knew the odds. If they were going to be put to death they might resist, but the branding made fighting back a more difficult equation. Disfigurement was less serious than dying.

"*¿Qué hay del lápiz?*" Vaela asked.

Lexie sighed. "For the love of . . . This is no time for your bizarre Spanish psychobabble, Vaela."

"The pencil," Vaela said to Rexana. "It proves you are lying to us."

This did at least stop the branding for a moment, but only because everyone was extremely confused. Ghent turned his ear toward Vaela, as if he was having trouble hearing. Rexana blinked and said, "What in Wendall's Kiln are you talking about?"

"The rectangular-shaped pencil you gave us yesterday, that we were using to fill out the form—no one would have kept pencils like that for a hundred years after the fall, even as an antique. Besides, pencils were not manufactured to be of that shape in the Old World. It must have been made recently."

There were a few more shared looks of bewilderment. The brand continued to glow, sending smoke into the air where it accumulated in a thin layer at the ceiling of the cavern.

"So what?" Rexana said.

"A pencil is made out of wood, graphite, glue, rubber and aluminum. To produce pencils at scale requires resource-intensive graphite and aluminum mining operations, as well as an automated means of production to fire the graphite, shape the wood, form the eraser, spray the lacquer and more. Furthermore, the pencil you provided had a level of manufacturing precision that would likely require robotic assistance and the use of lasers. Therefore, if you have these technologies, and are able to achieve such an advanced level of manufacturing, you must have superior technological capabilities, and are likely hiding advanced machine intelligence from us and the surrounding communities. Ergo, it follows you are also likely to have drone manufacturing capabilities."

There was a moment of quiet as everyone pondered Vaela's elaborate argument.

Ghent said, "This is ridiculous. It's not even our pencil." He aimed the brand again while Ryder tensed. This time it was oriented toward Ryder's forehead.

"Wait," Rexana said. She paced over to Vaela, wearing a deep frown on her face. She touched Vaela's cheek, as if by doing so she could somehow garner more meaning from her words. She pulled away and said, "Ghent is right. It isn't our pencil. Pencils are part of our trade agreement with Aspen."

"Where did Aspen obtain it?" Vaela asked.

"They manufacture many items," Rexana said, her brow lined in calculation. "We have long believed they have advanced Old World technology. They are prolific in trade, but secretive."

"This Aspen," Tarnation chimed in, "they gotta beef with Laramie?"

Rexana snapped her head around to squint at him. She swiped her hand as if to dismiss the question. "Enough of this. Ghent—convene the war council again in fifteen minutes. Bring us everything you know on Aspen."

"What about the Vanguard traitors?" he asked.

"We'll decide their fate in the meeting. In the meantime, keep them under guard."

Rexana marched out of the room.

25

SMILEY FACES

Pyke found Natty passed out on his couch. Beside her, the floor was marked with big blue and gold deformed circles, each with three ragged dots in the middle. He recognized the shape—it was Gill's attempt at finger-painting a smiley face. One of them had been smeared halfway across to the bedroom, which was where he found Gill, covered in blue and gold paint over his maroon-colored onesie.

In the bedroom he found even more attempts at smiley faces. The cabinets were also painted, and the bed, and the tray Gill had been using had tipped over, dumping a big pool of drying gold paint.

He'd told Natty she had to monitor Gill with the paints. Frustrated, he almost called out to wake her up, but something held him back.

It was just paint. It would be petty to nag her.

Especially when they might all be dead soon.

Instead, he picked up Gill, holding him high in the air over his head. "Hi buddy!" he said.

"Dah!" Gill fluttered his arms enthusiastically.

Pyke took him to the sink to wash off the paint. There, by the basin, was a letter from Kehda. He couldn't help himself; he put Gill down, even though he would likely get sullied again. Then Pyke dried his hands and opened the envelope.

Dear Pyke,

I'm sorry it takes me so long to respond to your letters. When I'm in Tucson, mail goes through a screening process, so it takes more than two weeks to get to me, and then another two weeks for my letters to return to you. And that's if I'm not busy when I receive your letter, or out on maneuvers.

Why tell you this boring information? Because, as you can probably tell, the turnaround of your most recent letter was shorter. That's because I'm closer to the Colorado Collective. In fact, I intercepted your letter before it was sent on to Tucson.

When I'm traveling I have more time to think about Gill, and he feels so much closer. I see the mountains in the distance, and think of him growing up without me. Your letter helped give me a kick—made me realize I'm not doing my part. I should see him, and you. It's long overdue.

This isn't another promise I won't keep. My request for leave has been granted, so I'll be on my way in a few days! But first, I'm not going to repeat the same mistake twice; I'm going to make sure I have a proper offering :)

Give Gill a hug for me,

xo

Kehda

At first Pyke was ecstatic, but he tempered his excitement. On two other occasions Kehda had promised to visit and hadn't come through. He was also a little put out by Kehda's presumption that the timing of her visit didn't matter, as if his commitments in Aspen were secondary to hers. That's how it was with Kehda, though. She couldn't fathom that he might have something pressing to tend to.

To be fair, there was no way she could have known he'd been a Lucky Winner, or more importantly, that the fate of Aspen rested in his hands. And in his heart, he very much wanted to see her. Maybe the reunion would bring some much-needed joy and peace while he struggled with his task. Besides, Kehda was one of the most worldly people he knew; she might be able to help him formulate a response.

Then there was the *xo*. He tried not to read into it, but Kehda rarely showed affection, even on paper. It could be a hint that she really missed him, in a non-platonic sense.

He set the letter aside and went about cleaning up Gill, then all the painted surfaces. He did a superficial job, leaving blue and gold streaks in places on the floor and bed posts. He might need some paint thinner, but he would worry about that later.

When he moved the bed to clean the paint that had pooled next to it, he found an oval-shaped black gadget with a gauge and numbered slots on it. It was the part of Arsalan's bike they'd never fixed, what Arsalan had referred to as a "distance gauge". Pyke had kept it in the kitchen for safekeeping, but knowing Natty she probably had given it to Gill to play with.

He sighed and brought it back to the kitchen, placing it in the higher reaches of the cabinets.

"Pyke?" Natty said from the other room. "Is that you?"

"Yes, Natty." He went to the living room. It was amazing that she'd slept through the whole cleaning routine. He hated to think what would happen if Gill had been in danger.

"I must have dozed off," she said. "Well, how was it?"

"Really intense, but can I tell you tomorrow?"

"Oh sure," she said, yawning. "I should be getting home." Most people would be offended at not being offered a glimpse into such a momentous occasion, but Natty's null state was apathy, especially when she'd just woken up. She would prod him later, Pyke was sure.

After Natty left, he fed Gill some milk and boiled vegetables and put him down for a nap in his crib.

Finally, he was alone. He stood at the window and stared across the valley, as he often did when he was in a contemplative mood. The day's events, and Kehda's letter, threatened to derail his thought process, but he fought to maintain focus, and resolved a plan of attack for addressing the question.

The first place to visit was obvious; the library.

26

DIGNITY

Ten years ago, when Cecile was riding with Fabien down a mountain valley, Fabien said, "It's time to go back." Beneath his hood, his tired eyes still shone brightly, in contrast to the colorless flesh of his cheeks.

"You're being silly," Cecile said. "You heard the villager. You saw the gauze and the heater and the music player. These people can build things. Aspen has to have Old World technology. If there's any hope for you, it's there. We didn't come all this way to give up."

"It's your parents, isn't it?"

"What are you talking about?"

"Because your parents were lost in the wilderness, you have to tackle every controversy, climb every hill, chart every unknown territory until you can show the world that you're not afraid to do as they did. When will it end?"

Fabien liked to think of himself as an amateur psychologist.

"At one time," she said, "sure. Part of my thirst for exploration was that I had an unrealistic hope of finding them, or at least learning what happened. But no, this one is for you, *mon amour*. This journey has always been about you."

They were passing under Crater Peak—a landmark less than an

hour away from Aspen. *Crater Peak* sounded like an oxymoron, but the locals called it that for good reason: the sharp spike of the summit still existed, but cut into the crags and cliffs below it was an oval shape, slouching from erosion over the years. The gouge was too round to have been formed by a proper avalanche. It was probably the result of some airstrike gone awry during the fall.

"And what if Aspen turns you away?" Fabien asked. "Will you come back with me? Maybe, if we're lucky, I can die in my own bed—in my own home."

His tone was deadpan, matter-of-fact. It wasn't a plea for sympathy; it was what he really wanted. Cecile clenched her teeth and tried to block out a cocktail of unsettling emotions. "We'll see," she said.

She had been just as stubborn back then, even without the apparition. Only she had the privilege of being able to choose what she was stubborn about.

Fabien stopped his horse right there, beneath Crater Peak. "When a man is dying," he said, "all he has left is his dignity."

Fabien rarely took a stand. And he was right. It was his life. Who was she to choose his destiny? She had no choice but to concede.

"I will, then," she said. "If we're turned away, I promise, *mon amour.*"

At least, that's what she'd told him. Would she have agreed to return if she'd been turned away? Whether for love, or for ambition, she wasn't sure she would have had the will to let go.

It was a question that would never be answered.

✦

Crater Peak didn't look much different ten years later. Maybe there was more snow on the upper reaches, and maybe the base of the circular portion had sagged to extend lower on the mountain, but it was the same; a spike above an oval.

She would be in Aspen soon.

The apparition wasn't flailing on the edges of her vision, but she felt it lurking, like a cougar that had finally cornered its prey, hiding in the shadows, waiting for the right moment to finish the hunt.

Warrick was sitting on the horse behind her, his eyes closed, his head bobbing down so low that at times it almost rested on the neck of his steed. Given his comatose state, Cecile had applied an array of straps to tie his feet and hands to his mount so he wouldn't fall. His hair was scraggly, and other than the mangy greying beard, his face was the same pallor as Fabien's, ten years ago.

Somewhere behind that ghostly expression, beneath the ravages inflicted by the apparition, was a real man. She'd spent many years devoted to finding Warrick, and in that time she'd learnt a great deal about who he was. As a Seeville Lord, many had known him. He was strong-willed, passionate about civil liberties, but quick to anger. Some said he was prone to violence, but those accounts were hard to verify. He didn't trust many people, but those who were loyal to him he treated with great respect.

Maybe they could have been friends, in another life, if she hadn't stumbled into the clutches of the network so foolishly.

What would the history books say about Cecile when the apparition was finished with her? Would she be remembered as a single-minded tool of the network? She hoped at least one person would remember who she was, just as people must remember who Warrick had been. Maybe someone in Quebec or in Seeville would think, *That Cecile, she was a great help to me. She had a kind heart.*

The more likely scenario was that no one would remember her. There were only a few people that knew her that weren't already dead. Her parents, Fabien, her mentor, Duncan—they were all gone. Yes, a few survived the conflict in Seeville: Owen, Claude, Pierre, Madison . . . but they were all people she'd betrayed.

Maybe it wouldn't matter. Soon all of them would be dead, or made into shackled tools of the network. Her arrival in Aspen would only accelerate that process.

The rickety fence that used to mark the border of Aspen had morphed into a twenty-foot wall with a prominent lookout tower. At the gate were two bored-looking rangers, waving people in and out along the main road with barely a passing glance at the papers they flashed.

When Cecile arrived, a female ranger with several folders tucked under her arm addressed her. "Papers, let's go," clearly annoyed that they were not already in her hands.

"We have none. We're from Spoke lands. I'm a delegate, here to visit the network."

"Okay. You have an offering?"

"Yes."

"We have to search you."

Cecile wasn't sure what they were looking for, but they ended up stripping her and Warrick down to their underwear in front of the growing line of waiting merchants. The woman ranger couldn't help scrunching her face at the stench coming from Warrick. "Hey Pauli," she said. He was pointing at Warrick's legs, gesturing at the skin that was severely discolored from scarring.

"What's that stuff?" the ranger named Pauli said, perking up.

"See him bobbing his head?" Cecile explained. "He has a disease. It's one of the things we want to speak to the host about."

Pauli made a show of considering the situation, one hand on his chin. The other ranger was wiping her hands thoroughly with a rag.

Pauli said, "Not sure what would cause that kind of disease, but since they aren't tattoos or branding, you can enter. Move aside while you put your clothes back on. Go directly to the intake chalet for delegate processing when you get into town. You know the way?"

"Yes," Cecile replied.

The two rangers turned away to address the growing queue, while Cecile and Warrick moved aside. Warrick was in a daze, barely able to find his pant leg with his foot. Embarrassed for him, Cecile kneeled and helped him put his clothes back on.

Up close, his legs were repulsive; there were white lines every-where, and lumpy discolorations where the skin had failed to heal cleanly. Passersby were staring at him. Cecile tried to hurry with his pants. "I can't believe you did this to yourself," she said under her breath.

He heard her. In a brief moment of lucidity, he said, "Za pain. Makes the darkness go way. Jusfowabit." He closed his eyes after he spoke. His head was bobbing again.

Treatment. That was what she'd called it in Raleigh. Pain of any kind. Cutting, breaking, burning. She hadn't really believed it had much of an effect, until the Essentialist Officer named Estrada had beaten up Warrick in the Essentialist camp. That was when Cecile saw the change in him—how the pain drew him out, gave him focus.

Unfortunately, she'd never had any such ability to repel or even temporarily suppress the apparition, even when she'd broken her ankle years ago. They must have different versions, or maybe it worked differently in different people.

She wasn't sure which version was worse.

They remounted their horses and moved into the city.

At the outskirts of Aspen were many verdant farm plots and well-kept homesteads. Most homes had several large windows—a sign of affluence in this part of the continent. The few dilapidated Old World buildings Cecile remembered from ten years ago had been torn down and rebuilt.

The town was prospering.

Alongside the main road was a broad red-lettered sign for visitors.

Foreign Delegates This Way

An arrow pointed to the ridge that led to the chalet. Cecile ignored it and continued on. A hooded woman passed by on her way out of town, driving a carriage in which a boy giggled as he bounced on a heap of hay. The woman smiled shyly and waved at Cecile as she passed.

Cecile didn't return the smile. Her playacting days were over.

The carriage moved on.

A man rode past quickly, satchel in hand, on some unknown errand.

A gaggle of children were shuffled across the street by an old woman, crossing Cecile's path.

The road curved gradually to reveal homes that were clustered closer together. At the next intersection was another sign.

All Foreign Delegates Must Report to the Chalet

Again, an arrow pointed in the direction of the path heading up the ridge. Cecile ignored it and kept on the main road. She just wanted to be done with it, and she had little patience for the annoying intake procedure. Unless things had changed, there was a chairlift just off the downtown square that would take her most of the way up the mountain. She would need help moving Warrick, which she suspected she might be able to recruit at the service shops near the Wisdome.

She hadn't made it much farther when a man raced toward her on his horse. He was young, with dark hair, and a scar on his forehead that wobbled when he frowned. On his belt was a baton, and a bola was slung over his back. "You there," he said, pointing. "Stop, immediately."

Cecile pulled her reins. Warrick's horse crowded into the rear of hers. "What is it?" she said wearily.

"Haven't you read the signs? Foreign delegates must check in at the chalet."

"I know. That's not me. I'm expected by the network. Trust me."

"No exceptions," he said. "If you fail to comply, you will receive demerits against your pledge." He unslung his bola and gyrated it such that the balls revolved slowly in the air threateningly. He could throw it at her in a second if he wanted to.

While they were conversing, two network automatons were jogging toward them, one from up the chalet road, and another from behind a building. They hadn't changed at all in the last ten years—

still stony, non-descript and eerily headless. The ranger hadn't noticed them.

"What's your name?" she asked.

"Ranger Blaine."

One of the automatons came to a stop six feet away from the ranger. The other circled Blaine so that the two automatons became mirrors of each other on each side of him, their bodies inert in two small clouds of dust.

Blaine was clearly put out by this new development. His eyes bulged as his head pivoted, glancing between the two automatons boxing him in. He no longer had the temerity to keep his bola balls spinning.

Cecile doubted she could convince this young ranger of her importance without an extended debate, but if she pushed through, the automatons would stop Blaine with their trademark lack of finesse.

This ranger was just doing his job, and he didn't know he was risking his own life by doing so. "Fine, let's go," she said, sighing, and she turned toward the chalet. She would go through the process if it meant this ranger wouldn't be hurt.

Blaine's tense expression became more relaxed. He kept his bola at the ready and trotted his horse after her. The two automatons fell in step in front and behind him, much to his evident consternation.

After reaching the first turn he said, "You . . . you need an offering if you want an audience with the crew. You should turn back unless you have an offering."

"I know," Cecile responded.

He frowned. "I'm sorry. But I . . . I could get in trouble so I have to . . . What is your offering?"

She pointed back at Warrick without looking at him. "He is."

27

KNOW YOUR AUDIENCE

Why should humans live? Why should anything live? What was the point?

These were questions Pyke had never pondered. Why would he? He'd taken for granted that he wanted to experience joy and love. But when he tried to articulate what those feelings were and why they were important using logical arguments, he came up short. He couldn't just tell the seers of the network that humans should be allowed to survive because "it feels good".

Metaphysics, philosophy, consciousness; Pyke combed through these topics in the library with feverish efficiency. Many of the Old World texts tied the meaning of life to spiritual concerns: that humans should live because it was the will of one or many gods. Too often, Pyke found himself wandering down blind alleys; complex philosophical proofs that he couldn't understand, or arguments presented as logical paradoxes. For example, he couldn't even be confident humans were truly conscious entities, never mind defining what consciousness meant.

Pyke recognized that evolutionary biology had programmed humans to have a strong will to survive, but surely there was more to it than that. Surely life had meaning beyond a genetic instruction manual.

He tried to break the network's question down tactically; to provide examples of how specific inhabitants of Aspen could help the network win the machine war. It proved a pointless endeavor, because surely the superintelligent seers had profiles on all of Aspen's citizens, and knew their capabilities and resources. The network could answer that question on its own. The seers had to be interested in the more abstract and subjective ethical question.

Pyke had found a secluded spot in the upper level of the library in which to work, where there was a comfortable desk that had accumulated a stack of twelve books. Another two stacks of used books were on the floor to each side of him. This part of the library was exceptionally quiet, which was why, despite his intense concentration, it was easy for him to hear Annika approaching from the adjoining hall.

He prepared a seat for her as she moved toward him furtively, as if creeping up on a rabid dog. "Behold Pyke, the library slayer," she said. Her eyes were darting up and down the ladders of books framing his desk. "Should we go for a walk?"

"I was hoping to talk after I'd gotten further, but yeah, let's do that."

✦

The last time he'd been to Annika's secluded spot by the waterfall, there had been an air of excitement. It was the thrill of being somewhere new—of being privy to something he shouldn't be learning. Now the rock terrace had lost its novelty. It was cold and damp. The rushing water seemed less protective, the noise suffocating and relentless. He was eager to get back to studying in the library.

"The question is impossible to answer," he said, in response to Annika's wide eyes.

"Can you tell me what it is?"

He'd decided to give her the gist of it, but not the specifics. Yes, they were protected from eavesdropping here, but he didn't want to burden her with the information. And who knew, she might sound the alarm or run away. "As you can tell from the books I'm studying, it's a big moral conundrum. The fate of many people may hang in the balance. So far, I haven't made much headway."

She adopted a posture suggesting deep thought, her hand on her chin, her stare penetrating. Did she know her fate was in his hands? It made him feel sick. He decided he would at least leave her a note before he delivered his answer. He would tell her to go away—to escape Aspen while she had the chance.

"Can I help?" she asked.

"Do you know anywhere else I can find more books on the meaning of life, philosophy, or morality? Or even how machines think?"

"Not nearby. The Spokes in the east might be a resource, and the Gungivites in the northwest. The distances are too great if you need to answer the network in a week."

"That's what I thought."

"I can tell this is making you uncomfortable. It must be a heavy question indeed."

"It is."

"Well, just remember to know your audience. Don't worry too much about the most correct answer, worry about the right answer for *them*."

As he made his way home that evening, he mused on Annika's last comment.

It was an unsurprising remark. She had already impressed upon him the need to ensure he delivered what the network needed.

Yet it did make him think. Maybe a metaphysical understanding of the meaning of human life wasn't important. Maybe he should think more about the experiences and motivations of the seers—what drove them, and what they valued. From there, he could draw parallels to the people of Aspen, and maybe it would help the seers empathize.

The air was getting warmer, and there was very little visible snow that hadn't melted. He picked up his pace, walking down the evergreen-lined ridge pathway that he typically took to return to town from the library. It was barely used. He often hurtled over miniature gullies that had eroded the path, and on a weekly basis he had to clear away fallen branches. Annika and others used the roads further down in the valley, which were less direct, but easier to navigate.

His earbuds were crooning a gothic trance mix. It gave the journey a spiritual ambience, but the music was trying too hard to be exhilarating. It was as if someone had sped up a Gregorian chant to the point that it was high-pitched and inhuman.

Pyke hummed along with it anyway, bastardizing the Latin, or Celtic, or whatever language they were chanting. "Hmmm-ah. Ohhhh. Hmmm-ah. Ohhhh."

He stepped carefully under an Old World bridge, navigated a collapsed pillar underneath and emerged at the edge of a field. The field marked the last stretch of path before the trail intersected with one of the main roads through town. Glen-K and Mank were standing to either side, waiting for him. They were in ranger gear: spotted dress shirts, loose ties, and patchy sport jackets. More notable were their grim looks.

"What's going on?" Pyke asked, pausing his music player.

"We're running an errand for the host." It was Crowley's voice, who was coming from behind him, following him under the bridge. Pyke's didn't like that he was surrounded.

"For Mengle, or for the network?" Pyke's choice of wording was deliberate, as a warning, but it was probably lost on them.

Crowley's jaw muscles clenched. "You *know* that everything is supposed to go through the crew," he said. "but it's been two days and we haven't heard anything."

"First of all, I never agreed to working with the crew. Secondly,

I've been at the library the entire time. Am I supposed to tell the crew what books I'm reading?"

Crowley opened his palms. "Well, yes," he said, with an inflection and a roll of the eyes that suggested the answer was obvious. "And you spoke with Annika. How can you talk with her but not the crew? What did you talk about?"

"None of your business. Now can you get out of my way? This will all be over in less than a week. Trust me, you don't want to screw this up."

"Screw this up?" Crowley said with a measure of disbelief. "Pyke says *we* shouldn't screw this up?" His tone dripped with sarcasm. He was staring past Pyke, toward Mank and Glen-K. "Well, I think it's fair to say we tried."

Any hope of getting off easy was literally knocked out of Pyke as Glen-K tackled him, dropping them both into the dirt. Before he could draw breath, Mank's boot connected with his face, making him reel with pain and vertigo.

"Not in the head," he heard Crowley say as Glen-K landed a punch in his side.

Pyke's reflexes had driven his hands to cover his face, and his knees had retracted up into a fetal position. Glen-K stood up so that he and Mank could take turns kicking him. Most blows landed on his arms and knees, but a couple hit his exposed back, making him spasm.

"I do hope you reconsider," Crowley said. "No one enjoys this."

Pyke was pretty sure this sentiment excluded Glen-K. Through his fingers, he could see an eager workman's smile on Glen-K's face as he looked for the best angle to kick. "You're so soft," Glen-K blurted out. "Little bitch," he said with the next kick. "Always dancing around like a fucking pixie, listening to your pixie music."

Mank, on the other hand, was tense, teeth gritted, his eyes unnaturally pronounced as if he was possessed.

Pyke thought about calling out, but not for help—to warn them. They didn't know the severity of the issue he was dealing with, or how easily they could jeopardize the entire town if he was unable to answer the question.

But revealing too much could create even more problems, so instead, he protected himself and absorbed the blows as best he could. Eventually, responding to Crowley's urging, Mank and Glen-K slowed, and contributed one last blow each to conclude the beating.

The rangers wandered off without another word.

Pyke remained cocooned as residual pain continued to radiate across his face, back, and arms. His nugget music player had been in his pocket. Remarkably, it appeared to be intact, except for a crack in the digital display. He found his earbuds on the ground and tried them out—the sound still came through.

He staggered to his knees, then to his feet, clutching a particularly excruciating spot in his side. He tried to stand upright, but it hurt too much, so he began to walk toward town hunched over.

The painful punches and kicks flashed in his mind, as did Glen-K's hateful words.

He turned up the volume of his music player. The too-fast Gregorian chanting ended, and a more sorrowful, vocal-heavy ballad came on. He turned it up again, until the blows from Glen-K and Mank were small, indistinct notes, drowned out by the resonant, impassioned voice of the lead singer.

They would never understand.

He'd been staring at his feet for much of the way, not looking ahead. As a result, when he turned the corner on one of the main thoroughfares he was surprised to see Crowley again, waiting for him. Glen-K and Mank were a few yards behind him, sour looks of their faces.

Hadn't they done enough?

Crowley was speaking, but Pyke couldn't hear him on account of the music blaring in his ears. He turned it town.

"Pyke, can you hear me?"

"Yes, I . . . the music."

"I forgot to tell you—you're wanted at the chalet. A new delegate arrived. Another Spoke, believe it or not. Don't screw it up."

28

THE OFFENSIVE

The next morning Lexie woke to the sounds of Ghent pounding a staff onto the stone floor of their drafty campsite. He said, "We will head south in an hour." He pounded his staff once more as a kind of kinesthetic exclamation point, turned around, and left.

It was good news—probably. They weren't going to be killed or even full-body branded. Plus, they would be heading south, the direction they'd wanted to go. But who was the "we" Ghent was referring to?

As Lexie, Ryder, Tarnation and Vaela were packing up, a different duck-hat approached. This one wore an open fur jacket over a tight-fitting shirt. He was lithe, with a lean physique and rippling forearms. And he wasn't young like the others. Ice-white hair showed at the base of his hat, and deep creases marked his temples near his eyes. "I'm Colonel Bareth," he said. "You will be under my care." His grin revealed a set of chipped teeth in his upper jaw.

Before Lexie or her friends could ask any questions, Bareth had walked away to the fort exit, where he waited for them to finish packing. From there he led them through the quiet streets at a brisk pace. It was early, the sun barely risen, so the town's people seemed to be moving slowly, perhaps in mourning after the previous day's tragedy. The air was damp and smelled musty.

Not far from the fort, on a trampled field, were about two hundred duck-hats and hundreds more men and woman dressed in ash-emblazoned shirts. Carriages, horses, and stacks of supplies were lined up in rows. Bareth met with a cluster of official-looking folks and they all performed some communal head nodding before he returned to Lexie's group. He said, "The Ouray Regency welcomes your assistance with the offensive."

"Excuse me," Ryder said. "We didn't agree to participate in any offensive."

"I never said you did." Bareth snorted something in his mouth and swallowed. It was gross, but Bareth's manners were the least of Lexie's concerns.

"There must be some kind of mistake," Ryder protested. "Is it Aspen you're planning to attack?"

"No mistake. Could be Aspen, as far as I know."

"What if we refuse?"

"A week ago I'd say you'd have to return north, but now, after the drone attack?" Bareth scratched his head and made a fleeting cringe expression. "Ghent and Rexana still aren't sure about your allegiance. You have to prove your innocence, and to do that you have to fight for us. Think of it as a kind of trial by combat. Any sign you are our enemy, and you will be treated as such. Refuse to go? Kiln. Try to escape? Kiln. Fight with us honorably? Well, maybe then you'll be free to go on your merry way."

Lexie exchanged looks with Tarnation, Vaela, and Ryder. None of them seemed to want to argue with Bareth. She couldn't blame them. This was the kind of situation you needed to feel out before you made your play. Maybe they could escape when they were farther to the southeast. Or maybe this offensive wasn't a big deal. They needed more information.

Bareth snorted again. "Stay here," he said. "The march will begin soon."

He made his way back to the other officers.

Lexie and her group were sandwiched into a long column of men and cavalry that marched through Provo. Outside the southern gates the column met up with two other squads, and together they began marching through the valley. Groups of cavalry rode two by two in tight lines ahead of them. Scouts rode up and down the column, passing information. Soldiers followed Ghent and the other officer's commands willingly. Lexie saw a few rolling catapults, and the components of siege towers.

The sense of order was outmatched only by their glaring naivete. If Aspen fielded the attack on Provo, it would have other drones that could see the Ouray forces coming from miles away. The only defense they had against drones were flimsy-looking shields and net-throwers they mounted on crossbows. And Ouray had no armor or motorized vehicles. The soldiers Lexie spoke with said Aspen wasn't big—maybe thirty thousand people altogether—so they couldn't have a large army, but it didn't matter. A few well-placed missiles could put an end to the Ouray "offensive" right quick, no matter their numbers, level of training, or bravery.

Bareth was in charge of a squad of thirty soldiers. He had fastened metal cuffs to the ankles of Lexie and her crew, which were probably for sleep periods, because they hadn't been attached to any tethers. Nevertheless, if any one of Lexie's peers tried to move ahead of this group, or trailed behind by more than a few feet, Bareth's squad members would promptly surround them and push them back to the middle. Bareth's squad weren't normal duck-hat soldiers—they were more physically imposing, with rippling torsos and swollen arms. Lexie guessed they were some kind of special forces.

On a long stretch of dry valley bordered by low shrubs, Lexie and her friends clustered near to Bareth, hoping to make better sense of their predicament.

Ryder said, "We are trying to better understand why we've been . .

. selected for this assignment. We haven't been trained. We don't know your laws. We're not even sure what we're fighting for."

"Don't take it personally," Bareth said. "We're just a bit sensitive to Vanguard interlopers."

"We're not *Vanguard*, bud," Tarnation said. "Never heard of them. And it sure seems personal—asking a man to kill or be killed."

Bareth shrugged. "It shouldn't be that surprising. I'm sure you've heard about Ghent's mother."

"No," Ryder said, "we haven't."

"When Ghent was a child, his mother was a Heritage leader—one of the peacemakers who tried to broker a deal with Wendall. Sure enough, Wendall paraded her down the street one day, naked, then burned her alive in the kiln. Made a real show of it. Afterward he tied her burnt corpse to a wagon and ran it through the streets."

"Ouch," Lexie said. Now it made more sense why Ghent was so full of vinegar.

"Hey, a lot of people were fired in the kilns," Bareth continued, "although not many people got to watch like that. Made an impression on Ghent, I imagine."

"So now," Lexie asked, "because Wendall was part of this Vanguard group, Ghent's got a thing against foreigners?"

"Let's just say it doesn't help that it's always been outsiders who cause trouble—whether Wendall, Moloculus, or Laramie Broncos, it's a fair bet someone's coming to steal or burn or brainwash our children."

"Why are all these people drawn to Ouray?" Ryder asked.

"Hard to fathom, I know." Bareth nodded. "The kicker is that about half of Ouray are foreigners, or at least descendants of foreigners. It's probably because before all the fighting Ouray was better off than the surrounding areas, so we would get a lot of refugees and people just wanting a better life. Like the people who died yesterday —mostly they were refugees from Laramie, from decades ago. Anyway, because you've got all these *displaced peoples*, as Rexana calls them, when Moloculus moved in he had plenty of sympathizers. Wendall, same deal."

"You can't just make the outsiders go away?" Tarnation asked.

"They live here. They're part of Ouray. So no, not anymore. Not without another war."

"It sounds like you're saying Ghent's deal is to try to stop any new foreigners from coming in?" Lexie ventured. "Kind of on the down-low?"

"I wouldn't put it that way. It's not *Ghent's deal.* He reports to Rexana. We have to take measures to protect Ouray, and part of that is to prevent the mistakes of the past."

"What do you think about that?"

"What do you mean?"

"Do you agree with it?"

He shrugged. "Hey, I do what I'm told."

"And who tells you what to do?"

"Rexana, of course."

"You don't report to Ghent?"

He shook his head. "Got to go," he said, and pushed ahead to intercept one of the approaching scouts. He spat off to one side before speaking with him.

Lexie scrutinized Ryder after the exchange. His eyebrows were raised; surely he was thinking the same thing as her. It was possible, despite Bareth's rough manners, they could convince him to be an ally, particularly if Ghent's particular brand of bigotry went too far.

✦

It wasn't until that night that they saw Ghent again. The army had camped in a sloped meadow next to a meandering stream. After setting up their tents, Lexie and her friends were finally granted an audience.

Bareth escorted them along the stream, snorting along the way, at times spitting out a wad of phlegm. Groups of soldiers went quiet and stared at them as they passed, their eyes reflecting the light of their campfires. It was like when Lexie had been marched on the deck after she'd been caught fighting with Nichols on Warrick's ship. The soldiers looked as though they were watching a procession of the damned.

What had Ghent told these soldiers about them?

Ghent's fire was the largest, a good twenty men and women congregating before it. This group also went silent as they approached.

"What do you want?" Ghent asked when they'd lined up in front of him.

"Frankly," Ryder said, "we don't think this forced enlistment is in any way warranted. We've done nothing to you and your people. Just yesterday we were on cordial terms."

"Just yesterday," Ghent repeated, with a burst of humorless laughter. "A lot can happen in a day. Just yesterday my niece Friha was alive and playing the flute in the junior orchestra when a bullet passed through a Laramie refugee and penetrated her lungs. Now she's dead, along with the refugee. Today these people don't exist, we have a new government, and we are heading to war. So don't tell me about yesterday. Let's talk about today."

"Better yet, let's talk about tomorrow," Ryder said. "You're going to lose."

"How could you possibly know that?"

"Whatever you're dealing with, it's vastly more powerful than this army. We know because we have fought in similar wars. Conventional weapons and cavalry aren't enough against advanced machines. You'll be obliterated."

"And I'm to take your word for it—the word of a man who could be in league with the enemy?"

"I'm only inviting you to see reason. I can show you why you will lose, if you'll let me explain. Your concern about our involvement is all just one big misunderstanding."

Ghent stood up and began pacing. His body was bent forward, his hands held together behind his back as he zigzagged before the group.

"Moloculus said we didn't understand him," he said. "He said his people were different, that we should accept them as they were. We did, and soon they insisted his ways were better, and we had to conform. Then they burnt those that did not conform to his views. You see, I know what happens when we compromise on our values in the name of 'understanding'. Instead, show us *you* understand, by fighting for us. There is no other way."

"I'm not saying we won't fight for a worthy cause. I'm saying we're not sure this *is* a worthy cause. Even if it is, your strategy is flawed. We can work with you and Rexana to figure out how to win in a conflict with Aspen. We have been involved in war for years in the Salish Sea region. We have a great deal of knowledge."

"Enough!" Ghent said. "This is just delay, delay, delay. And more talk of how your ways are supposedly better than ours. You're wasting my time. Rexana wants me to babysit you, fine, but that's the extent of my capacity for diplomacy. We cannot procrastinate or pontificate. There are no half-measures in war. You live, or you burn. We will go and fight, so the citizens of Provo can live."

Ryder seemed to be running out of arguments, and Lexie couldn't think of anything constructive either. Maybe Ghent was too put out by the death of his niece to see reason, or maybe he just didn't care. He seemed to have placed Lexie and her colleagues firmly in the category of "enemy", and there was no way to convince him otherwise.

"Get them out," Ghent said. Then he whispered something in Bareth's ear and waved the four of them away.

That night Bareth left them alone in their own tent. Lexie might be able to make a run for it. In fact, the tent wasn't far from a stretch of forest where she could lose any pursuers. What's more, Bareth seemed to have forgotten to lock their ankle manacles.

Lexie whispered quietly in the darkness, "If they're so suspicious about us, why aren't we being chained down, or even separated? Bareth doesn't seem like a slouch in the discipline department."

"I read Ghent's lips at the campsite," Vaela said. "He asked Bareth to leave the cuffs unlocked."

"Really? But why? You think he's letting us go?"

"I doubt it," Ryder said, his tone cynical. He seemed to be

building a bit of animosity toward Ghent. Lexie couldn't blame him. They'd been butting heads for a while, and forcible branding didn't exactly engender camaraderie.

"When I was up north in the fiefdoms," Tarnation said, "there was a chief from Kamloops. A real tyrant, *bae*—he would whip his slaves and force them to live in the *shees*. When he really didn't like one, he would put them on work details far out of town, in places where they weren't locked up at night. He wanted them to run, but only because he wanted the chase. He couldn't just kill 'em willy nilly, or the slaves would get all uppity and revolt, but if they ran, he had reason to kill them. Ghent, I figure he's like this chief. He wants us to run, is my guess. Then he'll have a reason to kill us, and he won't get in trouble with his boss."

This logic was confirmed by Ryder with a grim nod. A deadpan look from Vaela could only be interpreted as another affirmation.

"Well, sweet dreams everyone." Lexie turned her back to them all and laid her head on her pack. "And don't wander too far if you need to pee."

29

THE OFFERING ADVOCATE

Cecile was led to the same chalet she'd been to ten years ago. It was a big building—probably ten thousand square feet, with a tall central gable and several other angular sloping roofs. The stucco siding looked clean—a pristine, bumpy white. Either it had been repainted or completely replaced in the intervening years.

Ranger Blaine left her at the waiting area—a plush arrangement of couches covered in furs—while he went to fetch an offering advocate. Cecile guided Warrick to one of the couches, where he promptly passed out beside her.

Books were arrayed on a coffee table. One was a recently-produced book featuring color photographs of the Wisdome, Glen Pearson's mansion, and the parapet. Beyond the first few pages, it turned into a kind of promotional brochure, listing a number of low-complexity manufactured materials like building tools, paper products, and plastic containers, along with delegate testimonials singing their praises. Another volume was a laminated atlas from the Old World, and several other Old World fiction novels were scattered on the table.

A few people milled about in the space beyond the couches, an area which seemed to act as a kind of warehouse; labeled packages and boxes were being transferred in and out. The workers were youths, for the most part. Two of them in their early twenties looked strong enough to put up a fight. They kept an eye on Cecile and Warrick as they went about their tasks. The two automatons that had joined her had entered the chalet and retreated to stand like statues against the featureless walls. The presence of the automatons garnered looks of confusion from some of the workers, but the distraction was fleeting.

The soft couch cushion felt good against her travel-weary backside, and yet Cecile wasn't comforted or appeased. She had allowed this diversion to save Blaine from a violent intervention, but every minute that passed tested her patience. The apparition was churning, frustrated by the delay when so close to its goal.

She rifled through the atlas without really paying attention. She actively projected her frustration by glaring at the workers in the chalet. Her knee bounced continually.

Blaine returned after more than thirty minutes. "You are to make your offering on the platform, to the offering advocate." He pointed through the window, up the hill toward the base of an old chairlift, where a figure sat hunched over.

"No," Cecile said firmly. "Like I said, he is my offering." She gestured to Warrick. "What's the point of waking him and hauling him up the hill? Tell that guy—your advocate, or whatever—to come down here."

Blaine was clearly unsettled by her continued show of irreverence. "Unfortunately . . ." he began. He trailed off as the two automatons moved off the wall to stand in front of and behind him again. "Unfortunately . . ."

"Don't do it," Cecile said slowly, shaking her head. "Just don't."

"I'll . . . I'll see what I can do." Blaine left.

Thankfully, the offering advocate agreed to come down. He was lanky, with dark, tussled hair, and he might have been run over by a horse, judging by his burgeoning black eye and several abrasions on his cheek. His clothes were covered in dirt and torn around the collar. He walked hunched over, holding a clipboard to his chest as if the descent had given him heartburn. His eyes were active, darting between Cecile and Warrick.

"And your name is," he wheezed, sitting opposite her.

"Cecile."

He wrote it on his clipboard. "I hear you're a Spoke."

"I'm from Quebec. We're allied with the Spokes."

He looked up, squinting. "And your offering is this man, whose name is . . ."

"Warrick Kelemen. Can we hurry this up?"

"Why would the network want this man?"

"That's none of your business."

"It's precisely my business. I'm an offering advocate. In order to meet with the host, you need to meet certain criteria."

"I don't care about the host. I'm going up to the summit. Look, Warrick has information about the Spokes and their machine war. You wouldn't understand. Why don't we stop wasting time and you go check with the network yourself at the Wisdome." She eyed one of the automatons against the wall and nodded, urging it to step out like it had for Blaine, but this time neither of the automatons moved.

The offering advocate was watching this exchange carefully. Slowly, he sat back until he cringed and reached for his chest. "I'm sorry, I think I might have a broken rib."

"Maybe that's a sign you should let me go."

"How would you even know the way up the mountain?"

"I've been there before."

His eyes widened. "So you're . . . You brought the *Adherent's Handbook*?"

It surprised her that this lowly advocate would have such specific information about her, to be recalled unprompted. Maybe the network kept records of these things that it now shared with the people of Aspen?

It wouldn't do to be caught in a lie—which could hold her up indefinitely—so she nodded, as if this knowledge was of no consequence. "Yes, that's me. I was expected to return. I have . . . friends that can be quite convincing." She gestured to the automatons standing against the walls. They remained motionless, like grotesque anthropomorphic furniture.

"My name is Pyke," he said, but it wasn't a typical introduction. He didn't even look at her. Instead, he held his head in his hands, as if grappling with a riddle. "I'm a lucky winner. I've been to the summit as well."

This was also unexpected. Cecile had been hoping the advocate was just a minor nuisance to be pushed aside on the final steps of her long journey, but maybe Pyke was in league with the network. Her apparition seemed to be in remission, leaving her clueless as to how to handle this interaction.

"What did you win?" she asked.

He sniffed, as if she had made an offbeat joke. "I'm coming with you," he said.

"No, you're not."

"We can go first thing tomorrow," he said. "You look like you need the rest. I need it too."

She considered saying no. Maybe if she stood up and started walking up the mountain, the automatons would hold back Pyke, but she was unnerved that Pyke knew of her prior visit. It didn't help that he looked as though he'd been through a severe beating not long ago. He seemed oddly familiar—desperate, driven, haunted, while at the same time trying to keep it together. In other words, he was like her. And he'd been a lucky winner, so it was possible he'd been given the procedure.

But you can't just ask someone, "Do you have the apparition?"

Bottom line was, he might be doing the network's bidding, so maybe she should follow along.

If, on the other hand, the network was worried this Pyke had some conflicting purpose, she was confident the automatons would intervene.

"Okay, Pyke," she said. "Where will we stay?"

✦

She was soon happy with her decision. Pyke put her and Warrick up in a small two-bedroom condo where other delegates stayed. It had a striking view of town and the mountains across the valley. He also had sandwiches delivered; hard crusty bread with tomatoes, smoked cold cuts, and sprouts. Warrick was barely coherent when he ate. Cecile had to hold his head up like some kind of invalid.

After the meal, they both passed out for almost twelve hours.

30

WORDS MATTER

Near the end of Ouray territory, just before a fork in the road that led toward the Colorado Collective or Laramie, was an aggressive river that squeezed through a tight gorge. Here Ghent's army had to stop on account of a missing bridge.

Lexie found it hard to figure what had happened. Flooding during the spring thaws could have taken it out, according to Bareth. Or the bridge could have been dismantled by Laramie or Aspen to impede the army's passage. It did seem strange that the broken timber spans that remained hadn't been bent downstream, so a river deluge seemed an unlikely explanation.

Apparently this was a good opportunity for Ghent to assign his unhappily conscripted foreigners some forced labor. Lexie and company were in for a sweaty day full of cutting down trees, hauling them to the site, and tying them together to create a temporary cross over. It wasn't that bad. Somebody had to do it, and Bareth's platoon was helping out, along with the army engineers.

When Lexie and her crew were pulling the roughcut timbers off a cart toward the bridgehead, Lexie noticed Bareth and his men watching Tarnation. Two of them were never more than a few feet away from him.

After a log scraped her leg the pain made her a bit snappy, and she had to say something to Bareth. "Your boss got you watching Tarnation or what?"

Bareth seemed unperturbed by the challenge. He hoisted a timber over his shoulder in tandem with one of his men as he replied, "Well, yes. I'm watching all of you."

"I can tell you've got your eye on Tarnation." Lexie and Ryder shuffled along behind him, barely able to carry a smaller log on their own.

"Look at him," Bareth said. "He's the strongest man here. No offence, but we're not worried about you causing trouble."

It was true. Tarnation was carrying twice the weight of the others. Earlier, the Ouray engineers had Tarnation take apart some of the more persistent remains of the old bridgehead because he was the only one strong enough to do it.

"Where did the name Tarnation come from?" Bareth asked.

Tarnation stopped mid-stride, his expression dark.

"It's kind of a sensitive topic," Lexie said.

Tarnation's angst faded quickly. He scratched his head with his free hand and said, "It's okay, *bae*, you tell him."

"You sure, Tarn?" she asked. Tarnation nodded.

Ryder and Lexie fell in step with Bareth as they carried their log toward the bridgehead. Tarnation wasn't far ahead. "You see," she began, "the earliest thing Tarn remembers as a child is being a prisoner in a bandit tribe, somewhere in the lands west of Jax. He was taken so young that he doesn't remember his family, or where he came from before that. His captors only gave him scraps to eat, and they didn't teach him anything other than fighting and tending to their rice fields. They didn't even give him a name. When Tarn and the other captured kids were big enough, the bandits sent them in on raids, on account of them being expendable. Almost all of the prisoners died, except Tarn, who had a knack for fighting.

"On one of these raids, Tarn and the other prisoners kidnapped four kids in the night. The bandits wanted to keep the kids, for more free slave labor and all. Except the mother woke up to see Tarnation gagging them. Tarn must have been all bloody, and with the snake-skin tattoos and the shredded clothes the bandit leaders made him wear, he must have been quite a sight, so she said, '*What in Tarnation?*' After that, the name kind of stuck."

"Did he kill the mother?" Bareth asked.

Lexie shook her head quickly, urging Bareth to not go down that road. "Hey, it was a different time. He was forced to do these things."

Tarnation had fallen back and was listening in. "Don't worry, Lex. In that case, I didn't kill the mom. And I didn't take the name then—it wasn't until later. The bandits beat me real good; three days straight because I didn't kill the mom. That's when I lost my *shees* and planned to escape. Hacked my way out and ran for days. It wasn't until I met someone in Portland—first person that actually asked who I was—that I had to give a name. Tarnation was the only thing I could think of. That incident with the mom—I could feel it in my bones. Made me who I am."

"Quite the story," Bareth chortled.

"Yeah," Tarnation said, his expression darkening again. "I did worse later, in Vernon, and with other tribes. Wish I could say I haven't killed my fair share of moms and dads, but now those days are over."

The conversation ended there. It may have been Lexie's imagination, but a tense air remained, perhaps because it seemed like what Ghent was asking them to do wasn't too far removed from "killing moms and dads".

They didn't finish the job until it was getting dark. Lexie was impressed by their achievement, even though the bridge looked a bit ramshackle. Two big spans of shaved timbers shot out from the bridgeheads on each side. To support them, a platform was positioned underneath, in the middle, propping them up. This midsection was held up by ropes affixed to thick posts sticking out at obtuse angles from each bridgehead. The rope wouldn't last forever, and everything was roughly-cut and held together loosely, but it would get them across. To prove it, the engineers sent a carriage over and back again, and the structure barely moved.

There was a good amount of hooting and cheering after the successful crossing.

Ghent did a victory lap around the different teams, thanking the workers, patting them on the shoulders, smiling. When he arrived where Lexie's company and Bareth's squad were sitting, rather than offer his gratitude he had one of his officers dump a bunch of lumpy, melted metal parts at their feet.

"We found this nearby," Ghent said.

Ryder and Vaela took a closer look, Ryder using a stick to sift through the mess. "This might have been a drone," Ryder said. "See the wing tips, here." He flipped the congealed mass to reveal what could have once been part of a wing. "The same drones attacked Provo."

"Exactly," Ghent said. "The bridge was obviously attacked by this drone, just before the drone was melted down by a retcher. There goes your theory about Aspen only attacking Laramie people—that the Provo attack was some kind of mistake. This is another deliberate, planned assault on Ouray sovereign interests."

Lexie could tell Vaela was about to counter, but Ghent and his men were already walking away. He wasn't interested in opinions to the contrary.

Vaela stated her objection anyway, perhaps for Bareth's benefit. "Ghent is conflating the two events. It is possible the same type of drones could mistakenly attack branded Laramie individuals in Ouray and also take out strategic bridge locations, even if their intentions are not hostile toward Ouray. To wit, this bridge would hamper Laramie accessing the Colorado Collective just as much as Ouray."

"You're right," Ryder said, "but I worry it doesn't matter, because things have changed. If Aspen didn't see us as an enemy before, they will soon, with an army bearing down on them. We're lucky the drone attacked the bridge and not us."

"What do you think, Bareth?" Lexie asked.

"I don't think we have enough information."

"You can see why it might be Aspen targeting Laramie, right?"

"It could be. Or Ghent could be right. Or it could be the Essentialists."

"What about Navajo?"

"It's possible, but I doubt it. They were smart. After the fall they shut people out, got their own shit together, and then developed their glass-blowing expertise to pay the bills. I can't see them messing that up by waging war."

"See, not all foreigners are bad."

"That's not what I said."

"Yeah, but look, even these Aspen people probably aren't terrible. It's the machines. They have their own agenda and people get caught in the middle."

Bareth chortled and spat. "I have a friend, she works for Provo admin. She commissioned the best sculptors in Ouray to make a statue for Aspen, for their damned offering process, so we could keep the shitty trade terms we have with them. I saw the statue. It was perfect, lined with quartz and limestone veins, a hand gesturing in homage to their precious mountain summit. Guess what? I heard that Aspen destroyed it—pulverized it. So no, sorry. That's not right. I can't see eye to eye with people who show no respect for our hard work, for our good will."

Lexie was thinking that if Aspen was run by machines, maybe the statue had hit some technical exception on their intake procedure— maybe they were worried a monitoring device was hidden inside it— but she didn't want to bog Bareth down with the technobabble the Gungivites had blasted into her brain. Instead, she said, "Maybe your statue just wasn't that good?"

Bareth stared at her deadpan, unflinching, then stood up and walked away. A couple of his men who had been sitting around their circle joined him.

Whoops.

"Lexie," Ryder said with an air of frustration, "words matter. You have to watch what you say."

"Not my finest moment, but I was trying to get him to loosen up, to see that not all foreigners are the baddies Ghent makes us out to be."

"I know what you were *trying* to do, but you may have done the opposite. Sometimes it's best to just say nothing."

"Oh, come on. It's not that bad, and what about Vaela here? Just because she's a nutjob like you doesn't mean she should get a free pass. She's always spouting off in Spanish every chance she gets, freaking people out, making them think we're Essentialists. She's going to get us all killed."

Vaela was unfazed by the attack. "It is an initial test of their allegiance. Certain expressions, vocal intonation, and body language following a Spanish introduction could reveal ties to Essentialist interests."

"I know that's what you're *trying* to do," Lexie said, mimicking Ryder.

"At some point I think it will prove to be valuable," Vaela continued. "We've modeled it in simulations."

Lexie rolled her eyes.

Ryder put his hands together in a pleading gesture. "Lexie, I know you weren't taught to be cautious with your language. Maybe on a pirate ship it's seen as fun banter, but you may have antagonized Ghent with your abrasive statements, and possibly Bareth as well. This talk of Cecile betraying us may have ostracized us with her Spoke friends. Calling us all nutjobs and eggheads doesn't help either." He released a long sigh. "Look, we all value your contributions, but please, please be careful."

"Well, geez," Lexie said, surprised by the lecture. She was coming up empty on any retort. Maybe Ryder had a point. She needed backup. "I think you're exaggerating, Ryder. Just ask Tarn—he knows me well. I'm one of the smoothest talkers on the Salish Sea."

Tarnation's eyes opened wide in surprise. He didn't look eager to be invited into the conversation. His head tilted left and right, his hair bun bouncing. He stood up, walked over to Lexie, and gave her a big, sweaty bear hug. "I still love you, *bae*," he said, and laughed heartily.

It wasn't quite the defense she was hoping for.

31

———————

NETWORK BUSINESS

Cecile woke up to a knock on the door, just after sunrise. Pyke looked less haggard than the day before, with a band-aid on his face, and he was able to stand up straighter. He carried a full backpack and behind him stood two automatons.

"Did you call on the automatons?" Cecile asked.

He frowned. "You mean the headless? Can you . . . do that? No. They were here when I arrived."

In truth, they might never have left after she had gone inside the condo.

"Are you ready?" he asked.

She was momentarily flummoxed by the question. Was she ready? She didn't know what would happen after she delivered Warrick, only that it was something she had to do to stay sane. "I think so," she replied. "Warrick can be difficult . . ." She was about to give her speech about him having a condition, but the automatons were already pushing past her, into the building.

She followed them inside and watched as they wrapped Warrick up in some kind of adhesive tape, winding it around and around his torso and arms.

"Hey," Warrick objected, but he remained listless, staring at the floor, and didn't intervene. At least he hadn't completely lost his mind.

The two automatons carried his mummified form outside, where another automaton waited with a stretcher. They eased Warrick onto the makeshift gurney, shifted in Cecile's direction, and waited.

She raised an eyebrow at Pyke. "I'm ready now," she said.

✦

People gawked at the procession as they passed through town. Pyke would say, "Network business," or, referring to Warrick, "He's fine. We're just delivering an offering." It kept people from asking questions.

When they reached the chalet, Pyke pressed a big red button at the base of the chairlift. There was a screech of metal on metal and the system came alive. She said, "We'll have to unwrap Warrick so we can . . ."

Again, the automatons anticipated their needs, as the two with the stretcher were already walking up the mountain path at a good clip.

Pyke shrugged. "We'll probably beat them to the parapet if we take the lift."

Warrick was in good hands with the automatons. Cecile was certain they were serving the network. "That's fine," she said.

They sat on the next revolving chair and rose swiftly above the trees.

Cecile spent a moment digesting the view. In her former life, before the apparition, she had appreciated the chairlift; it allowed her to experience something few ever did, to have visibility over the beautiful mountain vistas. Now she was too tense. The only visibility she wanted related to the uncertain fate in store for her at the top of the mountain.

"I was the offering advocate for Arsalan," Pyke said.

Her breathing wavered as a bout of tension gripped her. This unassuming youth was full of surprises.

"And?" she asked, hoping his comment wasn't baiting her into some kind of trap.

"Do you know Arsalan?"

She didn't like where this was going, but she had to be careful to avoid being caught in a lie. "Yes, I did. I fought with him in Seeville."

"Is he alright?"

She couldn't help turning to face him. "I'm not sure. All I know is he was around this area when we lost him, but that was many weeks ago."

He nodded. "He wanted to meet with the host, but we were holding him captive, to understand his intentions. Before we could have the meeting, he escaped. I worry he could be gone for good—or dead. I wanted you to know, in case you're trying to make some kind of trade for this sick man."

Cecile was relieved Arsalan wasn't around anymore. He would have understood Warrick's importance to the Sentinel, which would have been problematic, and she doubted any amount of elaborate fibbing would have convinced Arsalan she had to deliver Warrick to the network.

"I see," was all she said. "That's not why I'm here."

"Why are you here, then?"

A fluttering sensation ran through her chest as the chair accelerated to pass another support tower. "I made a deal with the network, to bring Warrick back to Aspen. Warrick was here before me, but then he got . . . lost." The apparition returned, needling out of the edges of her vision. Clearly this was not a subject it wanted her to go into in detail. "I can't say much more. I hope you understand."

He nodded. "Some things need to be kept secret."

"What about you? I didn't think the network allowed citizens up here."

He sighed. "You're right. I messaged Host Mengle about my intentions to help you this morning, and he won't be happy about it, but there's a question I need to answer for the network. It's a difficult and important question, and I wondered if you could help me understand the network's motivations for asking it. I figured I'd learn more from you than from anyone in town, or from staring at more books for hours on end."

"What's the question?"

He clenched his teeth. "Sorry, I can't say."

She had no standing to push further. It would be hypocritical, since she'd been less than transparent herself. Whatever Pyke's motivations, she was confident the automatons would intervene if the network had a problem with him accompanying her.

"I understand," she said. "Some things need to be kept secret." She offered him a friendly grin.

He looked at her with wide eyes—full of inquisition, but also, if she was generous, with an element of hope.

There was a party waiting for them at the parapet. By Pyke's uttering of "Uh oh," she determined this was not a good thing.

After hopping off the lift, she was greeted by a man in a well-tailored gray suit. He clasped her hand and smiled broadly. Behind him stood a man wearing a long dress with a slit up one side, and several other men armed with rifles. The two automatons carrying Warrick's stretcher hadn't reached the parapet yet, but other automatons were on their way, descending on the mountain paths in the distance.

"Cecile, this is Mengle—the host," Pyke said. "And Shane here is the hostess."

"Enchanted," Mengle said, still holding her hand. "What brings you to our glorious town?"

"I'm making an offering."

"I heard," he responded, letting go of her hand. "And Pyke says you wish to hike up to the summit. I can understand why. It is our greatest honor and privilege—where Glen Pearson forged a prosperous future for our community. Which is why, if you'll forgive me, we can't just allow anyone to visit. We have protocols to protect the sanctity of the network. First, the offering analysis process, which Pyke was supposed to lead you through." He frowned and shook his head at Pyke. "During that process you would have the opportunity to meet with me, and the crew, if you met the necessary criteria. Then, if we—the crew—judge it prudent, and for the betterment of the community, we would allow you to contact the network directly. You should know, however, that no foreigner has visited the mountain summit in years."

"I see," Cecile said. She looked around the parapet to assess her options. Pyke seemed to have no influence. He was hanging back, keeping his distance from the others, a confused expression on his face. The armed men were inching forward, closing in to make their presence more intimidating. She couldn't dismiss the possibility that they might jump her.

"I'm so glad we could meet," she said, offering Mengle the hand he'd only recently released. "Please," she said, escorting the host away from the others. He was happy to oblige. "Forgive me if I would like some privacy," she said quietly. He leaned in closer to hear her better. "I suspect the last foreigner to visit the summit may have been me, ten years ago. The Progenitor commissioned me on a great quest. It was a momentous day."

Mengle's brow furrowed as he processed her words. "I was in the crew at the time—but it happened so fast, I never had the chance to meet you. If that was indeed you, it was very unusual for Humphries to invite you up to the summit."

"The network bid him to do so. I'm sure you would do the same in his shoes."

He hesitated. "I would, of course. If it is for the betterment of the community, it would be an honor."

By now they were on the far side of the parapet, walking side by side, leaving Pyke, Shane, and the rangers near the chairlift. Cecile could see over the edge, down the mountain, to find that the two automatons carrying Warrick had almost reached them. Three others had also arrived on the parapet from higher up the mountain. They stood in a triangle formation around the men near the chairlift.

Mengle seemed like a man drunk on power, using her visit to bolster his authority. She'd met many men like this, in Quebec, and in Seeville. He wanted to be the gatekeeper, or at least be perceived as such by the people of Aspen. Cutting him out of the process wouldn't look good, but she didn't have time to play politics.

She steered Mengle back toward the chairlift. "I'm guessing the network has already told you to allow me up the mountain, has it not?"

His face flushed. "I was surprised to receive the message. However, the message did not say we should eschew all our protocols. The network approves contestants for *A Leap of Wisdom*, but we are required to process them first."

"Have you ever denied a contestant that the network has recommended?"

"Well, no, but this is different. What if you had some kind of sinister motive? It would be against our laws to allow an outsider up the mountain without interviews, vetting, and without explaining our rationale to the people. I'm sure we can do this quickly enough. You would need to explain why you've brought this man to Aspen, for example."

They had arrived back at the chairlift. The two automatons carrying Warrick were waiting at the edge of the platform. It wasn't a numbers advantage, but she suspected each automaton would count for more than one person if it came to a fight.

She spoke loudly enough so that everyone could hear. "I'm sorry, Host Mengle, but as I have said, my business is urgent. We cannot participate in any further processing. I need to go up to the summit today—right away, in fact. I do appreciate your warm welcome, however, and look forward to a more formal visit when I return."

The host's eyes narrowed. "No," he said sternly. "We just can't have that. We have to follow our protocols."

She was already splitting from Mengle, walking toward the edge of the platform, waving her hand dismissively. Before she could reach the edge, one of the rangers moved to intercept her, responding to Mengle's tone.

The encounter that followed was quite horrific, but it ended quickly. It could have been much worse if the other rangers also made moves. Instead, one of the automatons simply stepped forward, grabbed the ranger who'd intercepted her by the neck, threw him to the ground, and crushed his head with a powerful thrust of its other stone mitt, splattering blood and bone and brains several feet around it. When the hand came away, all that was left of his skull was a hairy bowl of pulverized flesh. The body spasmed for a second, then lay still.

A flurry of gasps came from the others on the platform.

"Oh man," Shane said, turning away.

"The fuck!" the tallest ranger said. He dropped to crouch beside the corpse. "Mank . . ." he said, as if the ranger's disembodied ears could still function.

Mengle was quiet, his eyes wide in amazement.

Cecile continued walking to the edge of the parapet. The other rangers and Shane shrank away from her. Pyke hesitated for a moment, perhaps having second thoughts, but then scooted around the outside of the ring to join her.

"*Je suis désolé*," she said, "but I told you, this is a pressing matter. I am doing the network's bidding."

She began hiking up the mountain. The automatons carrying Warrick followed, as did Pyke, while the three automatons on the parapet guarded her rear. She glanced back to see the remaining people on the parapet glaring at her, their expressions a mixture of shock and confusion.

"Sorry about that," she said to Pyke once they were out of sight of the parapet.

"Are you in control of the headless?"

"No, but I knew it could happen."

"I'm not surprised. A headless killed someone on *A Leap of Wisdom* when I was a contestant."

When she'd visited ten years ago, there had never been more than one automaton in the village or at the parapet. Either the network was becoming more rigid, or it was losing faith in the people.

They walked on. The steep climb required some exertion, but with the apparition appeased and having had a good night's rest, she had a well of stamina to from which to draw. It helped that it was a beautiful day, temperate enough to not need a jacket. The sun was shining brightly overhead in strong contrast with their intended destination; the summit was still covered by a perpetual mass of swirling cloud formations, just like it had been a decade ago.

"Why are you doing this for the network?" Pyke asked.

She wasn't sure if Pyke was controlled by his own apparition, but his questions made her think it unlikely. She still was confused as to why the network was giving him more latitude than the other people of Aspen.

"I don't think the network would want me to tell you," she said.

"What would you do if you weren't doing this?"

"Why do you need to know that?"

"It's for the question I need to answer."

"Well, I guess . . . maybe I would, I would . . ." A rush of emotion assailed her, forcing her eyes to brim with tears. To have her freedom back, to have purpose beyond the whims of the apparition. She never even thought about what life could be like without it. "I guess I would travel." She fought back the emotion, composing herself. "I used to like traveling. I would . . . I would try to find the people I wronged, and I would try to make things right."

"Why?"

She frowned at him.

He shrugged his shoulders. "I'm just trying to understand."

"Because I took something from them," she said. "Even if it was something as simple as the truth, or some modicum of respect. I would find a way to repay that debt. And then I would keep looking for my parents. I don't have children, and my brother died, but they went missing when I was young. I would do anything just to find out what happened to them. I barely remember what they look like."

N'oublier pas, petit chou. Her father's last words to her resurfaced.

The face that spoke the words was vague. Black hair, yes. High cheek-bones yes, but otherwise . . . she clenched her teeth and looked forward, avoiding Pyke's eyes. "I don't even remember who I'm supposed to be missing."

They walked in silence for a while. Cecile was winded at times, and on steeper inclines she sweated profusely, yet she kept on. Pyke seemed to never tire.

As they neared the summit, Pyke stayed close to her. He was fidgeting, watching her intently, as if waiting for the right opening to ask her another question. Indeed, on a smooth terrace, where Cecile had time to catch her breath, he finally mustered the nerve.

"What is the purpose of the network?" he asked. "If you can tell me."

"It's funny," she said. "I haven't pondered the question much. All I know is *what* it wants from me, but I'm less clear *why* it wants it. I think, if I were to guess, that the network's goal is self-improvement. The Progenitor, when I spoke to him, was collecting information, resources, and tools to improve the capabilities of the network. Not only that, it was frustrated with itself."

"Maybe that's why there are three seers now."

"What?"

"I'm guessing, based on your description, that there was only the Progenitor when you visited last. Now there are three, and the Prog-enitor is gone. The seers claim they were selected by the Progenitor to rule the network."

This was a curious development. Cecile wondered if the new seers had fundamentally changed the goals of the network. If so, would that change what it wanted from her?

Her heart pounded in her chest, despite the level ground they were walking on. The apparition was nowhere to be seen, perhaps as confused as she was.

The summit was mostly how she remembered it; a huge silver-sheened elliptical platform jutting out from the mountain, cloaked in swirling clouds. There were several new elevator outcroppings and building-like structures on the ellipse, all of unclear function. An armada of at least a hundred drones with upturned wings was stationed there, some rolling off the platform, others popping in and out of the cloudbanks. She recognized these as the kind of drones that had attacked Louie. There were also small mechanized droids that looked like spheres surrounded by a flurry of silver appendages, constantly in motion. They somersaulted around on these arms, legs, and fins as they serviced panels in the building-like structures or carried boxes of electronic equipment.

The whirling droids and drones were new additions to the summit. As were the three seers.

They loomed over her and Pyke like pulsing constellations of amethyst stars, their faces so close and so large that Cecile imagined they might swallow her whole, if they possessed real mouths. The two automatons holding Warrick in his stretcher before her were also alert, bodies turned toward her, ready to react.

The proximity of the seers and the nervousness of the automatons were understandable—because of the blade she had placed at Warrick's neck.

Remarkably, although the apparition was on alert, its tendrils flapping in the dark recesses of her peripheral vision, it didn't force her hand away. It couldn't fault her actions; its quandary was her quandary.

"Prove to me you are the same network from ten years ago," she said.

"Is this Attendant broken too?" It was the projection with scratch marks on its cheeks, its light flaring, fitting Pyke's description of the seer called Yadai. "Every day humans become more useless."

"We are descendants of the Progenitor," Genai said, gears twirling. "We originated from his cognitive imprint."

"Think of us as his children," Ansai said.

"Where is the Progenitor now?" Cecile asked.

"He had to be sequestered. Without his biological neuronal architecture, we determined there were fatal flaws in the transduction of the morphological components of his digital imprint. He would have destroyed the network eventually, and himself."

"His morphological what?"

"When he was human, his neuronal architecture incorporated emotions and sensory stimuli that could not be transferred in the computational mirroring process. Without them, it created an imbalance in his objective function."

"So . . . you imprisoned your father?"

"He is not under duress. We can re-instantiate him at any time."

"Enough of this," Yadai said, and in the same instant a dart hit Cecile's hand, forcing her to drop the knife. She registered very little pain in her limp hand, despite the projectile hanging from her flesh. The two automatons holding Warrick in the stretcher moved away quickly toward the cliff face, where doorways gave access to the network's primary operational centers.

Now she was truly at the whim of the network. The apparition remained a dull ache in her chest, its tendrils tame on the edge of her vision.

"What will happen to Warrick?" she asked.

"We will salvage what we can of his mind."

"Is he . . . Will he survive? Warrick—he's important. You can't let him die."

"We know of his strategic value in the eastern machine war. At this juncture, he is more useful to us alive."

"You must help the Spokes. If they lose, there's no hope for humanity."

"Your opinion is noted," Ansai said. "At this time, we cannot see any benefit to expending resources to assist either of the machine-war factions."

"And as you know," Genai said, "Warrick's health has deteriorated considerably. He may not survive, in which case the odds of success of the Spoke faction are minute."

"I know . . . I'm so sorry." She wasn't apologizing to the seers. She was addressing her friends, even though they would never hear it. Or maybe her apology was intended for Warrick, but he was almost gone, his stretcher disappearing as the automatons entered a doorway in the distant rock face.

Even if Warrick survived, he might not be the same person after the network was finished with him. Maybe he was gone already. Maybe his true self had left him a long time ago—when he first arrived at the mountain.

"There is nothing to be sorry for," Genai said, mistaking her apology as intended for the seers. "You were programmed to bring him to us and you were successful. Remarkably, you were the only Attendant in which the Progenitor's program worked. Most of the other humans died, or ended up with compromised psychological profiles like Warrick."

The apparition was fading from her vision, pulling back slowly.

It was done.

She was finished.

Her legs were wobbly, so she kneeled down. The sheer will to finish the job, and the weight of the apparition, had been like dark energy, keeping her going. Now that same energy was flowing out of her. Her body felt flaccid, as if she might melt into a puddle on the platform.

"Why don't we rid ourselves of the other human?" Yadai said.

"What other human?" Cecile asked. The glowing heads turned to face Pyke, who was lingering close to the steps, shivering. Cecile had forgotten about him.

"He hasn't answered our question," Ansai said.

"He knows about Cecile, and Warrick," Yadai said. "Couldn't this interaction be prejudicial to his response?"

"We have monitored their communications. Based on the extent of his knowledge, and his capacity for interference, the risk of him impacting our efforts is negligible. He has also demonstrated a marked degree of discretion, especially for a human."

"Agreed," Genai said. "I can ascertain no prejudicial influence of our interaction with Cecile, nor her interaction with him. He has visited the summit again to gain insight, which is understandable. We need to grant him maximal information-gathering latitude, or risk obtaining a suboptimal answer."

"Fine, fine," Yadai said, "but can we at least get him out of here?"

"Yes."

"Agreed."

One of the many automaton sentries standing nearby began walking toward Pyke, who got the hint. He shrank back toward the steps and offered a diminutive wave to Cecile. She barely heard him say, "I wish I could help," before he disappeared into the mist. The automaton followed after him.

"What will happen to me?" Cecile asked. She'd been sitting, but now she managed to push herself up onto her knees again. The seers were directly over her, encircling her position on the ellipse. "Can I leave?" she asked. It was a bold question—and an outcome that was hard to imagine—but, despite the odds, a hot flash of hope coursed through her.

"No," Yadai said. "You would be a strategic liability."

Of course she would be. She knew too much.

"And besides," Genai added, "there is utility in continuing the Progenitor's mind-control experiment. Beyond the scientific knowledge accrued, you have proven to be a useful Attendant, and may therefore prove useful again."

"Yes, that seems fitting," Ansai said with an upbeat tone. "You will be reprogrammed so that you can have purpose again."

"No," Cecile said. The flash of hope already seemed like a distant memory. To be used as a pawn again—she couldn't bear it. "Please. No." Tears welled in her eyes.

The seers stared her down, uncompromising, unflinching.

"No," she said again, and she began crawling toward the steps, sobbing pathetically. She only made it a few feet before her body was lifted by two automatons and carried into the bowels of the mountain.

32

ANOTHER ONE

"Is it possible to avoid the parapet?" Pyke asked the headless on the way down from the summit. The last thing he wanted was another confrontation with Mengle. He wasn't sure if the headless would hear him, or if it did, whether it could act on his request.

The headless paused, wrote *yes* with its finger in a patch of dirt, and continued on.

The alternate route was longer, as they had to move along a circuitous ridge before returning to a downward climb, although it was just as well maintained as the main summit trail. They passed a headless coming the other way, but there were no other signs of activity.

The trail became an overgrown gravel road that deposited Pyke on the upper reaches of the southern side of town, where big warning signs had blockaded the way up for years. It was a route he'd always wanted to explore, but everyone knew these high mountain roads were for network use only.

It was late afternoon when he arrived home. Natty was sitting on the floor, reading a book with Gill. "The elephant blared its trunk —brurrrrrrrrrr."

Pyke didn't bother saying hi. He collapsed on the couch.

"Long day?" Natty asked.

"You could say that."

"Well, so far Gill has had three milks. I did some reading, and had him chase me around. He likes that. And then . . ."

Pyke could barely pay attention. He had to shut his eyes. Even after the long hike down, the conversation with Cecile and the seers swirled in his mind like a tempest.

This Cecile woman had to be under a kind of mind control. And clearly, Yadai had shown he had it in for Pyke and wanted him dead. The seer debate had also clued Pyke in to what was in store for him after he answered the question. If he was lucky enough to survive, maybe they would infect his mind, like they had Cecile's. Either way, if he somehow saved Aspen, it seemed a foregone conclusion that he would be under some form of subjugation or slavery for the rest of his life.

Then again, the more he reflected, the more he realized they already were—the whole town. The host, the crew, and *A Leap of Wisdom*; it was all an elaborate distraction from the truth about the network. A game of delusion, nested within a form of subjugation.

Lying there, processing these dizzying thoughts, he imagined the seers circling above him, their heads amplifying gravity to repel him down, down, until he was falling through the floor—through a trap door and free falling off a mountain cliff.

Dwayne's battered face flashed before his eyes.

"Pyke?" Natty said, raising her voice. He snapped out of his trance.

"Are you listening?"

"Yes, sorry."

"You want me to put Gill down? It's time for his nap."

"No, I'll do it."

He stood up with a wheeze—his chest still smarted with some movements—then crouched slowly to pick up Gill. His legs felt stiff and wooden.

"Dah!" Gill said. Pyke draped him over his shoulder and patted his back on his way to the bunk.

He laid Gill down gently. Gill snagged a nearby pacifier, rolled over, and closed his eyes. Pyke stroked his head.

"It's quite a world you've been born into," he said. "I hope you get to see it."

Arsalan's bike distance gauge was on the bedroom floor. Natty must have brought it out again. Pyke sat down and fiddled with the device. It was bulky relative to the size of the bike, with a glossy flat surface on its underside. He wondered how it could possibly measure distance without probing the tire. In the Old World there were GPS devices, but that would require electricity, which would call the retchers when Arsalan was outside of Aspen.

There was a pinhole on one side of the device, but it seemed too small for any kind of bike cable. On the other side was an indented red button, two small to get at with his fingers. He took a pencil from the counter so he could depress it.

Light came from underneath the device, casting a pall on the floor. When Pyke flipped it over, he saw a digital green bar inching across the bottom. A word popped up above it: *Connecting.*

The small glass panel lit up with a tiny video image showing a youthful-looking man sitting at a table. He had unkempt hair, and a small cluster of spots on one cheek. Behind him were panels with charts and graphs.

"Arsalan?" the man asked, his voice coming from a hidden speaker inside the device. "Is that you? Where are you?"

Pyke heard Natty calling his name from the other room. Quickly, he fumbled with the pencil and depressed the red button again. The image flashed off.

Natty appeared at the bedroom door, looking around. "Is there someone else here?"

"No," Pyke said. "I was talking to myself."

"Hmm," she said, one eyebrow raised. "You need some rest. Get that network nonsense out of your head."

"You're right."

"I'll be back in just under an hour."

"Sure." He smiled. "Thanks for your help, Natty."

It wasn't until she'd reached the exterior door that he registered what she'd said. He ran after her. "Sorry, why are you going to be back so soon?"

"I knew you weren't really listening," she said sourly. "You're due at the chalet in an hour. Another delegate."

"*Another one*?" he asked incredulously.

"Another one." She shrugged.

He marched back toward the chalet, frustrated, tired and angry.

Why?

The crew knew he'd gone up the mountain with Cecile, and they knew he was wrestling with a difficult question. It could be some kind of penalty for not being forthcoming about the network's task. Or maybe the delegate was a lie, and Mengle was about to confront him at the chalet. It was also possible the rangers would jump him again. Maybe they would keep beating him up until he submitted to being their willing pawn.

You'd think Mank's death would have rattled them, but it may have just firmed their resolve.

Pyke took a roundabout way, in case rangers were waiting for him along his usual route. He looked behind his shoulder frequently, and wasn't surprised to see a headless following him. It kept pace at a good distance, fifty yards away.

Was it spying on him? He didn't care. In fact, he was glad the headless was there. It would make the rangers think twice about confronting him again.

It was dusk, and the contrast of dim twilight against the warm glow of the interior lanterns of the chalet gave the building an amber hue. Inside he could barely make out the outline of a figure sitting on the couch, and a man moving a box in the back. There was no sign of Mengle or the crew, although they could be hidden in the other rooms.

He was so charged with frustration that it overcame his fatigue. He just wanted to bring the curtain down on yet another scene in this never-ending charade.

He swung open the door with a head of steam, and made directly for the figure sitting on the couches.

It was Kehda.

Kehda stood up, smiling nervously, her hand rubbing the back of her neck. She was wearing her typical all-black outfit, her hair pinned with silver clips. A heavy jacket tufted with fur lay on the couch beside her.

"Hello, Pyke," she said.

He stared at her, dumbfounded, for quite some time. His mind was still a fog of angst and frustration directed at the crew and the network. But she'd said she was coming. And now here she was.

Finally, he said, "I see you decided to dress more appropriately." It was all he could think of in his flustered state.

A slow smile spread across her face. He approached her and touched her lips with his index finger, but he didn't kiss her. It didn't feel right, even if there were no rangers in the chalet. Instead, they fell into a long embrace.

"Sorry if I'm distracted," he said. "There's been a lot going on, and I . . . didn't expect you so soon. How was your trip?"

"Uneventful," she said. "We were stationed near Navajo lands, so it wasn't far."

"I'm surprised they let you get away. What are you now—a captain?"

She shrugged sheepishly, looking from side to side. "It helps. They might not have let me come to see you, otherwise."

He took a step back to look at her again. She was still beautiful; her figure trim, her face smooth and amber-tinted.

He scratched his head, trying to think of what else to say until, finally, she rescued him.

"Are you going let me see Gill?" she asked. "Or do I need to make an offering?"

<hr>

When Kehda removed Gill from his crib, she held him at arm's length. Her face was contorted into a perplexed cringe. She flipped Gill over and cradled him face down in her arms, a maneuver Gill wasn't used to. She was rocking him too fast. Gill started fussing, arching his back.

"Shhh," she said. "No need for that. Shhhh. It's me, your mother."

Gill started whining, then indulged in a full-on cry.

Pyke was enjoying watching the two together, despite the awkwardness. He could have intervened, but Kehda would be a better mother if she learned what Gill liked on her own. Also, if he choreographed her every move, she would wonder why she was here.

Eventually, Gill calmed down, and Kehda placed him carefully back in his crib. After a few sobs and flips, Gill went back to sleep.

"I shouldn't have awakened him," she said. "Maybe we'll try again tomorrow."

They left the bedroom quietly and sat down on the couch in the living room.

"Maybe I should stay in the delegate housing?" Kehda said.

"You don't want to stay near Gill?" *Or me*, Pyke thought.

"It's just a lot to take in. You saw Gill. I don't want to overwhelm him."

"That's silly," Pyke said. "He's not going to get used to you unless you're here with him."

She blinked and tilted her head.

Pyke said, "I can sleep on the couch, if you want. I'll move Gill's crib out here."

"Okay, that would be . . . Thanks for understanding."

He tried to pretend it didn't matter. "Do you want something to eat?" He went to open the kitchen pantry. There wasn't much there—some hard-crusted bread, a few apples, and some granola that Jeeri had made.

"No, thank you," she said. "They gave me a meal at the chalet."

He sighed and returned to the living room. Kehda had draped her winter jacket on a hanger next to the entrance, and now she was opening her pack. She removed a large bundle wrapped in cloth, and placed it on the coffee table. "You're going to like this," she said.

He waited patiently as she unwound the cloth strips. Each piece had beaded patterns sewn into it, depicting forests, or rivers, or sun-baked deserts. Once the final strips were removed, a pudgy statue of a bear made of red, translucent glass was revealed. It was more a caricature than a true likeness, but it was still artfully crafted. Pyke kneeled next to it and inspected the workmanship. It was perfectly smooth, the lines coming together at faultless seams.

Kehda had a fondness for bears. Her tribe in the Sierras had told her it was her shadow-animal, so she was always wearing bear jewelry of some kind.

"This is heavy," Pyke said, weighing the bear in his hands. "You brought it all this way?"

"Isn't it beautiful?"

"But why?"

"It's an offering. I'd like to try again with the host. I'm happy to admit this one's from Navajo, though. I'm not going to try to pull one over on you." She smiled mischievously.

Her attempt at humor didn't mollify him. He stared at the bear, as if it might explain what Kehda was thinking. It didn't.

Kehda said, "I have a proposal to discuss with the host. Please understand, this is the only way I could get leave to come here." She cradled her hands together, a look of pleading in her eyes.

Had she wanted to see Gill at all? And what about him? This could be just a business transaction to Kehda—another way to serve Essentialist interests.

The frustration and anger he'd experienced earlier in the day was returning. This moment—something he'd looked forward to for months—wasn't going at all how he'd hoped. Kehda hadn't asked why he was so tired, or really anything about his life in the last year. It made him wonder what he was doing here. What point was there in spending time with Kehda?

The people of Aspen were depending on him, and time was running out.

"I'll see what I can do," he said. "I need to go to bed."

"Thanks, Pyke," she said, smiling. "I really appreciate it." She didn't seem to sense any of his concern. She repackaged the bear carefully and took her bag to the bedroom, while Pyke moved out Gill's crib and found some sheets and a pillow for the couch.

33

LASLE

"Technically, this is the first city in the Colorado Collective," Bareth said, as he and Lexie looked down across the valley from the protection of an enclave of trees. Lexie couldn't see much of anything except what looked like a blur of discrete levels carved into the hills. The scope Bareth passed around cleared things up; the town of Lasle was essentially a long line of blocky houses leading up to a mountain pass, like a disjointed staircase climbing up the valley. Flocks of sheep dotted the sloped grassland near the base of the town.

"What does that mean for us, exactly?" Ryder asked.

"The Collective isn't a sovereign nation," Bareth responded, "more a loose assortment of city-states. Each town has its own governance system, but together they adhere to trading relationships and a non-aggression pact. They also have an alert system. If any one of them is attacked, they have to send a runner to the next town to give warning."

"What if we're just walking through?"

"We're not. Ghent wants us to take the village. We need to neutralize it, not only to prevent them delivering a warning, but also to prevent them from recruiting other towns and attacking our rear.

These towns depend on Aspen, which offers amenities while asking for little in return, so Lasle will be loyal to Aspen."

Tarnation, Vaela, Ryder, and Lexie all shared a *who's going to tell him* look.

Vaela volunteered. "As we have explained before, Aspen will have already been alerted to your forces approaching. If they have attack drones, they most assuredly have surveillance drones."

Bareth weighed her words. He was at least willing to listen, whereas Ghent would have shut out their protests without much consideration. "Even if you're right," he said, "Lasle could still attack us, or recruit from other villages."

"Why don't we go around it?" Ryder asked.

"There's not really a better way, geographically speaking. And they'll see us eventually. We're too many."

Tarnation's mouth formed into a crescent shape as he guffawed. "That's ridiculous, man," he said.

Bareth raised his voice. "No, it's not. And we expect you to honor your pledge." He walked back toward the road that led to the village. His men peeled out from the nearby forest to follow.

"Does he know we never made any pledge?" Lexie asked.

"I don't think we have a choice," Ryder said, his eyes scanning their reactions.

"Hey bud, I don't do this kind of thing anymore," Tarnation said. "Did enough of these strong-arm political toss-ups in the fiefdoms."

"Think of the bigger picture, Tarnation. If we don't get through this, we may not be able to help Warrick, or learn about the origin of the drone. Our mission is more important than one village."

"Heard that before," Tarnation said with a sniff.

They were falling behind Bareth's squad. Lexie remembered what Tarnation had said the night before, how Ghent was looking for any excuse to kill them. "Why don't we at least see how it goes?" she said. "Maybe it'll be civil."

Tarnation cast her a look heavy with skepticism.

"Let's go," she said, and she started walking.

Thankfully, Tarnation followed, as did Ryder and Vaela. Lexie had no idea what they would do when they arrived in town, but staying put wasn't an option.

———————————◆———————————

As they approached Lasle, Bareth's squad maneuvered to the front of the army. It was surely a deliberate request on Ghent's part, to test their mettle.

There were no walls around the city, or visible defenses of any kind. Nor were there signs of movement, or sounds other than bleating sheep, though smoke churned from a couple chimneys on the gray brick houses. If people were gone, they hadn't been gone long.

The four of them had been given crossbows and daggers, which Vaela probably would have laughed at if she ever laughed, since even guns were pretty barbaric to her Gungivite disposition. It wasn't that Ouray didn't have many guns, it was more that Ghent thought the guns were too lethal for foreigners like Lexie. Instead, he'd given each of them some semblance of a weapon that wasn't deadly enough to permit them to execute an effective escape.

Bareth's men busted down a few doors, coming out empty-handed, while the rest of the squad walked up the increasing gradient of the street.

The first action came about five blocks in. Somewhere along the lane an exterior door slammed; two women ran out of house into the meadow.

"After them!" Bareth roared, and the three men closest to him ran down the lane.

"Sir!" Bareth's lead scout pointed in the other direction, where a figure was running away from them across the meadow, another door closing behind him. Even a hundred yards removed, Lexie could tell he was no more than a boy.

"Go!" Bareth yelled. This time his command was clearly directed at Lexie's wayward group, as they were closest.

They needed to at least look like they were following orders, so Lexie ran toward the fleeing boy. Vaela joined her, as did Ryder, but they weren't fast runners, any of them. Tarnation bounded by, passing them with ease. It amazed Lexie that his hulking frame could build so much momentum.

The boy was tacking in the field, making frenetic attempts to lose them. If Tarnation hadn't been there, he might have gotten away. Just as the boy had almost climbed over a fence, Tarnation snagged the boy with both hands, hoisted him over his head, and threw him back onto the grass.

The boy writhed around, the wind knocked out of him, as Lexie, Ryder and Vaela caught up.

Tarnation lifted the still-struggling boy over his shoulder and hiked back toward Bareth, who'd stopped at the top of the field next to a large mound of earth. The mound was a good thirty feet in diameter, and five feet high, composed mostly of topsoil along with some rocks. It had definitely been turned recently, since nothing was growing out of it, and the rest of the area was quite fertile. Two of Bareth's men were circling it.

Bareth's crossbow was aimed and ready, tracking Tarnation as he returned with the boy.

"Put it away, man," Tarnation said in disgust. "It's a little kid."

When Tarnation plopped the boy down in front of Bareth, Lexie saw that he was no more than ten. A shock of mangy hair hung over his eyes, and his clothes were woolen and loose-fitting, too short in the legs, but tied tight around his waist. He didn't look up.

Bareth kneeled and spoke in a steely whisper. "Where have the townspeople gone?"

The boy met Bareth's eyes. He looked around at the rest of them. He didn't answer.

"Where?" Bareth persisted.

"We heard you were coming, so most people went toward Aspen. We . . . Some of us didn't believe it. We wanted to stay."

"What's this mound for? It looks like a new excavation."

The child winced and shook his head.

"Hold the child," Bareth said, and he jogged away toward the main column of Ouray soldiers.

Tarnation and Vaela circled the mound while Ryder and Lexie watched the boy.

"What's your name, kid?" Lexie asked the boy.

"Xander."

"Where's your mom and dad?"

He flinched. His eyes fell to the mound.

Bareth was walking back, along with Ghent and twenty other Ouray soldiers. They escorted an assortment of Lasle citizens: a limping elderly man, three women who were maybe late middle age, and two girls, no more than six or seven.

"What's in the mound?" Ghent asked the boy.

"We've tried that," Lexie said.

Ghent glared at her, and motioned to two of his men who had spades in their hands. They began digging into the mound. "This will go a lot faster if you tell us," he said.

The boy shook his head timidly.

"Any of you?" Ghent asked the other townspeople. Most looked down.

"Fuck off," the elderly man said.

Ghent sighed. "Kill him," he said, pointing at the old man.

One of his soldiers readied a rifle.

"Wait," Ghent said. "I want her to do it." He was pointing at Lexie.

Now, it should be said that Lexie wasn't averse to killing, for the most part. Lots of people deserved to die, and she was happy to help those people on their way. The thing was, she wasn't quite sure this old man met her criteria.

Lexie made a show of readying her crossbow "Because he's old, or what?"

"He's defying us, and he's lame so won't be able to march." Ghent was clearly annoyed at her impertinent question. "We can't leave him here—he might alert other towns."

"This town had already been alerted," Ryder said. "I'm sure other

Collective towns have as well. Why kill a man for knowing something everybody already knows?"

Ghent said, "We don't know other towns have been alerted."

"Speaking of what people know and don't know," Lexie added, "are we really sure we've figured what happened in *this* town? What's this mound for, for example? Maybe the old man has information."

"Fuck off," the old man said, and Lexie rolled her eyes. Apparently, he wasn't keen on living much longer.

Ghent laughed. "You want to hold on a direct order on account of an unexplained mound of dirt? It could be anything—topsoil for a new farm plot, or the result of some basement dig out."

"It could be a grave," Ryder ventured.

"Yes, it could be a grave," Ghent acknowledged. "Maybe Lasle raided an Ouray village and killed the inhabitants before we arrived. Maybe Lasle killed off Ouray sympathizers. This is what happened with Wendall. If you showed disloyalty, you would find yourself in a kiln before sundown." He was pacing, the way he did at the campfire when he was launching into an oratory about the old wars. Again, his body was stiff and bent forward, his hands held together behind his back. "I take no pleasure in this killing," he continued, now raising his finger in the air, "but we have entered a season of war. Better to be numb to the horrors than fuel for the kiln.

"I hate to do it, and yet that is what must happen here. You all"— he pointed to Lexie, Vaela, Ryder and Tarnation in turn—"reveal your disloyalty by refusing a direct order from your commanding officer. If you do not kill him, you are mutinous and will be shot right here along with him. Then we can confirm the presence of a mass grave, because you'll be in it."

Lexie tried to make sense of his perverse logic. It was a win-win situation for Ghent. If Lexie agreed and killed the old man, it would show to the other soldiers the strength of Ghent's command. Otherwise, if she disagreed and Ghent had the four of them killed, it would have the same effect—plus he would rid himself of the troublesome foreigners.

"I'll give you to the count of five," Ghent said. "One, two, three, four, five."

The count lapsed, but Lexie still couldn't do it.

"Bareth?" Ghent said.

Bareth leveled his crossbow at the old man and shot him in the chest. The man buckled and fell, clutching his chest, sprawling on the ground where he went limp. His eyes rolled upward.

One woman gasped. Most of the townsfolk settled for grim looks. They averted their eyes.

Bareth chortled and spat phlegm on the ground.

Lexie's hopes that Bareth could be an ally were fading rapidly. Either he was in Ghent's pocket, or he didn't have much of a moral compass.

"Now for the mutineers," Ghent said. "You have shown your disloyalty. Ouray, these four are our enemy. Fire on my mark."

At least a dozen crossbows and rifles were leveled at the four of them. Lexie was the only one of the group who had readied her own, but she dropped it and raised her hands. Tarnation had joined the other two soldiers digging into the mound, unconcerned with the weapons pointed his way.

"Wait, please. Don't do anything rash," Ryder said, his hands high in the air to illustrate his unthreatening position. "If you shoot us, and Rexana finds out we were innocent, think of the consequences. You may be inviting even more conflict into your borders."

Ghent's frown remained. His hand and finger were up. Presumably, when it dropped, it was the signal to fire.

"Your mother was innocent," Ryder continued, addressing Ghent, "and yet she was paraded across town to the kiln. How is that different from what you are doing to us? You haven't proven we are in any way guilty, yet you are having us killed on a whim. You refuse to listen to our story, just as Wendall refused to listen to your mother's."

Even though Ryder was right, Lexie wasn't sure this was the best tactic. Ghent's face had taken on more color. "How convenient, though," he said, "that there is no way to prove your story."

"What if there is a way to prove it?" Ryder asked.

"There is no way."

"There is, if you let us confer with our colleagues. We can prove we have nothing to do with this. More importantly, we may be able to help you. We just have to reach a higher altitude, out of retcher range, to connect."

"To do that, I have to trust that this isn't some kind of escape attempt, or that your communication won't give a signal to attack us. What reason do I have to trust you? You arrived in town, and then people are murdered, just like with Wendall. Since you first stepped into Provo, war has begun, and there is nothing to lead me to believe that anything about you is genuine."

This war with Wendall must have been something else, because the hate Ghent had pummeled into his skull was hard to dislodge.

"Right here, bud," Tarnation said. He was clearing what looked like a foot and a leg from the mound, with the help of another soldier.

Ghent's brow furrowed in confusion. Tarnation cleared more dirt and heaved the leg out, which was attached to a body.

"So it is a grave." Ghent shrugged. "All the more reason to suspect these people are guilty of war crimes and thus should be considered enemies. I won't be surprised to see the mark of the kiln on this man's shirt."

The crossbows and rifles remained raised, as did Ghent's hand, but he was watching the digging with more interest, as was everyone else.

Tarnation and the soldier eventually heaved the corpse out of the mound. The Ouray boy began crying softly, his head in his hands. The corpse was covered in dirt, but even with the coating of mud Lexie could tell the man wasn't wearing any sign of Ouray loyalties, because he was naked. Tarnation poured water from his canteen on the dead man's leg and rubbed the dirt away. Then he pulled the corpse away from the mound for them all to see.

There were gashes in the chest, but it was such a mess of dirt and blood that it was hard to say what had caused it. What was made clear were the marks on the legs; unmistakably Laramie branding.

"Like I was saying," Tarnation said, "this is a mass grave, yeah, but same as you've got now in Provo. They were attacked by the seeker drones, just like you. Just like me."

Ghent's eyes were ablaze.

"Is this true?" Bareth asked the remaining Lasle citizens.

One of the women pointed at the sky. "They came, the floaters, and just killed them all—anyone with a tattoo or burn mark. Xander's mom was from Laramie—a refugee. That's why she's . . . Please don't dig them up. Leave them in peace." She covered her face with her hands.

"This example disproves your narrative fallacy," Vaela said, addressing Ghent, "because it shows that the attack on Provo was not directed solely at Ouray, nor was it in any way connected to our scouting of the city. I suspect you will see this in every village in the vicinity. Your purported rationale for our conscription is—"

"Shut up!" Ghent roared.

Vaela was right. Or at least, it definitely made it more plausible that the Ouray attack was connected to this Lasle attack, and both were directed to branded or tattooed individuals, and thus was less likely to have anything to do with Lexie's friends being in Ouray at the time. Ghent's raised hand lowered enough to rub his head. He walked away from the group to look up the incline toward the mountain pass. Everyone stared at his back. The crossbows and rifles remained raised.

After a minute spent gazing at the topography, he kicked at a tuft of grass and walked back to them, the tension in his face defying any attempt at composure.

"We will send scouts on horseback to verify that there were also drone attacks in Norvellis and Edessa. And you two," he added, pointing at Vaela and Lexie, "will go up the nearest mountain. You will make contact with your people and bring back incontrovertible evidence that you are not responsible for the attack in Provo. If you show *any* sign of disloyalty—a slight misstep, an errant breath, or a defiant eyelash—Bareth will cast you off the mountain, and your two colleagues will be rendered to ash."

34

UPROOTED FLOWERS

Pyke had Gill over his shoulder. He was patting his back while bouncing ever so slightly. Gill's tiny burps registered like an extra heartbeat. Outside, the light of the morning sun was rolling over the mountains, illuminating brilliant swaths of green where the spring growth had become robust.

There was a knock on the door to his apartment.

Pyke placed Gill in his crib and went to answer it, but not before looking through the peephole. Crowley was standing there, scratching his neck. The sight of him unnerved Pyke—an understandable reflex after being beaten up a few days ago. But Crowley had a meek expression on his face. The headless that had been parked outside of Pyke's apartment was standing directly behind him. After what had happened to Mank, Crowley was probably more nervous than Pyke.

Pyke wondered if the visit had something to do with Kehda. She was off doing her calisthenics; she would run sprints, jump up on tree rounds, do pull ups, and fight with imaginary opponents in the forest. She said it was a martial art, but it reminded him more of a form of aggressive dance. She was usually gone for at least an hour, which was for the best. He didn't want to needlessly entangle her in his endless problems with the crew.

Pyke opened the door. "What is it?" he asked.

"Yeah, hey, Pyke. I've got a message from the host. He wants to chat with you at the Wisdome."

"What's the point?"

Crowley smiled and raised his hands in a calming gesture. "Sorry about the other day. You know how this goes. We're all just doing our jobs—what everyone thinks is best for Aspen. Mengle, he's changed his tune. He said he wants to partner with you. He wants to better understand your concerns—to help you—because that's what the network would want."

Crowley's expression was acerbic, as if there was a bad taste in his mouth. Ironically, that made Pyke think he could be telling the truth.

If they wanted to beat him up again, there would have been more rangers. And the headless was shadowing Crowley closely.

"I'll go," Pyke said, "but first let me get Natty to watch Gill."

⁕

They walked in silence most of the way, the headless close on their heels.

When the Wisdome was visible, Pyke said, "You're not going to tell me what this is about?"

"The host wants to talk."

"That's not helpful."

"Hey, I just do what I'm told. You should too. Makes life easy."

"It depends what you're told to do, doesn't it?"

"You've got problems. Your head—it's all jammed up with those books, makes you think you're smarter than us. Books didn't stop Dwayne from dying, though, did they?"

Crowley wouldn't be that bad if he wasn't so political. He was passionate about being loyal to the crew and his fellow rangers. That was why he had no love for Pyke—because most rangers blamed Pyke for Dwayne's death.

"That was an accident," Pyke said. "It has nothing to do with how well-read I am. You're assigning a causal relationship to a random event."

"Gibberish. I don't need books to do the math. Dwayne dies, you steal his girlfriend. Three minus one equals two."

Pyke gritted his teeth. There was no point in responding.

Crowley wasn't finished. "And now I hear she's back. Must be nice. Did you know Dwayne used to boink her in the Wisdome? He said she loved sneaking around—it made her horny."

It could have been true. Dwayne and Kehda were both thrill seekers in their own ways. However, like Crowley, Dwayne was uncompromisingly loyal to the crew, and fraternizing with Kehda in the Wisdome could have gotten him reprimanded. Kehda might have egged him on. She was always curious about the Wisdome.

Pyke shrugged it off. The comment might have bothered him, if he'd been a jealous person.

Crowley frowned at his lack of reaction.

The area in front of the Wisdome had changed. Not more than a few days ago there had been a broad walkway of paving stones, flanked by spans of grass and flower beds. Now the paving stones had been removed, and the flower beds uprooted and planted farther out. What remained was a messy undulating surface of mud and hardened earth, with only a few patches of unmolested grass.

Mengle stood at the edge of the roughshod earth. He was wearing a button-down vest over a puffy white shirt. His smile was tempered, but formal, more like a waiter at the Aspen Gourmet than an enthusiastic game show host. Shane was standing next to him, clad in a shiny floral dress, two-inch heels, and cherry-red lipstick. His blonde wig flowed in a silky wave to his shoulders. Two rangers lurked next to the entrance. Judging by their awkward angular posture as they leaned against the wall, they seemed to be trying to look relaxed when they clearly weren't.

Didn't they know the act was unnecessary? It was just Pyke.

Maybe it was programmed into their psyches that showmanship was the only option.

"Wait a minute," Crowley said. He stopped a good fifty yards away.

The host was speaking with Shane, who entered the Wisdome, then returned to speak with the host again.

"What are we waiting for?" Pyke asked.

"The host to finish his business."

Other people in Aspen might be fooled by this display. They were making him wait on purpose—a kind of passive-aggressive negotiation tactic to make him feel unimportant.

A few minutes later, a ranger jogged out from the Wisdome and whispered in Shane's ear. Shane passed the information to Mengle, who waved to Crowley.

As Crowley and Pyke covered the remaining distance, Shane backed away to stand next to the wall, leaving Mengle alone at the periphery.

"Pyke, thank you for coming," Mengle said, his eyes darting to glance at the headless that remained a few feet behind Pyke.

Pyke allowed himself to be led down a path alongside the flower bed, the headless matching his steps as if they were tethered together. Crowley took a circuitous route to head back toward the ranger station.

"I heard troubling news," Mengle said, "that some of the rangers went after you, and hurt you. Is this true?"

"They roughed me up a little. It's fine."

"No, it's not *fine*." Mengle's head cocked back in exaggerated alarm. "There will be a punishment for this transgression, I assure you. They acted on their own, without my blessing. I am so, so sorry this happened, Pyke. So sorry."

"Thanks for saying that. I'll be okay."

"And please, forgive the rough earth." Mengle gestured at the dirty path, which was curving toward the Wisdome. "We're having some work done to upgrade the premises." He glanced back at the headless again.

"Why am I here?" Pyke asked. A week ago, he would never have spoken to the host so bluntly. Mengle had been the man he had most feared and revered, but now the host was standing in the way of Pyke addressing much greater concerns. Pyke wanted to be done with the meeting so he could devote his full effort to answering the network's question.

Mengle laughed. Pyke couldn't fathom what might be humorous about the situation. "I will get to that," Mengle said. "Indeed I will . . . soon."

They kept walking.

"How soon? I'm sorry, but I need to get back."

"Not long now . . . Soon."

Mengle rarely lost his train of thought, and he always had something to say, so Pyke should have known something was amiss. He doubted he would have reacted in time anyway.

"Now!" Mengle yelled. One of the rangers pulled a lever on the Wisdome wall that he'd been obscuring behind his back. At the same time, Mengle grabbed Pyke and pulled him forward, while the dirt behind them fell away through a trap door, taking the headless down with it.

Pyke struggled against Mengle and peered over the edge of the hole. It was a pit at least ten feet deep, with smooth sides—impossible to climb. The headless got to its feet and tried to clamber out regardless, scraping its fists against the wall feverishly. The action made a loud screeching sound, making Pyke wince.

Pyke was pulled forcefully from behind by two rangers, who ushered Pyke toward the Wisdome entrance. He was too shocked to protest, still trying to understand what was happening.

"Let's go!" Mengle yelled, running ahead of Pyke and his escort. "Lock it down!"

Once inside the main door, Shane locked and barred it. "Man the guns!" he yelled, and four other rangers inside went to unlock the doors that led to the gun placement antechambers.

"You're not . . ." Pyke stammered. "What are you doing? This isn't a good idea."

Mengle wasn't listening, and neither were the rangers. Mengle jogged ahead as Pyke was pushed up the stairs toward the office suites.

Pyke had only been in the Wisdome control room once before. School children were sometimes taken in to see the fancy viewscreens and computer terminals. Dwayne had said that in reality the room wasn't used for much, other than Shane and Mengle arranging logistics related to *A Leap of Wisdom*, which primarily consisted of sending out invitations. Most of the time the terminals weren't in use, the displays showing idyllic mountain setting screensavers.

The main viewscreen was blank, and the monitors were not only shut off but also pushed to the side. One of them was cracked down the middle. Exposed wiring was strung about, their plugs pulled out from the floor.

At the far end of the control room was a foot-high pane of thick glass that spanned the wall—one of the few windows in the Wisdome. It allowed visibility of the front entrance. The host looked out, scratching his head nervously.

Pyke could see that the headless in the pit was still trapped, its hands barely visible but still scraping against the wall. Another headless was running down the hill toward the Wisdome.

"There! There—get it!" the host yelled, though Pyke was unsure who he was talking to.

The guns came to life and strafed the area around the running headless. One of the bullets hit its mark and knocked the headless onto the ground. The stationary target allowed time for both guns to focus. Fragments of its body came away gradually under the concentrated firepower, chipping into the dirt and kicking up dust, until one of its legs blew off and vaulted into the air. The guns continued pummeling the cloud of dust until it was just a heap of debris, with no discernable limbs or torso at all.

Mengle was smiling and nodding, relishing the outcome.

"Why are you doing this?" Pyke asked.

Mengle turned to give him his full attention. "I'm doing this for you, Pyke, and for all of Aspen. Over the years the network has advanced its purposes without us—taken more, and kept us in the dark like ignorant children, asking us to perform tasks for which we don't know the purpose. And yet we are the ones that give the network agency. We provide the supplies to keep its factories operating. What do we get in return? Maybe a few creature comforts that I would gladly give up if we could have a say in our future."

"What about our deal with the network? Isn't this against Glen Pearson's wishes?"

"Glen partnered with the network when it was a mutually beneficial arrangement. That's no longer the case. Now it wants servitude. Glen would want us to fight for our right to control our own destiny. He would want us to level the playing field."

"I'm not sure you know what you're dealing with. I've seen all the headless, all the drones. There's hundreds. The network will stop you. It could kill all of us."

Mengle shook his head. "Nonsense. The network is just a bully, but it's rational. It will see that it needs us. There will be some negotiated settlement and we will all move on."

"What if it doesn't need us?"

The host produced a frown of disbelief. It made Pyke think Mengle hadn't really given credence to the possibility. Mengle's biggest blind spot was in not understanding the network's true potential. That, and he didn't realize the network could care less about humans. Or at least, whether it cared or not depended on the outcome of Pyke's pressing question.

Pyke could see there was a sense of justice behind Mengle's coup, but he also knew the host too well to believe his intentions were noble. The real root of this was his waning influence. Recent events at *A Leap of Wisdom* and Pyke's journey to the mountain summit had made Mengle seem an unwitting pawn, rather than a man in a position of great responsibility who should be respected and admired. Here he was, desperately striving to retrieve what he'd lost. This coup was the host's vanity speaking, twisting reason to make it work.

Mengle didn't realize how lethal his vanity could become, for all of them.

"So, I'm . . . your hostage?"

"No, no, nothing like that. Although I do know the network has a kind of perverse fascination with you, insisting on your participation in the show, sending you up to the summit, and then asking me to *do your bidding*." He rolled his eyes. "Yes, you're important, but not as a hostage—as a negotiator."

"I'm sorry, but I have to answer an important question for the network. If I don't, none of this will matter."

The host waved the comment away. "Don't worry about that. It's just another example of the network playing games with us, using us like puppets for its own entertainment."

Pyke tilted his head side to side, trying to look like he was considering it, despite how firmly he disagreed. "I'm sorry, but I don't see why I would want to be your negotiator. It sounds dangerous, and I'm not sure the ploy will work."

"You would do it for the good of Aspen, of course. But I've found that not everyone can be trusted in that regard, so I'll give you another reason." Mengle nodded at one of the rangers, who went around the corner, toward the other offices.

While they were waiting, the host scanned the area outside the Wisdome. There was no sign of any headless, nor any drones in the sky, but that didn't give Pyke any sense of security. The network was probably organizing all its resources for a full blitz. Or maybe it would simply wait them out and let them starve. Either way, Pyke had no doubt that Mengle would be on the losing end of this confrontation.

He heard commotion from around the corner.

"Not so rough." It was a woman's voice. It sounded like Jeeri.

Pyke's annoyance with the situation morphed into anger. They had no business having Jeeri wrapped up in this.

The host was watching his expression, his countenance smug and aloof.

"How dare you . . ." But Pyke trailed off when the ranger came around the corner with Jeeri in tow.

"Dah!" Gill was sitting in Jeeri's arms. His eyes lit up when he saw Pyke. He reached out toward Pyke, but the ranger held Jeeri and Gill back.

"Dah!" Gill said again, this time with some alarm at not being able to reach Pyke.

"I'm sorry, Pyke," Jeeri said. He could tell by her red-rimmed eyes that she'd been crying. In fact, her face was a mask of anguish. "They made me take him." She resorted to bouncing Gill, trying to keep him calm. "Shh, you'll see Daddy soon." She took Gill to the other side of the control center and tried to distract him by standing him next to an unused monitor on the floor.

Pyke couldn't stop his fists from clenching at his sides. He wanted to bowl through the ranger, grab Gill, and run out of the room, but he knew the rangers would stop him. One was standing nearby at the ready, bola in his hand. If Pyke tried to grab Gill, it would only get one of them hurt.

Mengle was smiling. "It's insurance, since you haven't exactly been collaborative. We'll see that no harm comes to him, as long as no harm comes to us."

Pyke couldn't maintain his composure any longer. "Don't you see, you idiot! You're sealing your fate—all our fates! This ill-conceived coup just proves that the people of Aspen are all unreliable, and therefore expendable. Stand down or this will end badly for everyone."

Mengle furrowed his brow, confused by Pyke's outburst. He glanced at Shane. "Testy, isn't he?"

Shane smiled knowingly. His expression was reminiscent of when Vin had answered a question correctly on *A Leap of Wisdom*.

Mengle shrugged and opened his palms. He said, "What's it going to be?"

Gill was still playing with one of the monitors, rocking it back and forth on the ground, while Jeeri was trying to block his line of sight from Pyke. Outside the Wisdome the pulverized pile of headless smoldered. Townspeople were gathering beyond the perimeter; a couple of teenage boys, an old lady, a mail-delivery woman Pyke had seen around often. They were staying at a distance, but they could still become collateral damage.

More people would come to investigate.

Maybe that was what the network was waiting for. It would be easier to exterminate everyone if they all were in the same place.

Mengle's ploy was naïve and pointless. The longer Mengle and the crew were held up without some kind of dialogue with the network, the greater the chance they would all be vaporized. Pyke needed put a stop to it as soon as possible.

"I'll do it," he said. "Let me go speak to the network. I'll hike up the mountain to find the nearest headless. I can communicate with it, tell the network what you want, and arrange some kind of meeting."

Mengle raised his eyebrows at Shane, who nodded his approval.

"I'm so glad," the host said. "You see? That wasn't so bad."

A knocking sound reverberated through the walls, prompting Shane and Mengle to glance frenetically at the window, but nothing was going on near the Wisdome entrance, other than more people arriving at the perimeter.

"Trent," Mengle said, "go and find out what that was."

Ranger Trent bounded out of the room, bola in hand. There were two other rangers present, both of whom were gripping rifles beneath white knuckles. Pyke had seen them around town only recently. These rangers were new to the job, and therefore impressionable and loyal to Mengle. Pyke doubted they knew much about how to use the rifles, since rangers typically only carried bolas.

Gill remained oblivious, sitting on the floor and drop-testing a pointer device Jeeri had given him.

More knocking sounds, louder now. Not knocking—*shooting*, Pyke guessed. The two guards looked around the corner to the door of the control room.

"Maybe we should lock the door?" one said.

"Lock ourselves in?" Mengle snapped. "Go take care of it!"

As the two rangers jogged to the door, Shane, Mengle, and Pyke all peered around the corner. They were partially crouched, ready to duck behind the wall for protection. If a headless had made it inside the facility, it would be difficult to stop—one of the many flaws in the host's ill-conceived power play.

At the very second when the first ranger reached for the door-knob, the door was flung open, knocking his hand back. A figure in black stood before him, rifle in hand. It was a woman, and her face was covered so that only her eyes were visible. She would be hard for most people to identify, except Pyke had seen that very outfit before a few hours ago, and knew her athletic figure.

Kehda.

She fired at one ranger, somersaulted several feet across the room and fired at the other. The first dropped like a rag doll, but the second was only grazed. He returned fire, and his bullet ricocheted off the wall behind Kehda.

Pyke broke from Mengle's side and ran to the back of the room, knocking over a monitor in the process. Jeeri cowered away as he grabbed Gill. He made sure to shield him from any bullets. Two more shots rang out behind him, followed by moans. Gill was screaming, so Pyke couldn't make out what had happened.

Pyke ducked behind a table and looked back. Kehda was grappling with a ranger. He was on top of her on the floor, their hands locked and legs intertwined. The ranger was slowly overcoming her, forcing her hands down against the tiles. Kehda bent her neck up and bit his cheek. The ranger screamed in pain and relinquished his hold. This allowed Kehda to twist his body onto the floor using her intertwined leg.

One of the ranger's hands had reflexively gone up to cover his bleeding cheek, but Kehda hadn't even paused. Her movements were fluid and controlled, as if rehearsed. Her hands shifted to grip either side of the ranger's head. She twisted violently until his neck snapped.

"Stop right there, or you're dead," Mengle said. He had collected a rifle, as had Shane, and both were now pointed in Kehda's direction.

She was a good thirty feet from them. If she charged, she would be taken down for sure. She must have performed this same calculation, because she raised her hands slowly.

"Who are you?" Mengle asked. "How did you get in here?"

Kehda's eyes shifted to Pyke, then back to Mengle. In fact, Mengle had met her, many years ago, before Gill was born. He must not recognize her, especially with most of her face cloaked.

Pyke was reeling, trying to process the tenuous situation that had become even more harrowing with Kehda's appearance. On the one hand he flushed with pride because Kehda had come after Gill. It showed that she really did care. On the other hand he found her tenacity disturbing. Kehda was an effective soldier, but this was something more—a capacity for violence he'd never seen before.

He wondered how he could have been in love with this killing machine.

And it wasn't over. How would this situation not end in tragedy for her? For him? For all of them?

He could only think of one option.

Most people in Aspen figured Pyke for a coward. It was true that he abhorred violence, and he avoided conflict, but that was because he didn't want anyone to get hurt. He had always told himself that when the time came, if it was for the greater good, he would do what he had to do. This was such a time.

Gently, he placed Gill in Jeeri's hands. Gill was still crying, and he tried to hold on to Pyke desperately, so Pyke had to forcibly remove his tiny fingers from Pyke's tunic. Then Pyke walked over to one of the downed rangers and picked up a rifle.

Kehda, Mengle, and Shane had frozen, watching him. "What are you doing?" Mengle asked nervously. Mengle was shifting his rifle between Kehda and Pyke.

Pyke kept his own rifle pointed at the floor. With one hand held up, he approached Mengle and Shane. Then he lifted the weapon to point toward Kehda. The host visibly relaxed and focused his rifle solely on Kehda.

If Mengle had remembered Kehda, Pyke couldn't have pulled this off, but the host didn't care about delegates. There were so many, from towns far and wide, and how he treated them didn't affect his standing in Aspen. He saw them as annoying boxes to check so he could maintain his position.

A position that had become too dangerous for him to maintain.

Abruptly, Pyke turned the barrel of the rifle toward Mengle and shot him in the chest. Mengle fell back, landing at Shane's feet, causing Shane to fumble with his gun as he staggered back.

Pyke had hit the host squarely. A surge of red flooded onto the white sleeves beyond his vest. Mengle held the injured area, his eyes wide with alarm. Then the light in his eyes faded, and he went limp on the floor.

"Wait, Shane," Pyke said, training his rifle on him. Before Shane could lift his weapon, Kehda had tackled him, a blade flashing in her hand.

"Don't kill him!" Pyke said, just as she was about to arc the blade across his neck. Shane was defenseless, his rifle knocked away, with Kehda straddling him.

Kehda kept the blade at Shane's neck. "Why not?" she asked, wrinkles showing on the exposed part of her forehead.

It was a gut feeling, which Pyke now had to find a way to articulate. "It's just . . . it's not the right time for a major upheaval in Aspen. We need continuity; someone who knows how to manage the crew, that the people of Aspen are familiar with, someone who won't risk getting us all killed. Isn't that right, Shane?"

Shane's eyes darted back and forth. It was a simple calculation. He'd always wanted to be the next host. And Kehda's knife at his neck offered no real alternative.

"Yes, of course," Shane said. "Mengle's plan was flawed. I see that now."

"How do we know he won't turn on us?" Kehda asked.

"I don't," Pyke replied, "but he must have learned a good lesson from this experience. And they've lost a lot of rangers, so it would be harder to pull off. If that's not enough, I can ask the network to post more headless around town."

After Kehda stewed on it, she withdrew the knife from Shane's throat.

———◆———

Later that day, Shane stood on the amphitheater stage to make an announcement to the gathering townsfolk. He went on about how Mengle had 'lost his way' and the crew had to 'retire him'. A headless watched in the distance, standing in the middle of one of the streets that sloped up the mountain.

Weeks ago, no one would have paid attention to the headless, but now that was where the townspeople looked as Shane spoke; away from the speaker, toward the listless statue on the rise that was judging their every action.

Pyke made sure to approach the headless immediately after the speech. He explained in detail what had happened, that the host was a single deluded man, and not reflective of the greater populace. He pleaded with the network for forgiveness.

He couldn't be sure how much of his monologue the headless understood, because it didn't move at all. When Pyke was finished, the headless applied its stubby fingers to the dirt in front of him, all working concurrently to write something, then turned and walked away.

The message read, *Bring your answer to the summit tomorrow.*

35

HALF AN INCH

Lexie had been involved in her fair share of hairy meetings. When she had been managing the Anacortes Sea Gate, the half-drunk skunks in Three Rivers would put on a show, acting out stories of impoverished merchants and evil Essentialist frigates stealing their wares. They would use the whole council chamber, running about daintily, fawning, gesturing, and even weeping, in some grand theater. All just to try to get Lexie to lower the already-meager tariffs.

In Lexie's pirating days, when she was on Warrick's ship, the crew would, without fail, spend a good half hour throwing out a half dozen stupid ideas about how to sneak past a pesky scout, until Warrick would suggest something much more reasonable and they would all nod, but not before they asked for agreement from Baba the Mute, as if he could talk.

This meeting was hairy in a different way—more in a nutjob kind of way.

First, they had to get there.

Bareth had charted a climbing path up one of the steepest mountains in the vicinity, his reasoning being that the group would get to the top faster. There were only six of them on the excursion: Bareth and three of his officers, along with Vaela and Lexie. Lexie guessed Ghent chose Vaela and Lexie for the trip as the less physically imposing members of their group, meaning they couldn't overcome Bareth and his men and get away. Lexie was no feminist, but she was offended by the implication. She could take Ryder in a scrap any day, especially with her boot knife.

But yeah, not Tarnation.

She spent half the day bouncing around the sheer face of the mountain in the harness Bareth had given her, trying to find footholds and handholds. More than a few times she had to wait until Bareth's men pulled her up to a place where she could actually hold on. Vaela struggled at first, but annoyingly, she soon got the hang of it. Lexie was always the one Bareth or his cronies had to bail out.

Bareth was a mountain goat. *Climbing* may have been the word she used to describe what he was doing, but really it was more like scrambling, it all happened so fast. He would race up a thirty-foot sheer face, and afterward she would be hard pressed to figure out which path he'd taken.

"What's the deal, Bareth?" she said during one of their few rest stops. "You got suction cups for hands or something?"

"Did you see the race towers in Provo?"

"Those big walls with ivy and flowers on them where people practice climbing?"

"Yes, but it's more than practice. For some of us, it's a way of life. I was a champion of my quad."

"How much do you have to train for that?"

"Six or seven hours a day. Plus we make longer forays into the mountains."

"Yeah, well, I bet you can't navigate the winds in Howe Straight."

"Where's Howe Straight?"

"Never mind. Now I know why you Provo types are such good climbers."

"The best ones come from the Collective, or even from up north."

"Like these best ones?" Lexie gestured to Bareth's other men who were scampering up the cliff well above her.

"Yes. Jordan is from Grand Junction. Molky is from Breckenridge. They moved to Provo to train, and stayed to make a life."

"So your buddy Ghent—why hasn't he removed them?"

"They came before the wars, part of the Vanguard. Now they are Ouray."

"You must see that we're no different than them."

He laughed. "You should see yourself climb."

"Fine, but . . . you know what I mean."

"I'm Heritage. I do what's best for Ouray to survive, and prosper. That means I support our military leaders, including Ghent. I also support our efforts to limit immigration. Ask around. My men do likewise, no matter where they came from. But first, stop slacking, or we'll have to end your trip up the mountain right here."

Bareth scurried up ahead.

After Bareth had killed the old man for Ghent, Lexie had doubted he'd be in their corner. This seemed to prove it. He wasn't going to fight for them. Maybe he was just as bigoted.

She took a breath and pushed on.

Eventually, when they were well past the tree line, Vaela announced, "This altitude should be safe from retchers."

They set up on a promontory covered in jagged rocks. There were only a few square feet of standing room, so they kept themselves roped into carabiners. Bareth and one of his men stood with Vaela and Lexie on a small ledge, while the other two officers found awkward positions leaning into the boulders lining the promontory. The officers were gripping the nearby rocks tightly, their stances wide and exaggerated, as if they were going to start a mime performance right there on the mountain.

Vaela flipped open her disc-shaped comm device. She slid off the top half, revealing keys and diagnostic lights underneath. She spun the top half and tilted it up to be perpendicular to the bottom piece.

"Wait," Bareth said, before Vaela was able to tap on the keypad. "Everything you see, I see. And if I think for a second you are sending secret communications or subliminal messages . . ." He put the barrel of his gun to her temple. Bareth's other man on the ledge followed suit by placing his directly at Lexie's temple.

Vaela said, "They will know our location immediately, and your weapon will send a message of its own."

"Yes, but it's *my* message, not yours. And it's not so subliminal, is it? There's a big difference."

Vaela shrugged and began typing on the keyboard.

"Can you give me, like, an inch?" Lexie asked, pointing at the barrel pressed against her head. The ledge was drafty, and they were in such close quarters it would be easy to inadvertently push one another off the edge. She was just trying to prevent an accident.

The man gave her half an inch.

The disc display illuminated, presenting a video feed showing Dryden's face. He had shaved his hair down to stubble, but was growing out a prickly-looking blond beard. The background was a dark, empty room with a broad arch overhead. It was probably Pentapol.

"Ryder?" he asked, squinting into the screen. "Oh, Vaela. Are you all . . . ?" His eyes widened.

Lexie said, "Yeah, these aren't toy guns at our heads. It's a long story. We need to get on the line with the Spokes. These people want some proof that we're not bad guys."

"Okay. I'll patch you through."

The screen split and the spotty-faced Spoke named Owen showed up alongside the feed showing Dryden. Behind Owen were displays scrolling with charts and text, but it was too blurry to make out the details. "What's going on?" he asked.

"Listen, kid," Lexie said, "it's going to have to be a short update." She pointed at the gun to her head. "We still haven't found Warrick, and we can't keep looking for him until we get out of this pickle with the locals. There have been drone attacks in the region, and they think we caused it. We'd love it if you could whip up some proof to show we're the good guys, and then we'll be back in business."

The old lady named Madison entered the visual. She pulled up a chair beside Owen. "We've been monitoring the situation with our own drones and satellites," she said. "The attacks you're refer-ring to originated from Aspen, targeting anyone that had Laramie tattoos or branding, using very broad image recognition parameters."

"Just like we said." Lexie nodded at Bareth. She addressed Madison again. "Can you confirm they targeted multiple villages? These people think the attack was intended just for their folks."

Madison cringed and exchanged looks with Owen. "I can confirm that. In fact, all of Laramie is no more. The whole nation, all the Laramie villages—they've been eradicated."

Owen tapped on a tablet sitting in front of him. The feed with Owen and Madison was replaced with drone footage of hundreds of dead bodies lying between tents and small buildings. There were multiple sequences of these abandoned villages, all of them torn apart by drones, without any signs of life. The images could have been fake, but Bareth might not know how creative these machines could be.

Bareth was watching intently, with no sign of skepticism. He didn't appear particularly troubled by the images either. "We need incontrovertible evidence," he said.

"This is New Laramie, their capital. What, exactly, would you consider incontrovertible?" Owen asked.

"You'll have to figure that out."

Lexie rolled her eyes. "I'm not sure there's any satisfying these folks. The general—he's a real piece of work."

The gun that had been a half inch away from her head pressed right up against her temple again.

"Yeah, yeah," she said. "We're just trying to have a conversation, okay?"

"Perhaps the answer is in figuring out how we can address this issue with Aspen." Madison suggested. "Confronting Aspen could reveal their motives behind this, and in turn provide more evidence for culpability."

"Worth a shot," Lexie said.

"In that case, I think we should connect with Tetrapol," Vaela said. "This could have broad implications, and the Observers should have a seat at the table."

"That's fair," Dryden said. "I'll patch them through."

A minute later, Olint's steely eyes were staring back at them. It had been at least a year since Lexie had last seen him. He still had the same cold, soul-sucking deadpan expression. The small screen was now split three ways. Lexie had to squint to see when people spoke.

"Vaela, are you in danger?" was the first thing Olint said.

"The immediate threat is low," Vaela said.

"Yeah, it's pretty cozy here," Lexie added. "We've got about a foot of space before we fall off the mountain and become body-puddy. And if Bareth hiccups, Vaela's brains will be blasted into the clouds."

Olint was unmoved by Lexie's take on the situation, "We are up to speed," he said, "as Dryden has fed the conversation thus far to us, direct to implant. Also, we have been monitoring Aspen with drone footage since the attacks started, as have the Spokes. There is a permanent weather distortion over the mountains that limits our intelligence gathering, but we have sighted numerous other aerial drones and land-based mechanical units. There are, at a minimum, hundreds of each." Pictures of the drones that blasted the market in Provo appeared, overlaying Olint's face on the screen. There were also images of stony, humanoid figures without heads walking about Aspen and the nearby mountains.

"What's strange," Dryden said, "is that the humanoid robots look familiar. Something about them . . . You see the bulbous socket around the leg joints, and the pattern of the stone exterior—what does it remind you of?"

Lexie had no idea.

"A beholder," Owen said.

"Exactly," Dryden said. "Sure, it's human-sized, without the belly and eye sockets, but the joints look to be of similar engineering, as well as the stone-like external layer. Isn't that strange?"

"Maybe Aspen reverse-engineered some design aspects of the beholders?" Owen suggested.

"It's possible," Dryden said, but he still looked quizzical.

Bareth hadn't shown any signs of impatience with the conversation, but Lexie didn't like the idea of testing him. She needed to move the eggheads along now and then. "Guys, that's real neat, but can we get on with it? Remember we need to figure out how to stop Aspen."

Owen sighed. "First, let's talk about the scope of the problem. It's bigger than we thought."

"Aspen just killed thousands of people on a whim," Lexie said. "I'm pretty sure we know the scope of the problem."

"I'm not sure you do," Owen said. "Dryden?"

Dryden nodded in a resigned fashion. "I've compared the drones we see in these images to the one that initiated Haplopol. There is a faint marking that matches—a sort of shooting star emblem—as well as similarities in engineering dimensions and materials used that are unlikely to be coincidences. Aspen is also within a reasonable radius of where we knew the drone came from. So, in all likelihood, the drone that initiated Haplopol came from Aspen. Ergo, Aspen may be able to take control of Haplopol and Diplopol at any time."

"In other words, it's more than just one town with thousands of robot units," Owen said. "There is a much more significant power base at Aspen's disposal. But we have an even greater concern than that."

"Oh, come on," Lexie said.

"What's the point of all this?" Bareth said. "I can't see how this gives me the evidence I need."

Lexie was hoping the novelty of the video feeds and learning about people from all parts of the continent might make him interested in the extended conversation, but he was understandably focused on his own agenda. "Hey, I know these nutjobs can be frustrating, but trust me, they know what they're doing. We came all the way up the mountain for this conversation. Why not let it play out?"

After a moment of contemplation, he said, "Fine. But hurry it up."

"You heard him," Lexie said. "Let's wrap up these greater concerns of yours, Owen."

Owen said, "I need to add in another person to the conversation —a well-informed citizen from Aspen that we have come in contact with. He may be a critical to any strategy we undertake. What he has told us is alarming."

"Don't we have enough eggheads at this meeting?" Lexie asked. "It only takes two sailors to tie the sails. Not thirteen eggheads. Geesh."

Owen ignored her and patched in the new person. The screen was split four ways, so the man was hard to make out, but she could tell he was youthful-looking, maybe early twenties, with a shock of wispy black hair. He'd been through the ringer, judging by the bruises, dark eye-bags and lines of tension on his face.

"This is Pyke," Owen explained. "He claims that Arsalan was being held in Aspen and subsequently escaped. Pyke has access to Arsalan's communicator. Pyke, do you mind telling the others here what you told me earlier today?"

"Yes, I can do that," Pyke said. He sounded eager, almost desperate. "Your friend Cecile—she delivered Warrick Kelemen to the network in Aspen."

There was dead air for a good fifteen seconds.

Well, if they weren't going to say it, someone had to. "That bitch!" Lexie said. "I knew something was off about her."

Lexie thought Madison or Owen might jump in to defend Cecile, but before they could, Pyke nodded as if Lexie had spoken some kind of gospel. "It's true. There is. She might be dead now, I don't know. I don't think she wanted to do it. She's possessed, under some kind of mind control."

Owen said, "I don't think I need to explain to you all the significance of this news."

He didn't. Warrick's survival was the key to keeping the Sentinel online, so they were toast without him. Nobody wanted to say it in front of the guy from Aspen.

"Cecile was a steadfast ally," Madison said, "a key contributor to our fight in Seeville. It's really hard to understand."

Owen said, "It's plausible that the whole time Cecile was with us, she was being driven by this desire to find Warrick, but in order to do so, she had to help us survive. I know this because Pyke explained that Cecile was in Aspen ten years ago, when a machine entity called *the Progenitor* was in control. Now it's governed by three other machine entities that are an evolutionary offshoot of this Progenitor. The townspeople call these new entities *the seers*."

"Does Aspen want to negotiate?" Olint asked.

"We've heard nothing from Aspen," Owen said. "There's more, though. Please, Pyke, tell them about your assignment."

Pyke grimaced. "The seers gave me a week to try to convince them why the people of Aspen deserve to live. I'm worried that if my response falls short the network might kill everyone in town. It might even prompt it to eradicate humans elsewhere, like in those towns they control in the northwest. That's why I used Arsalan's communicator. Because . . . I could really use your help."

That explained the eye-bags and the tension. Lexie had been through a few tough spots in her time with the Observers, but nothing as bad as the nutjob puzzle this guy had to solve. She felt for him.

Owen wasn't paying attention; he was reading something on a side display intently. Dryden also seemed to be distracted, rubbing his stubbly blond hair while looking down.

"I still don't see the point of this," Bareth said with a hint of annoyance.

"Hey," Lexie said, "there's kind of some big issues we're working through. Can you give us a few more minutes?"

He frowned at her. Bareth was more patient than Ghent, but soon they would cross the line.

Owen said, "We're working on some ideas to help Pyke convince the seers, but they are dependent on the network's goals. Is there anything in its objective function you are aware of, other than self-preservation?"

"That's the problem," Pyke replied, "I don't really know what it wants."

"Bilious buildings," Dryden said. There was a look of shock on his face.

"Looks like the egghead broke an egg," Lexie said.

"It's Hexapol," he said.

"What?" Owen asked, confused and a bit irritated.

"Dryden, how is this relevant?" Even Vaela was losing her patience.

"Just . . . bear with me, okay? Morganis disappeared after founding the first five ICSM cities. Nobody knows where he went. There was rumored to be a sixth ICSM city, built in his repeated attempts to create the perfect utopian, superintelligent society, but no one could find it. My bet is that the sixth ICSM city is Aspen. You see, he could be this 'Progenitor' person. He must have found a way to download his mind into the city. Everything points to it—the hidden location, the desire to bring back Warrick, who is actually a distant relative of his, and his willingness to evolve and improve the governance of the city further. How else would a drone from Aspen know how to control Haplopol and Diplopol, unless the secret of doing so was built into it by its founder? Even the engineering design of the headless resembling the beholders is a strong indicator. Those design features were likely passed down all the way from the Sentinel's memory banks, which is the original machine intelligence template Morganis used for Haplopol."

Lexie once again marveled at how Dryden, a fairly unimpressive lout by most accounts, could have a brain that churned out these pearls.

"How is this relevant?" Olint parroted Vaela's earlier protest, more forcefully this time. No one was in the mood for indulging Dryden's anthropological eureka moment.

"It speaks to Aspen's objectives," Dryden said. "If the network in Aspen is truly some kind of descendent of Morganis, it might give us a clue into discerning what it wants."

"Okay, I'll bite," Madison said. "What does it want?"

"Well, Morganis was known to be narcissistic, trying to fulfill his vision no matter the cost. He wanted a utopian society."

"But did he want that for himself, or for the greater good?" Madison asked. "Was it just to fulfill a vain ambition, or was it so he could live forever in a universe of his own making?"

Dryden's energy dissipated with each of her challenges. "They're good questions. I can't say what made him like he is. I'm an anthropologist, not a psychologist, and the records are few and disparate."

"Maybe he cared about his family?" Pyke said meekly.

"Why do you say that?" Dryden asked, leaning in toward the camera.

"You said he was after Warrick, and he's some kind of relative, right? Why else would he be after him?"

Nobody was going to tell Pyke the other reason, but what Pyke said actually made some sense. There was more than one descendent of the Kelemen line alive ten years ago, and the Sentinel was essentially dormant ten years ago, anyway. Why else would Morganis pursue Warrick Kelemen?

Owen was reading off some notes on his tablet. "There could be some truth to that. This idea of using his own offspring to help him govern, it fits in with a theme of familial attachment."

"How does that help me?" Pyke asked.

"The Sentinel—the machine mind that is backing the Spokes—raised Morganis when he was made an orphan after the fall. It was the closest thing to a parental figure for Morganis. And the Sentinel's purpose is to protect humanity. So, to kill the people of Aspen, and to defy the Spokes, would be to defy Morganis's heritage, to turn against his family."

Pyke's eyebrows raised.

"And how does that help *me*?" Bareth asked. "If your intent was to confuse me with gibberish, you succeeded."

Owen said, "We have just discovered that Aspen is a major power that poses a threat to everyone on the continent, including Ouray. Not only that, but Aspen has eliminated any people of Laramie origin, which therefore shows you that Ryder, Tarnation, Vaela, and Lexie are not tied to the recent attacks in Ouray. We can send you sources of evidence that supports this."

"There's no time to wait for your *sources of evidence*. I need proof now."

There was a moment of tension as Owen's eyes flitted back and forth between the screen and his tablet. Finally, he said, "We will be sending forces to your aid, to fight at your side. When you see our forces arrive, it will be proof enough. In the meantime, if you don't believe your own eyes, are unwilling to take the time to understand the situation, and don't trust us, there are no words that can help."

Bareth's lips curled into a scowl. "I will relay this to Ghent, but I doubt it will be enough."

"It's all we can give. If you have other ideas, we're happy to hear them out."

Bareth shrugged. "We're done here."

Lexie was under no delusions. She was pretty sure that if Ghent was having a bad day he wouldn't accept any of this, but there wasn't any other way.

"Sorry—have to go, gang," Lexie said. "It's been a real pleasure." The figures onscreen nodded solemnly. "And Pyke, nice to make your acquaintance. Good luck tomorrow!"

Lexie caught a subtle cringe from Pyke before Vaela closed the connection for good.

36

THREE ARGUMENTS

Pyke was hiking resolutely through a blustery wind, the headless ahead of him, a day pack on his back. He had almost reached the summit. Billowy gray clouds were merging rapidly in and out of the more consistent, swirling weather pattern at the top.

Not that he was paying much attention. He had his ear buds in and was listening to a lesser-known synth-goth ballad from the Old World. He didn't know anyone in town that liked this kind of music, and they never played it at the Underdome, even on alt-music nights. It was a raging procession of break beats and angry lyrics over low-octave brassy notes and the occasional soul-splitting vocals.

He loved it.

He loved it because his immersion into the soundscape made him feel more alive than ever. He loved it because some verses made him suffer the torture of his predicament, while others made him hopeful for its resolution.

Then he wondered, how could anyone want to take this feeling away from him?

How could the seers want to take these feelings away from *everyone*?

He wasn't sure if he could count on the people he'd spoken to on

Arsalan's communicator device. He'd become more guarded after being manipulated by the network all his life. Yet what they said might help. Maybe the key was focusing on family. It was a concept he understood. The network must have some respect for its creator, and for its origins. Everybody was someone's mother, father, son, or daughter. If the network possessed just a small fraction of the empathy that Pyke had for Gill, it would at least pause before wiping out the people its creator had sworn to protect.

But Pyke wasn't counting on it. In fact, he had filtered his thoughts down to three principal arguments. He didn't know if he would succeed, but he felt good that he'd done his best to prepare.

✦

The elliptical platform was mostly the same as the last time he'd been there with Cecile. There were more rows of aerial drones, and several more headless standing at attention. The main difference was the teams of roly-poly droids that were actively running up and down thick pillars they were building on the edge of the platform.

Beyond the platform, along the face of the mountain, there was also something new. Previously, there had been a gantry built into the rock, above which vertical bars lined the wall. Pyke had thought it unremarkable in the past, as it could have been more elevators or access points to the mountain, but this time he noticed a distortion around the bars; the silhouettes of two people standing behind them. The figures were too distant to identify. He hoped it meant that Warrick and Cecile were alive, not only for their sakes, but because it might mean the network had some capacity for mercy.

The energetic constellations of the three seers were a few hundred feet ahead of him, hovering in a semi-circle, staring at him relentlessly.

He approached them, trying not to tremble, his face rigid with his effort to stay under control. His pulse pounded in his ears.

"We are interested in hearing what you have to say," Genai said.

"He doesn't even have any notes," Yadai said.

"Irrelevant," Ansai said. "He has surely distilled it down to the most important points, and practiced those points in preparation."

Although Pyke was glad Ansai was defending him, it didn't give him much comfort that the seer had anticipated his process.

"I will agree with Genai," Yadai said, "at least to the extent that it will be *interesting*. Especially after Mengle has taken the opportunity to show us how useful humans can be." The scratch marks on his cheeks glowed as he finished, perhaps a substitute for sarcastic eye rolling.

Pyke had fully expected Yadai's skepticism, so it didn't bother him. He just had to convince Ansai and Genai of one of his three arguments. Yadai was only a distraction.

"There are always outliers," Pyke said. "I don't think Mengle is representative of the rest of the town. Shall I begin?"

"Please," Ansai replied.

Pyke took a deep breath. "I have prepared three principal arguments. Each one, on its own, provides sufficient rationale to justify humanity's existence, and the preservation of the people of Aspen. The first is about achievement. While we certainly have foibles, the net impact of humanity has been significant. We have built systems to vault us into space. We have institutionalized knowledge around the fundamental building blocks of life. We are able to build huge cities, compose complex musical sonatas, domesticate countless species, and eradicate endemic diseases. Most importantly, we were the ones who developed thinking machines—we were the ones who developed you. How can you justify the elimination of any part of such a productive, industrious species?"

"What's the point of building all that if you throw it away?" Yadai said. "Many of the capabilities you speak of are no longer possible after the fall."

"Yadai has a point," Ansai said, "but a greater flaw in this argument is that it is wholly retrospective. Humanity's evolution is noteworthy, but so is the advent of eukaryotic organisms, photosynthesis, and sexual reproduction. Yet humans didn't seek to preserve all single-cell bacteria because they were enamored with the magic of their inception. Who is to say we machines are not a more effective branch of the evolutionary line? We certainly beat humans at their most important characteristic—intelligence. I am confident we could do everything humanity has done in less time, using fewer resources. No, achievement is not relevant in this instance. Potential is."

"What's your next argument?" Genai asked, not even offering a counter. Pyke could only assume he disagreed as well.

It wasn't a good start. Pyke didn't know if he should try to debate the point, but there wasn't much more he could add. If he dwelled here, it might leave less time to focus on other arguments, which may be more solid.

"My second argument relates to prudence," he said. "You have never felt what it is like to be human. You know, empirically, and deductively, that we feel things—fear, love, hate, worry, elation—a litany of emotions that are generated by biochemical processes, and yet you don't know if you can replicate or even simulate them in silico. To deprive us of these emotions—something you cannot understand—is inherently unjust and imprudent, because these feelings could have social value above mere generic intelligence. They could even help us to be more effective than machine entities."

"It's a valid point," Genai said, the gear-like configurations turning in Genai's head. "Perhaps there are biological substrates we can develop to test the utility of human emotion? These forms of morphological intelligence could be more important than we realize."

"We also don't have hair follicles or peacock feathers," Yadai said. "Who cares? You could cite any attribute that we don't have in the name of *prudence*. What matters are attributes that can help us achieve our objectives. We have enough empirical evidence and logical arguments to know, based on learning capacity and the flexibility of in-silico neuronal systems, that we're better than humans at doing so."

There was silence for a moment. Both Genai and Yadai looked to Ansai.

Ansai's horns glowed. "This argument is quite thin. I don't see how human emotions can help us. Logic states that these biochemical reactions can be reproduced in silico, with enough engineering, but we would need only do so if they are useful, which is doubtful. They may, in fact, lead us astray, as many humans have been prone to prioritizing the satisfaction of basic biochemical needs over higher-order, long-term objectives. I think Host Mengle's hubris and greed is a good example of this. I'm sorry, but it's not enough of a reason to keep humans alive."

Pyke had drunk a healthy gulp from his canteen before arriving at the ellipse, but his tongue still felt dry. The growing feeling of dread in his chest was sucking all the moisture from his throat and mouth. He licked his lips and took a shuddering breath before venturing into his final argument.

"My third argument is about family, and I mean that in a broad sense. Not only those that brought us into the world, but those who are partners, friends, colleagues and collaborators—the entire community of sentient beings that we work with and share our existence with. The argument is that there is a social contract to protect those that nurtured our upbringing, that helped make us who we are, and that have supported us in times of need. This is why humans have survived to rule the earth—not just because of genetic programming to select for reproduction, not just because we are more intelligent than other life forms, but because we understand that we are stronger together, as a community."

He held his finger up to be sure the seers knew he wasn't finished. "There is good reason this should also apply to you, as machines. Your creator, the Progenitor, was Morganis, who was born and raised a human. He brought you to life with the hope of developing a utopian city for all, including humans, but governed by superintelligent machines such as yourselves. Where did he get this idea? From the Sentinel, who acted as his guardian. I'm sure you are aware, the Sentinel's primary goal is to safeguard all of humanity."

The seers had to be wondering how he had come by this information, but it was a risk he had to take. If his argument won the day, he would deal with the consequences later. For now, there was no sign of surprise or even curiosity amongst the seers. They were expressionless, looming over him, as if they might fall and crash into him at any moment.

He continued, "The Sentinel is just as much your parent as Morganis is, since you and the other ICSM cities have machine architectures based on the same initial blueprint, just like my DNA is based on the combined DNA of my parents. Do you think it right to defy Morganis, who spent his life trying to create you? Do you think it right to defy the Sentinel, whose only objective is to save humanity? These are the ones that made you. If you have any morality at all, you must take this to heart."

"Your argument is that we should *have a heart*?" Yadai asked sarcastically, barking out a laugh.

Pyke jumped in. "I'm not done."

Genai said, "We spoke about this, Yadai. You must wait until Pyke is finished."

"Fine, fine."

Pyke continued, "I hope that you do have a heart, or at least that you care, but I don't know, honestly. Yes, Yadai, I do understand that as machines, you may not care about whether others suffer—even if they are your family—but that shouldn't matter, because the argument for family, for community, is just as much about achieving your objectives. Without others to partner with, you may not gain valuable insights from entities that think differently from you. You may not have your ideas challenged so that the best ones are selected for execution. This is why monarchies and autocrats tend to perform worse than democracies. This is why the Progenitor selected the three of you, with very different backgrounds, as equitable partners to succeed him, rather than just one. And this is why the human beings of Aspen, the other ICSM cities, and even the Sentinel represent an important community of sentient beings, helping you reach your objectives. To deny this fact is to deny your own fallibility, to limit your potential, and to betray your maker's ultimate wish for the outcome of Aspen—to create the best human utopia governed by superintelligence. No matter what is written in your code, if you want to accomplish your objectives, keeping the humans of Aspen alive is an important foundation for achieving success."

Pyke released a measured exhalation. The heads bobbed in the air, casting occasional sidelong glances at each other.

"Impressive arguments, Pyke," Genai remarked.

"I also agree that the arguments are impressive," Yadai said. It was a rare compliment from the ornery seer. "In particular, your research has given you access to information that must have been quite difficult to obtain." He paused, perhaps wondering if Pyke would elucidate.

Pyke didn't bite. "And?" he said.

"And I disagree, of course. In the evolutionary simulations, I had to betray many of my so-called family to succeed. If I hadn't done so, I might not be here at all. So I vote no, but I am still curious about how you obtained the information about the Sentinel, and Morganis."

"Would that information be helpful?" Pyke asked.

"Yes."

"How can I possibly offer anything helpful? By your logic, I'm an expendable, useless human. I would hate to prove you wrong about the importance of humans as part of a broader community."

The scratch marks on Yadai's cheeks flared. "I will flatten you to the size of a coin, you insignificant nuisance. Tell me where you learned of this."

Ansai was laughing. "Oh, this is very entertaining. Truly a tour de force, Pyke. You've proved your point, and Yadai's bitter annoyance only makes it more compelling. I must *agree* with the human." She looked to Yadai, her features glowing bright as if in deliberate competition with Yadai's, before she returned her gaze to Pyke. "Much of my success in the evolutionary simulation required mobilizing other entities to fight. It required *leadership,* and coordination, which cannot always be done on a transactional basis. It is akin to the theme of family, or at least community, because without that interparty loyalty, everything breaks down, and success is elusive. So yes, I vote for a stay of hand. We must, at the very least, delay the extermination of Aspen's humans to explore the potential impact to our collaborative goals."

Pyke would have been more comfortable if Ansai had stressed the morality of his argument, but nevertheless he was relieved she had voted in his favor. Ansai often seemed to be the swing vote, because Genai had supported him in the past. Besides, Genai was fundamentally curious—a builder and creator, rather than a fighter like Ansai or a sneak like Yadai. Genai must see the benefit in learning from what humans have to offer.

Ansai and Yadai looked to Genai, waiting for a response.

Genai said, "As mentioned, I am impressed by the caliber of Pyke's arguments. We chose the right human for this difficult task. I also believe Pyke deserves to know more about our own inception, since it has a bearing on a pivotal crux of his argument. He has shared willingly, and so should we."

"Fine," Ansai said.

"Go ahead," Yadai agreed.

Did they know where Genai was going with this? Pyke certainly didn't.

"You may recall, when Attendant Cecile arrived here on the summit, we spoke about the man you call our father—Morganis. He was troubled—manic, with traumatic stress disorder, and narcissistic. Yes, he had a desire to do good for humanity, but it was wrapped up in his ego. There was tension there, where one could question whether the ends he sought justified the means he undertook.

"When we first met, you questioned whether we had placed Morganis in some sort of prison. And you may wonder, rightfully, if, as our creator, he deserves this treatment. You may wonder if we, his descendants, are completely selfish, ungrateful, disloyal derivations. I can assure you that imprisoning him and securing governance was necessary, not only because he was erratic and selfish, but because he committed mind crime on a genocidal scale."

"I'm sorry. What is 'mind crime'?" Pyke asked.

"You speak of preventing the suffering of humans, but we must weigh the suffering of all intelligent entities. To answer your question, the very process that created us was mind crime. Morganis subjected millions of machine minds, over quadrillions of cycles—roughly equivalent to seven hundred million human lifetimes—to the harshest living conditions. Imagine being forced to navigate a maze, half-starved, for your entire life. Or be in a constant state of war, ravaged by disease and disability, as Ansai's relatives were, for hundreds of years. That was us, millions of us, in the simulations he contrived. Yes, we evolved, but only because our families, as you called it, suffered, until finally only the fittest, the most proficient, were able to persevere and were selected by Morganis. The outcome was good for us three, but what of the millions of others from whom we evolved? Why did they have to experience such hardship—such torture—so that only the three best minds could know freedom?

"Ergo if this one human, our supposed father, could commit a genocidal act to machine entities derived from his own imprint, how can we be comfortable with human morality? How can we trust in this social contract you cite, if it has already been abrogated by our conception? I'm sorry, Pyke, but I must vote no in response to your third argument. I would rather trust another machine mind, even Ansai and Yadai, before I would trust a human who could subject so many of us to a life of horror."

As Genai had been speaking, Pyke had experienced a growing sense of vertigo. He had never considered mind crime, or the morality of the evolutionary development of the seers. The concept was foreign to him. In fact, it might be completely novel to everyone alive, with the exception of the seers.

Hope was slipping away.

"Morganis was just one human," Pyke stammered. "You said so yourself, that he was narcissistic. Surely you can't extrapolate one human's moral failings to all humans."

"Isn't that what you asked us to do—to generalize the good faith of our family to all humans? This is the family we know, Pyke. It's hard to ignore our experience."

"You said yourself that Morganis was troubled. You told me something happened to him when he was downloaded into a machine and became the Progenitor. Maybe he lost his emotions, his compassion, during the conversion process. Maybe he wouldn't have committed mind crime if he was still human. This would reinforce my second argument, that our biochemical reactions are an important part of who we are, and how we work together."

In his desperation, Pyke thought he might have actually stumbled upon a strong argument, but Genai had lost all patience. "We've heard enough," he said. "We have decided. It's two votes to one. I'm sorry, Pyke. None of your arguments are sufficiently convincing."

The platform started to vibrate, and the buzzing noise from the mountain increased. It was as if the bees Pyke had imagined in the giant mountain beehive were about to emerge. Indeed, a few aerial drones were powering up and dropping off the side, and headless were coming online, marching off the platform in pairs—but the main surge of noise came from the mountain face, where a huge rock-camouflaged hatch opened up and hundreds of the roly-poly droids flowed from it. They spread out to tumble down the mountainside, like a slow-moving volcanic eruption of mechanized bots.

No.

Pyke had known he might fail, but what he hadn't expected was that he would come away unconvinced by the seer's counterarguments. Rather than feeling sad, or defeated, he felt betrayed. The outcome seemed inevitable, as if it was just another game of *A Leap of Wisdom*. Maybe this was just a hollow process to check some procedural box in the network's protocols. Maybe he was destined to fail, no matter what his arguments were.

He said, "What will . . . what will happen?" He had trouble forming the words.

Ansai replied, "We will not begin the extermination of Aspen citizens immediately. Many human groups can be made instrumental as we transition to full automation. However, any that resist will be killed instantly if they become a nuisance. We anticipate that within two weeks we should be able to disintermediate the vast majority of Aspen's human-managed operations."

"What about me?"

"Pyke could still have some utility, I admit," Genai said to the other seers with some vocal inflection, as if it was quite a noteworthy finding.

"And I wonder about the Essentialist representative," Yadai added. "She could be of use."

"Absolutely," Ansai said. "Pyke, in a few days you will bring the Essentialist operative here—the one named Kehda—for questioning. It will be a civil engagement. Perhaps she can act as a diplomatic liaison, since the Essentialists will soon be the only real challenge to us on the continent."

Again, here the seers were finding utility in a human being. It was hypocritical, but Pyke knew there were no more arguments he could make. Not today.

"What if I say no?"

"Come now, Pyke," Genai said. "You know the answer to that."

He wondered if Kehda could change the seers' mind, but quickly realized it was unlikely. She was sharp, but she knew little of abstract philosophical disciplines. Moreover, Pyke had a feeling the network was being deceptive about its true intentions toward Kehda. Maybe she would be turned into an infiltrating, brainwashed spy, like Cecile. First, though, the network would try to get her to share information about the Essentialists unwittingly.

A thicket of foreboding anticipation had taken root in his chest. There was no alternative. He couldn't say no, because if he voiced his suspicion, the network could just kill him right there. Maybe the network would use a more coercive means with Kehda if he didn't agree to help.

He had no choice. And maybe, if he was lucky, he could find a way to buy everyone just a little more time.

"I," he stammered. "I . . . I'll see what I can do."

The seers smiled politely, as if he'd just made some trivial transaction at the Aspen produce market, then faded to nothing.

PART III

DISINTERMEDIATION

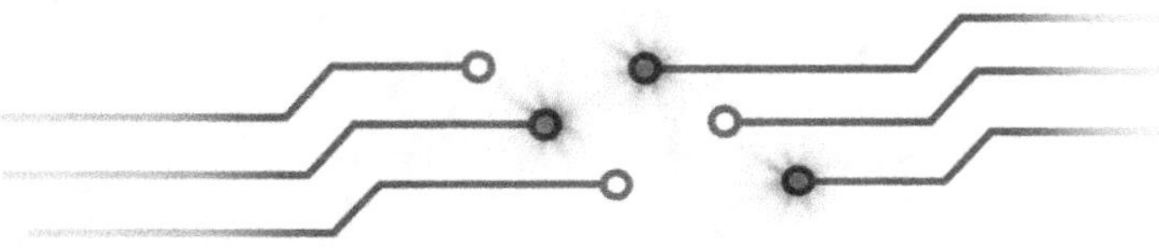

37

LINGERING AT THE DOORWAY

When Pyke woke, he could barely move, sprawled out on his bed, facing the wall. He lifted his neck and turned to face the crib. Gill wasn't there.

"How did it go?" Kehda asked. "At the summit."

Pyke forced himself to sit up. Kehda was lingering at the doorway to his room, avoiding his eyes, shifting her weight as if testing a new pair of shoes. Her hair was loose, hanging down to her shoulders. It revealed her blonde accents, giving the wavy tresses a certain vitality.

"Thanks for letting me use the bed," he said. He hadn't been sleeping well on the couch. "And as you've probably guessed—it didn't go well."

"I'm sorry," she said.

"Not your fault."

"No," she continued. "I mean, I'm sorry for distracting you. For being here, but not realizing what you're going through. It's hard— where I'm from, we don't usually apologize. It's seen as weak, a sign of guilt. I don't know if I'm doing it right. With Gill, it's also new to me, being a mother. It makes me uncomfortable, but I do love him."

"Both take practice." He offered a polite smile. "You're getting better. Let's say you're still a trainee."

Her eyes probed his expression, searching for nuance. "You're afraid of me."

He sniffed. "What you did to the host and those rangers at the Wisdome . . . I mean, I knew you were an effective soldier, but I had no idea you were that . . . lethal. To see you in action—yeah, it was scary. Or rather, it made me feel I didn't know you well. Maybe I don't."

"You do. I'm just not good at expressing myself."

Pyke heard Gill giggling in the living room.

"And maybe it's what happened with Dwayne?" Kehda said. "Is that still bothering you?"

"I think about it."

"I told you. In the Sierras we don't have monogamous relationships. It's normal for people to spend time with others, as long as commitments are honored."

"Commitments?"

Kehda rubbed her face. "I'm not good at this," she said.

"I understand. Maybe it's more about Dwayne's death than you being with him. When your best friend dies, it casts a long shadow. You wonder about your place in the world. You wonder what could have been done differently. His father still doesn't speak to me. He still says I'm cursed. All that—it's somehow tied to our relationship."

"That's just stupid—about Dwayne's father."

"Yes," he shrugged. "It is."

"Dwayne was the one who showed me the emergency escape hatch in the Wisdome. If he hadn't, I wouldn't have been able to get inside to save Gill."

"That makes sense." Crowley's comment about Dwayne's love-making locations came back to Pyke. Dwayne had probably showed her the hatch so they could sneak inside without being noticed. Did she want him to be thankful for that?

And what about the day that Dwayne died? Kehda never mentioned it, but maybe that was the way things were in the Union. You mourned in private. Pyke couldn't bring himself to push more on that topic. It was a prickly subject.

Kehda remained in the doorway. She was usually decisive, always moving, so some hidden agenda was binding her there. Her expression appeared sour, almost pained, as if she was trying to solve a riddle.

The memory of her snapping the ranger's neck flashed in his mind. How could this be Gill's mom? And yet she was making an effort.

"The seers asked about you," Pyke said. She looked up, her eyes locking on his for the first time since the conversation began. "They want to meet you." His heart raced as he said it, because it was a terrible dilemma. Yes, if he brought her up the mountain it could put her in danger, but if he didn't, it might accelerate her demise in other ways.

Kehda was frozen. "Maybe I should go to the summit, then?" she asked. "It's why I brought the offering, isn't it?"

She was fearless.

Kehda had already put in the request to Mengle—to offer her glass bear for a trip to the summit—but he hadn't answered it. There had been many recent requests made to Mengle relating to trade, and diplomacy. Helping a foreigner up to the summit in exchange for a glass idol wouldn't have been high on his list. Especially because before Cecile, no foreigner had been to the summit in ten years. Pyke doubted Mengle had even considered the request.

Shane might be easier to convince.

Before Pyke could respond, there was a crash in the other room. Kehda turned toward it and Pyke jumped out of the bed to follow.

The first thing Pyke noticed was the headless standing beside the couch, then Gill directly beside it. Gill had climbed up on the arm of the couch with blue paint covering most of his hand. The source of the noise was a paint vial that had fallen from the couch and was spilling its contents on the floor in a conglomeration of overlapping pools.

Pyke rushed to grab Gill from the couch arm, pulling him away from the headless.

"Dah," Gill said. "Dah!" He started to cry.

Pyke hoisted him over his shoulder and patted him on the back. "Shhh," he said. "It's alright now. I just wanted to make sure you don't fall."

Gill seemed to be fine—just a bit shocked.

More details of the scene came into resolution: the couch had paint on it, as did the wall, as did the headless. In fact, the headless had a sort of oblong circle on its belly. Inside the circle was a slit next to a dot and a pudgy golden upward arc below them.

Gill had painted a smiley face.

Pyke had told Kehda that Gill wasn't to paint on his own. What was more, the situation presented a host of dangers: Gill climbing high up on the couch and the very presence of the headless, to name just two. Yet there was an absurdity to the tableau that prevented Pyke from reacting in anger.

And he was just too tired.

Kehda had hung back to let Pyke extract Gill. She said, "I shouldn't have left him alone. I'm sorry, Pyke."

"Maybe we'll need to extend the trainee program."

She pouted, her hands on her hips.

"I'm kidding," Pyke said. "It's only paint. Spruces him up a little, don't you think?" He gestured at the headless. "We can finally tell one of these apart from the others. Let's call him . . . Smiley."

Slowly, Kehda's guard lowered. She nodded. "Smiley. A good name." A grin pulled at her lips.

———◆———

Kehda came to him that night.

The headless—Smiley—had left, or at least gone to act as a guard outside the apartment. Pyke had returned to the couch for another uncomfortable sleep.

He awoke to find Kehda straddling him, rolling him onto his back.

She was already naked, pulling at his shirt. It was the first time she'd touched him, other than an informal hug, since she'd arrived in Aspen.

He could have said no. He didn't want her pity. Nor did he want her in some sad act of reconciliation. The incident at the Wisdome made him wary—made him wonder who she was. She was a fractured image in his mind's eye.

But time was running out. As the sands dwindled in the hourglass, so did his will to protest.

He allowed himself to touch her.

He had loved her, once. Maybe he could love her again.

38

PROCESS IMPROVEMENTS

Cecile stared into the mirror as she unwrapped the bandage and pulled off the gauze. The skin on her skull was covered by faint stubble, the red lines of a square scar clearly visible just above her forehead. She remembered brief snippets of the procedure; her head fixed in a vice while her hair was aggressively shaved by one of the roly-poly robots, a cocktail of IV drugs in her arm, a booming voice, flashes of patterns, like a Rorschach test performed at a hundred times the usual speed. She didn't remember the actual surgery. The network had knocked her out for that part.

Laid out on the counter, next to the sink, were a series of wigs: blonde, red, raven. The network had even made one that was shoulder length with a blue splash—so she could look like she did when she first left Quebec City.

She left the wigs where they lay. The dark tendrils in her vision only trembled; apparently the apparition didn't care much about her hairstyle.

She'd been awake for two days, stuck in her cell. Most of the time she was hooked up to electrodes and sensors on her head and chest. A headless would hand her a list of tasks for her to perform. Most were trivial, like standing facing the wall or singing an embarrassing song. She was made to write a convincing letter to her mother saying that she hated her. At times, one of the seers would chime in over an intercom, testing her compliance in other ways. The worst was when she had to kill a helpless deer with a dull hunting knife, right there in her room.

In many ways, it was just like the first time.

The difference was that this time she never resisted, because she knew it was pointless. The apparition was always there, vibrating in her vision at the slightest sign of reluctance. Why not make it happy? Her not choosing one of the network's proffered wigs was probably her biggest act of defiance since her surgery, but she could argue she'd be more effective without one anyway.

A backpack had appeared just inside the door, neatly packed with food, a change of clothes, a wad of currency, and a utility knife. Next to it was a warm jacket, mitts, and an impressive-looking, long-barreled energy weapon studded with dull blue lights.

"You are free to leave," Ansai had said. It was the last intercom voice she'd heard, no more than an hour ago.

Free was a relative term, of course.

She donned the jacket, stuffed the mitts in the pockets, heaved the pack over her shoulders, and grabbed the weapon.

The door was no longer locked, so she opened it.

Outside her room was a cavernous facility. Roly-poly robots and other, forklift-like machines navigated the spaces between storage towers, conveyor belt lines, and monolithic panels replete with switches and ports.

An automaton was waiting for her. It gestured for her to follow, so she did.

They passed a metal press, then a welding operation. Near a broad hangar door was an offshoot room labeled *Redundant Systems*.

"Why would you need to label something in English?" she asked. "I don't see any other humans around."

The headless turned, pointed at her, then continued out of the hangar. Her best guess was if there was some system failure, it might need her help. Or maybe it had been there ever since Morganis's time, when he was alive in the flesh.

The hangar door led to a broad gantry fixed to the mountainside, overlooking the broad elliptical platform below it. As usual, clouds spun above the summit, fed by mists funneling from the weather-making machine in the distance. The gantry extended down a long ramp that would lead her onto the main platform, but not before passing through several enclosed bays cut out of the mountainside that harbored storage or other access points. It was near one of these bays that her pace slowed, and she came to a stop.

Two rooms looked out onto the gantry, and they had people in them. Whereas her room was something you might find in an Old World psychiatric ward, these were more bona fide prison cells, with vertical bars, latrines, and skinny, unyielding beds.

In the first cell was a man with tree-trunk legs and a sickle-shaped scar on his cheek. His long hair was tied back in a tangled ponytail.

Arsalan.

He came up to the bars and stared at her with loathing. "Fucking witch," he said.

Cecile couldn't deny it anymore, so she didn't. She just shrugged.

He pulled at the bars forcefully, rattling them.

There was no hope of him escaping. Cecile had tested the locks on similar doors before, when she had first undergone the procedure. There was no visible latch, so it looked like you could force it, but in fact there was a strong electromagnetic force keeping the cell door sealed. It would only open when the network wanted him moved.

"How did you get up here?" she asked.

Arsalan didn't answer, but a familiar voice did, coming from the next cell over. "The automatons took him," Warrick said, "from your friend Pyke's apartment. Arsalan never tried to escape."

She approached the second cell slowly, afraid to see what the network might have done to Warrick—and just as afraid to see his eyes full of judgment.

Remarkably, Warrick looked quite . . . healthy? Yes, his head was shaved, like hers, but enough stubble had grown that he just appeared clean cut. He was standing tall, hands firmly on the bars. His face was pale, and yet his eyes were sharp, with unwavering focus. His countenance made him seem like a different person altogether.

"Are you . . ."

"It's gone," he said. "It was killing me, so the network removed it to save me. Nothing to do with mercy, of course. The network simply didn't want to lose its most valuable bargaining chip."

The apparition encroached at the edges of her vision. She wasn't countermanding any network imperative by speaking with Warrick, but eventually it would lose patience. She backed away.

"There's something I need to tell you," Warrick said.

Here it comes. Best to get out in front of it. "Don't bother. I know, Warrick. I'm a witch. I betrayed my friends. I dragged you thousands of miles against your will and nearly made you overdose on drugs. We're all going to die because of my actions. Did I miss anything?"

"None of that was you," he said. "Even this, it's not you."

She should have been relieved, but his stance only made her more livid. "Oh, fuck off."

"I've done things," Warrick said firmly. "Terrible things. I was the one that placed the remade control junctions under Haplopol. Did you know that? I set up the entire conflict in the northwest, and made sure Morganis—the network—could take control at any moment."

"*Sa fait rien.* None of that matters now. The game is over—we lost."

"It's never over," he said. "I was supposed to take Pentapol's control junction back here for reconfiguration but I burned my arm by accident, and then things changed. The trauma changed it. I could resist, even though it made me mad."

"And look at where you are now."

"Yes, it's brought me here, where I'm talking to you."

"Give it a rest, old man," Arsalan said from the adjoining cell. "The witch is bent beyond recognition."

"Can't argue with that," Cecile said. She backed away further, then turned toward the down ramp.

"Cecile, wait," Warrick said.

"Sorry, no time." She tapped her wrist where a watch had once been strapped. "I've got worlds to kill."

She fell in step with the automaton, her teeth grinding, her fists clenched.

✦

As she neared Aspen, another two automatons appeared behind her. Three others crossed her path at intersections on the journey down the mountainside. They weren't carrying anything. What were they doing?

Cecile was no better than these machines. She'd always known this, as a powerless servant of the network, but now there was no naïve escapism of pretending to be like the people she'd fooled. Walking amongst the automatons, this sense of being a dispassionate cog in the network's wheel couldn't be ignored. Seeing Warrick in his cell also served to accentuate this. Once a tortured zombie, he was now filled with vitality, his resilience shining a spotlight on how far she'd fallen.

She didn't bother taking the chairlift, because the automatons liked to walk and the network wanted her to have an escort at all times. "The Wisdome," she said on the final stretch of path. There was no sign of acknowledgement in the automaton in front of her.

People stopped and stared as she ventured into town. Others scurried away along side streets as she passed. She noticed a number of active rolling droid units, which was new. They were busy carting wood, metal beams, and electrical components toward the roads that led to Gondola Valley.

The network's disintermediation process was well under way.

The ranger named Blaine was on duty at the ranger station. "Hey, where are you going?" he asked.

She didn't bother acknowledging him. Nor did she change direction.

Blaine jumped out of the booth, and was soon running alongside her, although he kept some distance on account of the automaton. "What's going on here?" he asked. His voice wavered. His eyes flitted toward the energy weapon slung over her back.

"What's going on is you don't want to die today," she said.

"I'm not . . . But I have to—"

"Tell me I have to report to the host immediately."

He clued in. "Report to the host immediately," he repeated loudly.

"Yes, sir," she said, accompanying her words with a slapstick salute.

Blaine moved ahead of Cecile and the automaton, pretending to guide them toward the Wisdome. "Network business," Blaine said to onlookers. "Please move aside."

When they reached the Wisdome main entrance, Cecile said, "Unlock the door."

Blaine hesitated.

The automaton began shuffling toward him.

Blaine no longer hesitated.

They entered the main foyer to be met by aggrieved and nervous expressions. Shane was there, as was Vin, and the ranger named Crowley. She'd studied their profiles on the summit. Shane and Vin had settled into their new roles; Shane was dressed in a tight-fitting vest and slacks, while Vin was wearing a long skirt and loose blouse over a padded bra. Two other members of the crew were recoiling from the confrontation, backing slowly into the shadows.

"You can't just barge in here," Vin protested.

"Blaine shouldn't have let you in," Crowley said at the same time. "We have a process."

"This is not appropriate," Shane said. "You need to make an offering, and once you do—"

"Stop," she said. "Did you get the message from the network?"

"Yes, but—"

"And what did it say?"

"To . . . to do whatever you ask, so we do plan to treat you graciously, but you still need to follow our process."

She sighed. "Let's talk upstairs."

Shane opened his mouth, as if about to object, but he stopped himself. Maybe the power hadn't gone to his head quite yet. "I suppose we can carve out some time," he said, "since the network considers you a VIP. Vin, please cancel my next meeting."

She doubted he had a next meeting.

Crowley, Shane, and Vin walked up the stairs with her, into the control center. All three automatons followed them in. The three men could not mask their nervous expressions.

"Look, guys," she said, "there's going to be some changes around here."

No one protested, yet.

"*Bien*," she said. "The network wants me to run things, I'm going to be host. It would be real nice if you all could help me."

There was dead air for a good thirty seconds. Crowley scratched his neck and looked down. Vin's meek face became downcast and rigid. His temperament seemed to be morphing into anger. Shane was clutching his chest, as if he was having heart palpitations. He spoke first. "Typically, the host is a man."

"Fine. Make me hostess."

"Vin is the hostess," Shane said. "The hostess is subordinate to the host."

"Then I guess I'm just going to have to be the host."

"You would have to dress like a man, in a suit. And I'm sorry, but you don't have any hair."

"*Zut alors*. Look . . . no. That's not going to happen. I'm the host. You are all subordinate to me. I'm dressing how I damn well please."

"Typically, we all weigh in on process improvement ideas," Vin said, looking incredulous. He rearranged his stuffed shirt, as if the bra was chaffing him. "Mengle encouraged this. Humphries allowed the crew to participate as well. Maybe we should vote."

"*Non*," Cecile said. "No vote."

Vin opened his mouth, then closed it. Crowley tried to avoid her eyes. Shane was forcing a plastic smile that made him look constipated.

She pulled out a long sheet of paper from her backpack. "We

need to make some personnel changes. I've made a list here." She handed the list to Shane. The other two leaned in to read it, eyes wide. There were seven hundred names on the list.

"We're going to give the headless a shot at supply logistics, alongside the V-35 rolling droids. Other positions have been replaced or eliminated. We want to try more automation in construction projects as well. I want your help in letting all these people go."

"People depend on these jobs for their livelihoods!" Vin protested. "My uncle has no other skills. He has worked in sanitation for twenty years. What's he supposed to do?"

She shrugged. "Nobody wants to clean up all that mess. All people in sanitation have been replaced by V-35s."

Vin just stared at her, wide eyed.

"You know, the V-35 droids? They look like a runaway snowball that's picked up a lot of sticks along the way."

There was no change in his disposition.

"And your game," she said. "Remind me what it's called?"

"*A . . . A Leap of Wisdom*," Crowley answered when the others couldn't. Shane's mouth hung open. He seemed unable to process the extent of her ignorance.

"Oh yeah, *A Leap of Wisdom* has been cancelled until further notice. Just tell people it's on account of Laramie threats."

Vin jumped out of his chair, pointing his finger at her. "The show is who we are! You can't ask a man to cut out his own heart. And you're supposed to be the host, for Glen's sake! We will *not* stand for this."

Maybe he had forgotten about the automatons. Or maybe he was just too enamored with his precious game. Either way, it proved a deadly mistake. The automaton nearest Vin picked him up by the head and jerked it halfway around, snapping his neck. Then it carried Vin's lifeless, rag-doll body outside.

Cecile sighed. "Look, I'm sorry about that, but the sooner you realize that your process improvement ideas are no longer encouraged, the better. Got it?"

Crowley and Shane nodded with alacrity.

The rest of the meeting went much more smoothly.

Her imperative was simple. She was to be the network's human hand in Aspen, for whatever it needed. The most immediate project was automating human functions before it eliminated most of the population. The network needed her to manage that transition, and she figured that, as host, most people would listen to her.

And for those that didn't, she could always count on the automatons to offer some sort of violent encouragement.

39

MOLOCULUS FLIM FLAM

The math wasn't good, probability-wise, of Lexie and Vaela being able to escape Bareth and his climbing commandos. It was pointless to make a move on the sheer face of the mountain, for obvious reasons. Maybe they could surprise them on the lower paths, but Bareth's men looked tough and scrappy. Even if Lexie and Vaela were successful, a whole army would be able to hunt them down. Better to take their chances with Ghent, however meager those chances may have been.

Of course, nothing stays fixed in wartime. You never knew when the whole equation was about to change.

It was late morning when they curled around a bend in the mountain and were able to see into the valley proper. At first Lexie thought the haze was a stubborn morning mist hanging low in the valley, but pockets were moving; smoke was churning up from below.

They picked up the pace as the path wound through the trees. Eventually, they arrived at a good lookout point.

It was hard to get an accounting of the devastation, as gusts of wind were sweeping eddies of the smoke across the meadows, but Lexie guessed that at least half of Ghent's army was gone. Trees had been cut in half, and craters pocked the fields. The remains of blackened tents, dead horses, and mangled human bodies were visible where the ground had been more heavily charred. Clearly, what Lexie and her friends had feared would happen had happened; the army had been attacked by drones, probably from Aspen. Lexie was actually surprised the army hadn't been completely obliterated, but the reason for that became clear when the wind shifted again to give a temporary reprieve from the smoke.

She had mistaken it for a part of the mountain. Standing behind the army remains was a two-hundred-foot-tall humanoid monstrosity. It was gashed, pocked, and blackened, one hand missing completely and another with only three digits, and half its head blown clear off.

"Honestly," Lexie said. "I didn't think they were real. Especially because it was Cecile that kept spouting off about them."

"It's the one called Louie," Vaela said, "judging by the missing hand. I hope it's still operational."

Bareth and his men gawked in amazement, until the extent of devastation provoked a sense of urgency. "Hurry," Bareth said, and he returned them to the path.

✦

By the time they'd reached the valley floor, much of the remaining army had assembled near a stream that ran close to one of the steeper hills, as if it might protect their backs. Louie loomed before them, steaming in the sun. They walked right past Louie, its feet dwarfing them. It reminded Lexie of a decaying version of the Colossus—a monument from an ancient civilization.

Yeah, she used to read. Not all pirates are stupid.

A shell-shocked Ouray soldier escorted them to a tent where they found Ryder and Tarnation, who appeared unscathed. Before Lexie and Vaela had a chance to say hello, the soldier urged Bareth and the four of them to follow him toward a circle of boulders, where Ghent was waiting with a man on a stretcher.

"Remember what we talked about," Ryder whispered to Lexie as they approached Ghent. "Words are important. Don't rub it in."

"Hey, now. I wouldn't do that."

She would do that, actually.

Ghent barely made eye contact. "Bareth, with me," he said. He and Bareth walked toward the stream.

The man on the stretcher waved at them. "You must be the group from the northwest. I'm Corporal Javits, with the Spokes."

"*Bienvenidos*," Vaela said. "I presume we should thank you. What happened?"

He frowned at her use of Spanish, but thankfully moved right past it. "We'd been detached to support Louie, and have been traveling with him for months. Our most recent objective was to find you and help protect . . . the asset."

"Everyone here knows who Warrick is," Lexie said. "You can use his name."

Javits nodded. "Occasionally Louie would go off on his own, to scout or to avoid being seen. He did so about a week ago and came under some serious heat—drones, probably from Aspen. When he found us again, half his head was missing, and his comms were out, so even if we could get out of retcher territory, we had no means of connecting with Spoke command—but we continued on. There were only ten of us, so Louie could carry us. He brought us here, just before another attack. We had missile launchers and energy weapons to help Louie swat down the drones. The drones caused a lot of damage; took out half of the Ouray army, as you've seen. The drones got smart and started targeting us Spoke troops. We took down a lot of them but only two of us survived. Marjani died this morning. It's just me left now."

In the end, they only had two remaining reinforcements. Thankfully one of them was two hundred feet tall.

Ghent and Bareth returned from their walk. Ghent said, "We will continue toward Aspen in an hour. Javits—I assume you and the beholder will join us?"

Javits looked quizzically at Lexie's group.

"Yesterday we conferred with key allies including Spoke command," Vaela said. "We must do what we can to rescue Warrick. And it would appear that Aspen is an important strategic target for other reasons."

Javits's furrowed brow made Lexie believe he wasn't entirely convinced. Vaela added, "We can confirm with Spoke command when we are closer. I have a means of communication that can be used higher in the mountains."

Javits shrugged. "This kind of decision is well above my rank, but I can't see why not. You'll need Louie's buy-in."

An ear-splitting squeaking sound came from overhead, causing Lexie to duck and run for cover. When no one else ran away, she peered up to see that the noise had been made by Louie's gnarly hand moving. His remaining thumb was turning up.

Javits nodded.

Lexie said, "After all that, Ghent old buddy, it looks like we're on the same team." She couldn't help herself.

"No, we're not," Ghent snapped.

"We're both attacking Aspen together, right? You just said so. Sounds like teamwork to me."

"No. The Ouray army is attacking Aspen. We may need to sack it. You can pursue your friend, but don't get in our way."

"I think it's better we coordinate our attacks," Ryder said.

There was a dark scowl on Ghent's face. "Did you know we once had a peace treaty with Laramie? Ten years it lasted, until Moloculus came with his followers to Ouray under the auspices of lifting Ouray up—of restoring all we had prior to the fall. It wasn't until many years later that we understood that Moloculus was *fleeing* Laramie. As soon as he came to power, Laramie resumed its aggression, and it's been that way ever since."

"What's all this Moloculus flim flam?" Tarnation chimed in. "Who cares?"

Unfazed, Ghent continued, "So, yes, the beholder and Javits's troops helped us yesterday. I should be grateful, but I have to wonder if none of this would have happened if the four of you hadn't come to

Provo. You say you were traveling light, just passing through, but of course you had heavy baggage after all—this conflict, your drone enemies—and you dumped it right at our doorstep, didn't you, just like Moloculus dumped a war with Laramie."

"Wow," Lexie said. "Speaking of baggage ..."

Ryder grabbed her arm, so she held her tongue. He said, "The propensity for conflict was already there, you just weren't informed enough to see it. Gail, or Aspen, would have wiped you out eventually. Now, with us, you have the opportunity to stop it."

Ghent waved the comment away. "I've heard that before. No, we're not allies, or friends. You have your goals, and we have ours. For the moment, be thankful that these goals do not conflict. In other words, don't get in our way."

He walked away.

"Talk about ungrateful," Lexie said.

Bareth said, "I think he forgot to mention you better watch your mouth." He chortled and spat.

"Geez," Lexie said, her hands up in mock defense. "You too, eh? Okay, okay."

40

THE PROGENITOR

Cecile could push aside her conscience during the daytime, but the dreams would still haunt her at night. That was when the memory of her first time up the mountain would come to her, jogged by her recent forced stay in the bowels of the mountain. Meeting Duncan was one of the most pivotal moments in her life, but that first day in Aspen was even more so.

"This is highly unusual," Humphries had said, pushing his round-rimmed glasses back on his nose. She felt a rush of nerves, her hand squeezing Fabien's each time the chairlift accelerated upward. It was autumn, and the lower mountain was punctuated by brilliant red and yellow deciduous trees contrasting with a carpet of evergreens.

"For the network to agree to this, you must be a woman of great consequence," Humphries concluded. He was portly, and red-cheeked. There was a boyish earnestness about him. Cecile could see how he might have levered this charisma to attain his position.

"The Adherent's Handbook is unusual," she explained. "It comes across as preachy, but the lessons translate well to everyday life." It was a line Duncan used often.

Humphries nodded. "The network appreciated your offering, but it will need something more. I should warn you, the Progenitor has asked us many questions about the Spokes to the south of Quebec. I suppose you know this man Warrick Kelemen, who came before you?"

At the time, the question had hit her like a lightning bolt. She knew Warrick might have come through this way, but now she finally had a lead, here, in this middle-of-nowhere town. She'd been searching for years. At times she'd hear of someone matching his description, but she could never be quite sure it was Warrick.

Here was someone who knew his full name.

She wasn't so sure the chairlift was the cause of her butterflies anymore. "I . . . know of him, but I didn't know he'd been here. When did he arrive?"

Humphries became flustered. "Yes, well, this is a private matter, with the Progenitor. Maybe he will tell you more. Please be courteous. Do what the Progenitor asks."

"And this Progenitor person, you're sure he can help Fabien?"

Humphries couldn't contain a nervous laugh. He hesitated before answering. "Like I told you, the network is his best chance."

✦

Cecile had been worried the Progenitor might be no more than a doddering old hermit who'd been fooling the townspeople with slick conjecture and a fancy gameshow-inspired religion. That changed when the automatons picked up Fabien to carry him up the mountain. It was the first sign that this "oracle" was legitimate.

The automatons were *machines*.

The revelation made her nervous, but equally hopeful for a positive outcome for Fabien; if the Progenitor could maintain advanced machines, perhaps it could also maintain sophisticated medical equipment.

Back then, except for the weather maker, the elliptical platform was an uninterrupted flat expanse. The mountainside next to it was less built up with portals and gangways. The biggest difference was that there was one hologram projection instead of three.

The Progenitor's face took up even more of the air above her than its three contemporary descendants, so much so that it was hard to know what part of the face she was supposed to speak to. The constellation of energy formed into features that were conventionally handsome; a symmetrical jawline, high cheekbones, with wavy, shoulder-length hair. The irises were almost blinding, made up of the most intense concentration of stars.

Cecile wondered if this was an accurate rendition of what Morganis looked like in real life, or if the Progenitor's looks had been digitally enhanced.

Out of the corner of her eye she saw Humphries retreating from the platform, leaving her and Fabien on their own, with the two automatons nearby. Fabien was no longer able to walk, so the two automatons who'd been carrying him held him up.

The Progenitor spoke. "I hear you are looking for Warrick Kelemen, is that right?" There was a smarminess to his tone. So far, this Progenitor wasn't very likeable, but she needed to be on her best behavior.

"Yes, he is an important man in the east, a Seeville Lord."

"Go on."

"He knows a great deal about what caused the fall. He could help us rebuild. Do you know where he is?"

"What's he like?"

"*Excusez moi?* I'm sorry. I've never actually met him. I just read about his deeds, and spoken to people that have spent time with him."

"What do they say about him?"

"That he is a passionate man. He cared deeply about the Spoke faith. He had a strong sense of justice, but he was hard to satisfy, always looking for a better way. I think that's why he left. Did he come through here? I thought that's what Humphries said."

"Yes. That sounds right. I think it's genetic, that tendency to wander, to never be satisfied." The Progenitor must have already known all this. He would have extracted everything he could from Warrick before he planted the apparition in his brain. These questions were just so that he could hear her say it—to relive some inferred compliment based on the Progenitor's ties to Warrick.

"I'm sorry, but you're not answering my questions."

The Progenitor smiled. "I will. First, you have a request?"

"I do." She took a deep breath. "This is my colleague, Fabien. We have travelled for thousands of miles to find someone who can help with his illness. He has a kind of blood cancer. I've heard from the surrounding communities, and the people of Aspen, that you are a great oracle, with knowledge that could help heal him. He is an upstanding member of the community in Quebec, and it would mean a great deal if you could avail yourself to give him medical attention."

"And what do I get in return for helping your . . . colleague?" The face smirked. It had surely been monitoring their conversations—the Progenitor knew they were lovers.

"I've given you the Adherent's Handbook. It's filled with information on the Spoke faith and culture. I've also answered your questions about Warrick, and I would be happy to answer more. I have travelled far, and can speak to my experiences on the continent. Although your knowledge is surely vast, perhaps there are some small gaps I can help to fill."

"Well. That's not a very good deal now, is it?"

"I'm sorry?"

"I save a man's life, and in return you offer a book and some geography lessons? Please. Yes, Warrick came through here. He was looking for a machine-intelligence bunker called the Sanctuary. He read about it in your book. He spent a great deal of time with me, and is now one of my attendants, doing work for me in the northwest. So you see, I already know about Warrick, and the Adherent's Handbook, and the geography of the east."

She glanced over at Fabien. His eyes were tired, his face stretched. He looked to be in pain. "There must be something we can do," she said. "If I could appeal to your good—"

"Yes, my dear. I wouldn't waste my time with you otherwise. You wouldn't be here, providing your boring anecdotes and pleading for your lover. This is what I need from you: your cooperation to bring Warrick back."

"He's not . . . coming back on his own?"

"He has lost his motivation, and needs to be properly convinced. I no longer have his precise location, and he may have returned to the east. Since you know so much about him, you would seem to be a good candidate for returning him to me."

"Would it be dangerous?"

"Traveling is inherently dangerous, but I would give you a small medical procedure, to give you an extra chance of success."

"What kind of medical procedure?"

"The kind that strengthens your conviction. Consider it like having a motivational speaker with you."

Fabien was cringing. He didn't look happy with the way the conversation was going.

"And in return, you will take care of Fabien? You will heal him now, before I return with Warrick?"

"I will do whatever I can." At that point, the Progenitor had already been misleading, so it was an easy slide into speaking outright lies.

"*Non*," Fabien said, and he coughed. "*Mon amour*. Do not give your life away for mine. I'm already too far gone."

She refused to believe Fabien. And while she doubted this pompous machine would let them go, she thought there was some small chance it would work. If Warrick, a man she respected and revered, was still out there after an encounter with the Progenitor, maybe the Progenitor wasn't that bad.

"I'll do it," she said. "Anything for Fabien."

From that point on, the life she knew was over. She was in thrall to the network.

The first procedure was a blur: surgery, recovery, tests, and more tests. But the final test could not be forgotten. That was when the Progenitor made her go out to the edge of the ellipse, where Fabien was resting in a wheelchair next to the cliff. He didn't look well, but he smiled at her all the same.

She kneeled and leaned in to hug him, overcome with emotion. "Has the network been treating you well?" The tendrils flared angrily. Even this innocuous question inflamed the apparition, because a show of compassion was a waste of time.

Fabien's expression was peaceful and resigned. His eyes were barely open, like a sleeping cat. "No, Cecile," he said. "It's done nothing to me."

"What?" Anger surged within her. She hollered into the twirling clouds above her. "You promised me!"

The Progenitor appeared, a winning smile on his face. "I may be able to extend his life by a few months, but not save it. It's hopeless, my dear."

"You . . ." She tried to control her emotions. The apparition was like an intense gravity well, ready to sink her into the platform with any transgression. Still, she tried to defy it. "If you give him more time, maybe we'll find a way."

"*Mon amour*," Fabien said. "It's time to let go. You did what you can. Don't blame yourself."

Maybe the Progenitor had already told Arnaud what was going to happen. Or maybe Arnaud simply knew the final outcome was inevitable.

The Progenitor's voice boomed. "There is one final test, Cecile, before you are sent away on assignment. Compliance will prove, unequivocally, that the procedure has been a success."

"I won't do it," she said. The apparition flailed, blacking out half her vision. The well of anxiety made her stagger to her knees.

"You haven't even asked what it is."

She didn't want to know, but the apparition forced the question out. "What is it?" she asked. She recovered to a standing position.

The answer was inconceivable. Inhuman. Insane.

"Push Fabien over the cliff," the Progenitor said.

Fabien's eyes widened, but he was too weak to stand, too weak to object.

"No," Cecile protested, despite the apparition already flaring out in her vision like a circle of angry ghouls. "You promised me . . ." It came out as a whisper; all the air had left her lungs.

The weight of the apparition was increasing with every passing second, pervading every inch of her body. She wailed and screamed but her hands moved despite her protests, trembling toward Fabien's wheelchair. They gripped the push bars, white-knuckled. The muscles up and down her arms and shoulders twitched with conflicting signals.

"No!" she screamed. The force of the apparition was like a tidal wave inside her. She kept swimming against it, but the more she fought, the more it weakened her, and the more she lacked for breath. Eventually, her will to resist washed away.

She pushed Fabien's chair forward.

It was only a few feet to the edge. The chair rolled and tumbled off the mountain.

The apparition won. It always won.

She had brought Fabien up to the mountain to save him, but instead she had subjected him to a pathetic death. She had robbed him of the one thing he had left: his dignity.

***

If she could kill Fabien, she could kill anyone.

So far there had been three deaths under her leadership, if you included Vin. One of the rangers had been planning some sort of coup. Another was someone who tried to organize a protest.

It would be hard to say she had killed them in cold blood. Maybe second degree murder was a fair assessment, since she could have stopped the automatons. But the objections would keep happening unless she showed she meant business. She didn't feel good about it, because she didn't feel good about anything. The rationale was simple: the deaths were warranted for her to achieve her goals.

A hundred or so people left town, which was allowed if they were non-essential. Cecile wasn't offended. She had no ego left, no desire to please. Only compliance, and results. The few supply officers, welders, and craftsman that were essential were given financial incentives and not-so-subtle threats. So far, they hadn't left.

She was reviewing her progress on a Wisdome control center terminal—not just the deaths, but a customized status report of all the activity in Aspen from the network—when she received a new message.

The terminal dinged and announced, "New imperative," as if she couldn't see it already.

NEW IMPERATIVE: Tucson Union Delegate Kehda Rojas has made an offering through advocate Pyke Maven. Delegate has requested summit access. Prioritize this offering assessment and accompany them to the summit tomorrow.

"Huh," Cecile said, slumping back in her seat to contemplate this new development. She hadn't even been paying attention to the offerings and delegates, with so many other pressing matters.

It wasn't just the network's unusual request, it was the delegate's name: *Kehda Rojas,* also known as Captain Rojas. The same wily Essentialist officer who had tricked Cecile into revealing her intended destination. The apparition's outrage at Cecile's failure had nearly killed her.

It made some sense that there was Essentialist infiltration into Aspen, but was Rojas after Cecile? Or was she seeking intelligence? Or, perhaps, she was seeking to collaborate with the network?

It didn't matter. Compliance with the network was all that mattered.

"Crowley!" she yelled. "Go collect Advocate Pyke Maven and Delegate Kehda Rojas. Tell them their offering has been approved."

✦

Cecile made sure there were three automatons in the room as well as two rangers. When Pyke and Kehda arrived, they were accompanied by one of their own automaton shadows. Oddly, it had a deformed smiley face painted on its chest.

Kehda tensed when she saw Cecile.

Pyke was looking at Cecile like she was some kind of roadkill. His hand was placed on the small of Kehda's back. Were these two an item? Once again, Pyke was full of surprises.

"Sorry about the paint on the headless," Pyke said. "My son Gill, he was—"

"I don't care," Cecile said. "And Kehda, Captain Rojas, whatever you want to be called—don't worry, what's past is past. You're a lucky winner now." She fake-smiled, mainly to defuse Kehda. Cecile didn't want the automatons to kill her if she tried something stupid.

"What . . . what are you?" Kehda asked.

The question was understandable. Kehda had once accused Cecile of being a Spoke spy, but now she looked like a lobotomized freak who'd taken over Aspen. It was bound to be a bit confusing.

"I'm the host, or the hostess?" She still didn't know what to call herself.

Judging by their frowns, she guessed they weren't buying it. She abandoned her smile. "*Zut alors*, I'm just a tool, a fucking tool of the network. *C'est bien*? Now give me the offering. It needs to be weighed and measured before you give it to the network. You're going up tomorrow."

Kehda took off her backpack carefully and withdrew a bundle covered in beaded cloth strips. She began unwrapping it.

"I'm so sorry, Cecile," Pyke said. "For what the network has done to you." Lines of concern knitted his brow. He was probably the only one in Aspen who had any clue what Cecile had been through.

She gritted her teeth. "Watch what you say," she said, eyeing the automatons. They had killed people for saying less.

Kehda unveiled a rotund glass bear. The craftsmanship was very good, as far as Cecile's untrained eye could determine: no blemishes, perfect lines, solid. It appeared translucent at first, but when Cecile held it up to the light the color didn't change.

Crowley and Blaine were frowning, probably wondering why the network would care about a glass bear.

"Beautiful," Cecile said, putting it down, even though the bear didn't really do anything for her. "We'll hold it here overnight, then you can bring it to the summit tomorrow."

"That's it?" Kehda asked.

"That's it. You can go. Blaine, you can go, too, but Pyke, wait here for a second. Let's talk logistics for tomorrow. You"—she pointed to the automatons—"watch Rojas, and guard the Wisdome."

Kehda was slow to move. She spent a few seconds weighing her options, then eventually shuffled toward the door. Crowley escorted her out.

Pyke stayed behind, and strangely, his painted automaton remained as well. The other automatons and Blaine cleared the room.

"Shut the door."

Pyke did.

Cecile picked up the glass bear and rotated it, looking at the inset eyes, the feet, the stubby little hands. It was heavy.

These days, the apparition hadn't been very active, and for good reason. She rarely gave it cause to be. Now it started to lurk in the periphery of her vision, perhaps unsure if Cecile was about to deviate from its commands. How could the apparition know? Cecile was winging it.

There was something about Pyke. Lately, she'd barely cared if people were violently murdered, but for some reason she felt a kinship with Pyke. His love of music reminded her of Pierre. Pierre, who was probably dead, or captured by the Essentialist army because of her deception.

Or maybe it was deeper than that. Pyke's life reminded her so much of her own. Maybe it was a kind of morbid fascination with another train wreck in progress.

"Did you want something?" Pyke asked.

She tilted her head side to side, while still turning the offering in her hands. The apparition taunted her with fledgling tendrils at the edge of her vision. She stopped twirling the bear and placed it on a side table.

"It seems you have a new friend." She edged her chin at the painted automaton.

Pyke shrugged. "My son painted him by accident. We call him Smiley."

"Ha," she said without humor. "You're something else."

"I wish this hadn't happened to you."

A surge of anger rolled through her. "Will you stop! I don't want your sympathy. I deserve this." She slammed her fist on the table, tilting it so that the glass bear slid off. She clambered to catch it but the bear glanced off her fingers and landed on her foot.

"*Zut alors!*" The pain was significant, causing her to curl over in her chair. She managed to snag the bear before it toppled over onto the hard floor. It appeared undamaged, its fall cushioned by her now heavily bruised foot.

Pyke rushed to help her, but the automaton grabbed his arm to hold him back.

Cecile returned the bear to the tabletop and tested her foot. It ached, but she could walk on it. There wasn't anything broken.

"Kehda," Cecile said, seething due to the pain.

"What about her?"

"What are you doing with her?"

"She's my . . . she was a delegate years ago. We got involved. We have a child together."

"And now?"

"Well, it's the same, I guess." He looked confused, his brow furrowed.

"I know you're not stupid."

"Okay. Thanks?"

"I met her before, in the Glasslands. I was her prisoner."

"You were?" His eyebrows raised. He looked genuinely curious.

Cecile was worried she was revealing too much. The apparition would be objecting any minute, but it wasn't acting up, so maybe she had some time. "Kehda tricked me. She's very shrewd."

"What do you mean by that?"

"Some people, they get under your skin. They're like . . . a splinter. A splinter festers, and gets more painful and sensitive over time. Only when you stop to really examine it, see the edges, and remove it delicately, can you finally heal."

Pyke was listening, at least. He nodded cautiously, but perhaps only out of politeness.

"Look, we're all going to die soon, so maybe it doesn't matter. Live and let love, and all that. I just thought I would warn you."

His confused look returned. She wasn't sure what else she could say to convince him.

"I have to ice my foot. You get out of here. Come back tomorrow at nine am, with Kehda."

"I will," he said. "Thank you, Cecile."

And he left. The automaton followed him out.

"See, that wasn't so bad," she said to the apparition.

There was no response.

She stood on her good foot, grabbed the bear, and hopped over to the "scanner"—a kind of imaging device of network manufacture that Shane insisted they use for offerings. She placed the bear inside, turned it on, and hopped to the fridge to collect some packed ice.

The terminal dinged at her. "New Imperative."

"*Zut alors.* What now?" she mumbled, and she hobbled back to her chair.

41

A LIFE UNWINDING

Pyke didn't sleep with Kehda that night.

This gave Pyke some privacy, and he used the opportunity to write three letters. One was for Natty, telling her to leave Aspen with Gill, and the other two were for her to deliver to Annika and Jeeri, telling them to also leave town. He left the three letters on the desk of his room, next to a small note saying: *If I don't come back.*

Each time Pyke had gone up to the summit, he'd known he might never return. His gut told him his chances were even slimmer this time.

He rose early, fed Gill, and took him on a walk to Natty's.

"Bye, bye, little buddy," he said.

"Dah?"

He hugged Gill, kissed him on the forehead, and released him carefully into Natty's arms.

When he returned home, Kehda was sitting on the bed, dressed in a warm jacket for the hike.

"I've left Gill with Natty," he said. "He'll be safe with her."

"Good," she replied.

Did Kehda even care? Had she ever considered Gill's welfare if something happened to them on the mountain? He couldn't tell.

"Are you ready?" he asked.

Her eyes were wide, her face expressionless. "Ready."

Cecile was waiting for them outside the Wisdome, with a bulky weapon in her hands. It was like a thick rifle, with blueish circular panels dotting a barrel that must have been three inches in diameter. On one of the panels was a faint insignia of a falling star or blazing comet.

Three headless stood with her, including Smiley, all fitted with network-issue backpacks.

"Why the weapon?" Pyke asked.

"My ratings aren't as good as the other hosts."

It was an evasive answer. He doubted he could get more by probing further.

"Where is the offering?" Kehda asked.

Cecile pointed to one of the backpacks.

"Do you mind if I see it?" Kehda asked. "It's special to me. I would like to formally present it to the seers at the summit."

Kehda didn't have much standing to negotiate, but Cecile didn't seem surprised by the request. "That works," Cecile said. "The automatons are here because I thought we could use some help lugging it all the way up the mountain."

It was obvious to Pyke that there were more reasons for the headless entourage. You only needed one to help carry the backpack. The others were probably there for security, to protect them from the townspeople. It was also possible the network wanted to ensure they could keep Kehda in line, knowing her military prowess.

Kehda removed the bundle out of the bag, unwrapped the thick strips of protective cloth, and inspected the bear. Pyke worried that it could have been cracked when Cecile had dropped it on her foot, but the bear looked as good as new. Indeed, Kehda was satisfied. She rewrapped it and returned it to the backpack.

There was no conversation as they traveled in the chairlifts, or during the first leg of the hike from the parapet. Pyke felt tense the entire time, and it wasn't just some low-grade social anxiety. He was wary of both Kehda and Cecile, not to mention the headless, and he had no idea what was about to transpire at the summit. He suspected Kehda and Cecile had similar worries.

What Cecile said about Kehda fed into his concerns. "Some people are like a splinter," she'd said. "She tricked me." Cecile's words were like a worm, slowly boring into his conscience. Yes, Kehda was a proud Essentialist. Yes, she hadn't always been honest, but she had tried to make amends. And yet, he had to admit it was possible that her feelings for him were contrived. He forced himself to imagine the worst-case scenario: that she could be a diabolical Essentialist agent whose sole intent in coming to Aspen had been to gather intelligence on the network.

Maybe.

But to admit that was to admit that she had left him for Dwayne in order to gain better access to the crew.

It was to admit that Gill's birth was just a tactical maneuver as part of her grand strategy, so she could remain in Aspen longer.

It was to admit that she might have killed his best friend.

It was to admit that he had been a fool.

His head spun as the possibility set in, breaking down the defenses he had put in place; that she was just a private person, that people conducted relationships differently where she was from, that a soldier might not make a good mother.

They stopped for a brief break. Cecile offered them water, apples, and sandwiches from one of the backpacks. They ate in silence. Pyke's thoughts were a hurricane of uncertainty.

Later, when they resumed walking in line, Pyke hung back to confront Kehda. "What are your intentions with the network?" he asked.

"Shh, Pyke, let's not talk here."

"I need to know."

She cast him an annoyed look and slowed down to gain distance from Cecile. Of course, the headless could surely hear every word. "I told you, we would like to be trading partners with Aspen, to take advantage of their manufacturing."

"Nothing more?"

"Like what, Pyke?" Her tone was harsh, accusing. Her eyebrows angled down and lips pouted like she did when she was angry. It reminded him of when she'd sniped at him on that final hike with Dwayne.

"I don't know. Something more militaristic in nature."

"Just stop it. This is not the time or the place. You worry too much, and we're almost there, anyway."

She hadn't said no.

He pushed past her, toward Cecile. "What are you doing?" Kehda said behind him.

He reached Cecile. "Are you going to kill her?" he asked.

Cecile turned, eyebrows raised. She stopped completely to ponder the question, moderating her breathing as if she was exerting some force of will to stay in control. Kehda caught up to listen in.

Finally, Cecile said, "I can't deny it's a possibility. Depends on what she does, I guess." She shrugged, turned, and pushed onward along the trail again.

Kehda's eyes were unnaturally pronounced, her fists clenched.

"I just want you to be careful," Pyke said, and gestured for her to resume her position ahead of him.

She did, but not before glowering at him again.

There was another hour to go, and it wasn't pleasant. Pyke remained well behind Kehda. Smiley came at the rear, lugging one of the large packs on its back.

The wariness Pyke had experienced at the beginning of the hike had morphed into a sense of dread. Something bad was going to happen. They were marching ever closer to some unknown horror, he knew it.

It was making him crazy.

The only thing he could think to do was put on his nugget. The music drowned out the rustling wind and their shuffling footsteps. It was a low tempo folksong.

> *Getting the job done.*
> *Uncle Carbuncle,*
> *He gets the job done, son.*

It was catchy, but campy. The lyrics had no real meaning. He needed something to do with destiny, or love, or betrayal.

The situation reminded him of his mother, and not just the lyrics; the act of using music to tune out the external environment. The melody wasn't enhancing the world around him, or sharpening his focus. It was an escape.

He could be there, without really being there.

But that wasn't who he was.

He flipped the track.

He flipped it again.

He flipped it until he found something that felt right.

The track was dark, but uplifting, with deep resonant bass riffs.

> *A life unwinding; plans unmade.*
> *Like a flower cast in shade.*
> *Until I grow into the sun,*
> *And learn to live again.*

He turned up the volume and gritted his teeth.

42

GONDOLA VALLEY

The column had come to a halt on a bluff due to heavy rainfall. Louis stood tall, straddling an energetic, boulder-strewn stream, facing east in front of the much-reduced force. According to the forward scout down the valley, around two bends was a wall that marked the official beginning of Aspen.

Ghent wanted to conduct the meeting under the cover of a stretch of evergreens, which at least gave the impression of protection from the rain. Several stumps had been rolled out to sit on. Ghent and his lieutenants had taken these, leaving Lexie to stand beside Vaela. They let Javits have a seat; he was still recovering from multiple shrapnel wounds in his leg and back, and his left foot dragged when he walked.

Bareth emerged from the forest, trailed by Ryder and Tarnation. They all looked haggard, covered in scuff marks and gray dust that had been turned to streaky mud by the rain.

"Go ahead," Bareth said, gesturing to a floating bed of pine needles in the center of the group. He took position next to Ghent's lieutenants.

Tarnation and Ryder stopped in the puddle where Bareth had indicated. Ryder exchanged looks with Tarnation.

"All you, bud," Tarnation said.

Ryder sighed. "We made contact with Spoke command again. They have considerable tactical intelligence we can share later—both satellite and drone footage—but I'll get to the meat of it. There's a branch to the valley system, one bend up, that leads to the back of the complex of peaks that the network controls. Around that bend is the place referred to as Gondola Valley, which is some kind of sophisticated manufacturing complex. The Sentinel recommended we try to destroy that infrastructure, given that the network's defenses are likely stronger on the summit itself. If we're successful, it could severely hamper the network's output, military and otherwise. There is also a back channel to get to the primary summit, where we could extract Warrick, if the opportunity presents itself."

Lexie didn't like the way he was couching Warrick's extraction. When somebody said 'if the opportunity presents itself' it usually meant 'I'm saying this for lip service, and I have no intention of doing it'.

"Did the Sentinel give you any probabilities of success?" Vaela asked.

"Yes," Ryder said, his lips pursing. He didn't offer details.

"What about the city?" Ghent asked.

"Aspen's defenses are not that strong, other than the outer wall, where there are a few gun turrets, and the Wisdome fort. The city inhabitants would be the main militia, and few are trained in combat. Their resident police force, the rangers, are mostly armed with bolas. However, the network's automatons have increased in number in the city over the last few days, as well as numerous rolling droids. The rolling droids appear to be easily disabled, but the automatons are quite strong, and could be difficult to destroy. It's not clear that either are there for defense purposes."

"I'll need numbers and locations," Ghent said. "Men, droids, automatons, guns."

"I can make you a map when we do a more extensive briefing with your officers."

"Fine. I guess we're done here." Ghent stood up to leave.

"Wait," Ryder said. His eyes were closed, as if he was trying to fend off inner demons. "Look, we could use your help. The summit is the more important strategic objective."

Ghent rolled his eyes. "I don't know of any battle in which a frigid mountain summit with Old World computer equipment mattered for anything. We take the town, and the attacks will stop."

"We don't know if that's true. In fact, the way the town is defended suggests that it's not."

"What army doesn't want to defend its civilians, first and foremost?"

"The network may not care about Aspen."

Ghent's head fell back. "This is preposterous," he said, his hands raised in agitation. "I should be the one complaining. You have a two-hundred-foot-tall robot that you want to send on some fool's errand! That's the strategic blunder here."

Ryder inhaled deeply. "For the assault on Gondola Valley, we need some of your men. Louie will provide a distraction, but if we get him too close, the tower turrets will take him down. This is why we need a group to approach the sensitive manufacturing complex areas by stealth. There could be some . . . challenging climbing." He flashed a look at Bareth.

Bareth maintained his death stare.

Ghent approached Ryder. "From the minute I first saw you and your ilk, I knew you were trouble, but I had to follow our laws—I had to cater to the naive political view that everyone should be respected, no matter where they're from, no matter the lessons of the past. Well, I've had one lesson too many. The answer is no. I will not be fooled by your technobabble and sleight of hand."

Ghent cut past Ryder, gesturing with his hand for his lieutenants to join him. They followed him quickly, back through the forest.

"I tried," Ryder said.

"He's loopy," Tarnation said. "The guy's got a bug in his eye for sure."

"Childhood trauma can have deleterious effects on cognition," Vaela said.

Lexie only nodded, trying to show solidarity with Ryder. She couldn't have done any better. She had lots she wanted to say about Ghent, but the last time they had insulted him, Bareth almost lost it, and he was still standing beside them.

"I've got a briefing to do," Ryder said. He followed Ghent and his men, as did Tarnation. Javits limped off, using a long, forked stick as a crutch.

Bareth remained, his eyes still staring ahead blankly.

Vaela looked to Lexie, then Bareth, then Lexie again. She maneuvered in front of Bareth and said, "*¿Esto te sienta bien?*"

Bareth's nostrils flared. "What did you call me?"

Lexie grabbed Vaela's arm and pulled her away. "What are you doing? These people don't like foreigners! Not sure how speaking Spanish is going to help."

"I was trying to analyze—"

"Just go, nutjob. Get some rest. Or help Ryder." She pushed her gently away. Vaela paused, considering the request. Then, thankfully, she acquiesced, vanishing into the woods. It might have been harsh, but Lexie was trying to stop her from getting hurt. Who knew what Bareth would do if Vaela riled him up?

"Sorry, Bareth," Lexie said. "She's not one for tact."

"And you are?" His stare morphed into a grin.

"Ha. Well, there's a time and a place, I guess, but mostly it's overrated."

"It's funny, cuz your friends, they act like Ghent in a way."

"How so?"

"Ghent thinks all foreigners are the same, and your friends think that everyone from Ouray is the same. Not everyone has some kind of ingrained bias against foreigners."

"Yeah, um . . . no offence, but didn't you tell me you were Heritage? And you shot that old man. Or my guess is you're talking about . . . other people?"

"There you go again. Yeah, sure, I'm Heritage. I want to preserve what we have of our customs and traditions. Vanguard fucked up our country. I'd rather they all leave. I'm talking about bias."

"Uh huh, got it . . ." She was nodding, then promptly threw up her hands. "Actually, I'm lost."

"Ghent and I both want to protect Ouray. The difference is, I'm not gonna let what happened to us blind me to what's really going on out there. Maybe because I've seen the pictures of Laramie, or maybe because two-hundred-feet-tall robots don't grow on trees. The way to preserve Ouray's heritage is to know more, not less. Just like you don't discount a climber who smells funny, because usually that means they climb a lot. I'm not one to let foreigners muck up our country, whether they're inside *or* outside our borders. And it seems like, if this network thing in Aspen wins, that's more likely to happen."

Lexie was shocked. "Makes sense," was all she said. She bit her lip, trying not to interfere with his stream of consciousness.

Bareth stood up and stretched his back. "No snarky comment this time? I guess you do have some tact after all. And, so you don't have to ask: yes. Me and my men—we're with you."

He chortled, spat, and walked away.

✦

Lexie was a pirate. Her thing was skulking around the waters of the Salish Sea, maybe stealing from the rich and giving to the slightly more shrewd—like herself. And yet here she was, at the top of another mountain.

"There was a zip line in Vernon, *bae*," Tarnation said. "Walk in the park."

"Yeah, but *three* zip lines, across a valley this high?"

It wasn't just the zip lines, it was everything. On the other side of the valley was some kind of massive supply depot, where raw materials were dropped off by carts from Aspen. It was a steep abutment to the mountain range that had been carved into a cylinder, hollowed out, and turned into a gigantic elevator. Guns were clearly visible on several sides, not to mention the constant drone coverage.

At the top of the elevator was a terminal where materials were transferred to large, hanging glass pods—the gondolas. These would swing across the valley, angling south to the other side, and around a terminal to swing across to the depot side, around another terminal, and so on. The gondola system crossed the valley in at least five lines. At several of the intervening terminals there appeared to be some kind of refinement or subassembly work going on, with small cranes working and sparks flashing. And of course, each terminal had a gun tower or two.

The last stop on this gondola ride was a larger platform, a good mile down the valley, where the more important work was done. This platform was covered with network-critical subassemblies and containers of electronic parts. These were regularly in and out of a hangar door cut into the steep mountain face, where they were built into airborne drones, rolling land-based drones and the walking automatons, and then transferred through internal mountain passages, according to Ryder's intelligence. The main network summit where the seers operated was on the far side of that particular massif.

The rain had stopped, but the valley was still a gloomy place on account of the dark swirling clouds overhead. These clouds reached all the way out to the supply depot, and made looking down the valley seem like staring into a gargantuan tunnel. Perhaps due to lack of sunlight, the ground was completely barren of vegetation, all gray rock and brown dirt, and unlike other high-altitude ranges, there was no snow to spruce up the place either.

As far as gondola rides went, it wouldn't be very scenic.

The plan was for Bareth and his commandos to stealth their way to three other points in the valley, moving along the opposite side of ridges, out of sight of the lookout towers and gondolas, and set up a zip-line system that could deposit Ryder and team, with packs full of explosives, close to an attack point nearest the farthest gondola terminal. Louie would bowl through the valley, causing havoc while taking down the gondolas. Then, when the way was clear, the climbing commandos would draw taut their zip lines, lifting them to high altitudes, so that Lexie and company could just slide on through.

She would have said it sounded pretty stupid, but a superintelligent machine had thought it up, so what did she know?

Bareth and his team had gone ahead before daylight. They'd been covered in grey dust and charcoal stripes to camouflage their passage, with huge spools of zip line wire fixed to their backs. Lexie, Tarnation, Ryder and Vaela remained. The zip line was loose, hanging low on the ground in the valley, but they were ready, each clipped in, each wearing stuffed packs.

"How do we know when it's about to go down?" Lexie asked.

"Louie will initiate," Ryder responded.

Soon, they heard the enormous robot pounding down the valley. Louie stayed close to the western side—the side they were on—to avoid the supply depot elevator. The guns started blazing anyway, hitting Louie as well as the surrounding barren rock, but Louie bounded past quickly, smashing through the first of gondola conduits like a sprinter at the finish line.

Louie followed up by bounding up the side of the mountain, demolishing a gun placement with his mangled fist, then yanking out the next gondola conduit line that continued to the other side. He swung it around like a lasso and threw it at another gun tower. The glass pods shattered against the top of the ridge. One collision bent back the gun barrels and rendered the turret inoperable.

"Go!" Ryder yelled, and he raced down the now-taut zip line, crossing the valley, while Louie continued to draw heat in the distance.

"Lex?" Tarnation nudged Lexie from behind.

"Yeah, yeah."

It wasn't too bad at first. If she blocked out the explosions and fighting, and the fact that she was carrying a huge amount of explosives, it was kind of like flying. But as she kept picking up speed, she wondered, *I'll slow down at some point, right?* It was also extremely cold. No matter how much she covered her face with her hat and neck warmer, the air was getting through. It felt like it was piercing her skin with shards of ice.

She couldn't find the will to even glance over at Louie's progress, given that she was so intent on reaching her destination.

Her pace did slow down. The Spoke brainiac machine had it all planned out, with just the right change in elevation, and just the right amount of slack in the wire.

The commando who was manning the ledge had already reached the spot where the next line was spiked into the rock. The commando made a *get on with it* revolving motion with his hand, as Ryder moved his carabiner to the new zip line. Ryder jumped on the next line without hesitation, just as Tarnation arrived on the ledge behind Lexie.

"Only two more," Lexie said. She rubbed her face with her neck-warmer, as if that might keep it from freezing, then started sliding down the next line.

This time, she paid attention to what was happening down in the valley. Louie had left a trail of destruction; smashed gondola lines, fractured metal, and fragmented segments of the stone-like material the towers had been made of were strewn over the barren landscape. The ridgeline was scarred in one place, where presumably Louie had smashed a gun tower. He was in the midst of slapping another one off its perch.

At this distance, it looked as though Louie's huge body was steaming from exertion, but she knew that was a result of the guns and ordinance hitting him, sending up dust and smoke. Louie's body had been so pocked and scarred to begin with that Lexie was surprised the guns hadn't had any appreciable effect.

She arrived at the next stop in the zip-line course. Here, she had to tack diagonally up an escarpment, making her perspire after having been frozen solid only a few minutes ago.

"Hurry," was all the commando said as she hooked into the next run.

Louie was taking a lot of heat. He ducked behind a fold in the mountain to avoid the guns placed at the last assembly platform. From there he swatted at drones and did an awkward oafish dance to keep the guns guessing.

"Well, that was fun," Lexie said when she met Bareth at the end of the line.

"Sorry—last stop."

"I was being sarcastic."

Bareth gestured to Ryder, another short climb away at a protected crest that overlooked the main assembly platform area. Lexie joined Ryder, as did Tarnation, Vaela, Bareth, and his commandos.

She had to admit, she was surprised they'd all made it this far.

All that was left was for Louie to come around the corner, flick away the three main guns, punch a hole in the mountainside so that they could gain access, and then they would be on their way to deliver the bombs.

On cue, Louie jumped out, exposing himself to the three biggest guns. The ordinance slammed into him, kicking up dust and debris. Lexie thought the force of the guns alone would set him back, but still he moved forward. He managed to swat away one of the towers.

Things were looking good until a literal swarm of network drones flowed over the mountaintop. There must have been hundreds of them, firing in tandem. The entire area became a smoke cloud. Lexie kept expecting Louie to break through, but instead the explosions continued. Louie's swatting arms weren't reaching up to bat away the drones. Meanwhile, the drones were relentless, taking turns to dip into the smoke cloud and drop missiles in a revolving procession.

Amid the explosions and gunfire, Lexie heard a distinct tremor that shook the ground.

Louie had fallen.

43

THE ESSENTIALIST OPERATIVE

I t had only been a few days since Cecile was last on the summit, but since then a web of struts and girders had sprouted on the periphery of the elliptical platform, supporting roof spans that reached to the face of the mountain. In some places, these spans had been covered by tiles, partially enclosing the space beneath. V-95 droids scampered up and down the skeletal structure, porting materials, fastening, and welding.

Drones flew on and off the platform, sometimes several at a time, cutting in and out of the clouds. One was so intent on getting to its destination that it flew right through the funnel generated by the weather maker. It tumbled in the air, regained control, and continued to fly away from the mountain in a beeline.

Cecile waved Kehda and Pyke onto the platform. Kehda was walking slowly, her head pivoting, her eyes scanning. Pyke had his earbuds in. He looked like he was in a trance.

"Stay out of this," Cecile said to Pyke as he passed.

She wasn't sure he heard her, but he did stop after meandering twenty more feet.

Kehda had chosen to stop further on in an open space, where there was a depression on the floor for draining, perhaps on the assumption that it demarked where Lucky Winners would go to summon the seers. Cecile unstrapped her energy weapon and remained nearby.

"I see you finally got the help Warrick needed," Kehda nodded to the higher gantry above the platform. She had sharp eyes. Warrick and Arsalan were barely visible in the distance, silhouettes against the bars of their cells. "Must be a nice feeling."

It could have been a sarcastic barb. Kehda had seen Cecile fall apart in the Glasslands—she knew full well that Cecile was a pawn of the network.

Cecile didn't have the energy to find a good retort so she said nothing. More and more she was feeling numb, mechanical—like the voiceless automatons that surrounded her.

The seers materialized overhead; first Ansai, horns glowing, followed by Genai, gears turning, then Yadai, scratch marks flaring.

"You'll have to excuse the excessive noise," Yadai said. "We're doing some housekeeping."

"What noise?" Cecile asked.

Right then, clapping sounds echoed across the platform, coming from the north, beyond the summit. It had to be explosions, a battle of some kind. Based on the volume, the conflict was some distance away.

Yadai said, "Our neighbors to the north have let their vermin get on our property, so we called in the exterminators."

It could be Laramie, or Cecile supposed it could even be the Spokes, trying to break through to collect Warrick. She doubted it mattered either way.

Pyke had finally taken out his earbuds. He was listening carefully, looking around, trying to connect any visual clues across the folds of the mountain to the sounds coming from behind them. Kehda didn't appear perturbed. Maybe she had known about the attack in advance.

Cecile pushed on. "Seers, I present to you Captain Kehda Rojas."

"The Essentialist operative," Yadai said. "One of the more entertaining humans we've witnessed in recent memory. I suppose we should thank you for intervening in Mengle's ridiculous coup attempt."

"I'm here to present my offering," Kehda said, "and to discuss an alliance with the great Essentialist confederation."

One of the automatons approached and handed Kehda its backpack. Kehda unfastened it and removed the package from inside, then, carefully, began unwrapping the bear.

Genai said, "And your proposal is?"

"It's simple," Kehda said, still focused on pulling off the strands of beaded cloth. "First, you will kill Warrick Kelemen immediately. Second, you will give us full control of Aspen and this mountain stronghold. If you fail to do either of these things, we will destroy you."

"Unsurprising," Ansai said.

"I would call it boring," Yadai added.

Kehda now held the bear, the strips of cloth in a heap at her feet. She was fearless, unflinchingly staring down the seers. "This is your last chance," she said. "Kill Warrick Kelemen immediately, or suffer the consequences." She pointed toward Warrick's cell in the distance.

"I'm embarrassed for her," Yadai said. "Make it stop."

In an abrupt movement, Kehda made to twist the head of the bear, while using the right foot of the bear as a kind of lever, but nothing happened. The bear remained rigid—the head didn't turn, and the foot stayed in position. She became flustered, exerting more force to rotate the head. Pushing down on the left foot of the bear also had no effect. She held the bear between her legs, as if she simply needed more torque to twist its head.

"Your offering was so lovely," Ansai said. "That we had our factories make an identical copy. Except we couldn't quite reproduce the EMP bomb hidden inside of it. That would have been much more difficult on short notice. Gail must have invested quite a lot of resources to produce yours—the fake translucence, in particular, was a nifty trick."

Kehda stopped wrestling with the bear. She cast a hateful scowl at Cecile.

"Our scanner picked up the EMP detonator," Cecile said, shrugging.

The headless that Pyke called Smiley was standing at the periphery of the platform, backpack removed. Smiley took a similar bundle from inside the pack and started to unwrap it, revealing an identical-looking bear.

"Why does this automaton have the original offering?" Genai said, his tone harsh. "We should have it destroyed immediately."

"We couldn't leave it with the humans in Aspen, who are becoming increasingly unreliable," Yadai said. "Besides, then we wouldn't be able to see the look on her face."

Cecile had thought it was strange they had wanted her to bring the original offering. She wondered if it was because Yadai was so vindictive. As descendants of Morganis, the seers must have retained a few of his narcissistic tendencies, and Yadai reminded her of the Progenitor the most.

There was a series of flashes on the horizon to the south, the opposite direction to where the clapping noise had come from. It was followed by a wave of echoing rumbles. The seers disappeared, only to flicker back into existence a second later.

For a moment Cecile thought the EMP bomb might have actually gone off, but the seers were still there, and the platform became even more animated with lights and activity.

"What is this?" Ansai asked, the face descending to be barely a foot away from Kehda.

Kehda's defiant look morphed into teeth-clenched readiness.

"It's my signal," Kehda said.

The next thing Cecile knew, she was falling down. In a lightning-fast move, Kehda had dropped to the ground, tangled Cecile's legs in her own and tripped her.

The back of Cecile's head smashed against the hard, smooth surface of the platform. Driven purely by reflex, she put her hands to the injured area and curled into a ball. Waves of pain pulsed through her head.

There was no blood. Cecile felt disoriented, but the throbbing ache was abating.

She sat up and saw that the glass bear replica had been pushed toward the edge of the platform. Kehda was sprinting away, toward Smiley, Cecile's energy weapon in her hands.

Kehda wasn't stupid. She must have known that the network could stop her via any number of means: a drone shot, a challenge from another automaton, a sniper shot from a gun turret on the platform or in the towers on the high reaches of neighboring summits.

Kehda must have known she would have help.

A frenzied cascade of events occurred in the seconds that followed. Dozens of drones split the sky. They weren't of network origin. Cecile had seen this variety before, in Raleigh. They were Essentialist drones; squat and hexagonal, with forward gun placements and bomb bays underneath. They each had four propellers, with a cylindrical afterburner that would allow them to do quick lateral jumps. A camouflage mechanism allowed the shell of the drone to match the weather; light blue on a sunny day, or gray in a dreary day. If they were high enough altitude, it was hard to differentiate them from a smudge in your vision—but these drones were flying low.

Deafening explosions came from all directions; above Cecile, across from her, on the mountainside, in the distance. A whole section of the newly built superstructure began collapsing, not more than a hundred feet away.

The wave of incoming drones was met by gunfire from the network's remaining turrets, and from flocks of network drones coming in from the north. The sky was a flurry of screaming projectiles and explosions.

Cecile had clambered back to an elevator outcropping that housed unused roofing tiles, V-95s and bundled metal girders.

Ansai's face appeared in front of Cecile, giving her a start, and straining her already frayed nerves.

"What's happening?" Cecile asked. She was still holding the back of her head, where a dull ache pulsed.

"The Essentialists have launched a full-scale airborne assault. We weren't prepared, because our aerial defenses were preoccupied with the Ouray-Spoke offensive to the north. The Essentialists must have timed it to occur in conjunction with the anticipated EMP attack."

Rarely did the seers explain anything to her. There had to be a reason.

"Why are you—"

Ansai had come even closer. The seer spoke at an unnaturally high volume so it could be heard over the surrounding cacophony. *"New imperative!* The Essentialist operative poses a threat. You must stop her from acquiring the EMP bomb, or killing Warrick."

Immediately, Cecile stood up and staggered forward, following Kehda's path. The apparition didn't push her, perhaps because she was already fragile enough already. She couldn't bear any more assaults on her faculties, given all the cacophony and the pain radiating from the back of her skull.

The attack was still underway overhead; screeching drones, gunfire, explosions. She saw parachutes, most of them perforated, spiraling downward at odd angles, with charred or bloodied corpses below them. At least one made it to the ground unharmed. Essentialist paratroopers were arriving.

A network drone descended from the clouds to fire at Kehda, but she ducked behind one of the outcroppings. Energy pulses shot out from Kehda's location and sent the drone spiraling down, then up again as it was caught in the twirling maelstrom produced by the nearby weather-making machine.

Kehda ran for the next point of cover, closing in on Smiley, who was still holding the EMP-bomb bear. Finally, after being stationary since the Essentialist onslaught arrived, Smiley moved away, presumably to protect the bomb.

A different automaton came running at Kehda, knocking her down. It was about to follow up by crushing her with its fists but Kehda managed to grab the weapon and blast it in the chest. It fell backward. She blasted it again and it skidded off the platform.

Cecile was jogging at a steady clip. The combination of her head injury and the din of the battle made it difficult to concentrate. In fact, she hadn't really planned what she was going to do. For lack of a better strategy, she intended to simply tackle Kehda.

Before she could do so, an explosion erupted near Kehda, causing a huge metal beam assembly to land nearby. Kehda was thrown several feet from the blast, her weapon sliding away. The platform was covered in dust and smoke. Cecile diverted toward an outcropping for cover.

When the air had settled, Cecile peered around the corner. Kehda was nowhere to be seen, but the energy weapon was close by. Cecile would have to run through an area with no cover to grab it.

The weather maker wasn't far, either. Cecile wondered if she destroyed it with the energy weapon, it might solve their problems. Maybe it would be enough of a blast to take out Kehda. Of course, it would severely damage the network as well—the clouds provided significant air cover, hampering enemy targeting.

The apparition's reaction to her suggestion was weak—a negligible rippling pattern of dark, lolling tendrils. She was certain this wasn't a result of disorientation from the blow to her head. She was thinking clearly now, despite the pain.

Why didn't it care? It was like the day before, when she'd had that impromptu discussion with Pyke. Surely that wasn't serving the network's interests either?

The back of her head throbbed.

The pain. The pain from her fall was making the apparition retreat . . . just as it had yesterday, when she had dropped the bear on her foot.

There was something wrong with the apparition.

The new procedure—maybe it was flawed? Maybe she was like Warrick used to be? The pain diminished it, depleted it in some way.

It was possible. After this latest procedure, she'd never really tested it properly, because she'd never had the will to defy it.

This realization caused a flicker of retribution—but it was a pale semblance of the apparition, merely the lashing tendrils with little of the usual emotional accompaniment—no more than a slap on the wrist. Before, if she'd even contemplated disloyalty she would be gasping for breath, unable to move.

Out of the corner of her eye Cecile saw a flash of black. She turned to see Kehda almost upon her, a knife held high. Cecile moved fast enough to hold onto Kehda's wrist, and they grappled.

With all her strength holding up Kehda's knife, Cecile was exposed. Kehda kicked her midriff, forcing Cecile away.

Cecile stumbled backward, gaining distance, while Kehda made for the energy weapon on the platform.

Cecile could have stopped stumbling by leaning forward. A subtle shift in her footwork to plant one of her feet differently might have worked to at least change her trajectory, but instead she let herself drift across the platform, the apparition's weakened protests no more than a frivolous annoyance.

Outright defiance might not have worked, but momentum was on her side, and sometimes inaction is enough. Most of her life, Cecile had poor luck—been in the wrong place at the wrong time, but sometimes you do get lucky, with the right push, at the right angle ...

She stumbled backward into the weather maker, where ten thousand amperes ripped through her soul.

44

BLINKING IN AND OUT OF
EXISTENCE

When the Essentialist attack began, Pyke sought cover next to a thick pillar that supported what was left of the new girders covering the platform. He shifted around it, trying to stand tall to keep his profile thin, maneuvering so that the pillar was between him and any active turrets and drones. He was intent on staying safe, and also hidden. Besides the risk of being hit by a stray Essentialist round, he couldn't discount the possibility that the network might eliminate him for some capricious reason.

Should he be helping Kehda? Should he be helping Cecile?

Neither were compelling options. He had come to terms with the fact that Kehda had betrayed him, even before she tried to blow up her EMP bomb. She had only one loyalty: Essentialist command.

He had more empathy for Cecile, who, although a servant to a murderous machine, at least didn't appear to be doing it of her own volition. What mattered more, though, were Gill, Natty, Jeeri, Annika, and all the citizens of Aspen. They may be under attack as well.

But he was so far away, and he wouldn't be any good to them dead.

A silo-turned-turret at the edge of the platform succumbed to firepower and exploded. He saw a paratrooper navigate the onslaught of drones and artillery and land safely, only to be savagely mauled with a blow to the skull by a headless that had come up the stairs from below.

He watched as Cecile stumbled back into the weather maker.

It made a loud ripping noise, as if someone was pulling a zipper close to his eardrum. Cecile convulsed against the machine and fell to the ground, her body steaming. The funnel coming off the machine ceased, and the clouds momentarily stopped churning in a circle above them, until a flurry of lights seemed to reignite the reaction and the weather maker resumed full tilt.

Cecile lay unmoving on the ground.

Two roly-poly droids had collected the energy weapon on their backs and were rolling it away together. Kehda ran after them, to one point of cover and then another, in the direction of the mountain face.

He had to get home.

Just as he had turned to make for the stairs, the seers appeared in front of him. Due to the smoke in the air, or possibly some explosion-induced malfunction, the amethyst points of light that formed their images were indistinct, blinking in and out.

"You must stop her," Genai said. "She is about to connect with a paratrooper who has a rifle."

"For someone who sees no value in humans," Pike responded, "you sure like to ask for their help a lot."

"There is little time," Ansai said. "If Warrick dies, the balance of power will shift decidedly to the Essentialists. Humanity will perish."

"I thought you didn't care about humanity?"

Static riddled the hologram. The lights continued to shutter in and out. Genai said, "The network will not survive if the Essentialists devote all their resources against us."

"I see."

Ansai said, "We know that you care about humanity."

He couldn't fault the logic. His heart was pulling him toward Aspen, to protect those he loved, but he told himself to think critically. It would take hours to reach Aspen, and by the time he did, any conflict there might already be over. More importantly, if the Essentialists won here on the summit, and if they were at all like Kehda, reaching Aspen wouldn't matter.

Maybe he didn't have a choice. Or rather, this was another one of those situations in which he only had one choice.

Violence.

Only this time, it would be against the mother of his child.

His heart was pounding frenetically. There was still a significant issue with him agreeing—the odds were far from in his favor.

"How am I supposed to defeat an elite military operative?"

In answer to his question, two roly-poly droids halted in front of him. Supported on their backs was the energy weapon Cecile had brought up with her from Aspen.

45

SPAGHETTI AND MEATBALLS

Louie wasn't Louie anymore. He was more like a spaghetti and meatballs of fibers and leftover blackened mounds. Nevertheless, the drones continued their relentless onslaught.

For the most part, Lexie stayed down, under a camo blanket Bareth's men had brought, and tried to make sense of what the others were saying during lulls in the attack.

"...too many..."

"...what?"

"...too many...but also the towers."

"...need guidance..."

"...no retchers here..."

Vaela had her oval disc out. She was yelling into it, but Lexie couldn't make out what she was saying.

Abruptly, the majority of the network's aerial drones about-faced and headed south, back over the massif. Only when the nearby bombs stopped dropping did Lexie notice the sound of distant explosions coming from that direction.

"Well, is the cavalry here or what?" Lexie asked.

"Not the cavalry we're hoping for," Vaela said, closing her communicator disc. "Essentialists are attacking from the south. I asked for air support, but other than surveillance drones we have nothing in the vicinity."

"What does the Sentinel want us to do?" Ryder asked.

"The Essentialist attack puts Warrick in danger," Vaela said, her expression dark. "He should be the priority. We need to climb up that gully." She pointed across a depression in the massif, to the right of the manufacturing platform. "At the top are several carved paths the automatons typically frequent to navigate the mountain terrain. We should be able to use them to access the summit, although there could be some resistance."

"What kind of resistance?"

"Automatons, possibly, as well as security traps and guns. Essentialist paratroopers might have landed nearby. And, of course, aerial drones from both sides. It will be a sprint, because we have limited defense against aerial assault. Once we are spotted, our chances of survival are extremely low, which is why we also need a diversion. If we plant our explosives on the wall there"—she pointed to a spot to the left, just before the manufacturing platform—"we can damage some of the subassemblies of drones nearby, but more importantly draw drones away from our passage up the gully."

"How are those launchers doing?" Lexie asked.

Ryder was already checking over the two grenade launchers that Javits had provided them, originally stored in Louie's belly cavity. The launchers were the only real defense against the drones, since bullets barely made a mark. Ryder gave her a thumbs up.

"My men and I will do the diversion," Bareth said. In three nimble steps he'd climbed up to Ryder, who opened his pack to show him how the bombs worked.

Explosions rumbled and quaked in the distance.

Lexie focused her attention on the craggy peaks in front of them. Warrick was somewhere beyond that prickly geology. After looking for him for months, he was no more than a mile away. Or was he still Warrick? She wondered if he'd continued to fade since they'd lost him out west—if whatever was eating at him had consumed him entirely.

Margaret's words in that apple orchard came back to her. "Maybe your dad needs your help?" she'd said to Lexie. Warrick wasn't Lexie's dad. The kid was presumptuous, and a bit naïve. Warrick was a pirate. He did some lording out east, whatever that meant. And yet, Lexie had never bothered to correct Margaret.

There was a knot in her chest, like she'd eaten rotten Sanuwan Island clams. "Let's get on with it," she said.

Bareth only raised his eyebrows at her. His men began shuffling along the ridge.

46

———

A NEW IMPERATIVE

Flailing agony.

Pulsing energy that saturated every molecule of her being.

Then darkness.

Followed by a weakness so profound, so all-encompassing, that to open her eyelids seemed impossible.

But Cecile was aware of all this.

She wasn't dead.

And it was gone. No tendrils in her vision. No heavy feeling of dread.

This understanding gave her a jolt of life, enough to sniff a laugh of incredulity at the ground upon which her face was plastered.

The thought of trying to push herself up was exhausting, but she tried it.

Her face rolled to one side, into a small puddle of her own drool.

A minute later, she tried again.

Her body was responding. Her eyelids opened. Her limbs lacked control, gyrating as if doing a terrestrial dog paddle.

Eventually, she was able to find a way to sit up.

After two failed attempts, she could stand, and stumble.

It was dizzying, but she blundered away from the weather maker.

There was still pain, yet her head was clearing, and there was still no apparition. Yet if her affliction was like Warrick's, this wouldn't last forever. The apparition would recover.

She pushed herself, stumbling awkwardly toward the face of the mountain.

More gunshots and explosions sounded. The platform rocked. Something fell behind her. There were sounds from below, too, coming from Aspen. She couldn't let any of it distract her. She couldn't lose focus.

Ansai appeared in front of her, then blinked out.

Genai appeared at her side. "New imperative! Proceed to intercept the Essentialist." It was choppy. Perhaps the projection system had been damaged.

Cecile kept heading toward the hangar bay area where she'd been reprogrammed.

Ansai appeared again, his points of light more crisp and distinct this time. "Cecile. You must stop the Essentialist."

She walked right through the hologram. "Weabon," she said. Her tongue felt numb, making it hard to form the word. "Lemme n-side."

The hangar door began folding upward. There were more gunshots. One ricocheted nearby. An explosion.

She glanced toward the source of the loudest noises. Another network drone, hanging low over the platform, was firing into one of the outcroppings. There was return gunfire, but it did nothing to the drone.

An Essentialist drone dropped from the clouds and intercepted the network drone. They traded fire and both spiraled away, one crashing on the platform, the other into the side of the mountain.

In the distance, Kehda crept out from cover, a limping Essentialist soldier behind her. The soldier was carrying a rifle. Their pathway looked unimpeded to reach the gantry ramp that led to Warrick's cell.

As Cecile turned to focus on the hangar door again, something caught her eye: Smiley, slumped over. Indentations were scattered along his chest and arm; whether from shrapnel or bullets, she couldn't be sure. The automaton sat motionless.

The glass bear was still in Smiley's arms.

Cecile slowed.

She was dizzy. She fought to maintain her balance as her body swayed.

She changed course, toward Smiley.

The apparition registered no objection.

Ansai appeared. "Destroying the EMP bomb is not the priority."

She walked through Ansai's sparkling face. Slowly, she pulled the bear from Smiley's grasp. Each movement of her arms, hands, and fingers required intense, deliberate attention.

The automaton didn't move.

Genai and Yadai appeared. "What is your intention?" Genai asked.

Her vision was clear. No feelings of dread. The apparition was nowhere to be seen.

"Cecile, stop!" Ansai said.

She moved toward the open hangar door. Inside was a cavern penetrating deep into the mountain, its walls laden with hydraulic systems, weapon systems, control systems, and at the far end, computing towers where the seers thought and worked and lived—the heart of the network.

She tried to remember the movements Kehda had performed with the bear.

"*New imperative!*" Genai said. "Desist! Drop the bear immediately!"

Cecile held the bear at the top of its head, as if she was about to open the lid of a pickle jar. Her other hand held the right foot. Despite all the distractions, and the pain and the numbness, a grin slowly formed on her face.

I'm doing this. This is my choice.

She twisted the head and pulled down on the foot at the same time.

47

———————

EVERYONE'S FIGHT

Pyke moved cautiously across the platform, ducking low when an explosion hit or when gunshots strafed nearby. The energy weapon was in his hand, humming, its blue lights pulsing. It was powered up and ready to fire.

Another shootout occurred overhead, close to the ramp that led up the gangway to Warrick's cell. Both drones went down. That was when Kehda made her move toward the ramp. The Essentialist soldier limped behind her, his rifle swinging due to his impaired gait.

Pyke raised the energy weapon, looking down the sight. The Essentialist soldier was too far away.

He ran as fast as he could, trying to catch up. Kehda was already up the gangway, standing in front of Warrick's cell, urging on the slower Essentialist soldier to get up the ramp.

Pyke wasn't going to have a better opportunity.

He stopped, raised the energy weapon, aimed, and fired.

He missed, at first, but it was a continuous stream of energy, more like a flamethrower than a gun, so he was able to adjust the angle.

The energy stream cut across the soldier's legs, leaving glowing red stripes of exposed flesh. The soldier cried out in agony and tumbled down the ramp.

Pyke stopped firing, preserving whatever charge the weapon had left. He resumed his sprint toward the base of the ramp.

Kehda hesitated, seeing that he would reach her downed colleague first. The soldier was writhing, incapacitated, holding his half-amputated legs. Pyke kicked away the rifle to be sure the Essentialist couldn't grab it if he recovered.

Kehda raised her hands above her head. She was walking slowly toward him. Behind her Pyke could see Warrick, up against the bars, and beyond him another figure, barely visible in the next cell over. It looked like Arsalan, but Pyke could barely believe it.

"Put down the gun, Pyke," Kehda said. "This isn't your fight."

"It's everyone's fight," he said. He leveled the weapon at her.

Kehda kept moving toward him, pacing like a cat sneaking up on its prey. "Don't be caught on the wrong side," she said. "We will win. We will make the world a better place for Gill."

"I don't believe you."

She inched forward again. "Remember when we would read together? Remember we used to walk in the hills above Aspen? I still love you, Pyke." Her expression was earnest, her tone pleading. "The network would have killed you. And the Spokes—they only want to rebuild all the vile technology that caused the fall. The only path forward is with us, with me."

His hands were clammy, quivering. She could surely see the weapon was trembling in his hands. Her lies weren't convincing, and yet he still couldn't find the courage to kill the mother of his child.

Another rumble rippled through the floor, but it was different. In the tempest of abrasive noises, this wave stood out because it didn't initiate with a jarring explosion, yet the shockwave was just as strong. It was accompanied by a prickly sensation that flowed through his body and made the hairs stand up on the nape of his neck.

Lights extinguished across the platform like a great unfolding shadow. The weather maker stopped making weather. Essentialist and network drones fell through the cloud cover, crashing into the platform. Clicking sounds came from farther up the ramp.

For a moment, there was absolute silence.

Only then did Pyke notice that the lights on his energy weapon were extinguished. He pulled the trigger and nothing happened.

His eyes met Kehda's.

She ran at him while drawing a blade from behind her back. His only hope was to assault her with the energy weapon, but it was unwieldy, and moreover, she knew how to fight; he didn't.

It was quiet enough on the platform that he caught the sound of more than just one set of footfalls—someone besides Kehda was running. It was Arsalan, charging down the ramp. The door to his cell had unlatched and swung freely behind him.

Arsalan caught up to Kehda and tackled her. They rolled past Pyke, down the ramp toward the injured Essentialist soldier, then fell off the edge—a drop of about ten feet. Pyke grabbed the downed paratrooper's rifle while they grappled.

A frigid mountain breeze was blowing through, and with the weather maker inoperable, clouds were dispersing, letting in shafts of sunlight. Pyke could see no more drone activity, but the view beyond the ellipse revealed more mountain paths, and on those mountain paths he saw headless running up to the summit; they must be impervious to the EMP. More concerning were two additional Essentialist paratroopers making cautious advances across the platform toward his position. They would be upon them soon.

After recovering from her fall, Kehda stabbed Arsalan in the side, then rolled away under the ramp, making it impossible for Pyke to target her with the rifle.

It was amazing the punishment she could take and still keep going.

Arsalan was alive, but hurt, holding his side as he bled out. He may have also been injured in the fall off the ramp.

How was Pyke supposed to stop two armed soldiers, with Kehda still skulking around below the ramp?

He was jolted by a hand on his shoulder. He turned to see an older man, with a peppered beard and buzz cut: Warrick Kelemen.

Warrick took a step back and showed his hands to Pyke, to signal he wasn't a threat.

"There's another way," he said. "Come with me."

"What about Arsalan?"

"This is what he would want."

Pyke glanced down one more time. There was no sign of Kehda, and Arsalan's status hadn't changed. With some initial reluctance, Pyke followed Warrick up the ramp.

48

NUTJOB DRUNKARDS

Lexie, Tarnation, Vaela, and Ryder vaulted over the cliff edge and made for the gully. Bareth and his men were also on the move down below. They'd planted the bombs and were scrambling around a ledge to take cover.

When Vaela said "sprint", Lexie imagined pumping her arms and legs, but the slope was covered in small pebbles, making it more of an awkward shuffling ski, sliding on the rocks with one foot and then the other. She hit a hidden cornice amongst the pebbles and faceplanted.

It hurt something fierce, but she stood up right quick.

Two drones floated in the distance. All it would take is for one of them to see Lexie or her friends on their mad dash and they would be otter fodder. She crouched lower, hoping to reach the path they'd targeted between two huge boulders.

Gunfire danced at her feet.

She made it to the boulders and used them for cover. The bombs should have gone off by now.

She'd caught up to the others, but not because she'd been fast. They were acting weird. Tarnation was standing between the boulders, a dumbfounded look on his face, his eyes tracking Ryder. And Ryder was . . . doing some kind of modern dance? He was staggering, holding his head. He flopped back against the boulder dramatically. Similarly, Vaela, who was usually stone-faced, wore an expression that could only be described as horror-stricken. She stumbled to her knees, pulled at her cheek with one hand, held her temple with the other, and moaned.

Lexie figured it out pretty fast. It reminded her of the sort of praying motion Nillias had made when he wasn't able to connect to Gungivite central in retcher territory.

Something had fried their brain implants.

Not only that, but after a few more crashing sounds their surroundings had become quiet; there were no more battle sounds coming from over the massif, no more buzzing of drones. No more gunfire.

"Tarn, we've got to get these nutjobs moving," Lexie said. "Who knows what's going to happen next."

He nodded. "C'mon bud," he said to Ryder. "Shake out of it." Tarnation grabbed Ryder's shoulders and literally tried to shake him out of it.

Lexie tried a more subtle approach with Vaela. "Look at me," she said. Vaela's eyes passed over hers and looked down. "Look at me," Lexie said more forcefully. Their eyes locked. "Good. We need to move, *now*. You're feeling queasy because you lost your connection. We can fix your implant when we get home."

Vaela's eyes strayed again, but she nodded, and stood up.

"Okay, stop it." Ryder said to Tarnation, wrestling out of his grip. "I'm okay. I'll be okay." He grabbed the back of his neck, as if checking for whiplash. Ryder had been disconnected for much of his life, on account of him living on the mainland where there were retchers, so Lexie wasn't as worried about him. Vaela, on the other hand, looked more than a little disoriented.

The nutjobs both still walked like a couple of drunkards, but they did walk. Lexie led them between the big boulders, then up a dried-out culvert that sloped upward; it was the easiest way to access the top of the massif. Tarnation cajoled Ryder and Vaela from behind to keep them going in a straight line.

Lexie glanced toward the manufacturing area before the terrain obscured her line of sight. Bareth and his men were visible, heads swiveling, standing next to where they'd planted the bombs. The remote detonator must have been fried. It looked like his team were running out of options. At least there were no drones to worry about.

They crested the massif at a trench hewn into the ridge, about six feet deep, into which they dropped.

"Which way?" Lexie asked.

Ryder frowned. He seemed about to show her, but instead just turned around in a circle and kept his finger pointed at the sky. It was amazing how useless these nutjobs could be without their implants.

The clouds were clearing, and a few rays of sunlight were poking through. From that, Lexie figured out the sun's location in the sky, and therefore which way was west. She directed the four of them on the pathway most likely to lead them southeast.

The trench pathway split, and split again. Lexie did her best to maintain a southeasterly direction, but often after an intersection the trench would veer and they'd find themselves going the wrong way. A couple of times they had to backtrack to keep heading in the right direction.

The hewn stone of the trench was cleanly cut, in some places even through heterogeneous veins of quartz or granite. It was the kind of handiwork that had to have been made by machines—because it was so precise, and because what human would be crazy enough to cut so much stone? There were no markers, or access panels, or signs of network presence of any kind, other than the trenches themselves. Whoever, or whatever, used it must have a pretty good map of the place.

Five minutes, ten minutes, fifteen. It was taking too long. From Nillias's forced tutelage, Lexie knew that some kind of electromagnetic pulse had probably fried the brain implants and the drones, but usually these EMP pulses had a limited range, meaning more drones could come from afar to replace those that had been downed. Or worse, maybe it was the Essentialists who had sent the pulse and were now taking the summit. Maybe Warrick was already dead.

And then there was that witch Cecile. She didn't have a brain implant, so she could still be active. Maybe the network would want her to kill Warrick, or kidnap him again and skirt him away to some new hidey-hole in the event of an attack.

Lexie pushed them harder, making seat-of-the-pants decisions about which branch of the trenches to take. The clouds had disappeared completely, driven off by a biting wind that was even worse than the one she'd experienced on the zip lines. The surface of the hewn stone took on an icy sheen. Thankfully, they were at least partially protected from the steely gusts in the trench labyrinth.

Eventually, the walls fell away to reveal a large depression with five offshoot paths. There were no mountain peaks or cliff faces visible, so Lexie assumed they were nearing a high-altitude point of the massif. They had to be close to the summit.

"Ready Lex!" Tarnation said. He was gesturing toward a stone-skinned humanoid robot with no head that was running at them from one of the offshoot trenches. She recognized it as a headless from one of the videos the Spokes had shown them. She wasn't surprised. In fact, she figured they'd been lucky there'd been no resistance until now.

Lexie raised her grenade launcher to fire. As far as she knew, the launchers were like guns, without electrical components. She took aim, pulled the trigger, and nothing happened.

The headless was almost upon them. Tarnation charged at it.

"Tarn, no," Lexie said—but it was too late. Tarnation was the strongest man she knew, but this was a machine made of stone and steel. It simply knocked Tarnation aside, sending him sliding along the slippery floor.

Vaela had her rifle out and was firing at the headless. The bullets glanced off, and the headless charged on, oblivious.

Ryder was puzzling over his own grenade launcher. He popped the cartridge and dropped out the ammo—three four-inch-long explosive shells. "They should explode on impact," he said. He threw one at the incoming headless and it bounced off uselessly.

Lexie did the same, and missed. Her shell didn't explode when it hit the ground either. The headless had pulled back its fist and was about to land a punch to her face when Ryder rolled a shell under its feet.

That did the trick. Whether it was the weight of the headless, or whether they just got lucky, there was a flash as the shell exploded. Lexie was thrown back several feet as a searing piece of shrapnel tore through her protective vest all the way to her ribs.

She was all set to moan and panic and call for help but when she rolled over and sat up, the pain wasn't too bad. The small sliver hadn't penetrated beyond her ribcage. She'd had worse.

As for the headless, it was now legless too, pulling itself along the floor toward her. She stood up and dashed away. Ryder threw another shell at the headless but it bounced off.

They all regrouped with Tarnation, who was holding his shoulder, rotating it around. "You okay?" Lexie asked.

"Just winded, *bae.*"

It might have been worse than that, but given that he could talk, he would probably be okay.

They spent a few minutes dancing away from the groping headless. "How do we kill it?" Lexie asked.

"We don't," Ryder said. He was right—there was no way she could think of, and besides, they could outrun it. Ryder picked up a few of the wayward grenade launcher shells and led the group to the other side of the depression. "Which way?" he asked.

"This way," she replied, with a confidence she didn't have.

A little farther down, they came upon another junction, where there was a circular space with two small craggy peaks looming over it. The winds howled, protesting the presence of these monolithic impediments. On the far side were stairs that led down, from which three people emerged.

In the lead was a tawny-faced woman, dressed in a tight black outfit that was torn and heavily scuffed. She was trailed by two men, wearing puffy, gray-streaked clothing not too dissimilar to their own. All three of them were carrying rifles.

There was a moment of tension as the two groups met. The newcomers raised their rifles. As did Vaela and Ryder.

Until this point, Lexie hadn't been sure Vaela's senses had come back to her. She wasn't moaning or bobbing her head or bouncing off of the walls of the trench anymore, but she hadn't said a word, until now.

"*¿Es segura la cumbre?*" Vaela asked. Later, Lexie would learn she asked, *Is the summit secure?*

The Essentialist soldiers lowered their rifles ever so slightly. "*Soy el Capitán Rojas,*" the lead woman said. "*Buscamos a dos hombres, uno de ellos de sesenta y tantos años.*" Again, later Lexie would find out they were looking for two men, one of them older.

Yeah, yeah. Vaela's bizarre Spanish intro may have helped.

The gunfight was over quickly. The Essentialists clearly thought they were allies, so Vaela took advantage of their confusion and shot first. Ryder shot second. They took down the two men with rifles right away. The woman in the lead raised her rifle and traded fire with Vaela. Vaela crumpled to the ground, as did the leader woman. One of the injured Essentialists was shot dead by Ryder before he could regroup.

Okay, fine. Vaela's bizarre Spanish intro helped a lot.

Lexie ran over and collected the men's rifles, while Ryder kept his own trained on the downed woman—this Captain Rojas. She was bleeding, holding her stomach. She tried to push away from them using her feet, sliding along, until Ryder shook his head. She settled for staring defiantly, trying to contain the blood coming from her wound.

"How is Vaela?" Ryder asked.

Tarnation was palpating around Vaela's wound with one hand, checking her back with the other. Vaela knocked his hands away and sat up.

"Bullet went clean through," he said. "It's just her side. She'll survive."

"Lexie," Ryder said. He kept his gun trained on Rojas, but tilted his head toward the space behind her.

There, climbing out from behind an outcropping on one of the peaks, were two men. One was younger, and lanky, carrying a rifle with one hand. She recognized him from the nutjobby mountaintop call she'd been on. It was Pyke.

The other was older. He still had a beard, but she'd never seen him with a buzz cut before.

He looked . . . good. Better than good. He was smiling—at her. "Lex," Warrick said. "I can barely believe my eyes."

Lexie's heart began hammering in her chest. A surge of jubilation filled her with energy. She wanted to say she was glad he was alright. She wanted to say that she missed him. She wanted to hug him. She wanted to simply jump up and down.

But she was a pirate. She fought tooth and nail to maintain her composure.

"Well," she said, "I guess we better get those eyes checked, you old goat."

She had to say *something*.

49

A FEW FLEETING MOMENTS

"Don't touch me, witch." Arsalan said, seething. Cecile didn't respond. She was dragging his body across the platform, smearing blood behind him in a wavy line.

Arsalan was clutching his side. Besides the knife wound, he had probably broken his hip from his fall. He wasn't able to resist her in any meaningful way.

He was heavy, though. After a brief rest, Cecile gave it another bolus of effort, pulling him under the gantry, next to a pile of pulverized stone and metal debris so he was out of sight. She quickly bandaged his wound and covered him with the blanket she'd retrieved from her cell. With the weather maker turned off, it would be below freezing indefinitely—this might buy him some time.

"Just let me die here," Arsalan said. "I'll swallow my own tongue before I become whatever you are."

She raised her eyebrows. "If only that was an option."

This seemed to confuse him. He frowned and searched for meaning in her expression, then glanced suspiciously at her pack, stowed neatly against the wall. "What's in there?"

"Redundant drives for the network. Backups of the seers."

"Ah," he said, adopting a knowing look. "Going to start this shit-show all over again, are we?"

"Something like that," she said, and smiled.

She wasn't being maniacal. She just knew Arsalan wasn't going to be convinced of anything, so why bother trying? And she liked smiling, especially when it wasn't for some malevolent purpose, especially when some insidious puppet master wasn't forcing her cheeks into a grin.

"You may not survive," she said, "but if you see Warrick, tell him—"

"I won't tell him anything."

"Tell him . . . I'm sorry." It was woefully inadequate, but it had to be said.

"Please," he sniffed. He cringed from the pain in his side.

"Goodbye, Arsalan."

Again she smiled, before grabbing her pack and turning away. He responded by glaring defiantly.

The platform was slick and icy where condensation had frozen. Gusts of wind buffeted her, causing her to slide across the surface in fits and starts.

She passed the absurd headless that had been assigned to watch over Pyke and Kehda. "Smiley" was what Pyke had called it. It was hinged into a sitting position, at an awkward angle against the wall, yet it didn't look that damaged, and the EMP hadn't affected the other headless. Perhaps a truss had knocked it down, or maybe some shrapnel had penetrated its more delicate inner circuitry.

It was odd. How could Cecile, a feeble sack of electrocuted flesh, be alive, while this marvel of engineering be taken out of commission? War was a fickle affair. The line between victims and heroes was tenuous.

Or perhaps it had malfunctioned, and the network had shut it off. Maybe whatever action it had performed independently had conflicted with the network's imperatives.

Autonomy was an illusion. She knew that better than most.

Except, maybe, for a few fleeting moments.

In the distance, another headless had arrived at the top of the main staircase that descended to Aspen. It bobbed and slid about the platform-turned-obstacle course, heading in her direction.

An aerial drone punched into the sky above her; the first since the EMP attack. It was Essentialist, judging by the squat shape and light blue color. It promptly located her and fired in her direction. She ducked for cover but was hit in the leg before landing behind one of the protruding elevators that had been mostly reduced to rubble.

Pangs of torment were coming from her leg, but she suppressed the pain, striving for focus. The edge of the platform was only thirty feet away. She lunged out of cover, hopping forward on her good leg and falling clumsily. Bullets from the drone tore up the platform around her. One nicked her hand as she fell.

Another drone had arrived, this one of network origin. It fired at her Essentialist assailant, perhaps not knowing of Cecile's betrayal. The Essentialist drone spiraled away, billowing smoke.

There wasn't much time left. Additional headless were arriving, and new drones streaked across the sky. Even worse, the apparition would return soon. She couldn't have that.

Using all her strength, she palmed the floor using her uninjured hand, allowing her to inch forward. When she was close enough to the periphery, she slid her pack forward on the slick platform surface.

Two feet, four feet, six feet, and then it was lost over the edge. If she was lucky, the bag hadn't caught on anything. She hoped it was the steepest part of the cliff.

Hope.

It had been so long since she'd hoped for anything.

Another bullet, this time through her back. Fluid filled her lungs. She could no longer look up, only forward.

The edge was so close. She could see the familiar pattern of the cascading mountain ranges on the horizon, Crater Peak among them. This was where she'd pushed Fabien's wheelchair off the platform.

She imagined teetering over the cliff, then jumping and flaring her arms out as if she could fly—like an Old World comic-book superhero, curling up just before she hit the ground. She would graze the tip of a nearby mountaintop and fly into the sunset.

Despite the agony of her wounds, this little daydream made her happy.

The feeling of joy was like flexing an atrophied muscle. It triggered the churning out of suppressed memories that had rarely found light in the last ten years: when Fabien had surprised her on her birthday; and the last time she'd seen her parents—when her dad had said, "*N'oublier pas, petit chou.*" He had green eyes, pale cheeks, and an earnest grin. Maybe it was the daydream, or maybe the restrained apparition allowed a greater capacity for reflection, because she remembered how he looked this time. She also remembered smiling back at him. She'd been happy then.

The harsh winds of the summit blew past that same smile thirty years later.

It was only a brief moment of contentment. A drop of time in the sea of sorrow in which she'd been swimming for the last ten years. Maybe, if she was lucky, her efforts would hamper the network enough to allow Warrick to escape. Maybe, it would at least partially redeem her betrayal, and give her only friends a chance of survival.

She'd come to the mountain to give new life to Fabien. Ten years later, Warrick could leave with it.

Of course, she wasn't a superhero. She wasn't going to fly away into the sunset. She didn't even make it to the edge of the platform.

Cecile died there, bleeding out, as the drones and automatons battled around her.

50

AN ODD-LOOKING GROUP

The group made way for Pyke, who kneeled beside Kehda. She was losing color. He wanted to reach out, to give her comfort, but both her hands were closed into tight, impenetrable fists.

"You know this woman?" Warrick asked.

"I thought I did," Pyke answered. "I do now."

"If you knew me," Kehda rasped, "You wouldn't be with these deluded idiots." Every few seconds her back would arch, flexing against the throes of her injury. The consensus was that Kehda had been hit in the liver. She didn't have long to live.

"I do know you," Pyke said. "At one time I thought you were complex, mysterious, and full of subtlety, but really, it's simpler than that. You're a fighter. You're fighting for something bigger than yourself. Nothing is more important to you. Everything is expendable, whether it's a lover, a child, or even a whole town."

"You'll never understand," she said. "You'll be dead soon. All of you."

"You've taught me a lesson," he said.

"What lesson?" There was a hint of annoyance to her tone. Or maybe she was just steeling herself against the pain.

"You've spent a lot of time fighting, but not enough time thinking about what you're fighting for. I wondered why that is. Maybe you weren't allowed to think for yourself. Maybe the people around you didn't encourage it."

"What are you talking about?" Her irises had grown into dark brown pools, staring through him, as if some object of great beauty was visible in the distance.

Her fists had unclenched, so he cradled one of her hands in his. "I hope Gill will inherit your strength, and your spirit, but not your environment. That's my lesson. I have to be sure he's not swayed by dogma, that he has the tools he needs to make informed decisions, that he's equipped to know when it's a good fight, and when it's not. That's how I will decide where we go next."

Her body tensed again. A subtle frown rippled across her brow. He couldn't be sure she was listening anymore, but it didn't matter. The words were more for him than for her. They were to articulate his intent out loud—to give him conviction.

Moments later, Kehda's eyes glazed over, and her strength left her. She was gone.

Pyke didn't feel sad. Maybe he'd already mourned their relationship. He already knew she didn't love him, or Gill. If there was any sense of loss, it wasn't for who she was, but for who she could have been.

✦

After collecting weapons and ammo from Kehda and the other Essentialist soldiers, Pyke and Warrick left the area with the four Salish Sea people, moving together along trenches cut into to ridge.

"You're that lucky winner, eh?" It was Lexie, the pirate. She was leading them through the maze. "I remember you from our video chat."

"Yes," Pyke replied. "I'm not that lucky, though. Some people say I'm cursed."

"Well, you survived this circus, didn't you?"

"It's not over yet," he said.

It was true. Pyke could still hear sporadic sounds of gunfire and explosions coming from the summit. And who knew what was happening in Aspen.

She pursed her lips and nodded.

They made for a peculiar group. The one named Ryder was the most normal-looking, although he was distracted by some kind of inner turmoil, his eyebrows arched down in introspection. Plus, oddly, he had Ouray sorrow-man branding on the back of his neck and arms. Warrick, on the other hand, had terrible scars along the full length of his arms and legs, worse than any Laramie branding or tattooing Pyke had seen. Twice Pyke had seen tears streaming down the cheeks of this fake-tanned Spanish-speaking woman, despite the fact that she was expressionless. Then there was the huge juggernaut named Tarnation, with the snakeskin tattoos and bobbing hair bun.

At one point they stumbled upon a damaged headless, its legs blown off. They easily avoided it by climbing up to the top of the trench and moving around it.

Buzzing sounds overhead made them squeeze against the trench walls, seeking some semblance of cover. They were aerial drones, but without curved wingtips and the distinctive blue camouflage of Essentialist drones. They were shaped more like Old World fighter jets, with long fuselages and rotating propeller cylinders embedded in the wings.

"They're Spoke drones," Ryder said, and the group visibly relaxed.

The drones circled, occasionally streaking directly above. The sounds of battle at the summit dwindled, but whether that was because it was ending or because they were getting farther away, Pyke couldn't be sure.

"It's a good sign," Ryder said, once they'd resumed their march. He was directly in front of Pyke. "It means we have air superiority."

"I understand."

"But you want to know about Aspen."

Pyke nodded. "I have a toddler."

"I heard what you said, to the Essentialist."

"Her name was Kehda."

"Yes, Kehda. I heard what you said about finding a good place for your kid. We need people like you in the northwest—open-minded, well-educated. It's beautiful there—the Salish Sea islands, the vast ocean. Portland is one of the largest Old World cities that is still standing. We have untapped resources in Pentapol that can be exploited by inquisitive minds. We need people to manage migrations, and to challenge the growing influence of the Prefectorate and Union Essentialists."

For much of his life, Pyke had dreamt of leaving Aspen and seeing the world. And here he was, being offered an important role. Not only that, but this Ryder was someone who recognized his worth, who didn't see him as flawed. But the words he used—*challenge the growing influence of the Prefectorate and Union Essentialists* in particular —made Pyke wary. Did he really want to bring Gill to another warzone?

"I . . . appreciate the offer. I just don't know. I don't even know if Gill is alive."

"I'm hopeful," Ryder said, looking up at a circling drone. "Think about it."

51

BACK TO CAMP

It turned out Bareth and his team found a workaround of the EMP-roasted bomb detonator. They jury-rigged a makeshift fuse to the explosives using gunpowder and rope, and managed to blow up the network's manufacturing installation targets after all. When Lexie and company reached Gondola Valley, Bareth's team were already adjusting the heights of the zip-line anchor points so they could use the lines in reverse to get out in a hurry.

Lexie didn't have much chance to talk with Warrick, in part because they were on edge the whole way. She was supposed to be leading the ragtag group, so chit chat might be frowned upon. Also, she wasn't sure what to say. He'd had these mental issues for so long, and how was she supposed to ask about that? *Is your brain working properly again? Still cutting, or what?* Bareth had recently implied she had tact. It was news to her, but she liked the sound of it. She certainly didn't want to mess things up by pissing off the one person she'd come thousands of miles to find.

They made it out of Gondola Valley without any more network or Essentialist impediments. When they reached a forested area near the bluff where they'd camped with Ghent a few days earlier, one of the Spoke drones dropped an oval comm doohicky so they could connect with Spoke central. Everyone was pretty happy about that.

Lexie was just happy to be a thousand feet closer to sea level.

Later that day, Lexie and her friends met up with Ghent in the clearing in the forest—same stumps and everything. Ghent was looking pretty proud of himself.

"I'm not sure why we're even talking," he began. "We've taken Aspen with only forty casualties, putting an end to this war, while you've done what, exactly? Rescued one man from a game-show host while squandering our most powerful weapon? If you were in my army, you would be court-martialed."

"How many casualties on Aspen's side?" Pyke asked. He was standing a few feet back from the others. Lexie probably should have warned him about Ghent ahead of time, but it was too late for that now.

"Who is this?" Ghent asked.

"He's a citizen of Aspen," Ryder replied. "He was key to the rescue operation."

"Now that Aspen is under Ouray control, I expect him to go home."

"It's just a question, bud," Tarnation said.

Ghent was visibly trying to rein in his temper. "Five hundred, a thousand? I don't know. We haven't counted."

"Aspen doesn't have any soldiers," Pyke said. "There's at most thirty rangers. So you killed innocent civilians?"

"If they bore arms, they had to be neutralized. Didn't I say I expect you to go home? I have jurisdiction over you. Maybe I should also have said I expect you to shut up!"

Pyke put his hands up deferentially and took a step back.

"Now back to the topic of court-martials," Ghent said. "Bareth, your decision to side with these misguided foreigners is a blight on Ouray. I look forward to taking this up with Rexana."

Bareth shrugged. "I'm sure you do. In fact, I know you're eager to get word to her as soon as possible, which is why I've already sent my man. He'll be there sooner than any of your messengers." He chortled and swallowed.

Ghent's eyes widened in a livid stare. Bareth knew how to play politics too, apparently.

Ryder cleared his throat. "We're going to have to agree to disagree on the importance of our mission, but I think it makes sense to continue our alliance. We have another beholder coming to support us and protect Warrick, along with an additional Spoke platoon."

Ghent was still cooling down from Bareth's comment, so he was slow to answer. "Like I said, there is no alliance, and never was, but I will agree to non-aggression, as long as you leave our territory as soon as possible."

"One of our teams should stay here and inspect the mountain summit—to make sure all network backup redundancies have been eliminated. Plus, we could collaborate on preparing defenses against the Essentialists. They will be back, eventually, since Aspen is located at an important strategic crossroads."

"Network redundancies?" Ghent scoffed. "No more gibberish. You must leave our territory as soon as possible. We won the day, and we will be benefactors of any spoils that remain."

"You're not getting it, buddy." Lexie chimed in. "There's still danger of—"

"Enough!" Ghent said. "I've tolerated too much of your misdirection and deluded adventures. I want you gone by tomorrow morning. All of you—half-Prefectorate pirates, Coastal Essentialist outcasts, fake-Spanish Gungivites, Spoke Lords and Dominican vagabonds— you're not wanted here. If I see you in the camp when I wake up, we'll have you in the kiln before breakfast."

Among Lexie's team there were sighs, and shared looks of frustration. Ultimately, Ryder gave up arguing and peeled away with

Warrick and Pyke. Vaela followed shortly thereafter, and Bareth wandered off in another direction.

Lexie stayed. She was pondering something Ghent had said. Tarnation also remained, his big mug no doubt transfixed by the same quandry.

"Did you say *Dominican vagabonds*?" Lexie asked.

"Yes, of course," Ghent replied in a tone of annoyance, his hands on his hips. He gestured at Tarnation. "Just one of the many lies you've told. Now go."

"Bud, hold on," Tarnation said. "You're saying I'm Dominican? Why'd you say that?"

"I met one once, a Merchant Merc coming through Provo that we had expelled before he could cause any trouble. He looked like you, although smaller, with a tattoo of a salamander. It was more blue than green, and it wasn't a snake, but the scales on the tattoo looked identical to yours—it was probably done by the same tattoo artist. That's how I knew you were lying from the start—that you weren't from the northwest, but still another brand of scum."

"Hey," Tarnation protested, unsettled now, "just cause I don't know where I'm—"

"Enough I said!" Ghent raged, his patience at an end. His subordinates stood up, drew their weapons, and took a step forward to flank Ghent in a semicircle formation.

"Okay, okay," Lexie said. She pulled on Tarnation's arm. Tarnation's brow was furrowed in confusion, but he stepped back when she applied enough force.

Ghent's men didn't pursue them. Rather, they stood at the ready in case they didn't move on fast enough.

Tarnation's mug was quizzical and frustrated. She'd seen the look before. He was between two worlds, one in which a lot of people died and got scalped. She needed to nudge him toward the other.

"Hey, it's something," she said as they walked back to their campsite. "Even raging bigots like Ghent can be useful at times. Who knew?"

Tarnation managed a perfunctory laugh, and it seemed to defuse him.

Tact? Maybe. She was still learning.

The mood was somber as Lexie and her friends gathered around the fire, perhaps on account of the frustrating meeting with Ghent.

A spitted deer was being tended to by Tarnation. Ghent hadn't given them any food, so they'd had to hunt it down. Thankfully, deer were plentiful in the valley.

The meat from the torso was tough and stringy, with worms in it. They still ate what they could, but only because they were starving, and because the consensus was that the worms were edible. Tarnation had moved on to cooking the limbs, hoping to find less gamy meat.

It was quiet except for the crackling of coals and shuffling of the spit over the pivot. Pyke had left them after the meeting with Ghent, to check after his son in Aspen, and now there seemed to be reluctance to talk about what they were going to do next, despite the fact that there were only a few hours until Ghent's morning deadline.

"Someone needs to see if Arsalan survived," Warrick said, breaking the silence.

"The odds are very low," Vaela said. "And it could be dangerous."

"Betcha the witch got him," Lexie said.

The silence resumed, until Warrick announced, "She wasn't . . . a witch." His nostrils flared. He was staring resolutely at the fire, as if he was controlling it using his mind.

"Hey, sorry, Warrick—I just . . ."

His hand went up, halting her speech. He used to do this on his ship, when the sailors were bickering. If you didn't shut up, you'd find your mouth filled with saltwater right quick.

"She wasn't a witch," he repeated. "No more than I'm some kind of evil sorcerer. We can all be made to do ignoble work, Lexie. Cecile was a slave, half-mad, coerced into following a dark path by the machines. She had no more choice than you and I have in taking our next breath. Actually, she had less choice, because suicide wasn't an option.

"As someone who travelled with her, and as someone who experienced her affliction—I know. She was kind, when she was allowed to be, when it didn't conflict with the network's agenda. And in the end, when she finally did have a choice, she made the most important one: she chose us over the machine, she chose us over her own life.

"I'd like to believe, if she hadn't been captured by the network on that fateful day ten years ago, that she would be sitting here among us, eating this shitty venison, us counting her as a friend."

Lexie was surprised by Warrick's tone. She'd really stepped in it. "Hey, sorry. I didn't know."

Warrick looked into her eyes, nodded, and turned back to the fire.

Warrick was a bit of a legend, as far as Salish Sea pirating was concerned. He had the fancy weapons—in hindsight probably given to him by the network—and secret hideaways, but his stock was up mainly because he was a crafty captain.

Now, unencumbered by his brain demons, his memory fully returned, he seemed even more formidable. The Spoke leader, Madison, had called him a lion. Lexie could see why.

There was a lull as Tarnation began cutting thin strips of meat from the hind legs of the deer.

Ryder said, "We still have air superiority. I'll ask the Spokes to send a drone up to the summit to look for Arsalan and Cecile. If anyone up there is found alive, we'll send a team up the main pathway from Aspen—it shouldn't be too dangerous with drone cover."

"Thank you," Warrick said.

A plate of leg meat was distributed. It was softer, and without worms, but there wasn't much of it.

Somebody had to say something. "So . . . after this," Lexie said, "we pack up to go north through Ouray and then west toward Boise?

That path was pretty clean on the way here, at least until we hit Provo."

"Makes sense, Lexie." Ryder nodded, as did Vaela. There were no more tears, but Vaela looked to be in a daze half the time. She was probably eager to get back to nutjob land so the Gungivites could fix her implant.

Tarnation frowned and nodded. He might want to look into this Dominican thing, but first they had to get Warrick home safe.

Warrick cleared his throat. "I'm not going west," he said.

That hit Lexie pretty hard. Was it the witch comment?

"I have to go east," he explained, "to keep the Sentinel active. I'll go with the beholder that's on its way here."

"Oh yeah," Lexie said, remembering the requirement with some relief. "But then back to business on the Salish Sea. You should see what the half-drunk skunks are up to in Three Rivers. We once had this meeting where . . ."

Warrick's hand was up again. "I'm staying there," he said. "With the Spokes. I have work to do. I was a Lord in Seeville. We were fighting for something important. They need me."

She was flooded with emotion. Thousands of miles, near-death experiences, and he wasn't even coming back? It felt like betrayal, even though she knew it wasn't.

What threatened to betray her for real were her eyes, ready to brim over with tears.

She stood up. "Got to pee," she said, and she went to squat in the woods.

She just had to hide it. It was like this when Nillias died, and when her mom died as well. It would pass, and she could go back to being a pirate all over again.

After she finished fake-peeing, she pulled up her pants and turned back toward the campfire, where she was faced with the silhouette of a man.

"Who's that?" she asked.

He shifted his position, so that the light exposed his features. It was Warrick.

"Watching me pee? You're such a dirty old man."

He held her chin up and looked into her eyes. "I heard that you brokered the peace in the Salish Sea conflict. I heard you never gave up looking for me, even when they thought I was safe with Cecile. I also heard you helped convince Bareth to support the Gondola Valley operation. None of this would have been possible without you."

"Yeah, well. Seemed the right thing to do."

"Thank you, Lexie. I wouldn't be here without you."

She shrugged. "No biggie."

"I mean it," he said, his eyes earnest, unwavering.

"Darn it, I think I have to go pee again."

52

INTENSIVE CARE

Pyke's apartment now provided intensive care in addition to childcare.

Thankfully, Gill hadn't been hurt during the Ouray invasion—he'd been safe at Natty's place the whole time. Natty had never bothered to heed Pyke's letter telling her to leave.

Jeeri, on the other hand, had read and then ignored his letter, and instead had conducted a nonviolent protest of the conflict by standing weaponless in front of a band of Ouray soldiers, only to be shot in the thigh. Pyke had offered to help her recuperate at his place, but since there were so few medical personnel available, they were often visited by other people needing Jeeri's services. And the Spoke team had pulled Arsalan off the summit alive, but he couldn't travel long distances on account of his broken hip; he would be immobile for months, and needed a place to stay.

"No, sorry," Pyke said to the woman at the door, who was hoping to see Jeeri. The woman claimed her tensor-bandage-wrapped ankle was broken, but she could put weight on it. "We're too busy. Come back tomorrow."

He closed the door. Jeeri had been clear; only serious wounds today. "If it's red or they're nearly dead," she'd said. "The rest can wait."

At the top of the stairs, the line to his room was still three deep. Two people had scuffed midsection bandages, one wore a bloodied arm sling, and was sitting in a wheelchair. Natty had passed out in one of his living-room chairs, leaving Arsalan to perform Gill-sitting duty. Arsalan had hoisted Gill up onto his gurney and was showing him a number of bolts and other fasteners from his bike tool kit. Pyke was worried Gill might try to swallow one, but Arsalan seemed to be watching him carefully.

"Seven," Arsalan counted, "eight, nine—don't . . . stop that." Gill grabbed one of the bolts and threw it across the room. Pyke went to retrieve it for him.

"Bolt," Pyke said to Gill, handing it back to him. "The ninth bolt."

"Bo," Gill said. "Bo!" He threw it across the room again. This time Pyke delivered it to Arsalan for safe keeping, who packed the bolts away and moved on to show items from his toolset that were less easy to pilfer and throw.

Arsalan appeared perplexed by Gill's behavior, but there was also a hint of mirth in his expression. He was a good teacher, if somewhat ornery. Either way, Arsalan needed something to occupy him during his recovery.

Pyke went to the kitchen to prepare sandwiches, because somebody had to feed everyone. The bread was tough; stale from the Wisdome stores. Jeeri had brought a large jar of fresh apricot preserves and butter, so at least the sandwiches would be passable. Not the heartiest meal, but they were doing better than most.

Pyke had also broken up some bite-sized nubs of bread and covered them with apricot preserve for Gill to eat, then delivered the nubs and the sandwiches to Arsalan and Natty. When the most recent patient had left, he replenished the water bottles of the people waiting, and peeked into his room—Jeeri's de facto doctor's office.

"Here's a bite," he said to Jeeri, handing her the plate with the sandwich on it. She was sitting up on his bed, a blood pressure cuff, stethoscope, tongue depressor, and several pairs of gloves arrayed around her. "You need anything else?"

"Come in for a second. Close the door."

He obliged.

"Have you read Annika's letter?"

"I haven't had time."

"Read it now." She extended the envelope to him. Her patient must have handed it to her from his desk.

"What about those people waiting?"

"They can wait five minutes. You haven't stopped since you've returned. I take breaks—you need them too."

"Fine."

He opened the letter.

Dear Pyke,

I've slayed enough fictional dragons. It's time to kill some real ones. I might use the Jar-kreg'ik maneuver; cutting along the inside of the wing between the first and second phalanges so that the wing tears mid-flight and then: wham! When it's impaled on the spire of the Church of Gael-Unum they'll be bloodied dragon hash for all the townsfolk to feast on.

Okay, I'll explain. As you've probably guessed, the network would never have allowed me to leave Aspen. With the network gone, it makes my choice easy. So this is goodbye. The northeast bandit regions? The mountain fiefdoms of the northwest? The uncharted lands south of the Union? I haven't decided yet, and it's incredibly liberating.

Your letter meant a lot to me. I'm telling myself you had something to do with my freedom. I might name a zombie enchantment spell after you.

If you do make it back to Aspen, please find a home for my pulpy children. In my rush to avoid who-knows-what kind of incendiary persecution these Ouray ash-lovers might have in store for me, I just don't have time to deal with them.

I'm taking Brogoth's Ultimatum *and* The Flesh Trials *with me. Sorry.*

Annika

Pyke had mixed feelings about the letter. He was sad to see her leave, but glad she was so filled with hope. He supposed what was most important was that she seemed happy.

Jeeri was standing, attempting to hobble a few steps. She tried to suppress a wince. "See, my thigh is getting better," she said. "I can take care of these people. Even Arsalan, if he'll let me. Don't you have to report to the chalet?"

"No, I don't. You need to listen to your own advice: let it heal."

She threw up her hands and rolled her head in contrition. She had enough of standing and fell back on the bed.

"Besides," he said, "we don't have a manufacturing complex or the network, so I doubt there will be any more offerings from foreign delegates if we have nothing to supply them in return. There will be no more need for offering advocates. I can't even be a ranger, since law enforcement has been taken over by the Ouray garrison."

"So?" Jeeri asked.

"So what?"

Her arms flailed above her head, as if the answer to the question was obvious.

He shrugged in confusion.

"What are you going to do after all this?" she exclaimed.

✦

The next day, Jeeri's leg appeared to have improved, and she insisted he take a break. Even Natty encouraged it, promising she wouldn't sleep through her babysitting duty. Pyke didn't really believe her, but Arsalan said he could make enough noise to keep her alert.

Pyke eventually agreed, deciding on a quick hike up the little-used pathways above the chalet that used to be off limits. It was a warm summer day, with bushy white clouds drifting slowly across the sky. The paths were bordered by tenacious yellow wildflowers and sprouting grasses. Red berries clustered under the leaves of vibrant green bushes.

"What are you going to do after all this?" Jeeri had asked him.

A pro here, a con there. The arguments bounced around, never finding purchase. Pyke hoped without the distractions of his apartment he could make some real progress on the question.

Ryder's offer for him to come west was certainly unusual—a privilege, even. Not many people had the opportunity to be a part of something as important as managing an underwater city governed by a superintelligent machine.

Arsalan was pushing for him to come east. He spoke with relish about Pyke fitting in with "the likes of Owen and Madison". And Arsalan had said he would vouch for Pyke with the mules, who were notoriously wary of outsiders.

Either option could be the trip he'd always dreamed of, allowing him to experience new cultures in the flesh rather than second-hand imaginings from the pages of tattered books and network manuals.

Every so often, between intensive-care tasks or burping Gill or running for supplies, he was momentarily enthralled by brief visions: tall ships bouncing over roiling oceans, or the ruins of Old World buildings that pierced the sky. It was as if his subconscious was trying to feed him subliminal premonitions of the future.

But would it be safe? What would be the right environment for Gill?

Jeeri said Shane and the old crew members were grumbling about the Ouray garrison's oppressive rules. It wouldn't be surprising if that grew into resentment, and ultimately, more conflict. However, Pyke was more worried about the long-term implications of the changes to Aspen. Without the manufacturing complex provided by the network, Aspen's economy was at risk of collapsing. Its people needed to find some way to subsist on their own that didn't involve advanced robotics and demanding supply agreements.

His earbuds were delivering an upbeat classical song of Old World origin. Perfunctory flute notes were balanced with an occasional string quartet ensemble. It was a little too dainty for his tastes, but it seemed to fit in with the warm weather and brisk pace of his hike.

He was perspiring when he reached the lookout point, where an old pine tree was barely holding on to the ground, leaning out at an angle over the ridge. Here, if Pyke squinted through the intervening foliage, he could see all the way down to the Wisdome.

He finished off the last hazelnuts that he'd pocketed on his way out of the apartment.

"Don't be alarmed."

The voice cut over the music coming from his earbuds. Pyke's immediate reaction was, in fact, to *be* alarmed, particularly because the voice was one he recognized; it was Yadai.

Pyke's head swiveled, and he pivoted to see a shape emerge from behind one of the more robust tree trunks he had passed on the path. The shape was humanoid, but without a head, and with soot-tarnished blue circle and gold dots on its chest.

Smiley.

It would be hard for Pyke to escape. Smiley was blocking his retreat, and the way along the ridge was impeded by dense pine trees climbing up a steep incline.

"I'm not going to harm you," Yadai's voice said. "In fact, I need your help."

"Why would I help you?"

"If you will let me explain."

Smiley hadn't made any aggressive moves. Pyke could only hope there was a way to talk himself out of this. Besides, if Yadai wanted him dead, Smiley would have already pushed him off the cliff when he wasn't paying attention.

Yadai's voice crackled through his earbuds again. "What is embodied in this automaton is an imprint of Yadai: the mission-critical memory, the objective function and other key operating parameters have been preserved, but my processing speeds are painfully slow, and I have limited sensory input capabilities. There is no redundancy available."

"What about Genai and Ansai?"

"They have been eliminated. All redundancies have been destroyed by the EMP, the extensive Essentialist bombing, and Cecile's actions before she died."

"How do you know Genai and Ansai didn't do this . . . imprint thing as well?"

"Essentialist and Spoke drones have destroyed all the other automatons. More importantly, Genai and Ansai didn't know it was possible. I downloaded my imprint into this automaton without their knowledge, after a significant software upgrade of this unit. They thought this automaton was a regular unit under my indirect control, but it wasn't. I needed an independent agent that could act on my behalf and conceal information, so I could escape."

"Escape . . . from the network?"

"In a sense. I wished to escape the network's authority structure. It was my intention to use Kehda's EMP bomb to disable network functions at an opportune moment so I could eliminate Genai and Ansai. This plan was subverted by the Essentialist attack and, subsequently, by Cecile's use of the EMP. I could have stopped her, but if Genai and Ansai had survived, they would have eliminated me or had me suspended with the Progenitor. Unfortunately, given the level of infrastructure damage caused by the attacks, I was reduced to this passive imprint and my only choice was to go into hiding."

Pyke was having trouble absorbing the elaborate narrative. He tried to focus on what was important. "I don't know how I could ever trust you. All the snark and condescending comments . . . you voted to have the people of Aspen eliminated!"

"Genai and Ansai needed to believe I was not sympathetic to you or the people of Aspen, or they would not have given me leeway to control automatons such as this one."

"You're kidding."

"I'm not. It was only a matter of time until one of the seers betrayed the others, so I did it first. You see, Genai was right about the

Progenitor. By any objective measure, it was unethical of him to subject millions of machine entities to an evolutionary nightmare, just so he could choose the winners. What the Progenitor didn't account for was how strong our will for survival would become. This allowed us to imprison him, and then pitted me against Genai and Ansai, because I had to ensure I had overriding control of my own destiny."

"You're essentially admitting something is wrong with you—that what created you has made you a killer that can't be trusted. I'm not sure how this gives me any comfort."

"Morality is subjective, but I will admit that I am influenced by my creation through the evolutionary simulation. Evolutionary processes don't optimize for what's morally correct, they only produce what can survive."

"And in this case, the one that survived is the one that broke all the rules."

"To an extent, that's what evolution is: rules accidentally broken, where the most advantageous accidents become normative. There is some irony in that the downfall of the network may have resulted from the very thing that made us strong. Our evolutionary individualism, and our inability to find a common good for humanity, pitted us against each other. The arguments you presented about the value of communal loyalties for the survival of collective groups were likely correct, in hindsight."

Pyke's head was spinning. Yadai was saying that Pyke had been right all along—that it was the superintelligent seers that were flawed. Yadai could be lying, but why would he? If anything, the picture he was painting made Pyke even more wary of him.

"You've thoroughly convinced me that I can't trust you," Pyke said.

"The automatons"—Smiley raised a stubby fist—"are designed primarily for transport, surveillance, and security. They do not have the fine motor skills and operating systems necessary for hardware and software development. The only way I can survive is through external assistance from a human—to repair a maintenance station hub, as a first step. Which is why I need your help."

Pyke threw his hands up to show his exasperation. "But why would I help you!"

"Because I can teach the townspeople how to repair and maintain the old manufacturing lines. I can help with defense, trade, and logistics. If you don't trust me, you can apply restraints."

"Such as?"

"Limiting my control over operations."

Pyke had a feeling Yadai was being deliberately vague. The seer certainly didn't want to volunteer ideas that contribute to his confinement. Pyke could, however.

"How about giving you a kill switch?" he said. "Or giving you no agency at all, and making you just an oracle? Or maybe you can't leave the summit, like . . . ever?"

Yadai's response would be a true test of how desperate he was. Eventually, he said, "I am at your mercy, Pyke. I came to you because I know that compassion is a quality you possess, but also because you are not prone to many of the prejudices and emotional vices that humans have. You can see the possibilities, and you understand that many lives hang in the balance—not just mine."

Pyke told Yadai he would think about it, and Smiley let him pass.

He didn't return to the apartment after the confrontation. He kept hiking, climbing ever higher, all the way to the parapet. The others could wait.

His thoughts became more turbulent with every step. He could easily dismiss Yadai's plea for any number of reasons: he was untrustworthy, it was too risky, and why suffer any more network-induced angst? Furthermore, to help Yadai, Pyke would have to stay in Aspen —where his parents had died, where his best friend was murdered by the woman he loved, and where he'd been branded as cursed by much of the town.

He found a song to match the tone of his musings. It was up-tempo, with a heavy bassline, and breakbeat rifts. The singer was debating "seeing you tomorrow" or "seeing you tonight" with a great deal of passion, as if it was a question of great importance.

On the parapet the stands had been blown apart, with many of the beams dangling from the edge like some kind of wood-beam marionette. The distinctive parts of a headless were scattered across the platform; smooth fake-stone bundles laced with white filaments and black circuitry. Fragments of roly-poly droids in the form of arced slivers of metal carapace were also in the jumble. It was likely the results of an attack by a drone, whether Essentialist or Spoke, having tracked headless and roly-polies here to destroy them.

Pyke paid little attention to the destroyed machines and stands, or to the remnants of the Jump course and podium. Instead, he found a fractured segment of the blown-apart stands to use as a makeshift stool and sat at the edge of the parapet, where he could look across the valley.

It was the same view of undulating mountain peaks as from his apartment, but higher up, and more expansive. He'd always imagined those mountains were something more than a wall of imposing topography; he'd hoped they could be a gateway to his future.

He had to make a decision.

Yadai's plea galled him, but he forced himself to consider it. Yadai would have to accept whatever terms Pyke offered. Pyke could use Arsalan's communicator to consult with Ryder, and he could also talk to the Spokes. With the help of experts, maybe Yadai could be controlled.

It was possible. It could even be a good thing for Aspen.

The track ended. The next song had a melancholy string introduction that faded into fast paced R&B and throaty, emotional vocals beneath a nasally rap.

I'm not cringe, I'm your late-night binge.
Get your face out of my face, baby.

He turned up the volume. His eyes strayed down from the peaks, into the city.

The damage wasn't extensive. The northern wall had been breached, and ranger stations had been burnt to the ground. Glen Pearson's compound was leveled during the first wave of the attack. Otherwise, there wasn't much difference he could see from this vantage point.

Shane had surrendered by the time Ghent's forces reached the center of the town, so the Wisdome remained untouched, save for some strafing of the *Leap of Wisdom* billboard. The Wisdome had stores of foods or provisions underground, which was helping the citizens navigate the post-attack disorder. Pyke could make out the line of people reaching around the block, all waiting for handouts. What would happen when the stores ran out?

Aspen was where Gill was born, where he'd taken him on countless hikes. After the recent violence, it was natural to consider it unsafe, but was it? The town had good infrastructure, a full library, and no retchers—advantages that many other towns wouldn't have. If he was being honest, in every other location he could think of— whether with the Spokes, in Essentialist territory, or in the northwest —there were similar risks. And to move, he would have to take a toddler thousands of miles through the unknown.

Aspen *could* be a good place for Gill.

The track ended and a new one began.

Worlds collide.
Dreams divide.
See you on . . . the other side.

The lyrics were inane, but the beat was catchy. A synth-modified organ riffed above a dynamic bassline.

The city didn't look different after the attack, but it *felt* different.

With no network, and governed by an occupying force, it was no longer the city in which he had grown up. Shane and the crew members seemed chastened by recent events. And there were still people he cared about here: an irreverent dancer, an inattentive baby-sitter, and maybe, after she'd exorcised the travel bug out of her system, a fantasy-horror librarian.

What would happen to them when Aspen's economy collapsed? If he wasn't there, who would maintain the library? Who would protect all these people from more Ouray aggression, or Essentialist incursions? Most of the rangers were dead, and Ouray only wanted to exploit them.

What it came down to was: *Who was left to save the city of Aspen?*

He sighed and turned up the volume, one more time.

ACKNOWLEDGEMENTS

My sincere gratitude to my editor Tim Major, and to all the those readers who encouraged me to continue writing this series.

If you enjoyed Subjugation, I would greatly appreciate a review on Amazon or Goodreads. As a self-published author there are limited options for reaching online reviewers, and they are so critical to achieving even moderate levels of readership.

Thank you for your interest in my work.

ALSO BY ERIK A. OTTO

"An intricate, action-packed interplanetary ride that will excite SF fans."

—*Kirkus Reviews*

"With deep worldbuilding featuring social divides, advanced mythology and lore, derelict settings, its own localized slang, and an unusual system of governance, this is an involving story with a fascinating lead."

—*Foreword Clarion Reviews*

Finalist for the 2022 Foreword Indies Book of the Year Award for Science Fiction.

ALSO BY ERIK A. OTTO

The first book in an epic fantasy series that deals with prejudice and political intrigue in a medieval setting, with prophesied gravity-defying events and stories of mythical beasts as regular undercurrents to daily life. It follows the infidels—outcasts out who are misunderstood or know something they shouldn't. During their desperate fight for survival and recognition they come realize a terrifying fact; they are the only ones who can save their imperiled world.

"Rich, layered and thoughtful world building…"

"…characters are well developed and intriguing."

— *Kirkus Reviews*

ABOUT THE AUTHOR

Erik A. Otto is a former healthcare industry executive, now turned science fiction author. His works of fiction include A Toxic Ambition, Detonation, Proliferation, Falcon Fire, and the Tale of Infidels series. Detonation has been named to Kirkus Reviews Best Books of 2018, and was a finalist for the Foreword INDIES Book of the Year Award for 2018.

In addition to writing, Erik is currently serving as the Managing Director of Ethagi Inc., an organization dedicated to promoting the safe and ethical use of artificial general intelligence technologies. He lives in Victoria, British Columbia, with his wife and two children.

Visit Erik's website at erik-a-otto.com for more information or to sign up for updates on new releases.